False dawn began to lighten the sky and Gralyre risked a glance behind. Horror almost stole the heart of him.

Eight figures ran effortlessly along the snowy track, easily gaining on the foundering horses. Their legs cycled tirelessly, never faltering, never slowing.

Their arms dangled limply at their sides. They ran not as men ran, for men would be using their arms vigorously, pumping them up and down in an effort to gain more speed. These creatures ran using only their legs. Their slack jaws bounced with their rough gait, but no fog of breath exited. Some bore gaping wounds from their deaths earlier in the evening, but the injuries hindered them naught. Without a pause in their mechanical strides they lifted their heads and screamed at their fleeing prey. The panicked horses leapt ahead even faster.

Ahead of them, silhouetted black against the bruised sky was Hangman's Tor It was at least fifty feet to the crest upon which Gralyre could make out metal cages swinging from poles.

He glanced back over his shoulder. Gods! 'Twas going to be close; a race between the horses, the Deathron and the Dawn!

For André

Exile is a great read. I look forward to reading your work someday!

The Exile

Lies of Lesser Gods

Book One

L.G.A. McIntyre

Per Ardua Productions Inc.
Vancouver, Canada

For information about special discounts for bulk purchases please contact
Published by Per Ardua Productions Inc
103-1450 Laburnum Street
Vancouver, Canada
V6J3W3
www.perarduaproductions.com

Printed in the United States of America by CreateSpace
Trade Paperback edition September 2013

ISBN: 978-0-9919120-0-1

For all the strong women in my life

You inspire me

the Sister, the Mama, the Barbies and the Whores

Love you all.

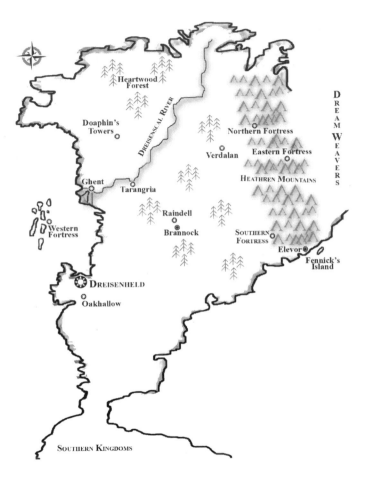

PROLOGUE

Men scream rage and fear. Sword smashes against sword in chaotic battle. Raw grief and despair; his men die, one by one. He stands alone in a sea of blood; the tide is against him. The wave of evil cannot be stopped. It crashes over him, crushes him, brings him to his knees. A prisoner.

A Demon's face slowly emerges from a boiling red mist. Its eyes burn with evil and triumph. An executioner's sword hangs suspended for a wild moment.

Terror! Cannot move! Cannot Escape! I will not cry out!

The sword drops. Sunlight sharpens the edge; his terrified visage, a distorted reflection in metal, chases the blade towards his neck. The sword bites and he is wrenched into the swirling blackness of forever... forever, but not the end...

Agony harries him into an infinite night, a void that has never seen starlight. All is pain. The void pulses, the chamber of a giant heart, flaying his soul in a savage rhythm.

I am lost, I am everywhere, I am the universe...the void pulses...I am nothing, I am smaller than the smallest grain of sand.

For brief flickers between he is himself, eroding with every violent cycle to slip away into the grinding maw of the voracious darkness.

This then, is death; this then, is my punishment for failure.

Wildly thrashing limbs produce no movement. They do not

exist here. Screams from blinding suffering go unheard. Infinity swirls and boils, terrifying, with no eyes to shut against it. Whatever power tortures him, forces him to gaze into the face of eternity.

Torment and time. It is forever; it is a split second. Sanity slips further from his grasp. Madness degenerates into soundless howls and disembodied thrashings.

Into the black chaos, colors swirl, growing brighter, forcing the darkness to recede. Vivid greens and yellows, blues and reds, swirl faster and faster.

He fights to escape as he is sucked into the vortex of color, birthed back into the land of the living...

DREISENHELD - SPRING

The Master sits the throne with regal boredom. Interest flits from one distraction to the next. After so many years, familiar vices lack the excitement and intensity of old, yet they beckon still. The ritual has a life of its own.

Even the assembled creatures mirror their Master's mood. Their half-hearted tortures do little to lift the ennui. The rhythm and horror of Dreisenheld goes on, a habit, an addiction that no longer sates the Master's appetites.

Distraction arrives from an unexpected source. It is a tickling of the senses only, nothing more, yet it persists like a fading note struck off key. Gradually the dissonance draws the Master's attention. Something has changed in the world.

The dawning of recognition sears away the tedium and the Master surges from the gilded throne. The assembly cower and squeal at the unexpected movement. But they are not the targets this time.

The Master weaves magic, straining, seeking. But the trace is too small, is fading, is gone.

Frustration lashes out at demons foolish enough to have crept closer. Blood sprays the walls and floors, overlaying other, more ancient stains.

"Get out! All of you, out! Send me a Stalker! Send me Sethreat!" The command rings out over the moans and cries of adulation.

ഏ

The Master's red lips part, teeth bared not as a smile, but as a threat of aggression. A long, sharpened fingernail, gilded in purest yellow gold, traces ancient blade scars that mar each reptilian cheek of the Stalker, Sethreat.

"You, my hunter, have been with me from the beginning," the Master croons. "He gave you these scars No one knows him as you do." The golden nail re-opens the scar tissue as it passes, and draws forth a thin bead of blood from the Stalker's scaled cheek; a warning of greater magic that could be unleashed. "And no one is to know that he has returned." The now bloody nail passes between ruby lips, a tongue flicks forth to taste.

"Yes-ss, Master!" Sethreat quivers in ecstatic horror of the

Master's threat, of the Master's touch. The Master's word is law, and the law is absolute.

The Master stares deeply into the Stalker's eyes, measuring the creature's compliance, savouring the absolute terror. *The most terrifying killer in all the lands trembling in fear of my touch. Is there more delicious ambrosia?*

The Stalker cannot hold the Master's burning gaze for long. Sethreat's gaze drops, awaiting the Master's pleasure with tail cowered tightly between legs. Blood drips from snout to floor, a quiet splash to the demon's preternatural hearing.

Satisfied, the Master stalks back up the stairs to the dais, and reclaims the throne in a flurry of ermine. "Seek out unrest. That is where you will find him. His coming is the dawning of an epoch. The end of days has come, but not for us… no, not us! He has returned, and we shall live forever!"

The Stalker flinches from the exaltation in the Master's voice, a sound more terrifying than rage, but the echoes resonating within the empty marble chamber are inescapable.

"Bring him to me alive. Only then will the world be remade in our image. Fail me, and I will slit your throat and slake my thirst with your blood!"

Sethreat cringes low, belly to floor, backing away through silent pillars until passing through the massive bronze doors where the Master's burning gaze can no longer be felt. Only then does the Stalker dare to stand and shuffle quickly away down the filthy corridor. Grating sounds of claws on marble echo amongst the silent, watchful columns of Dreisenheld. The Stalker's throat is tight. It must find The Man. It dares not fail.

THE HEATHREN MOUNTAINS - SPRING

"What is this foolishness?"

Catrian Kinsel glanced up at the demand, but did not cease saddling her mount. "Uncle." The high mountain breeze teased fitfully at her chestnut brown hair as she cinched a strap tighter.

"Answer me." The Commander of the resistance reached out and stilled her hands. "Ye are going after the Tithe."

Catrian stiffened but did not look at him. "We have talked o' this."

"I thought ye had abandoned this nonsense. It was decided."

Catrian jerked her hand out from under her uncle's and spun to glare up at him. "No. Ye decided! Every year, we grow weaker! Hiding! Waiting! And still ye will no' see reason. The secret o' the Tithe is pivotal t' breaking Doaphin's hold upon the land. I can feel it, I have seen it."

Commander Boris Kinsel's face creased into a scowling map of hard roads taken. "Then let someone else unravel it. Ye are too important t' risk."

Catrian was shaking her head in denial before his words were finished. "We have tried that. No one ever returns. 'Tis useless!" she dismissed.

The wind stilled for a moment as they glared at each other.

The sudden quiet shifted her gaze to an inner distance that only she could perceive. Her voice softened, hushed by despair and prophecy. "I see tides o' destruction and pain bearing down upon us, and we are no' ready...we..." Her awareness refocused on Boris as she drew a deep breath to calm herself. "I look t' the future, and all I see is death." Her voice resonated with the strength of her distress.

Boris' weathered hands came to rest on Catrian's shoulders. "Ye think that ye are indestructible, that your magic protects ye, but ye must see reason. Ye must remain hidden! Safe!"

Doaphin the Usurper would allow no challenge to his power. In a land where a talent for magic carried an edict of death, Catrian was a precious rarity, a prized asset of the resistance.

She glared at her uncle, unwilling to allow the old arguments and fears to sway her this time. "What use am I as a weapon, if ye will no' use me?"

Boris' hands flexed at Catrian's challenge. "What use is a weapon that is thrown away? A weapon wasted? The Tithe is naught but Doaphin's plague! Another way t' lessen and abase mankind."

Catrian shrugged her shoulders out from under Boris' grip. "If that is all it is, why does he guard his secret so tightly? What becomes o' the women?"

In the face of Boris' tight closed expression, Catrian sighed heavily and rubbed a tired hand across her brow, marshaling her arguments. She did not want to fight with her uncle, but she would have her way in this. Her nightmares of late had been consuming. The implications were clear.

"I have tried, but even my power is no' strong enough t' pierce the shroud o' magic within which he hides the truth. If the Tithe were unimportant, there would be no reason t' guard the secret so closely. There is only one path left untaken. My gifts place me in a unique position t' unveil the truth and return."

"And should ye fail? Should ye disappear, as has every other who has taken this journey? What will become o' the resistance then? What good does the truth do us if we canno' make use o' it?"

"Look around, Boris. Should I stay, or should I go, we have already lost the war! If the resistance ever challenged the Usurper's rule, those days are long gone, generations past. Every year, we become weaker, and he becomes stronger. Ye see me as some sort o' magical charm t' stave off extinction, when the truth is that Doaphin takes less notice o' us than he does a fly buzzing round his soup.

"The Tithe is something important t' him, something that can truly hurt him, and 'tis a victory that only I can win! 'Tis the key t' everything! Without the Tithe, Doaphin will be diminished, and perhaps defeated! I promise ye!"

Boris glared down at her for a long moment, before his rigid back seemed to cave slightly. "Ye will bring a contingent."

Catrian knew capitulation when she heard it, and had to work to keep the excitement from her voice. "Agreed."

"Ye will take no unnecessary risks. If ye are discovered…"

Catrian looked up at her uncle with great affection. "I will be careful. If anything feels awry, I will abandon my plans."

"Where will ye allow yourself t' be taken?"

"Verdalan's Tithe is due within the month."

Boris was shaking his head. "No. 'Tis too soon. Ye will no' go until I am certain all eventualities have been planned for, until I have hand picked your guard, and until I am certain ye will be as safe as possible."

Catrian felt a momentary flash of anger at her lack of autonomy, but recognized the wisdom of Boris' words. She had been foolish to think she could leave quietly. There was little that escaped the old warrior's notice.

Suppressing a sigh, Catrian's gaze turned inward for a moment. "The Tithe will strike Raindell in the fall." As she suggested the small village, something clicked in her mind, as it often did when a path was rightly chosen. Raindell was deep in the heart of the enemy's territory. The Usurper would not expect trouble from such a pacified area.

Boris nodded once in agreement. "Raindell. We have a good man there. Wil Willson. If ye do no' abandon this nonsense, he will see ye safe."

CHAPTER ONE

RAINDELL - FALL

Enigma rise from out o' mist,
Spirit waken with a roar,
Dragon perched on vengeful fist,
Fell Usurper rule no more!

The snippet of child's rhyme cycled in Dara's mind, spinning her further away from the world of hysterical weeping and screaming. She curled tightly at the bottom of the caged wagon, trying not to remember that her mother had not survived this journey.

Tithe or annihilation. That was the choice given to the peoples of this benighted land; the choice always given, the shameful compliance always granted. The women of child-bearing age were herded into the Tithe wagon, ripped away from husbands and children, from fathers and brothers. It was the price of existence under Doaphin the Usurper's rule.

Dara clung to the memory of the promise in her father's eyes, the rage in her brother, Rewn's, tight clenched face. They would come for her. They would rescue her. None of the other women present could boast so.

Dara squeezed her eyes tighter, her hands clamped to her ears, the rhyme repeating, blocking the screams.

The wagon careened down the ill-kept road, the horses blowing and grunting in an effort to keep the pace. A wheel hit a large rut, bouncing the women high into the air before slamming them back into the wagon bed. Dara whimpered and grabbed her bruised shoulder, curling tighter. They would come for her. She need only endure for a while.

Her father had made plans to send her to the mountains, to go to the Rebels, where she would have been safe from the Tithe. She had dreaded the journey, had dreaded leaving her family, and had fought with her father over the decision.

She had been but four years old when the Demon Riders had last visited Raindell, and had only a vague memory of the loss of her mother. As such, the Tithe had been naught but a nebulous, far off threat, and her father unreasonable in his fear. Dara wiped her tears, leaving dark stains on her cheeks from the filth of the wagon. Now she understood.

Strong arms reached out and gathered her into a comforting circle. "Hush now, all will be well."

Dara bit her lip and clung to Catrian, the mysterious woman who had arrived at their farm in the dark hours several days past. Her father had said she was a Commander in the resistance. Dara could well believe it. Even now, there was little fear in her face.

Dara was too ashamed to speak. Her voice would betray her terror. She had fought hard against this woman, had treated Catrian with terrible rudeness, for she had suspected that her father had summoned her to carry Dara away to safety.

"I will no' let them harm ye," Catrian promised softly.

Dara glanced wildly at the whooping, laughing Demon Riders

accompanying the caged wagon. Then back into the calm hazel eyes of the woman comforting her.

"Trust me. All will be well. Keep down, and do no' draw their attention."

"I want t' go home," Dara whispered.

"I know."

Catrian cuddled Dara closer, stroking her hair soothingly, while her thoughts roiled and thundered at the injustices of life. Home was no longer safe. Every season there were fewer safe places in the world. Catrian feared that all too soon, no refuge would remain, and the age of man would be over. The wagon thundered onward, for the horses were unable to feel the terrible weight that bowed her shoulders.

Catrian sighed heavily, regretful that she had not told Wil Wilson of the coming Tithe so that he could see his daughter safely out of harm's way. But she had learned early that survival meant keeping her own council. Her role within the resistance was too important, her power too vital to the rebellion, to court a chance at betrayal, not even for someone Boris trusted as completely as Wil.

She could only pray that, when the time came, she would be strong enough to save not only herself, but Wil's daughter as well.

When the sun was high, the Demon Riders halted the wagon briefly to swap out the exhausted horses. Food and water were tossed at the women through the bars of the cage.

Catrian stopped Dara before she could lift a fatty chunk of meat to her lips. "Drink the water, but do no' touch the meat."

Dara looked at the meager food in her hand and her stomach rumbled loudly. The other women were tearing into the meal, fighting for the last scraps. "Why?"

Catrian's lip curled in disgust. "'Tis no'…meat."

Dara's fingers squeezed the lump of flesh. Not meat. Not meat one should eat. The impact of understanding made her gag and drop the scrap. Three women dove for the chunk. Dara gagged again.

Catrian quickly passed her the water skin. "Drink. Drink and breath," she hissed.

"But the others!" Dara whispered hoarsely, "We must stop them. They must no'…"

"No. Let them be. We must no' draw attention. And this poor soul is already gone. Let them find what comfort they can."

Dara glared at Catrian with disbelieving horror. Only the squelched tears of rage in Catrian's eyes had the power to stop her from screaming the truth at the other prisoners.

Catrian took back the water skin, saving it against their future need. She hoped that one of the abused horses faltered soon. To what lengths would they be driven when starvation took hold?

The brief rest was over. The wagon set off at the same reckless pace. The outriders took up their positions, to taunt and abuse.

Through it all, Catrian's hard fought calm was tested. With a mere flexing of power, she could destroy the 'Riders and free these women, but that was not why she was here. She looked down at the young woman huddled across her lap. Not even for Wil's daughter could she be so reckless. The Tithe had to end.

And she was the only one who could end it.

Many weeks of abuse lay ahead before they would reach any destination. And then the Gods only knew what she would have to endure. She, who had never been helpless, would have to play her part carefully lest she betray herself.

The butt of a spear glanced off her chin, knocking her sideways into the opposite bars of the cage, punishing her inattentiveness. Catrian gritted her teeth to control her instinctive rage, schooling herself to cower and scream, as were the other women.

The Demon Rider laughed, well pleased with her performance. He did not look closely enough to see the calculation in hazel eyes. He had already turned his attention to a new victim.

Dara had also believed the performance. Her terror ripped sobs from deep within as she helped Catrian to right herself.

Catrian drew her into a tight hug. "'Tis alright, I am alright." Her jaw hurt to talk, but she had to calm Dara. One misspoken word would betray them to their deaths. "'Tis an act. A play," she whispered urgently, "They need t' see what they expect t' see. That is all. If I do no' behave as the others, I will stand out. We both will. Just an act, just a play." She repeated the words, over and over, until Dara stopped sobbing.

"Just an act. Just a play," Dara echoed numbly.

"That is right." Catrian drew back and was encouraged by the color returning to Dara's face. "If we cry, 'tis only for their benefit. Fool's tears for fools!"

CHAPTER TWO

The man dismounted from his tired horse after yet another long day of riding. He stretched and yawned as he stood upon the rough track, surveying the immediate area as best he could through the encroaching trees and bushes. His fingers combed absently through his luxurious black beard as his keen blue eyes scanned the area for dangers.

Ever present by his side, Little Wolf sported an ecstatic look, eyes half closed, as he chased an errant itch under his chin with his back paw. He halted and stared up the road, ears cocked, before giving a jaw creaking yawn of his own and setting about marking his territory for the evening.

The road had led deep into the forest over the last few days, offering none of the ruins of villages and crofts that had sheltered them upon previous nights in this abandoned and forlorn land. They would make their camp in the open this evening, but it had been a fine, warm, late summer day and it would be a warm night to sleep under the stars.

Satisfied with his choice, the man wearily began the routine of setting up camp. A stray branch at the side of the track snagged his shirt as he passed, adding yet another rent to the threadbare black fabric. He shrugged. There was no one to care except the wolfdog.

He had no more than pulled some packs from his horses when the sound of a wagon, pelting at a mad pace down the rough road, reached his ears. He froze as the unexpected noises organized themselves in his mind. The jingle of harness and thunder of hooves almost drowned out the screams. Almost.

With the instincts of the feral animal he was, he whirled, searching for a place of concealment. Even if he could not hear cries of distress, after long days of travel in this deserted, wartorn countryside, he was not about to risk being caught in the open. His stomach churned with uneasy excitement as he pulled a sword from the saddle of one of the horses, and a crossbow and quiver of arrows from the pack of another.

He scattered the four horses into the brush with a wave of his arms. *'Danger! Hide in the woods and stay quiet!'*

The pup loitered until commanded away firmly. *'That means you as well, Little Wolf!'*

He could feel Little Wolf's discontent at being sent to hide, but if it came to a fight he would be more hindrance than help. He was too young, and the man too protective of his last living pup. He needed Little Wolf safe.

The man scooped up his loose packs, tossed them into the thick foliage at the edge of the track, and dived after them as the caravan hove into view.

First to appear around the bend were two of the familiar, red-coated soldiers, riding point for a wagon pulled by a four-horse team. The wagoner whipped the horses as they faltered upon the poorly maintained path, keeping them at a near run.

The ill-used horses were blowing and sweating. Blood dripped down their flanks from the merciless whip. The horses grunted and whinnied in distress as they were beaten for more speed.

The wagon bed was caged, and imprisoned within were many women. Four riderless horses were lashed to the back of the wagon, spares for when the others would falter.

Riding rearguard were four more soldiers, who amused themselves by poking the blunt end of their lances through the bars to strike at their prisoners.

The women were helpless against the assault. Many of them screamed as they bounced and cowered within the jolting wagon, slamming against the bars and each other in their efforts to escape the blows. Their terror fed the enjoyment of the soldiers.

The man's lip had curled into a snarl when he had spotted the first despised, red uniform, but as he witnessed the treatment of their defenseless prisoners, the tides of rage rose higher within him. The evil pleasure on the soldiers' faces, in their cruel laughter, reminded him too strongly of those who had massacred his family.

Rage cooled to ice, crystallized into lethal purpose. Revenge was at hand. The man's eyes narrowed dangerously, and his nostrils flared and quivered with his quickened breathing; a predator scenting his prey. He raised his crossbow, and sighted down the shaft at a soldier, riding alone on the near side of the wagon cage, who was about to strike a woman.

The impact of the quarrel sent the soldier flying off the side of his horse. He landed heavily and moved no more. The horse took its chance to escape, bucking and kicking as it left the trail and crashed into the woods.

The other three rearguards laughed uproariously and jeered, at what they thought were poor riding skills. In the mellow glow of sunset they had not seen the arrow, nor heard the sharp hiss of its flight over the screams of the women and their own raucous laughter.

One soldier spurred his horse around and dismounted to check on his unmoving comrade, while the other two continued to follow behind the wagon, unwilling to give up their sport. The wagoner and the two point guards were as yet unaware that two of their number had fallen behind.

The wagon thundered past the hidden man as, with an effortless flexing of muscle, he reset his crossbow. As the two mounted rearguards following the wagon drew even with him, he sighted down the weapon and shot the closest rider. The death cry mingled with the shout of alarm from the dismounted guard as he turned over the first fallen soldier and saw the arrow lodged under his breastbone.

The wagoner sawed the reins cruelly to drag his team to a halt while yelling forward to the two leading guardsmen. "We be under attack! Get back 'ere and 'elp! Move! Move! Move!"

The red-coated soldiers still outnumbered the man five to one. If given a chance to come against him en masse, he would surely be overwhelmed, but with the alarm given there was no longer a reason for concealment.

He charged from the bushes, his attack focused upon the dismounted rear guardsman who still lingered over his dead companion. With sunset at his back, his sword blazed red in the slanted light while his shadow raced long ahead of him, a black giant wielding a blade of cleansing fire.

At first sight of this apparition, the dismounted guardsman froze in surprise before fumbling for his weapon.

One violent slash ended the soldier's life, with sword still in scabbard. Before the body finished falling, the man spun lightly to meet the charge of the last rear guardsman, who rode at him with lance angled in lethal purpose. The ground shuddered from the force of the horse's hooves.

The sun was now to the man's disadvantage, showing the blazing outline of the horse and rider, but hiding the lance within its shadow. The man lifted and angled his sword to shade his eyes, squinting to spy the glinting spearhead levelled at him. At the last possible second he leapt from danger's path, rolling to avoid hooves as the horse thundered by.

The two forward guards had lost precious moments thrashing the thick brush for more attackers to materialize. They finally realized that they were fighting a lone man, and wheeled their horses about on the narrow track to squeeze past the wagon and join the fight. The wagoner continued to scream at them, shouting invectives and using his whip to hurry them along.

The last rearguard, cursing at missing his mark, pivoted his horse, dragging at the bit cruelly as he set himself for another pass with the lance.

The man turned to face him, but a black, horse-shaped cloud, seared into his eyes by the brightly setting sun, made it difficult to see. From the corner of his eye, where his peripheral vision remained unaffected, he saw the two point guards ride out from around the cage.

He was trapped between an anvil and hammer!

Inspiration struck. The man sought the minds of the horses.

'HALT!'

All of the horses in the cavalcade balked in terror, not knowing if they should obey their riders, or the commanding voice inside their heads. The soldiers could not spur them forward, and the horses were too distressed to attempt a dismount. The wagoner whipped his team, swearing viciously at them as the horses reared and screamed.

The last rear guardsman lost his seat and crashed to the ground. He landed hard, but sprang to his feet with a battle yell. He had maintained his grip on the seven-foot lance, and the iron point led the charge.

The man waited until the spearhead almost brushed his chest before striking it downwards with his sword as he leapt to the side. Overbalanced by the long pole as it rammed into the earth, the soldier stumbled forward, and the man cleaved him from shoulder to hip with a fierce overhand strike.

The women had stopped screaming to watch in fearful fascination as the huge, wild-looking man easily dispatched the Demon Riders. Remnants of black cloth, that may have once been a shirt, clung to his muscled frame, but did little else. His hair hung in a tangled, black mass down his back. His beard was so unkempt only his wrathful eyes, and his teeth bared in a snarl, were visible. He fought in eerie silence, unlike the soldiers who cursed and screamed as they died.

Catrian stood at the bars of the cage, watching the battle's grim progress. Dara, beside her, smiled hopefully. "Who is he?"

Catrian glanced down at the younger woman. "A fool," she

muttered. A fool with magic, she amended to herself. Her skin was still swarming as with the crawling of ants, from the residue of magic the stranger had wielded.

While the milling, spinning horses kept the two remaining riders well occupied, the man sprinted towards the front of the wagon to gain a respite for his eyes to recover before the next engagement. He almost paid for the miscalculation with his life, for he had forgotten the driver.

The wagoner leaped from his high seat, his naked steel aimed for the man's heart. If his timing had been better, the outcome would have been far different.

Instinct got the man's weapon up in defense at the last moment, and he caught the wagoner mid-air upon his sword. The shock of the impact swept painfully through his shoulder, wrenching his sword from his numbed fingers as the wagoner's weight carried them both to the ground in a tangled heap.

Though mortally wounded, the driver went for his throat, hands snapping and closing in an effort to tear and maim.

The man found himself pinned and disarmed, unable to free his sword from the wagoner's breastbone. The wagoner's sword had landed too far distant to be of use to either combatant.

The man struggled to keep the soldier's clawing fingers at bay with his numb arm while reaching with his free hand towards his worn boot for his dagger. Straining with effort, his fingers brushed the ornate hilt, once... twice.

The wagoner's struggles increased tenfold as he realized the man's intent. Bloody spittle sprayed from the soldier's cursing mouth.

The man stretched for that last minute distance, and suddenly had it. He swung his knife in a savage arc, again and again, until the wagoner's struggles ceased. He heaved the corpse's weight off his chest and rolled painfully to his feet.

During the battle with the wagoner, one of the panicked horses had thrown its rider, and careened into the brush. The second guardsman had managed to jump free of his mount. Shoulder to shoulder, the soldiers now slid around the side of the wagon to take the man from behind.

'They attack you!' Little Wolf warned.

In one quick move, the man cleaned and replaced his dagger, then braced a foot on the wagoner's body to jerk loose his sword. Through Little Wolf's eyes, he watched the two soldiers' stealthy advance. He sensed Little Wolf sneaking from the bush to join the fray.

'Get back!' He did not wait to see if the pup had obeyed him. He could not afford the distraction.

The man claimed the driver's fallen sword, and spun to face the direction the attack would come. A sword in each hand, he let his mind empty and his breathing calm. The curious stillness of the Sword Dance swept through him as his concentration narrowed upon the two soldiers about to appear from behind the wagon.

He circled the swords lazily with a flexing of his wrists, like a big cat sweeping its tail before it pounces, letting his body learn the balance of each weapon. The dance pulsed in time with his steady heartbeat. His vision sharpened, his heartbeat settled.

The soldiers sprang from concealment in a rush, thinking they had taken him by surprise. They skidded to a confused halt when they beheld the waiting swordsman. Still, it was two on one, and their confidence was high. They grinned nastily as they moved to flank him.

The guardsman on the right twitched his sword, but the man moved not a muscle. He sensed the first attack would come from the soldier to his left. His blade was there to block the wild slash when it came.

The first guardsman thought him distracted and stepped in, sword raised absurdly high to deliver a killing blow.

It was an invitation that the man could not refuse. He swung his free sword in a vicious backhand that chopped the guard through the midsection.

Blood gushed from the soldier's mouth as he folded over his mortal wound, trapping the man's embedded blade.

The remaining guardsman, seeing the imminent death of his comrade, disengaged to flee down the road.

The man waited until the soldier had gained a fair distance, before hurling his unfettered sword with a flickering, silver whine into the back of the coward, felling him mid-stride.

Panting lightly from exertion, the man turned back to the whimpering guardsman bent over beside him. With extreme contempt, he kicked the soldier free of his blade and stood a dispassionate watch over his death throes.

The wind stilled and even the forest bore a frightened hush. It was this silence that finally penetrated the mists of the man's battle madness, and brought him back to himself. Shocked by his own ferocity, he blinked at the carnage he had created. Seven.

He had just viciously killed seven men.

The tip of his bloodied blade hit the ground. Numbly, he released it completely. It landed against a rock with a discordant clang that made him flinch. His head swam and his stomach heaved warningly as the coldness of his battle fury wore off. He hunched over and braced his arms on his legs, blinking back tears and gasping for air, as bile pushed at his throat.

His eyes chanced upon the familiar serpent crest on the breast of a bloodied red uniform. His mind flashed back to the murder of his pack, his family, and then to the abuse he had witnessed these very soldiers inflicting upon the female prisoners within the caged wagon.

One of the savaged wagon horses faltered in its traces, trying to lie down but kept upright by the harnesses of its mates.

A hardness of will descended upon the man then, quieting his stomach. He straightened. As he gazed again upon the dead, he saw not murders, but executions.

He turned his attention from the carnage, and looked instead upon the wagon's occupants. The women were cowed and silent, their eyes round with fright, as if to make a sound was to invite his wrath next.

He retrieved his bloodied sword, and walked to the back of the cage. With one strong blow, he broke the padlock and swung the bars open. There was a scrabble of movement as the women cowered as far from him as possible.

Unsure what his next course of action should be, he took time to examine their frightened, exhausted faces. The women were all fairly young, in their prime, and two looked pregnant. They

were pitiably thin and filthy. Overwhelming compassion engulfed him. What crime could they have possibly committed to
deserve this fate?

'Get out!'

He frowned as none of the women moved. They had not
heard his thought command, nor could he hear their thoughts as
he did the animals around him. The man shrugged the matter
aside as he cleared his throat, concentrating instead on how to
form words he had not used aloud for several months.

"Get out!" Unsure if they would understand his language, he
sounded harsher than he intended. His unused voice rasped
darkly.

The women jumped and cringed as he spoke, but otherwise
moved not a muscle.

"You are free! Come out from the cage!"

One of them shook her head, her face terrified.

Well at least that settled it. She had definitely understood
him. Red embarrassment caressed his cheekbones as he recalled
his ragged appearance. They would not risk coming near to him.
He left the cage door ajar, and strode to the front of the wagon to
see to the injured horses, giving the women the space they
needed to feel safe.

As he worked on the harnesses, he tried to ignore the scared
prisoners, who had yet to move. He really did not care why they
were in the cage. It was enough that their release would inconvenience his enemies. But it did bother him that the women
feared him, though they could not be blamed after witnessing the
battle. They had no more cause to trust him than the red soldiers.

His hands stilled in their task. Clenching his teeth, he tried to block the sudden influx of memory sense; *death screams, the give of flesh as his sword pierces bodies, the metallic sharp odour of blood, the excrement of fear.*

As he blinked rapidly to clear an unexpected film, the man's attention returned to the abused animal he was releasing. His mouth thinned to an angry line as he pushed away his revulsion for the last time, concentrating instead upon soothing the tortured beast trembling under his hands.

Catrian sighed in frustration as her plans crumbled to ruin. The mystery of the Tithe would have to wait. She stalked to the entrance of the wagon, and jumped to the ground.

How could this have happened? All of Boris' careful planning, and neither of them had thought to account for this! The slow burn of anger brought a spark to her eyes. How many months would this cost? How many lost lives would measure that price?

She turned to help Dara down from the wagon before pulling the girl closer so that the other prisoners could not hear their words. "I sense your father and brothers are nearby. I must lead the women away, so that they do no' carry tales back t' Raindell about your family. If they were t' see that they have followed the wagon..."

Dara nodded her understanding. "I will wait here for Da, but what o' him?" Dara glanced meaningfully at the warrior.

Catrian drew lightly upon her power and skimmed the surface of the man's thoughts, like a skeeter bug upon a still pond, leaving no wake to warn a fish of a meal to be had. Even so, the stranger shivered and stopped what he was doing to rub his arms as against a chill, the back of his neck, his forehead. He was powerful indeed to sense her so easily! She dared not linger lest he suspect what was affecting him so.

His was an oddly calm mind. Despite the hatred he bore the Demon Riders, Catrian sensed a deep well of stillness within him, something she had never noted in another. But now was not the time or place for a deeper reading. She had what she needed. She drew back into herself. "He will no' harm ye. His only interest was killing Demon Riders."

Catrian turned to face the wagon. "Come!" she said to the women who still refused to move. "Come out from the cage! We are free t' go home!"

"But they will only come for us again," sobbed a woman, "and next time the 'Riders will kill everyone! We must stay t' protect our families!" There were nods and murmurs of agreement from within the wagon.

"Your people sacrificed ye t' this fate! What care ye if they now have t' face the same death they were so eager t' condemn ye to?" demanded Catrian coldly.

"'Tis no' like that," chimed one woman.

"We have t' protect them, and protect our children," claimed another.

"'Tis our birth purpose," came a hopeless voice.

Catrian made a sound of frustrated disdain at the indoctrinated stupidity of their beliefs. Her words, when she spoke, were harsh, born of her disgust. "I will no' bide here 'till the Deathren arise with the night and slaughter us, or worse, cart us off t'

Doaphin's Towers! 'Tis almost sunset, so stay if ye wish t', sheep!" she said scornfully. "But if I were ye, I would flee t' the Heathren Mountains, where the men do no' trade the lives o' their women so cheaply!"

The man was captivated by this commanding woman, surprised by her forceful speech. She was garbed in soft leather trousers and a brown, flowing shirt, different from the home-spun dresses of her fellow prisoners. Her shoulders lacked the defeated slope of the other women, and though she was thin, her leanness was due to muscle, not starvation. Her voice, when she spoke, was strong and compelling, as though well used to issuing orders.

His pulse jumped as she swung around. The meeting of their eyes was a physical blow. She vibrated with energy. It was in her words, in every movement she made. His blood grew hot with an unexpected rush of remembered images, *soft limbs, softer sighs.* Woman. In his sudden fascination, he forgot to breath.

She left off trying to motivate the unmoving prisoners, and advanced upon him. Her bold stare raked him, weighing and dismissing his worth with a glare. Her burning eyes bespoke anger under rigid control.

Recalling his scruffy exterior, he suddenly felt unsure and his ardour rapidly cooled. Suppressing the urge to fidget, he stood tall and returned her look, stare for arrogant stare.

"Who are ye? Are ye an idiot, or merely mad?" Catrian hissed quietly as she neared.

The man took umbrage at her tone. He had expected no

gratitude for saving them, but nor had he expected a rebuke! His expression settled into that which he had once practiced so long ago at a river's edge; arrogant and disdainful.

Her expression went from merely angry to outright incensed. "Obviously an idiot!" she gritted out the answer to her own question, her grey-green eyes narrowed dangerously. "By rescuing the women so close t' the village, ye have invited retaliation upon them all."

The man had tuned out her speech after hearing the word "village". It was what he had been searching for, hoping for, a living, breathing village! Would it be a safe haven or would it be infested with more of these red soldiers?

Catrian opened her mouth to say more, but changed her mind. There was something disquieting about this man, something simmering beneath his wild, unkempt appearance, that made her leery of challenging him. He had used magic during the battle. That made him unpredictable. Dangerous. Without her men to back her up, she was in no position to seek answers, nor did he seem inclined to provide them.

Not taking her eyes from him, she bent and stole a sword from one of the bodies littering the ground. The blade glinted dully in her hand as she backed towards the opening in the cage. Her eyes stayed riveted to him, even as she turned her head slightly to make one more overture to the women huddled within. "Follow me if ye would live! Stay here if ye crave death!"

She did not wait for an answer before giving the man one last glare. "Do no' forget t' finish them off, warrior!" she ordered, then loped into the bush.

Her hazel eyes left the man with an impression of iron willed determination, and diamond hard intelligence. His last sight of her was her long braid flipping on her shoulders, as she was absorbed into the forest's gloaming.

His eyes flicked disbelievingly towards the caged prisoners. Did she expect him to kill the women? His outrage grew proportionately. She was obviously the mad one, not he. Shaking his head, he returned to his task of releasing the horses.

"Rebel bitch! Go on and hide in the mountains where ye belong!" a prisoner yelled after her. Despite her hard words, she cautiously exited the cage, and ran into the encroaching forest, chasing after the direction the woman had taken. Her flight released the others from their paralysis and they swarmed from the wagon, tripping over each other to be first from the cage. They gave the bodies on the ground a wide berth and followed their leaders into the forest.

Dara watched the last woman disappear into the brush. Silence settled over the battleground. Surely, her father and brothers must be near?

As minutes stretched, and the stranger continued to ignore her, Dara grew curious. Cautiously, she approached the wild-looking man. "I am Dara. By what name are ye called?"

He glanced up from the tight buckle he was working. His hands faltered to stillness. His tongue stuck in his mouth, for he did not know what answer to give, what answer would be safe.

Her smile stuttered. "Ye do have a name, do ye no'?"

"Gralyre," he blurted, before he knew he was going to. His unused voice pronounced the name hoarsely.

"Like the Lost Prince?" She dimpled at him prettily. "Your parents were the cocky ones!" She skipped lightly to one of the dead soldiers and began to riffle his pockets.

'Gralyre. Gray...leer...' He mulled the name over in his head, testing the syllables for hints of the familiar as he watched her cheerfully robbing the dead. She might be young in years, but there was nothing youthful about her practicality.

She momentarily ceased her pillaging to look him over. "Ye do no' look like a Prince!" she teased him further.

Worried that he had taken an unwitting misstep, he changed the subject. "What were they doing with you?" He gestured towards the dead soldiers. "Why were you a prisoner?"

"Where have ye been for the last three hundred years? 'Tis what they do. About every fourteen years they take women from the villages, and they are never seen again." Her voice turned grim and serious. "'Tis ransom for the life o' all in the village." Her eyes narrowed as she cocked her head. "Ye must be from the Kingdoms in the South to no' know o' this."

He answered her guess with an evasive shrug. "Why would people pay such a price?" he mused as much to himself as to distract her with a question.

"Because the 'Riders would kill everyone, and then take the women anyway. By forsaking the lives o' a few, the rest continue t' live," she stated, matter-of-fact.

The man frowned at the horror of such a practice. The taking of childbearing women explained the empty villages he had passed during his travels. Populations throughout the lands would be decreasing rapidly as fewer children were born. It also explained the burned crofts and townships he had seen, victims of old wars, many years gone. Those who had fought the Tithe had been destroyed. So people had stopped fighting, and were facing destruction anyway. Just at a slower pace.

She looked at the ground, scuffing her bare toes in the dirt. "My Da promised he would hide me when they came, but he did no' have the chance. I was caught in the village, no' at our farm, and was forced into the cage with the others. When ye attacked the Demon Riders, I thought 'twas he and my brothers come t' rescue me."

She cautiously sidled nearer, and then spontaneously grabbed one of his hands in both of hers. "Thank-ye," she said simply. "My family owes ye a life debt. We will no' forget," she promised earnestly.

She was gazing at him sweetly, something akin to hero worship burgeoning in her eyes. He raised his free hand and flicked a finger down her tear stained cheek. He did not know what to reply, so he just smiled.

A rustling in the woods sent him whirling away, smoothly retrieving his sword as he pivoted. He stepped protectively in front of Dara as he awaited the revelation of this newest threat.

Materializing from the forest, three men stepped from the thick brush bordering the track. He felt Little Wolf's surprise and realized he was not the only one caught off guard.

The strangers were dressed in forester green, and had approached from downwind, which was why Little Wolf had not noticed them. They were obviously seasoned woodsmen. The older man held a sword, while the two younger men had short bows with arrows nocked and ready. Judging by the resemblance, they were the older man's sons.

The father thrust out his free hand. "Hold, stranger!" he cautioned. He held his sword out to the side, at the ready, but not threatening as yet. "Ye have my..." He was interrupted by a high-pitched squeal.

"Da! Da!" Dara pushed around the protective bulk of the strange warrior and flung herself into her father's outstretched arms.

'Da?' the man silently mouthed to himself. His lips curled in amusement at the happy reunion. The two brothers received the same enthusiastic greeting after her father managed to fend her off.

"Are ye alright, Dara?" inquired one brother protectively. He was tall and straight, with light brown hair that mirrored his sister's.

"Yes, I am fine, Rewn! Ye should have seen him fight! He is as good as father!" Dara gushed.

The father looked the stranger over, guardedly. "We saw him fight," he said noncommittally. "Rewn, Dajin, better be getting the heads off these Demon Riders. 'Tis almost sundown."

"Come on, friend," invited the older son, Rewn, as he pulled a short sword from his belt. "Since ye created this work ye can do your share o' it. If they get up, they will no' be so easily put down again. Even for someone with your skill." So saying, he decapitated the wagoner's corpse with one hard stroke.

"Why must they be beheaded?"

"They are Demon Riders," said Dajin, the younger son,

rolling his eyes at the stupidity of the question. He was a lesser version of his brother in stature and colouring.

"How could he know, when he is from the Southern King-doms?" Dara defended her hero hotly.

The father and brothers' eyebrows shot upward at her tone of voice, and as one they turned to glare at the stranger.

Their glowers left the man feeling a fool and not even knowing why. The last thing he needed were overprotective men after him for turning the head of a lass. He moved away, and swung his blade, taking his part in the gruesome chore. Far be it for him to question the rituals of this land.

Still shooting suspicious looks at his back, the brothers moved amongst the corpses, participating in the mutilation as their father and sister finished releasing the horses. There were only the four abused wagon horses, and the four spares tied to the back of the cage to see to, for the rest had scattered during the fighting.

While they worked, Little Wolf, unable to keep from the excitement a moment longer, slunk onto the road. The man turned and gave the pup a fierce frown.

'What did I tell you?'

Little Wolf whined pitiably and sank to his belly, tail wagging furiously as his front paws worked busily at moving him forward and keeping him in place at the same time. *'I could not stay.'*

Behind the pup, the man's four horses jogged onto the path. It was open rebellion, no doubt about it.

Smiling, the man relented, hunkered down and opened his arms. The huge, black pup immediately cavorted at him, hitting him full impact in the chest. With a grunt, the man went over in a sprawl, but got Little Wolf in a headlock on the way down and took the wolfdog with him. Grinning, growling and snapping at each other, they wrestled for a moment.

The man finally got on top and forced the wofdog into submission. The pup gave the wolf equivalent of surrender, panting happily from the play.

He looked up to see four identical expressions of incredulity and blushed slightly, although his grin stayed firmly in place as he got to his feet. Little Wolf leaned heavily against him, tongue lolling in contentment.

He felt compelled to offer an explanation. "He is my...mine."

The father looked at him with interest. "Ye keep unusual company, stranger." For a moment, he had been challenged to discern man from beast.

"He is no' a stranger, Da. His name is Gralyre," Dara spoke in the man's defense once more. "He comes from the Southern Kingdoms!"

"I heard ye the first time, daughter."

As the father approached, Little Wolf, timid of this stranger, ducked behind his master's legs.

For a lengthy moment, the father stared into the man's eyes, taking his measure. "Is this true?"

The man shrugged. He could neither confirm nor deny the notion. He held his tongue lest he choose the wrong answer.

"Perhaps, ye would no' be knowing then, but Gralyre is a forbidden name here in the north. Were ye t' reveal it in the wrong company, it would mean your death." The father continued to study him as though expecting a response.

The man had none to give. His stance was loose and relaxed as he returned the father's stare with a calm level gaze of his own.

"My name is Wil," said the father, and thrust forward his arm in greeting.

The man took the firm grip. "I am Gralyre." Despite being outlawed, it was as good a name as any, and to change it now would provoke too many questions with answers he could not give. Having been warned, he would use a different name for the next people he met.

They maintained their clasp for several moments. Gralyre did not flinch away from Wil's probing glance. He had nothing to hide.

Wil had thought the stranger's eyes black, but they were actually an unusual midnight-dark blue. There was an air about this man, this Gralyre, that belied his rough exterior, a quality that Wil could not put his finger on. A mystery.

"Why is the name forbidden?"

Wil let their arms drop away and frowned. Surely even the Kingdoms to the South had heard the tale? Surely even the Kingdoms to the South had heard of Demon Riders? "How is it that ye do no' know of these things?"

Suddenly on his guard, Gralyre stepped back. With the instincts of the feral creature he was, he scented the tension in the air. He did not know these people. It would be dangerous to trust them. What if they only pretended their friendliness?

"I am not from here," Gralyre reminded in such a voice as to discourage all further interest.

Little Wolf, responding to his master's sudden tension, slid out from behind Gralyre, his head lowered, his hackles up. Eerily silent, the wolfdog stared fixedly at Wil as he circled the man in a large arc, stepping sidewise to maintain a forward posture, awaiting a command to attack.

A frisson of fear went down Wil's spine at the man's flat, arctic tone, the wolf's stalking presence. He backed slowly away, and felt his sons move to flank his shoulders protectively. The stranger had gone from a curiosity to a threat in a heartbeat.

"I see that ye have your own horses. We will be taking these four rested ones t' make good our own escape. These others who were pulling the wagon are done in."

The wolfdog returned to Gralyre's heel. Man and beast both remained alert and fixated upon Wil.

"Sons, daughter, time t' go. Farewell Gralyre," said Wil. "Heed my advice about your name." He ushered his children onto the horses and steered them back up the road in the direction that the wagon had come from.

Before they had completely vanished around the bend, Dara turned and waved with a sweet smile, either not sensing the tension, or ignoring it. "Farewell!"

Gralyre did not smile in return, although he raised his hand. The question of forbidden names plagued him as he was left standing alone on the road, the dusk casting a shadow shroud over the mutilated bodies of seven Demon Riders.

Demon Riders. The name certainly matched their nature, but why behead the corpses?

Little Wolf sniffed one of the bodies. *'They still smell wrong.'* His muzzle crinkled in a snarl of distaste.

ഇരൂ

When Wil and his family arrived at the rendezvous point, Catrian and her men were already waiting. She looked dainty compared to the dozen warriors surrounding her. Dainty, until you met her eyes.

Catrian did not waste time with pleasantries. "Is he one o' yours?" she asked as she caught the horse's bridle, stilling the beast so that Wil could dismount.

Wil did not ask to whom she referred as he swung his leg over and slid to the ground. "No."

Catrian jerked her chin to indicate Dara, dismissing the stranger from her mind for now. "She canno' stay with ye. The Demon Riders will be back."

Wil nodded. "I know." He glanced up at Dara, his heartbreak plain to see.

"Da?" Dara asked tremulously. She bit her lip. She did not want to go. She could not stay.

Wil raised up his arms for his daughter, and she leapt from her horse into his hug. "I love ye, girl, but ye are no' safe here!"

Dara nodded against his shoulder. With the terror of the Tithe wagon clear in her mind, she at last understood why she must obey his edict. "I love ye, Da!"

Dajin snorted from atop his horse. "Ye are only going t' the mountains. Ye are the lucky one. Da will no' let me go t' fight with the Rebels. I have t' stay in Raindell."

Dara glared at her twin. "I wish that it were ye, and no' me, that had t' go. I wish it were ye who had t' fear the Tithe!"

Dajin rolled his eyes. "That is no' what I mean, and ye know it!"

Rewn sighed heavily. "Leave it Dajin." He slid from his horse and hugged Dara close. "Keep safe. We will join ye soon."

Dajin's lips pressed together mutinously, but he kept further comments to himself as he dismounted and joined his siblings.

Dara hugged her older brother for a long moment before pulling away. Rewn brushed her hair back and gave her a kiss on the forehead for luck.

Dajin gave his twin a perfunctory embrace and then pushed her towards the man holding the fresh horse for her. Three other men were already mounted and ready to lead her to safety.

The Rebel warrior boosted her into the saddle and passed her the reins. Dara glanced at her family with panicked eyes. Everything was happening too fast. She wanted to slow it down, make the moment last. But time would move at its own pace, not hers. "Farewell!" she gasped around her tears.

Rewn took a step forward, his hands clenched tight at his side, helpless to ease his sister's distress.

Dajin waved negligently, looking bored.

Wil smiled encouragingly. "Ye will be fine. Ye will be safe."

Dara smiled through her tears, a poor attempt. Then the horses were in motion, spurring down the track, taking her to the safety of the Heathren Mountains, and the stronghold of the resistance.

CHAPTER THREE

Gralyre jerked awake, stifling his bellow of fear so that only a low, grunting moan escaped. The nightmare again. Every night. Would it never cease?

He wiped the terror sweat from his face, and rolled from his bedroll, panting lightly as his heartbeat slowed its frantic pace.

'All is well. There is no danger,' Little Wolf reassured. The pup lay nearby, his eyes bright upon his master's face, his muzzle resting along his front paws. The sun had not yet arisen, and the black wofdog was all but invisible against the ground.

Gralyre patted his thigh to invite the pup for a morning scratch. His restless gaze went to the valley below, where darkened buildings still lay in slumber.

He had begun to encounter inhabited lands by noon of the day following the battle. The farms, though poor, had shown signs of cultivation. Sickly crops had rippled in the breeze as scruffy sheep and emaciated goats had chewed their way through the sparse fields. Smoke had even curled from the chimneys of some of the farmhouses, proving themselves occupied.

He had seen no people though many times he had felt eyes follow him as he passed. If not for the animals and the planted crops, he would have thought the area as deserted as the lands he had travelled from.

His eyes flicked towards a light that appeared in the pre-dawn darkness. The village was beginning to stir. Still he waited. After months of being alone he thought he would have been anxious for civilization, but instead he was unaccountably nervous.

As the sun made its assent into the sky, Gralyre continued to study the town from the edge of the forest where he had camped. His concealment lay about a quarter of a mile across an open green space from the walls. Though the village was quite large, there was almost no traffic in and out of the gates. A pall of thick smoke hung over the town, spewed forth by many chimneys. It seemed a grim and unwelcoming place, and he was consumed with skittish reasons to go no nearer.

People would be surrounding him, talking to him, maybe touching him. He shuddered in claustrophobic dread.

What if he made a misstep, as he had with Wil, something as simple as his name?

What if Demon Riders occupied the village?

All other excuses fell by the wayside, and this became his primary concern. He was left to ponder again why their heads had to be removed before sunset.

After the massacre of his family, Little Wolf had made him burn the bodies of the soldiers he had slain.

'They smell wrong,' the wolfdog had insisted.

Gralyre's mind shied away from the painful memories. His chin lowered to rest on top of Little Wolf's head as he continued to contemplate the village. His hands sifted deeply through the wolfdog's luxurious black coat.

Even the compelling woman from the wagon, he now clearly understood, had been alluding to the Demon Riders when she had said to *'Finish them off.'*

Why?

He rubbed a hand over his face, and through his beard, sighed heavily, and made his choice. Though he was more than willing to risk his own life by going into the town, he was not about to place Little Wolf in danger.

Gralyre gently rubbed the pup's soft ears. *'If I do not return, wait here for no more than two days, then return to our farm. If I am dead you will need a safe place to live. You must obey me in this, Little Wolf. I want you safe.'*

'I will wait two days for you,' promised Little Wolf solemnly.

The two-day wait would allow the four brutalized horses from the caged wagon to recover their strength. There was plenty of rich forage for them here.

Gralyre had every intention of returning by nightfall, but should the worst of his imaginings come to pass, he could depend upon Little Wolf to see his instructions carried out.

He debated donning his chain mail, but his threadbare shirt would no longer disguise the rich shimmer of the silvery armour. If he appeared too prosperous he might become the target of thieves. Yet he did not want to be separated from any important artifacts of his past, so he packed the bundle carrying his most precious belongings onto the horse he had decided to ride.

The packs he would bring also contained items scavenged from the ruins he had passed, that he might be able to trade for food or coin. He also had hopes of finding a horse trader so that he could unburden himself of his growing herd.

It was with fearful anticipation that Gralyre departed. As the road curved away from view, he glanced back for a final farewell to Little Wolf.

The wolfdog waited stoically, ears and tail drooping, as he watched his master ride away. Sad and lonely thoughts were already drifting from the pup.

In sharp contrast, the horses were complaining resentfully about being left behind in favour of Gralyre's mount. That one made a big show for their benefit, lifting its hooves high and tossing its head airily.

Exasperated by their unceasing jockeying for status, Gralyre put his heels to the side of his horse and forced it into a canter down the track.

He reined in at the edge of the forest and once more scrutinized the treeless fields surrounding the small township. From here, it was a short ride to the open gates of the wood and stone palisade surrounding the town. He would be in full view, and unprotected, as he crossed the fields, an easy target for any soldier upon the walls.

From a distance, nothing seemed amiss. Smoke curled lazily from chimneys, and he could see laundry flapping in the stiffening breeze. His tightened lips betrayed his anxiety, as he set the horse to a slow walk out into the open.

Gralyre was the only one traveling the road. Even the sparse traffic he had observed the evening before had evaporated. For a town of this size, he thought the lack very odd. He continued to scan the open space for danger as he cautiously approached the palisade.

As he neared the gates, he was struck by the rundown poverty of the town. The villagers had done their best to repair the tumbled stone and crumbling mortar of the protective wall with wooden posts, though even these were rotten and sagging, and missing altogether in places, leaving large gaps in the defenses. He could have arrived the previous night and had no trouble leaving at any time he wished.

He passed through the unmanned gate and was assailed by filth such as he had never beheld. The street was an open sewer. The stench made his eyes water, and he wished fervently that he had approached the village from downwind, though it would hardly have mattered. The ramshackle buildings were well steeped in the thick stew of odors. A flea would have more success moving its dog, than the fitful little breeze had of clearing the thick miasma.

Rough lumber and other odds and ends leaned against the inside of the palisade wall. Gralyre thought it discarded debris until he saw a man dodge furtively into an opening and realized that they were dwellings. White mold seeped high upon the boards, the sickness of the place infecting everything it touched.

The horse danced sideways around a rotting bundle of rags. The moldy cloth undulated as rats scurried away from the vibrations of the horse's hooves. The horse gave a low grunt of disgust and, silently, Gralyre echoed the sentiment.

Two and three-storey buildings crowded over the street, blocking the cool sun. The sky narrowed to a blue slit of beckoning cleanliness as he moved deeper into the town.

There were few people about. Those females he spotted were either ancient crones or very young girls, neither fit for the Tithe, he supposed. The predominately male population was gaunt and hollow-eyed, and looked to have never seen a decent meal in their lifetime. Many sported horrible sores and deformities. Those he made eye contact with immediately dropped their gazes and scurried away in a manner akin to the rodents his horse had disturbed. As he passed, he could feel the eyes of the more feral villagers coveting even his poor belongings. Ragged beggars gave way grudgingly before his steady progression.

Some of the villagers eyed him with distrust while others stared blankly as though their minds were so consumed with the need for survival that they could not spare the interest. A few naked children, little bellies distended by malnutrition, pushed the muck of the street aside with sticks as they searched for scraps.

Nothing that Gralyre saw made sense. The village had not seemed large enough to support poverty of this magnitude, but as he moved further into the town, the prosperity of the place was little better than what he had just seen. The weathered and rotten buildings were collapsing around their occupants. Some of the structures seemed abandoned, as though their owners were already dead and laid to rest in their own hovel. The stench of the place certainly supported the presence of death. Other buildings seemed empty until a furtive movement gave away a skulking presence.

The street was fetlock deep in muck and refuse. Gralyre was doubly glad he was riding, not walking. Flies rose in angry clouds as the horse set its hooves into the sucking mud of the open sewers.

The horse complained bitterly about the filth. It wanted the man to dismount and pick the muck from its hooves.

'Later.' Gralyre was sorry for the horse's distress but was not about to come nearer to the diseased ground than he had to.

The horse shifted sideways and its ears canted back in anger at Gralyre's refusal. Craftily, it rolled one eye back to check on its rider's state of attention.

Gralyre caught a flash of the horse's intent and tightened his thighs against the saddle and his grip on the reins. *'Do not even think of trying it!'* he warned sternly.

The horse started in surprise that Gralyre had guessed its intention to unseat him. It blew out a gusty sigh and its head drooped in resignation as it continued to plod with sucking steps through the filthy street.

Gralyre searched for an inn or, at least a tavern, as he explored the town's three main streets and numerous side passages and alleyways. As he wandered up and down the crooked byways, his was the only horse in sight. He was not surprised. When people starved, dray animals would be of more use as food. His was doubly glad he had left Little Wolf behind.

At the centre of town he entered a market square. The people selling wares, although in slightly better health than the other poor wretches he had thus seen, were still marked by the surrounding poverty. They half-heartedly tried to interest him in their scant products, poorly tooled leather belts and rough bolts of raw cloth, gourds, squashes and potatoes from late autumn harvests, but with a shake of his head he declined. Like beaten animals, they cowered back to their stalls.

He was doubly confused by the lack of traffic if this was what

passed for a market day. It made no sense. Nor did it make sense
that the starving people of this market had given up so quickly to
try and sell their wares. A pall of despair, hopelessness and fear
hung over this place, defeat of the very worst kind.

On the edge of the square, he finally spied what appeared to
be an Inn. As he moved towards it, the breeze died and the
horse's hooves, sucking wetly in the muck of the street, sounded
too loudly into the silence. Shivers crawled up his spine as
Gralyre glanced around uneasily.

He was in time to watch the last of the people disappear
into their hovels, and down alleyways, leaving him alone in the
square. Even the vendors had packed up their stalls and carts,
and vanished with astonishing speed.

Discomfited, he halted his horse and continued to scan the
empty market square. Why had the people left the street? Was
this a normal occurrence at mid-morn? If all the towns were
alike to this one he definitely preferred the cleanliness of the
forest he had lived in for the last few months.

After a moment of indecision, Gralyre walked his horse
forward the final few feet and dismounted in front of the likely
looking building. It was a large, rudely kept structure in better
repair than much of the rest of the village. Its carved wooden
sign of a running wolf hung crookedly from the eaves on its
rusted chain, and swung like a squeaky wind chime as the slack
breeze pushed at it fitfully.

Gralyre looped the reins of the horse loosely around the
unused hitching post and paused once more to assess his
surroundings.

'*Be careful,*' he warned the animal, sending it images of what the population of the town might try, reinforcing his command.

The horse laid its ears back and cocked one hoof threateningly. It was not about to become somebody's meal.

Gralyre trod carefully up the three rotting treads leading to the stoop and reached for the handle of the heavy oak door. He pushed it open and stepped inside.

The babble of conversation ceased and silence reigned, giving the heavy door, booming shut behind him, an ominous emphasis.

Gralyre paused, waiting for his sight to adjust to the gloom. The dark shadows slowly resolved themselves into row upon row of occupied trestle tables. Two large fireplaces at opposite ends of the large room spewed smoke and heat while potboys cranked rotisseries laden with scant chunks of meat.

The room was overly crowded and every eye was upon him. Gralyre was surprised to see so many people when he had seen so few since he had entered the town. He shrugged away his misgivings. They were likely staring because he was a stranger. He doubted this impoverished place received many visitors. As yet, he had seen no sign of the hated Demon Riders. There was no reason to be on guard. Despite reassuring himself, the hairs on his nape sensed the tension in the air that he chose not to acknowledge, and bristled with foreboding.

His boots sounded heavily as he walked across the hard packed dirt and stone of the floor towards a slat-wood counter, behind which a man with the look of an Innkeeper stood.

Gralyre had long since given up hope of selling his goods and horses here, but it would not hurt to socialize with the villagers to discover more about their customs. The more he learned, the less likely he would be to make mistakes.

People moved from his path like cockroaches scurrying from the light. There was still no conversation. The men standing at the rough counter shifted to make room for him as though he were a disease they were afraid to catch. Compared to the poor wretches he had seen in the street, these men seemed almost prosperous. Their clothing was in good repair, and some of the raw wool had been given dye so that muted yellows and reds decorated some of their tunics. They were without the sickness afflicting the people he had seen on the street, and their faces, though lean, lacked the extreme gauntness of starvation.

The Innkeeper gave Gralyre a flat-eyed stare of expectation. As casually as possible, Gralyre glanced into the tankards of the men surrounding him.

A flash of memory; *Bubbly, amber, intoxicating.*

"Ale." That one word dropped sharply in the silent room.

The Innkeeper dipped a pewter tankard into a large barrel set at his feet and smacked it down smartly on the slat-wood counter in front of Gralyre. Conversation in the room resumed quietly, furtively.

Gralyre reached for some coin but the Innkeeper waived it aside.

"No need for that. No need for that." He shooed his hands at Gralyre. "Ye be the boyo what saved the women from the Tithe." It was a statement, not a question. Word of the ambush had roared through the town like a violent storm. "Ye rescued m' daughter. Your coin's no good here." His tone of voice was hostile, at odds with his words, as though he resented the hospitality he felt obliged to show.

It took Gralyre a moment to translate the man's thick accent. "Thank-you," he said simply and took a swig from his mug. The ale was young and very sour but for Gralyre the familiar taste was an awakening. He was left wondering what other tastes he had forgotten.

From the back of the room, Wil and his sons craned to watch the stranger, cursing the man's folly in coming here, to this place, at this time.

The town meeting had been called to find a way to save Raindell from the avenging wrath of the Demon Riders over the ambush of the Tithe Wagon. Already, the families who could afford to do so had fled into the forest, creeping secretively from the town and outlaying farms overnight to avoid the spying eyes of the collaborators, leaving Raindell deserted but for the sickly or civic minded.

"If 'twas me, stranger, I would drink up fast an' leave," stated the Innkeeper, interrupting the savouring going on in front of him.

Gralyre glanced up in surprise. "Why?" As his lips formed the word, he already knew the answer. Ugly muttering had sprung up around the room. He caught snatches of conversation as the men's ire arose, their bravery augmented by their neighbour's and the liquid courage they consumed from their tankards.

"...bastard, showing 'is face here..."

"...be the death o' us all..."

"...He has brought the doom upon us, and no mistake..."

Muscles bunched in battle readiness, Gralyre carefully placed his tankard back upon the bar. Casually, he gripped the rough plank counter and assessed the situation, trying to think of a way to get back to his horse without being slaughtered. His eyes locked with those of the Innkeeper, but it was obvious that there would be no help from that quarter.

"Ye saved me daughter," stated the Innkeeper with much dignity, "and for that I thank ye. But ye have also brought the wrath o' Doaphin down upon us by offing the 'Riders!" His voice rose, becoming dirtier, meaner. "By saving the few, ye condemned the whole, boyo!"

The Innkeeper swept Gralyre's tankard from the bar and dumped the contents to the floor, obviously regretting his largesse of moments before.

The muttering grew louder. The men were flogging their courage, and it would not be long before they acted.

Gralyre nodded his thanks to the Innkeeper, as though he had received the most pleasing of meals and service. Without a word, he turned and strode casually back through the crowded room towards the exit, exuding as much confidence as possible. It was a delicate balance. If he went too fast, or hesitated even a moment, they would be on him like a pack of starving dogs. He had almost made it to the door when the spark hit the kindling.

"The only way t' save ourselves is t' show the 'Riders that we be innocent! If we kill him maybe they will let us live!" A roar of approval went up from the assembled men.

Gralyre dived at the entrance. The heavy oak door had not

latched properly behind him and it crashed open as his weight hit it. He rolled out onto the front stoop, two steps ahead of the mob, turned to grab his horse and found it gone.

Someone had nicked it while he had been inside. He paused in stunned surprise, a moment that allowed the mob to catch him.

A villager spun him around and threw a punch at his head.

Gralyre saw stars as the meaty fist struck home. He ducked the next blow and sent back one of his own. The man gave a startled yelp, went down, and did not rise again. But another man took his place, and another and another. They slowly began to overwhelm him. Gralyre had to fight his own panic. It was his nightmare brought to life!

Gralyre's nose broke with stunning pain as someone clubbed him with a rotted plank wrenched from the Inn's stoop. He stumbled back and his groin exploded from a blow by a knee. He fell, helped along by a blizzard of clouts and kicks.

Unable to protect himself from the enraged mob, he curled into a tight ball and tried to shield his head with his arms. His legs were grabbed, and jerked as his boots were stolen. His dagger fell away, lost to him even as he tried to reach for it.

A kick landed in the small of his back, blasting it with agony so extreme he scarcely felt several ribs break from another well-placed boot. He fainted, unaware now of the further beating he endured. His slack body twitched and heaved with the blows.

"Wait, wait! Stop!" commanded a voice from the crowd. "Do no' kill him! We must give him t' the 'Riders alive, as proof o' our innocence! They will be more lenient on us then! If he is dead, they may no' believe us!"

"Good idea, Wil!" Some of the saner men took up the cause.

It took long moments of yelling for the idea to seep fully into the mob, and several shoves and kicks to quell the bloodlust of the men. Grudgingly, they backed off from the bloody, torn figure on the ground. Many gave parting kicks to the unmoving man as they went.

"I only hope he is no' already dead!" Wil's voice was heavy with condemnation as he pushed forward, moving quickly to the body and kneeling down. The men parted for him, for he was well respected. The excited babble of their voices died away as they awaited the verdict.

"Well, Wil?" First Councilman Cramer prompted. As de facto mayor of the township of Raindell, he had been most concerned with finding a way to save the town and with it, his position of importance. Collaborator or no, he was as expendable to the Demon Riders as the next man.

"He still breathes!" Wil announced. "Quick! Get him inside. We will hold him in Dolper's stillroom. 'Tis the only place in town with a lock!" The crowd muttered its approval as two men stepped forward and roughly dragged the unconscious stranger back into the tavern.

The Innkeeper, Dolper, reached into a pocket of the large smock he wore and brought forth an oversized iron key. The men watched reverently as he inserted it into the imposing padlock hanging off of a door behind the bar. The brewery lock was to keep thieves from sampling his ales.

The two men dragged Gralyre into the room and dumped him

on loose grain sacks.

"Out, out!" Dolper ordered.

The men retreated and Dolper locked the door behind them. "He will no' soon get free from there!" He dropped the key back into his pocket and patted it reassuringly.

The men laughed their agreement, slapping each other on the back. Drinks were served all around, on the house, which was unheard of. It was time to celebrate. Raindell was saved.

While everyone was fully occupied in telling the tale of their part in the capture of the dangerous stranger, Wil summoned his sons with a subtle twitch of his chin. Unnoticed by the rowdy crowd, the three men exited the tavern, heads held conspiratorially close.

ဆာလ

Excited by the afternoon's events, the villagers who could afford to splurge continued their impromptu celebration. As their money ran out, the men gradually trickled from the tavern and back to their families, secure in the knowledge that they had rescued their village from certain annihilation at the avenging hands of the Demon Riders.

CHAPTER FOUR

Dara groaned inwardly with relief as the leader of her three-man escort, Derek, finally called a halt. The Rebel had kept a brutal pace today. She leaned forward and swung her leg stiffly over the saddle and winced as her knees and chaffed thighs protested. Slowly, she lowered herself to the ground. She kept a tight hold on her patient horse as her muscles released their cramps. She could not walk. She was too stiff.

She glanced up in time to see Thomas and Gert nudge each other and smirk at her. There was no kindness to their teasing. She faced her saddle, clung to her horse and worked to keep from crying as she swayed in place. It was not her fault that she was saddlesore! When had she ever had cause to ride a horse, day in and day out, as these men had? Her spine straightened and she took a step.

Her legs collapsed, and she dropped into an undignified heap. Thomas and Gert guffawed loudly. Derek sighed loudly as he scooped Dara up and sat her on a log next to the unlit fire. Moments later her bedroll landed in the dirt beside her.

"Thank-ye," Dara said politely. She was almost too tired to feel ashamed of her fragility.

Derek grunted back and led her now unsaddled mount to join the other three that were already staked and grazing.

Dara sighed and set about rolling out her bed. She wanted nothing so much as to curl up and sleep.

Exhaustion claimed her as she stretched out and closed her eyes. After that, her evening passed in flashes of awareness.

...The firelight, a bowl slaps down beside her... She sits upright and takes a couple of bites of thick stew... The bowl is snatched away... A rough hand pushes her to lie flat... The low conversation of the three men... Words, harmful as darts, penetrate her restless, exhausted dreams...

"...Pathetic lowlander... Babysitting the no good little twitch... Pull her own weight... Bloody sheep to the slaughter... Should have left her to the Tithe..."

...A scrape of boots, her eyelids flutter up, looking beyond the coals banked for heat, as one of the two sleeping men is roused, Thomas, she thinks, to stand his turn at watch. Her leaden eyes drift closed...

Before she could believe it, she was roughly shaken awake and boosted back onto her horse. A hard biscuit was shoved into her hands and a skein of water slung from the saddle. Then it was ride, ride, ride, as if the Deathren dogged their heels.

The three men spared her little sympathy. They had made it abundantly clear that they were not pleased with the escort duty they had been given. After several overtures of friendship were rudely ignored or outright scorned, Dara fell silent and did little but pray that the long journey to Verdalan would be over quickly.

Derek kept them to the backcountry and avoided all roads. There was no explanation to be made for a group of human's on horses and their numbers were too few to win a fight, so furtiveness was their ally.

They rode in silence, leaving Dara's thoughts to wander as they would. To distract herself from the agony in her flanks, she thought often of the heroic warrior who had saved her from the Tithe. Her young imaginings would sometimes leave her sighing and blushing.

She tried not to think about her father and brothers. Sometimes the homesickness would choke her, and she did not want the Rebels to think her weak if they caught her crying.

She would grow stronger, and she would work harder. Maybe then they would not look down on her so. She would prove her worth or die trying.

ଟ୦ଔ

Gralyre awoke gradually, swimming slowly up through thick layers of pain. He could not open his eyes. It took more strength than he thought possible to painfully, hesitantly, reach up a hand to investigate.

He discovered his blood-matted hair pasted thickly across his face. The blood had congealed, though not quite dried. He had been unconscious for at least an hour.

He moaned from the light pressure of his quaking fingers against his battered features as he peeled the strands away from his eyes. Even with the hair gone, his eyelids were still sealed, swollen and tender. Tears and fluid oozed from the corners, burning into cuts and abrasions on his cheeks.

His body palsied with suffering and shock as he lowered his hand and sought to catalogue his injuries.

He knew, from the stabbing pain coming from his nose, that it was broken. Unable to breath through it, he panted lightly through his mashed lips.

His jaw was sore, but seemed only bruised as he closed it momentarily to swallow the blood rich saliva that had accumulated in his mouth. His tongue had a large wound where he had bitten it during the beating. Some of his teeth were loose, but seemed resigned to remain anchored within his mouth.

A firebrand pierced Gralyre's chest as he tried to draw a deeper breath. His body contorted to escape the torture, which caused even more suffering. Some of his ribs were broken, the rest were badly battered. He wrapped his arms tightly about his chest, trying to ease his ribs so that he might breath, trying to relax his body from his tight convulsion of pain. Every shallow breath was a hard fought victory.

His arms, though bruised and painful, seemed to have survived the beating intact. His knuckles were scraped raw from defensive blows and the little finger on his left hand was dislocated.

The worst of the agony screamed from his lower back. This injury concerned him the most, but he thanked the Gods of Fortune that he still had feeling in his legs. As he tested those limbs, bone deep bruises made their presence known.

Gralyre eased over onto his side to relieve the pressure upon his back and lay as still as possible, made helpless by agony.

Why had they not killed him? What were they waiting for?

ಐೲ

"He looks dead," came a dispassionate observation. "Be ye sure he yet lives?"

Gralyre awoke groggily as the voice penetrated the thick fog of pain. Light flared behind his swollen eyelids, telling him of a lantern. He could sense someone peering into his face from a short distance. He kept his shallow breathing to the same pace so they would not know he had awakened.

"Yea, I can see 'is chest movin'." It was a different voice. At least two men were in the room with him. "Just ye hope 'e stays that way 'til the 'Riders come." The man's breath puffed down upon Gralyre's face as he spoke.

"What should I do with this?" asked the first voice.

"Leave it on the floor. If 'e wants water, 'e can get it 'imself. I be no nursemaid," said the second man, from further away now. He must have straightened from his close perusal.

There came a loud, sloshing thump as a pail dropped heavily. "Come on. We do no' want t' be here if 'e wakes up. Do no' want t' hear 'im beg!" They chuckled and took the light with them when they left.

The door opened and Gralyre heard the murmur of voices. It banged shut and a lock scraped into place. All was dark and still. He may even have succumbed to his injuries again before, deep in his subconscious, the word *water* finally took on meaning.

The swelling in his right eye had subsided enough that he was able to slit it open. His vision jittered and swung as he tried to find the bucket. Across an impossible span of rough plank floor, a leather pail had been left near the entrance to his prison. He could see its outline in the spill of light from under the door.

Gralyre lost sight of the pail as the room spun and lurched. He growled in despair, but stopped the sound immediately as his ribs protested this unauthorized use of air. He cursed his infirmity as tears of agony streaked from his eyes.

After several long moments spent recapturing his breath, his thirst came to overshadow his pain. As slowly as possible, he eased himself onto his stomach and began an excruciating crawl towards the bucket. His abused body forced him to halt and rest after each small movement, but his iron determination kept him moving.

Over time, the murmur of voices in the outer room ceased. The guiding light under the door went dark. Yet he stubbornly refused to be defeated in his quest.

Time took a leap forward, telling him that he had fainted. Morning had arrived, seeping a faint glow through the cracks and knotholes in the outer wall, lightening the dark room to grey. And still he fought his way, inch by painful inch towards his goal until finally, after a pain induced eternity, he reached the water. So frail was he, it had taken the night to cover a distance of less than ten feet.

Gralyre lifted himself feebly upon his elbows and choked back a scream as agony tore through his injured back. He hung his head and retched, but that caused even more pain to explode from his broken ribs. He panted lightly, keening in distress as he waited for his body to adjust to this new level of suffering.

When he felt able, he leaned into the pail and took a couple of small sips. As he lifted his head to swallow painfully, he saw swirls of blood pirouette into patterns within the water. He lost his focus on the bucket as blackness formed in front of his functioning eye. He fought the darkness as the room pirouetted and his stomach heaved and threatened.

He must escape! They had not allowed him to live out of kindness! He vaguely remembered the overheard conversation from his jailers. They meant to ransom him to the Demon Riders!

Overcoming his pain one last time, he stretched upward for the handle of the door, but it was useless. He could not rise high enough to reach. Pain detonated in his body and he fainted.

৪০৫৪

Days passed hazily as fever racked his injured frame. He would lose consciousness then awaken to find watery gruel lying beside him or fresh water. At first he tried to count the number of meals in order to track how many days he had been held prisoner, but his delirium made the task impossible.

During a lucid moment, Gralyre managed to reset his dislocated finger. The relief from that one small pain was worth the agony of the procedure. His other wounds were beyond his ability to aid. No healers were sent to minister to his injuries. He had been left to suffer and whether he lived was up to his own stubborn will to survive.

Often, the man he remembered as the Innkeeper, named Dolper, he soon gleaned from overheard conversation, would accompany his jailers as they brought food or water. The Innkeeper did not speak to him, and Gralyre was too proud to beg for aid. Apparently Dolper's gratitude for the rescue of his daughter had been paid in full with a tankard of ale.

His periods of lucidity grew and his situation became clearer. His thoughts revolved constantly around escape, but weak as he was, Gralyre could find no way out of his cell. Walking was beyond him, so he worked to perfect his crawling.

Little Wolf would be gone by now, and for that he was grateful. To make certain, he opened his mind wide, but could feel no response from his dog or the horses. All he could sense was the large rodent population thriving within the village. Despite the thousands of small minds that teemed through his, he had never felt more alone. The beasts were too low to communicate above the instinctual need to forage for food, to protect territory, and to mate.

His connection to the minds of the army of rats did grant him a way to seek out hidden passages, to figure out where he was imprisoned and how he might effect an escape. From his sickbed, he explored the village in exquisite detail. Within a few days he knew every passageway and escape route out of town, even the ones that the villagers knew nothing of.

For instance, there was a tunnel running from the Inn to an abandoned hovel across the square. The opening lay just beyond the locked door to his cell, hidden behind the Innkeeper's bar, less than twenty feet from where he was confined. It might as well have been a thousand miles distant for all the good it did him.

As a prisoner, Gralyre did not rate a candle, but during the day, anemic light filtered into his cell through chinks between the rough planks of an outside wall. It was by this meager glow, during one of his alert periods, that he finally made note of the hogsheads of ale ageing in the corner. The barrels were stacked three deep against the wall.

He had not smelled the fermenting grains due to the swelling in his broken nose, and his brain had been so addled he had not made the connection before now.

A demonic grin flitted across his swollen and cracked lips as he crawled slowly, painfully, towards the barrels. Gralyre found a mallet and spigot set aside for just the purpose he had in mind. The Innkeeper was about to pay a hefty price for locking him within his thief-proof brewery.

Heartened by the small revenge, he hammered the spigot into a keg with feeble strikes, biting his lip to endure the pain the movement caused. The barrel successfully pierced, he sagged to his belly and rolled painfully to his back, maneuvering himself under the tap.

The ale was as sour as Gralyre remembered, but after swallowing as much as his belly could hold, his pain eased and his hunger melted away. The respite from the agony soothed him into a deep, healing sleep.

ഇരു

Dara was numb with exhaustion. She kept her eyes riveted to the haunches of the horse in front of her. Three more days, and they would reach the city of Verdalan, and she would never need to ride this horse again.

Three days…. Three days Counting days had become her personal mantra, just as yesterday it had been *four days* and tomorrow it would be *two*. No torture lasted forever; the end was nigh. *Anything can be endured for three days…. Three days.*

It was a moment before she realized that the horse leading hers had stopped. Dara perked up. Anything that paused the ceaseless impact of hooves was a good thing.

Derek held up a hand, halting all three of the trailing riders. Dara's horse snorted, and Derek whipped around to shoot her a glare. Dara felt absurdly guilty. It had been the horse after all, and not her, that had made the offensive sound.

But then the unnatural quiet of the forest penetrated her mind. No birds chirped, no insects buzzed. The hairs on her arms bristled as her sixth sense trumpeted to her that danger was near. She held her breath.

Slowly, Derek drew his sword and pointed it at a deadfall. Piles of churned, clumped earth and uprooted brush covered the roots of the felled forest giant. He glanced over his shoulder at the other two warriors, and nodded. The men quietly pulled ropes from their saddlebags, made loops, and swung them lazily overhead.

With barely heard rustles, the ropes slewed through the air and landed amidst the debris. Quick jerks set the loop of ropes around thick branches. The men wrapped the near ends around their saddles. Clicking quietly to their steeds, they began to back the horses away. The ropes creaked as they took up the pressure and strain. The debris pile shifted.

A snarling roar rumbled out from the pile, setting the horses to dancing with fear, a voice of evil playing against pitches that could not be produced by anything but the throat of darkness, a demon's call.

Dara covered her ears to block the sound, but it did no good. The malignant sound resonated against her skull, her chest, and froze her heart with terror.

"Now!" Derek yelled.

With whoops and hollers, the men broke their silence and drove their horses back. The debris under the deadfall pulled free and broke apart.

Sunlight fell into the previously shielded place. The creature hidden within screamed as it burst into flame. An inhuman sound made by an inhuman beast. Abandoning its hole, it charged out into the clearing, slashing and snarling, trailing blazing debris and thick, oily smoke in its wake.

"Ride!" yelled one of the men. Dara put her heels to her horse. She glanced over her shoulder in time to see the creature's flame wrapped arm swipe through the spot where her horse had stood moments before. Razor claws parted the air, and scaled skin sloughed off the arm in the maelstrom of flames. Maddened eyes glared at her from a reptilian face aflame with sparks and smoke.

Dara shrieked and faced forward, concentrating on staying in her saddle as her horse leaped a deadfall and careened around a tree.

The creature took three shambling leaps after the fleeing

horses, staggered to a halt and collapsed. Fire continued to eat at it as it twisted and writhed. Its roars ceased.

"Hold!" yelled Derek. He leaned down and grabbed Dara's reins, dragging her horse to a halt along with his. Both horses kept stomping and blowing, eager to be away from the scene. Dara felt their urgency as her own, and took deep sobbing breaths to keep from defying Derek and continuing to run.

"Thomas, Gert, go make sure," Derek ordered.

The two men swung their horses about and trotted the thirty or so feet back to the burning carcass.

The Rebels dismounted and used the tips of their swords to poke and prod the cinders and ashes into more direct sunlight. The pyre shifted and sank as the flesh continued to be consumed. Soon there was nothing left but the scorched earth where the creature had died, and a thick haze of smoke that drifted through the sunbeams that penetrated through to the forest floor.

"Ye alright, girl?" Derek asked gruffly.

Dara nodded, though she felt shaky and scared to death. She tried to match the Rebel's cool tone. "What was it?"

"A Stalker nest. It was holed up for the day. We did no' want that beast on our trail come nightfall. 'Twas pure luck from the Gods o' Fortune that we came across this one and killed it." He pointed an admonishing finger at her. "Remember girl, only sunlight or Maolar blades can kill one o' Doaphln's hounds."

"Do we have any Maolar blades?"

Derek snorted. "No one has Maolar blades anymore."

"Sunlight and Maolar," Dara repeated dutifully, but inside all she could think was, *Three days... Only three more days.*

ༀ

More time passed in an alcoholic haze, which did no good for Gralyre's already spinning head, but at least deadened the agony in his body. Finally came the day he awoke with a pounding in his head that was more hangover than concussion.

Groaning, he got to his scabbed knees and swollen hands, and crawled to the bucket in the corner he had designated for his bodily functions. He cursed that his memory had not warned him of the drink's revenge, even as he was pleased to see that for the first time there was no blood in his urine.

After he had relieved himself, he carefully tried to stand, as he had done every day since his beating. The pain in his back had receded to a dull ache, although any exertion brought back the searing brand. His ribs were his real problem now. With any movement, dagger thrusts of agony snatched his breath and strength. But today, to his joy and amazement, he shakily gained his feet.

Standing meant that walking was not far behind. Escape was now within his grasp. His mind turned to the logistics of gaining his freedom as he swayed in place.

The brewery was windowless and had only one entrance, which was always locked. Gralyre had tried the latch at every opportunity. Even if the door were to be left open, Gralyre would still have to pass through a gauntlet of drunken villagers. The last time he had tried that had left him beaten and bloody.

The outside wall was also a vulnerable point in his prison. The gaps bespoke poor construction. Were he at his full strength he had no doubt that he could kick out a loose board and flee. However, it was then a hike across the wide town square to reach the nearest empty building and cover, leaving him vulnerable to recapture.

It was a moot point for now because of his injuries. The door was his only viable option. He would have to leave at night, when the Inn was at rest, in order to avoid the villagers. How was he to get through that door?

He could set some of his little friends to watching the Innkeeper. Perhaps he could use the rats to steal the key? But then how would he use the key to unlock the padlock? Perhaps he could incite the rats to chew through the hinges if they were made from rawhide and not iron?

His head swam sickeningly, and the room tilted alarmingly, as he steadied his body against the wall and took his first hesitant step, then another, towards the door. It was poorly done, but it was walking, and it would get better with practice.

As it had been each time before, the door was locked. On further examination, the hinges were made of iron. Cursing in disappointment, Gralyre braced against the wall, using its support to ease into a sitting position. He would think of something. Now that he could walk he would find a way to escape. He was already dreaming of freedom as his eyes drifted closed.

∞CЯ

Gralyre awoke to conversation. Two men were standing over

him, discussing his fate, and he realized his time had run out.

"Ye see, your Worship, just like I told you. Here is the man what kilt your soldiers!"

"How do I know this is the right man, worm, and not some luckless stranger you would foist upon me to save your own hide?"

Gralyre cracked open his good eye, the other still being too swollen to open beyond a slit, and stole a brief look at the two. They had brought a lantern into the small room and the strong light pierced his throbbing head. In that one quick peek, he recognized neither of the men. They were neither his regular jailors, who brought water and gruel, nor Dolper the Innkeeper.

One was obviously a local. By his hefty, well-fed bulk, and quality of clothing, Gralyre assumed correctly that this man was a collaborator, and recipient to many favours for his betrayals.

But the other man was a quality above. He was dressed in dandified fashion from his flowing blue cape to a diamond ornament that flashed at his throat. Pale blond hair fell away from his forehead in artful waves, pulled back by a strip of blue ribbon at his nape. Creamy satin pantaloons were tucked into tall black boots, the high heels of which gave him intimidating height over his common companion. His accented voice was cold and arrogant. He was handsome in a petulant, boyish way. His features were stamped with the surety of his own superiority.

"The women what come back to town identified him as the traitor, your Worship!" said the local, ingratiatingly. "We be good, loyal subjects here in Raindell, and when we heard what the man had done to the Tithe Wagon, why we was outraged! Outraged! So we captured him for ye."

There was a moment of silence, as the gentleman considered the validity of the testimony. "I believe most of what you say, First Councilman Cramer." His voice sounded dangerously flat within the confines of the room. "That is why I have decided not to destroy the village."

"Thank ye! Thank ye, Lord Mallach! Ye are a kind and wise master!" Cramer bowed and bobbed like a fat sapling in a high wind, beaming happily with relief.

After allowing the man to fawn and gush for a moment, the gentleman continued. "But, I cannot have such crimes occurring without public atonement."

"Oh no, your Worship, no! That would not do at all," the First Councilman immediately agreed. He rubbed his hands together in a greedy fashion "'Tis why we kept him alive, ye see, so ye could make of him an example!" Cramer presented the town's strategy to the gentleman with the flourish of a third rate magician pulling an apple from up his concealing sleeve.

"You are eager to sentence this man to death, First Councilman." The gentleman's eyes narrowed cunningly. "I become suspicious of your motives. I must be certain that you are not guilty of trying to deceive me." He paused to draw out the suspense of the moment. "So, I have decided 'tis you who will burn, as a warning to the rest of the villagers."

"Me?" squeaked the councilman. "Wha' abou' 'im? Why no' make an example o' 'im? Have I no' always been a good an' loyal servant? Have I no' done everything ye 'ave ever asked o' me?" In his panic, Cramer's cant became pronounced and Gralyre realized that the man had been trying to ape the gentleman's upper caste accent in order to ingratiate himself.

"Oh, he will pay for his crimes. He will be taken to the Towers and questioned as to the whereabouts of other rebels. Then he will be publicly executed, to warn all who would act against mighty Doaphin, not just the few wretches in this back-water village. But you," Lord Mallach smirked. "If I would execute my own little pet, why imagine the terror that would spread among the ones I care nothing for."

As though in afterthought he decreed, "For questioning my wisdom in this matter, your family will join you upon the fires!" Lord Mallach considered for a moment. "Except for your wife and daughters. They will go to the wagons. How many generations has it been since your family has paid the Tithe, First Councilman?"

First Councilman Cramer fell to his knees and groveled, kiss-ing the man's boots and the hem of his cloak. "No' me children! Please yer worship! Take me! Burn me! Please! Spare me family!"

The gentleman soaked up the Councilman's despair with ruthless pleasure curdling his face. "Enough!" He kicked Coun-cilman Cramer away.

Cramer cowered for a moment then crawled back, still beseeching his master for clemency. "Please, yer worship! Please! Mercy!"

Gralyre could stand no more. Even though these people had beaten him to the near door of death, then kept him prisoner without aid, only to hand him over to his enemies, Gralyre found he did not have it within him to sit idle while an even worse atrocity took place. Ultimately, he would be responsible for the death of this man and his family, through his own unknowing actions of attacking the Tithe Wagon. The thought was unbearable.

With a burst of energy, he rolled himself to a sitting position. The pain from the movement cost him dearly, but if he was going to have any influence upon these proceedings he had to appear as strong as possible. Through lips pinched tight with pain, he confessed forcefully. "No one in the village had anything to do with the attack! I worked alone! Let this man be!"

Cramer clutched at Gralyre's unselfish assumption of blame and continued to wail. "Listen to 'im please! 'E tells the truth! Please, yer Worship! Please spare me sons! Mercy! Mercy!"

The gentleman looked down on Gralyre with lured displeasure, completely ignoring the sobbing Cramer in light of a new distraction

"So, you have awakened at last. I am Slanew Vad Pewers, The Count of Tac Mallach, Demon Lord of the Province of Mangeres. And you are..."

Lord Mallach waited until Gralyre was about to speak before interrupting him. "A nobody, an inconvenience, a bug! You dare to order me?" He lifted a highly polished boot and kicked Gralyre in the face.

Gralyre sprawled. His breath hissed out at the additional pain caused to his damaged body, but he made no other sound. A warm trickle of blood seeped from his already broken nose.

Whatever setting it had begun over the days of his incarceration was undone. Gritting his teeth against the pain, he forced himself back to a sitting position.

"I said let him go," Gralyre dared to order again, in a voice like rough granite. "This man has nothing to do with me. I have never seen him before today."

Lord Mallach's face registered shock that iced over with rage at Gralyre's temerity. He turned his attention back to the groveling Councilman, the easier victim. He sneered down at the shuddering, fear-filled face of Cramer. "Your partner in crime makes a case for you. You must be someone important to the resistance if he is willing to sacrifice himself on the fires for you."

Lord Mallach flicked a dust mote off the luxurious sleeve of his blue silk shirt. "I wonder if he expects me to listen to him? Does he think me an idiot? 'Tis inconceivable that one man could kill seven of my soldiers," he sneered petulantly.

"It be the truth, yer Worship, the truth!" Councilman Cramer sobbed.

"The truth! The truth!" hissed Lord Mallach. "There must have been at least ten or fifteen men involved to kill seven of my men. That is the truth!" His voice softened dangerously. "Of course you did not mean to infer I was wrong, did you Cramer?"

Cramer immediately tried to placate the count. "No, yer Worship, no. 'Tis no' what I meant!"

"Then you are saying he did not act alone, and that you helped him! You are guilty, Cramer! Guilty by your own confession!" Lord Mallach triumphantly pronounced. "You and your family will burn for your treason!" His face glowed with mad power.

At his words, Gralyre's eyes became as stone. He was stupefied at such an evil that would condemn an entire family to death on a whim. He did not know how or when, but he would see this monster dead for what he did this day!

Lord Mallach turned and looked back through the door at someone out of Gralyre's line of sight. "Take the First Councilman and his sons to the town square and build a pyre! His women are to go to the wagon!"

Over the First Councilman's incoherent pleas, two Demon Riders entered and grabbed his arms. As they dragged him from the room, there came the sounds of struggle, screams and sobs, as the councilman's sons in the common room of the tavern were dragged away to join their father's fate.

Gralyre hung his head in impeded rage. It was intolerable to be so helpless, especially in front of this fiend! His hands clenched and unclenched in fury.

"It bothers you that you cannot save Cramer and his family." A smile flitted across Lord Mallach's too perfect features as he realized this fact. He bent low to examine Gralyre's battered countenance more closely. A lock of pale blond hair fell across his forehead, its boyish innocence at polar opposites to the nature of this beast.

"He is one of mine, you know," he continued conversationally, "a collaborator. He deserves this punishment. It was his job to ensure that the worms in this town did not seek to rise their heads from the muck in which they fester. He failed me by allowing you to exist."

Gralyre could do nothing but glare. His chest rose and fell in painful agitation. Through the deep swelling bruises on his face, a muscle leaped in his jaw as he ground his teeth in frustrated violence.

"Ah, I can see that makes little difference to you. Ti-ton, come here!" Lord Mallach ordered to a presence lurking in the door to the tavern.

Gralyre broke contact with the Lord's eyes momentarily, to glower at the Demon Rider who entered with crisp military steps at his master's command.

"Look closely, Captain," ordered Lord Mallach. "'Tis rare in this day and age to find a man who thinks himself a hero!"

Captain Ti-ton laughed, a hissing obnoxious chuckle that set Gralyre's teeth on edge.

"Observe the weakness of a Hero!" Lord Mallach said this as though Gralyre were not in the room to hear his taunt. The Count's cold eyes did not stray from his prey. "Captain, I want you to randomly select four, no... eight people from the village and have them join the First Councilman upon the fires." Lord Mallach's smile was full of gleaming teeth. "This will be done because of your insolence, Hero. You will learn the conse-quences of defiance!"

Gralyre's fingernails dug deeply into his palms as rage fisted his hands. He started upwards in an uncontrollable urge to attack, but the flaring pain in his body aborted the move. He growled invectives through his set teeth as he fell back weakly.

He knew he was giving Lord Mallach and his lackey the

reaction they sought, but he was helpless to prevent it. He was confounded by the undiluted evil of the man standing before him. To his very soul, Gralyre wanted nothing more at this moment than to destroy Lord Mallach. But his strength was waning, and soon he would disgrace himself further in front of this creature.

"You dare to try and attack me?" Lord Mallach laughed. He made a small gesture with his finger and Gralyre shot backwards, slammed into a wall and fell loosely to the rough planks.

Gralyre retched and gasped, trying to keep from loosing consciousness. His head buzzed like a hornet's nest, making it difficult to concentrate. Goosebumps roughened his skin as he tried with little success to control the absolute terror gripping him at the Count's negligent show of power.

'*Magic!*' his memory screamed.

"You have your orders, Ti-ton," laughed Lord Mallach.

"Yes, Your Worship!" Ti-ton snapped his heels together smartly, reeled and left the room, still hissing his strange laugh.

After watching Ti-ton's snappy exit, Lord Mallach returned his attention to Gralyre's discoloured features. "You must be in pain?" asked the gentleman solicitously. The note of caring in his voice almost sounded sincere.

"'Tis nothing I cannot handle," Gralyre gritted out as he forced himself to breath. Rage and terror warred inside of him. Rage won out.

"Be not aggrieved by the Councilman's fate. Of his and yours, he has received the better death!" Lord Mallach chuckled nastily.

He made a beckoning gesture and Gralyre tumbled forward to land at his feet. With a flick of his wrist, Gralyre rose to his toes, hovering in place as Lord Mallach seized his beard and forced his head roughly from side to side to better examine his battered face. "'Tis difficult to tell beneath the bruising, but you may be a handsome boy when this swelling goes down." The Demon Lord leaned closer, his mouth going soft. "I like handsome boys…"

Gralyre twitched with aborted effort as he tried to struggle against the Demon Lord's magic. For a moment, his feet scrabbled to find purchase, but only his toes could touch the planks. His eyes, Gralyre realized. The pupils were wrong, oblong, like a cat's. They were not the eyes of a man. What was he? How did one fight such a creature?

And fight him he must! Since he could not attack physically, he must let words be his weapons. His mind cleared of rage and fear as he embraced the rhythm of the battle dance. The name *'Demon Rider'* finally struck a chord of understanding within his mind. *'They smell wrong...'*

He skewered Lord Mallach with his diamond hard glare. This monster would have no more enjoyment at his expense nor excuses to pull innocents into the fire.

The Demon Lord frowned, and his head reared back in confusion. This was not the reaction that he had been expecting. "Do you not fear me?" he demanded petulantly.

"You are not quite human, are you?" Gralyre taunted with a question of his own. There was a note of real condescension in his voice but no fear, and no anger.

Lord Mallach loomed menacingly, clearly displeased by

Gralyre's blatant lack of intimidation. He had the innocent, un-
lined visage of a boy, but there was nothing but death in his
eyes. "Why ever would I wish to be human? Humans are so very
fragile. They never last long during...questioning," Lord Mallach
gazed intently into Gralyre's face, examining his demeanor
microscopically for any reaction.

His hand tightened in Gralyre's beard as displeasure chased
disbelief across his innocent face. "You think that you do not
fear me, but you will," he purred. "I am sending you to the
Towers!" Lord Mallach was expecting a flinch of fear. His face
fell in sullen disappointment, as the dreaded name elicited no
response from the prisoner.

The Towers, held no meaning for Gralyre. For once, his lack
of memory did him a service. He allowed an eyebrow to climb
high in arrogant disdain, even though the movement caused
twinges of pain from his broken nose.

Frustration skittered through Lord Mallach's eyes. "So, Hero,
you are still not afraid?" Lord Mallach's hand, still gripped
tightly in Gralyre's beard, pulled down and Gralyre was driven
to his knees.

Gralyre bit back the cry of pain that tried to escape.

The Demon Lord dropped to his haunches, bringing their
faces to a level. He jerked Gralyre's beard, forcing his head
back, exposing his vulnerable neck.

In his debilitated state, Gralyre could do nothing to prevent
this exercise, so he went passive of body. Fear meant much to
this monster. Lord Mallach fed off it like a babe did mother's
milk. His continued lack of reaction was a victory of sorts within

this wretched situation.

"Shall I describe to you what you will face in Doaphin's Towers?" Lord Mallach whispered dramatically, punctuating himself with a light slap across Gralyre's abused face.

Gralyre remained stolid, though inside he howled in pain. He stared disdainfully into the eyes of Lord Mallach, and for added effect, forced a small, insolent smile to play around the corners of his split and bleeding lips. Even as Lord Mallach had divined his weakness, so had Gralyre discovered his.

Seeing the hint of disdainful smile, Lord Mallach's face contorted in rage and he punctuated his words with more forceful blows, dragging his victim's head back to a painful angle to gain freer access. "The keepers of Doaphin's Towers believe in making their prisoners support their own upkeep!"

WHAM!

The heavy fist caused bursts of light to explode in Gralyre's vision. The battle dance pulsed, stilling his emotions, deadening the agony.

"Every day, a strip of flesh will be sliced from your body."

WHAM!

"It will be boiled in front of you, and you will be forced to consume it."

WHAM!

"You will live off your own body and its broth until the last of your flesh has been stripped from your bones! In between feedings, they will of course ask you questions."

"How troublesome," Gralyre said with as much sangfroid as he could muster.

His insolence was rewarded with another blow. Gralyre was fading. The pulse of the battle dance slipped the fetters of his concentration. His stomach roiled at the grim insight into his future as the agony from his abused face rapidly sapped his remaining strength. If the creature did not finish with him soon, he would disgrace himself.

"Yesssss!" hissed Lord Mallach in triumphant satisfaction, mistaking the paling in Gralyre's face as fear. He raised his fist and slammed Gralyre's head one more time.

Gralyre felt a tearing in his chin, a small pain when compared to the rest. Part of his beard had come away in the creature's fist.

Lord Mallach pulled a hanky from his sleeve to delicately wipe soils from his hands as he let the hairs of Gralyre's beard flutter to the floor. With a flourish of cape, he strode from the room. "Put him with the women, and make them dress his wounds," he ordered two Demon Riders as he passed them in the door. "I want him in peak physical condition by the time we reach the Towers."

The Demon Riders stomped forward, grabbed Gralyre under his arms and dragged him roughly from the room. Black spots danced invitingly in front of his eyes as he sagged between his captors. Gralyre shuddered as he glanced into their faces. They seemed more or less human, until one looked closely, then little inconsistencies appeared. *They smell wrong. Why did I not notice this before?'*

When one caught Gralyre's sidelong glance, he bared his teeth in a horrible grin. He had two rows of serrated teeth, pointed and angled inward. A forked tongue pattered in and out.

Gralyre's skin crawled. If the Demon Rider sought to intimidate him, it was working.

They passed through the common room of the tavern, and the assembly of people shuffled from their path. As Gralyre glared at the villagers, their eyes dropped in shame. After experiencing a strong dose of the horrors of their lives, he could almost find it within him to forgive. Almost.

Out the door they went, down the rotted stoop, and into the street. Gralyre, who had been dragging his toes, chose this moment to use his legs. The Demon Riders were too strong to break free of, but since there was nothing worse than the fate they planned for him, whatever he did could not worsen his situation. Indeed, if he were lucky, he could anger them into killing him quickly, here and now, and avoid the torture awaiting him in the Towers. He was no sheep to go quietly to his slaughter.

Gralyre thrust his foot through the legs of the creature walking on his right, blocking his next step. With a hiss, the Demon Rider tripped and took all three of them down into the muck of the street.

Because Gralyre did not have the use of his arms, he landed painfully on his face and ribs, but as he spit dirt and pain borne curses from his mouth, he could not help laughing in insane triumph.

The Demon Rider he had tripped jumped to his feet and kicked Gralyre hard in retaliation. Gralyre grunted in pain, but it had still been worth it. He covered his head to protect it, chuckling maniacally. In that moment, he decided, he had finally gone mad.

"No!" came an icy command, as the offended Demon Rider pulled his sword. It was Lord Mallach. "I told you that I want him for the Towers! Harm him again, and you will join the villagers on the pyre!"

Growling to himself, the soldier released the blade back into its sheath and motioned for the other Demon Rider to pick Gralyre up. His reptilian glare promised further retribution when Lord Mallach was not looking.

Gralyre smiled back. A long journey awaited him, plenty of time to seek a quick death.

As Gralyre was dragged away to the caged wagon, he noticed villagers being herded into the market square, forced to congregate around the stacked wood of the pyres on which thirteen people were bound. One of the abandoned hovels fronting the square had been dismantled to supply the fuel. The villagers stood in unnatural quiet for a crowd of such a size.

His anger towards them evaporated fully in the face of understanding. They were only trying to survive in any way they could. Looking at their downtrodden and defeated stances, he wondered what it would take for them to revolt against their inhuman masters.

The Demon Riders threw him into the cage amongst the women who had been recaptured. As he landed upon the rough slats of the wagon bed, his great strength finally gave out. His head swam sickeningly as he fought the familiar fog of unconsciousness.

Gralyre scanned the faces of his cellmates as he lay panting, but saw neither Dara, nor the mysterious woman with the commanding presence. Neither had been recaptured. He felt a certain satisfaction that, despite everything, he had managed to help at least a few escape.

The cage door clanged shut, accentuating his prisoner status. Able to concentrate only upon his pain, he ignored the women prisoners, just as they ignored him. From his vantage point within the wagon, his last view before darkness claimed him was the grizzly spectacle of the First Councilman, his sons and eight unlucky innocents being put to the torch by the Demon Riders.

The villagers watched in silence, not daring to look away for fear of joining the councilman on the pyre.

Guilt reverberated in Gralyre's mind. *''Tis my fault.'*

ᔓᔕᔓ

Wil and his sons peered secretively between rotting boards of an abandoned hovel, watching as Gralyre was dragged towards the Tithe Wagon. Their attention was diverted momentarily as the 'Riders lit the pyres. Wil averted his eyes, shaking his head at the senseless horror.

"Have ye seen enough, Da?" Rewn asked quietly.

"Enough t' see that he is no friend t' Doaphin. But is it pretense?" Wil craned his neck to watch the Demon Riders sling Gralyre's limp body into the wagon cage.

Rewn turned away from the atrocity outside to watch his father's grim profile. "Can we afford that risk? If he is from the Southern Kingdoms, he may be the most important contact the resistance has ever had. We have had no word from the King-doms in four generations. It could mean reinforcements for the fight! If he is killed before the resistance gets a chance to question him..."

Wil gripped Rewn's shoulder, cautioning him to silence as six 'Riders marched past. They held their breath, heartbeats pound-ing, until they could no longer hear the purposeful strides.

Behind the two men, Dajin released his breath explosively. They turned in time to see his grin of excitement flash in the musty darkness.

"That was close!" Dajin whispered theatrically.

Wil exchanged a speaking glance with his older son, Rewn, before they both turned back to the view. The victims on the fires had ceased their screams, which was a blessing. Their contorted features could no longer be seen through the searing flames and thick black smoke.

The last of the women were being herded to the Tithe Wagon. Not so many as before. Many had not returned to the village to be sacrificed again.

"He must be rescued," Wil decided, "but we will keep him with us until we are sure he is no' a spy. Better that we expose only ourselves t' the danger."

"We should have just kept him with us in the first place," Dajin grouched.

Wil turned a stern look on his younger son. "And then how would we have saved Raindell from the Lord's retribution." He pointed back towards the fiery stakes. "We were lucky t' have gotten off so lightly."

Dajin could not hold his father's eyes, and turned to glare sulkily at the toe of his boot.

Rewn turned his back on the horrific sight of the burning bodies. The smell of roasting flesh permeated the air, inescapable. "We will need help. The Demon Lord travels with the Tithe this time. We will no' get near the stranger without magic."

Wil motioned to his sons that it was time to leave. "I know just where t' go for the help we need, lads," he whispered.

ဆာ

Dara glared at Derek's uncompromising back. "But why are we no' going into Verdalan?"

All that had kept her spirits up for the last few weeks had been the promise of a soft bed in the city. Now that dream was falling to dust around her. She could hear the whine in her voice, and could not muster the will to care.

Thomas strode past, buffeting her almost off her feet with a strike from his shoulder. "Out o' the way," he muttered.

Dara glared at him, before Gert caught her attention with the smile he was trying to hide. Her glare switched targets.

Derek sighed. "We can no' take ye into the city because ye are a woman, and Verdalan saw the Tithe only a few short months ago."

"Like t' start a riot," Thomas growled as he walked past Dara again, this time with a stack of firewood in his arms.

Dara stepped from his path to avoid yet another *accidental* collision with Thomas' shoulder.

"And the horses," Gert asserted his opinion.

"The horses?" Dara asked. She jumped when Thomas dumped the wood in a loud clatter.

"Yea, the horses. Only Demon Riders and Collaborators ride. Ye enter Verdalan with a horse, ye might as well just kill yourself and get it over with before the Demon Riders or the thieves do."

Derek grunted his concurrence. "We will meet our contact tomorrow. He will bring ye the rest o' the way into the mountains, t' the Northern Fortress."

Thomas gave her a hard smile. "And we can finally be rid o' ye, and return t' our mission."

Dara glared at him. *'And I will be quit o' ye, and your hostility!'* She lacked the courage to say the words aloud

CHAPTER FIVE

Gralyre awoke when his nose was reset. He yelped loudly and then groaned quietly as his ribs protested.

"I thought it best that I set it while ye slept."

He opened his watering eyes and glared briefly at his pain giver. With trembling fingers, he examined his throbbing nose. It was now straight, but he could feel the bones grinding within as he probed at it.

"Do no' be giving me that look!" she warned him. "If it were up t' me I would have left ye as ye were, but that one," here she nodded towards Lord Mallach, who was riding beside the wagon, "wants ye healed. Wants ye healthy for your torture so that ye will last longer," she jeered unkindly.

Now that Gralyre was fully awake, the jouncing of the ill-sprung wagon caused new degrees of discomfort within his body. "What have I ever done to you but try to help?" he muttered resentfully.

"Ye have no' helped, ye have only made things worse!" she said scornfully. "Ye had t' know they would come back and take us. And now more are dead!"

Gralyre adjusted his position so he could face her directly. "Why did you return to the village if you knew they would come for you again?"

"T' save me kin. We are the sacrifices so that the others may live." She sniffed righteously, settling the cloak of martyrdom firmly about her shoulders. "I watched me Ma and me sisters taken. I was too young t' Tithe the last time the wagons came. No one knows what they do with us." She paused and there were tears in her eyes. "Maybe, wherever they be takin' us, I will see them again."

"There are not so many women this time as the last. Where are the missing ones?" Gralyre asked in an effort to distract her before she began to bawl.

"They took that Rebel woman's advice and headed for the Heathren Mountains, I suppose. They still fight there, and 'tis said the 'Riders have never collected a Tithe from them!" There was a terrible longing in her voice to belong to a people that put more worth on their women then the extorted peace they could buy.

She turned her back to him then, and crawled away across the bucking floor of the wagon. Quiet sobs drifted from her as three other women cuddled beside her, offering comfort though, from the looks on their faces, they were as terrified as she.

Gralyre wondered grimly what the Demon Riders wanted with the women. Judging from past experience with the creatures, the women's lots were about to worsen.

✺

As the days passed, Gralyre recognize abandoned towns and crofts and realized they were journeying back down the same track he and Little Wolf had travelled from their farm. The Tithe wagon crossed the side trail to his burned home on the tenth day.

Gralyre watched with tired eyes as it sped by and thought of his pup. Had Little Wolf made the return journey safely?

He resisted the selfish desire to reach out with his mind and check, for Little Wolf would chase after the wagon, and in doing so, be placed in terrible danger. Better for his pup that he stayed safe, and returned to the wild life that was his by right of birth.

Gralyre had come full circle and could not help but feel the Gods of Fortune were toying with him. But though the direction he had initially taken had resulted in his capture, he was glad he had not traveled towards this other place, for it was a stronghold of his enemies.

Doaphin's Towers. Thoughts of what awaited him there sent fingers of horror throughout his body.

⬧

Escape was impossible. They were never allowed out of the cramped, wheeled prison. Food scraps and water were tossed at them through the bars. Filth and offal became their constant companions.

The women ostracized Gralyre from their group. After some aborted attempts to initiate conversations, Gralyre resigned himself to being the pariah. He was not sure if the women blamed him for what had happened in the village, or if they feared too much contact with a condemned man. Whatever the reason, it made for a comfortless journey.

They covered distances rapidly for the Demon Riders had no care for the stamina of the horses. They halted at dusk, and were away again as dawn pinked the horizon. Whenever a wagon horse stumbled and went lame, the outriders quickly slaughtered the beast and harnessed a spare to the traces. The hard pace continued with scarcely a stutter.

In a fortnight they arrived at a crossroad, and turned north onto a well-maintained highway. The traffic upon it, while still not heavy, was more plentiful. Most of the travelers were Demon Riders. What few humans there were, mostly slaves chained together and working to maintain the road under the ready whips of bored Demon Riders, or self-important collaborators who watched with ingratiating smiles as the Tithe Wagon passed, would give way, walking into the ditches so as not to offend with their presence upon the road. At such times, the Demon Riders kept their hands close to their swords, but none had the nerve to challenge them.

They passed through only two other peopled villages, the inhabitants of which were in an even more desperate state than those of Raindell. The rest of the land they travelled contained only ghost towns of rotting buildings. This land was empty of human settlements. The Woman Tithe was an effective tool of genocide.

When they ran short of horses, the cavalcade was forced to make a stop at a Demon Rider garrison. They paused for only the short time it took to trade for fresh horses before the wagon was away again. They moved as though the whips of the gods licked at their feet as they traveled north for another fortnight, losing two more horses along the way.

After over a month, the prisoners were sick and frail. The

cramped wagon gave no ease. Inevitably, the lack of food and the filth saw one woman die.

Gralyre braced himself to rush the cage door when they came to remove her body, but the guards were indifferent to the corpse, leaving her to rot amongst them.

To spare the women, Gralyre wrapped the body in its own threadbare cloak, as a shroud, and did his best to anchor it to the bars with the ends of the fabric so that the jolting of the wagon would not move the corpse amongst them. He could not feel sorry for her death, only envious. She had escaped the horrors that awaited her.

There finally came a night when the prisoners could see the lights of a larger city glowing on the horizon. Gralyre wondered what it was called, and if there were any men there, or if it was a city full of Demon Riders. Gralyre looked up from his defeated contemplations when torchlight shone brightly into his face.

"You have failed in your task, Hero," Lord Mallach taunted.

"What task would that be?" Gralyre asked with studied boredom as he picked dirt from beneath a fingernail.

"To save the women of course." He swept out his arm to indicate the twinkling of lights on the horizon. "The City of Tarangria. This is where they will be left!" The Demon Lord exalted, moving closer. "This is where they will face their fate! You, however, will continue onwards, north to Doaphin's Towers!"

One of Gralyre's fellow prisoners released a terrified sob that another woman quickly hushed, lest she draw the Demon Lord's attention.

But there was only one that Lord Mallach was interested in bedeviling. He lifted his torch higher to better illuminate Gralyre's face. "Does this thought not bother you, Hero?" he asked as he tried to read the emotionless features of his prisoner. "Or do you call yourself Hero no longer?"

"It would bother me more if I knew what the women's fates were to be. Why not tell me what it is? I am sure the agony of knowing would be intolerable." Gralyre waited with a sick feeling in his stomach, suddenly wishing he had not uttered that particular taunt.

"S-s-s-s-s," laughed Lord Mallach and wagged a finger at him. "I wish that I could tell you, Hero! Really I do! But, this is the greatest secret that we hold!" Lord Mallach's face was alive with evil enjoyment. "You play the game so well that I have decided to take personal charge of your interrogation when we reach the Towers!"

"I am honoured, I am sure." Gralyre inclined his head in a mocking bow.

"Oh, I shall have such pleasure as I have not known in years breaking you!" exclaimed Lord Mallach with true anticipation. Hissing his strange laughter, he walked away.

When the creature had receded beyond sight, Gralyre grasped the bars of the cage in his fists and rattled them angrily. He was so enraged he could barely contain himself!

The women huddled away into the farthest corner of the cage, making themselves small, as helpless beings were wont to do, so as to not draw his ire.

Flopping down against the bars of the cage, he angrily gave

them one more shot with his back. Gralyre ignored the burst of pain brought about by his foolish action. His injuries had healed little without rest and proper food. He still had not the strength of old.

"Stop cowering. I would not hurt you," he growled at the women. He watched with stormy eyes as their fear relaxed, before he ignored them to glare out into the darkness once more. His mind flitted from one desperate plan to the next.

Even if he could escape this cage and steal a horse, he could never outride the pursuit, not as weak as he was. And what of the women? He would not leave them behind.

Longingly, he thought of Little Wolf, glad the pup had not been caught up in his foolishness, yet contrarily wishing for that familiar voice in his head. In the distance, he heard the sound of wolves. Lonely for the company of a pack, he opened his mind to them, trying to hear their thoughts, and started in surprise as he reached a familiar consciousness instead.

'I come!' Little Wolf told him jubilantly.

Gralyre had a sense of the pup leaping through the darkness. *'No! Stay! Danger! Why are you here?'* His heart pounded with fear for Little Wolf's safety.

From his comfortable seat next to the cook fire, Lord Mallach leapt to his feet with a shout of anger. "Who dares to use magic in my presence?" His padded stool wobbled and overturned. The Demon Lord kicked it into the flames, scattering the burning wood in all directions.

'The horse you rode returned. He said the men in the village had eaten you. I did what you told me. I went home. I made the

horses come with me. I was lonely. I felt you pass by. I followed. You were hurt and could not hear me.'

The Demon Riders fled with cries of alarm as the Demon Lord stalked around the cook fire, lashing out at any who were not fleet enough. "I will find you! Who is it? I will eat your heart!" he roared.

Gralyre spared only a passing glance for the chaos, lacking the curiosity to discover what the display was about in his anxiety for his pup. *'You should not have followed, Little Wolf.'* Gralyre told the wolfdog angrily, though a small petal of hope unfurled within his chest. Perhaps the pup could help him escape?

Reading his thoughts, Little Wolf burst out, *'Others follow. They hide themselves.'*

Into Gralyre's mind materialized images of the three woodsmen he had met before. The father and two sons had with them a large group of men and one female. He recognized her as the fascinating, buckskin clad woman he had saved when he had attacked the Tithe wagon.

Gralyre quickly evaluated the situation, trying to dampen his excitement. *'If they mean to rescue us, they must attack before the women are delivered to the nearby city. It must be tonight or tomorrow morning, for it will be their final opportunity.'*

Lord Mallach grabbed a burning brand from the remnants of the fire and stalked towards the cage. Flames and sparks trailed to the ground in his wake. "Who is doing this? I will find you!" he bellowed as he came. "You cannot hide from me! You cannot escape me!" His eyes ferreted out the terrified faces of each woman as they screamed and cowered. Like a ravaging beast, he circled the cage, searching for the one he would feast upon.

'Go now, Little Wolf. They take me to an evil place. Be very careful that those that follow do not see you. Stay away unless I say otherwise!' Gralyre commanded protectively.

Lord Mallach dropped the torch, seized Gralyre's head and mashed his face against the bars. "You! 'Tis you! I feel your power! What are you doing? Tell me! Do you think to escape?"

"What are you talking about?" Gralyre mumbled against the cold iron bars as he released his contact with Little Wolf.

Lord Mallach shook his head, a smile on his lips as he relaxed fractionally. His gaze caressed Gralyre's face like a lover. "No. It was you. No one else here would have dared. I wonder how you survived to manhood without being discovered and put to death?" He brushed a lock of hair gently from Gralyre's brow. "I cannot wait for the Towers. I need a taste now. Let us seek our answers, shall we?"

His hands tightened in Gralyre's hair. "This is going to be good, so very good!" Light pants of excitement came from between his lips. "You have no idea how happy you have made me. Now hold still. This is going to hurt." He gave an excited giggle.

Gralyre screamed.

Lord Mallach's fingers seemed to push through his skull and claw into his mind. Like a sharp knife filleting a fish, Gralyre's defenses were slashed, exposing his thoughts, his most private *self*.

The Demon Lord stomped through Gralyre's memories,

brushing aside all resistance and ripping the truth from his mind. From far away, Gralyre heard Lord Mallach exclaim, "A wolf? You were talking to a wolf? What did you talk about?"

At all costs, he had to protect Little Wolf! Gralyre lashed out instinctively, using the only weapon that he had. He summoned his nightmare.

This time it was Lord Mallach who shrieked. Gralyre held tightly to the Demon Lord's presence in his mind, not allowing him to escape, ruthlessly forcing the evil creature raping his memories to experience the terror of the beheading, and of the void. Only this time it was the Demon Lord who was beheaded, the Demon Lord who was torn and shredded by the eternal empty place. He would cast this beast into the abyss and abandon him there!

Light and pain exploded in Gralyre's skull. When it cleared, he saw Lord Mallach shaking his head dazedly and clinging weakly to the outside of the wagon for support.

Gralyre leaned his head against the bars and retched heavily. He did not try to stem the tears streaming from his eyes. He felt violated, filthy. This creature had left behind a cesspool in his mind. His limbs shook so badly he had trouble lifting his hand to wipe the bile from his mouth.

Had he betrayed the men who followed the wagon? Did Lord Mallach now know of the rescue? Had he managed to force the creature from his mind soon enough to protect this knowledge?

Lord Mallach laughed thinly, triumphantly, as he recovered his strength. He suddenly lunged at the bars, his face close to Gralyre's.

Gralyre was too overcome to flinch.

"It cannot be, and yet here you are," Lord Mallach whispered closely. "You sought to hide yourself, but you have been unmasked! You will be my little secret for now, but soon the Master will grant all I desire!"

His eyes glowed with maniacal fire in the flicker of the fallen torch. As he left, Lord Mallach stomped it out with his polished boot, extinguishing the light. "Use magic in my presence again, and I will do far worse than steal your thoughts." The warning drifted back to mingle with the black smoke that rose from the snuffed flame.

ಬಂಐ

The morning dawned bright and sunny but Gralyre looked at the clear day with sunken eyes. Shudders still quaked his body as he clenched and relaxed his fists. Sleep had been impossible. He had waited all night for the rescue that had never come, eager to discover if he had betrayed his one chance at freedom, and those who would bring it to him.

Throughout the dark hours of his vigil, his thoughts had sunk deeper into despair. He could not forget the Demon Lord's parting words. Lord Mallach had recognized him. Now, more then ever, he feared his hidden past.

Despite the chaos of the night before, the morning routine remained fixed. Demon Riders approached, poking the blunt end of their spears through the bars to rouse the captives. The abuse was so common, that the prisoners now endured it stoically.

Tiring quickly of the sport when there was little reaction, the Demon Riders pelted the prisoners with what passed for breakfast.

Gralyre gave his measure of stale, moldy bread to one of the women. He could not endure food. The charity elicited no response. The women avoided him more than usual, scared to associate with the one who had earned the personal attention of the Demon Lord.

The morning routine ignited a flickering hope within Gralyre's chest. There did not appear to be any undue attention being paid to increasing security, or arming for battle. It spoke well that the attack - if it was even going to occur - remained secret. Perhaps the Count had not ripped the knowledge from his thoughts?

They had just started down the road, on their final leg to Tarangria, when they heard the singing. Stirring with hope, Gralyre crawled to the front of the cage for a better view of what they were about to encounter.

It was the rescue! It must be! Now would be revealed the Demon Lord's ignorance or knowledge of the incipient ambush. Gralyre closed his eyes briefly and sent a desperate prayer winging towards the Gods of Fortune.

The song was a ribald tune, sung off key by an inebriated female voice. It grew steadily louder as they approached.

"The Prince's Cock was a very fine bird, a very fine bird was he,

Chased he was by the Cook's Pussycat, across the land to

sea! Oh! Sea-ee-o! Across the land to sea!

The crafty Cock was tireless, strong, and did dodge hither and yonder,

But smart Pussycat kept chasing along, ne'er two paces beyond! Oh! B'yo-ond-o! Ne'er two paces b'yond!

Then the Cock could run no further, his feet were in the water!

As Pussycat sprang to catch 'em, his wings began to flutter! Oh! Flut-ter-o! His wings began to flutter!

Out 'ore the sea flew the crafty Cock, as happy as could be!

Poor Pussycat, missed her mark and fell into the sea! Oh! Sea-e-o! Fell into the sea!

'Tis often the truth in this struggling life, so listen well and make mark,

Wherever you find a wet pussy, you'll find a happy cock! Oh! Co-ock-o! You'll find a happy cock!"

During the off key singing of the off colour ditty, the wagon had rounded the curve of the road and revealed the unlikely pair sitting on a log by the ditch. Gales of laughter followed the song's flourishing finish.

"Shing us anotter one, darlin'," demanded the drunken man.

"I shink ye 'av 'ad enough fer one night," slurred an equally smashed woman. "Ye gods! Where did daylight come from?"

The woman wore a dirty, low cut dress, her filthy cleavage rounded high above the torn bodice. Her stained skirt was raised well past her knees as she sat with legs splayed wide for balance. She held her head in her hands, groaning and cursing the mercilessness of the morning sun, as she worked with fumbling fingers to rid her unkempt hair of debris from the forest floor.

The knees of the man's homespun trousers were grass stained and his rough woolen shirt was ripped and torn. He blinked owlishly through bloodshot eyes at the wagon as it rumbled into view, rubbing a hand over the black stubble on his chin. It took little imagination to discern what they had been about.

Which was exactly the picture they were hoping for, Gralyre thought, recognizing the bold Rebel woman he had rescued previously. His heart stuttered. Had he betrayed them? Had he betrayed her?

"'Ere now!" exclaimed the bawdy woman. "Oo's 'at comin' up the road?"

The entourage slowed but the soldiers did not seem to be unduly concerned. The proximity to their final destination had relaxed their guard.

Gralyre's eyes shifted to the bored features of Lord Mallach. Did he know? Would he now kill this woman and her men?

Lord Mallach raised his hand, and the Tithe Wagon came to a shuddering halt.

Gralyre's hands tensed upon the bars of the iron cage as hope and fear lashed through him in alternating waves. His hands squeaked as his tight grip wrung the bars. The next few seconds would tell the tale. Did Lord Mallach know?

"Should we take her, m'lord?" Captain Ti-ton asked.

"She hardly looks worth the effort, but I suppose we should. Be quick about it. I want to push on towards the Towers tonight!" Lord Mallach glanced back at the wagon with an intimate smile for Gralyre's eyes alone.

Gralyre trembled at that look, releasing and scrabbling away from the bars before he could control himself.

Lord Mallach's smile widened with delight, as his prisoner displayed fear for the first time. He turned his horse so that he might continue to revel in Gralyre's distress, completely ignoring the two humans sitting by the road.

Ti-ton slipped from the saddle and strutted up to the drunken pair. He booted the man in the face, tumbling the drunk over into the brush and out of the way of his intentions. He grabbed the woman and stood her up.

She sagged into his arms, unconcerned over the plight of her beau and her own proximity to a Demon Rider. "Yer a big one ain't ye?" she charged, her hands busily working him over. "It be a copper fer a tumble, and a silver if ye want somethin' special!" she announced with blurry enthusiasm, winking outrageously. "What say ye, darlin'?" she asked, touching the Demon Rider's cheek with her palm and forcing his gaze to hers.

Ti-ton flinched slightly as their eyes met.

Gralyre shivered away a strong, buzzing vibration at the base of his skull. It pulsed off so quickly he doubted he had sensed anything at all. He shook his head as the odd sensation faded.

Lord Mallach's smile for Gralyre hardened into a glare. "Talking to dogs again?" he asked snidely as he snapped his fingers.

Gralyre felt the buzz again, as a familiar force slammed his body to the back of the cage, high against the bars. He grunted as the magic released him to tumble down to the wagon bed.

"You will learn, Hero, that any defiance will be met by punishment! I warned you of what would happen if you used your magic again!" Lord Mallach snarled. He flicked his wrist, and Gralyre was hurled back up into the bars.

A terrible pressure on his chest held Gralyre in place before driving him back into the wagon bed. He gasped for air before the Demon Lord's power slammed into him anew.

He had not used any magic. If it was not him then... Gralyre's eyes flicked to the Rebel woman before once more being slammed onto his hands and knees, spitting blood into the rank straw at the bottom of the cage.

Gralyre finally recognized the odd vibration for what it was. He was sensing the use of magic by those around him. This must be how Lord Mallach had known he was talking to Little Wolf the night before. When Mallach had sensed the small burst of power he had mistaken it as Gralyre's. Was it the Rebel woman? Had she been signaling to her men? Was she even the one who had used magic, or had it been one of her men? Or perhaps one of the Demon Riders?

Captain Ti-ton had slung her over his shoulder and now strode towards the cage. She kicked and squirmed, shouted vile threats, and threatened to lose the contents of her stomach. Ti-ton ignored her contentions completely, easily carrying her struggling form.

Ti-ton did not sheath his sword, though most of the others in the dangerous party had. One or two Demon Riders hooted and hollered encouragement as the woman continued to struggle and scream. The rest of the mounted soldiers either grinned at the spectacle the woman was making, or enjoyed the enthusiastic beating that Lord Mallach was giving Gralyre.

Gralyre narrowly held onto consciousness as his head bounced off the bars. Mallach did not know of the rescue! A smile stretched his mouth despite the pain that drew spots in front of his eyes. If he could keep the Demon Lord's attention focused upon him, it would grant the rescuers a valuable distraction. If magic was what it took…

'Little Wolf! Keep a safe distance. Await my call!'

"Defiance!" screamed Lord Mallach. "If you refuse to bend to my will, then perhaps your travelling companions will convince you otherwise!"

The women in the wagon began to scream and writhe. Blood flowed from their nostrils and eyes.

One of the prisoners clawed at Gralyre's arm. "What are ye doin'?!" a woman wailed at him. "Do as he asks! Save us!" Her eyes rolled back in her head and pink froth began to spill from her mouth.

Gralyre had done what he could. He could not risk the women's lives. He had to give the Demon Lord what he wanted. "I comply!" he shouted at Lord Mallach. "I comply! Please! The women have done nothing!"

Lord Mallach sniffed, and the women stopped screaming. "You will learn, Hero, you will learn. I release the women because the Tithe quota must be fulfilled. However, I will find you a new whipping boy when we reach the Towers." He turned away, losing interest now that his will had been imposed. "A Hero's weakness," he jeered.

From hands and knees, Gralyre's split lip twitched into a hard smile and his eyes flicked from the drunken woman slung over Ti-ton's shoulder to Lord Mallach. Anticipation burned through him. *'I will see you dead this day!'* he vowed.

As the women began to pull themselves together, they took up their accustomed huddle as far from Gralyre as possible. Knowing him to be the cause of their suffering they cursed him and threw handfuls of the rotten straw in his direction. Several of the prisoners still retched through the bars, as bloody tears flowed down their faces.

"Enough!" Gralyre's growl cowed the bloodied prisoners. He had no time for this. The cage was about to open and he readied himself to rush the gate. If he could not get away at least he could die fighting in aid of the rescue!

The wagoner climbed down to unlock the cage for the new prisoner.

Ti-ton slung her off his shoulder and propped her against the wagon as she sagged drunkenly. When the wagoner turned his back on the pair to insert his key into the padlock, Ti-ton coldly ran his sword through the wagoner's back.

With a surprised cry the driver fell and the key to the cage slipped from his limp fingers with a discordant clatter. The women prisoners screamed and fell back at the unexpected violence. Gralyre threw himself to the bars and reached through, but was unable to touch the fallen keys.

"Get back!" the Rebel woman hissed as she deftly dropped and rolled beneath the wagon, safely out of the way of battle. The keys went with her.

Cursing, Gralyre was left with no recourse but to watch the battle unfold. This, then, was the magic the woman had wrought. She had subverted the will of the Demon Rider Captain and turned him into her puppet weapon.

As Ti-ton pulled his sword from the wagoner's body, a Demon Rider shouted his challenge and spurred his horse forward to ride his Captain into the ground. His attack was tentative, and his face showed his uncertainty.

There was nothing tentative about Ti-ton's reprisal. He cut the horse from under the Demon Rider, and then ran him through as he lay pinned beneath the thrashing beast.

Gralyre remained poised at the bars, unwilling to miss a single moment. His grim smile widened to a feral baring of teeth as Lord Mallach screamed in rage.

Lord Mallach stood high in his stirrups and bellowed at his troops. "Get him! Get him! The one who brings Ti-ton down will be the new Captain!"

The Demon Riders dismounted in a rush, for the narrow track prevented a cavalry charge. Screaming fearsome battle cries they attacked on foot.

Ti-ton was in the grip of a berserker's fury and no sword could touch him. Two more of his soldiers joined the ranks of the dead before the attack disengaged. Ti-ton came to rest with his back to the side of the wagon, breathing harshly as his previous comrades in arms faced him in a half circle of drawn steel. His face was blank of emotion as if he did not see the carnage he wrought.

Lord Mallach howled with rage. "What are you waiting for,

cowards? This is what you were created for! Kill! Kill! Kill!"

Unwilling to get close, but wanting the promotion, a Demon Rider shot the traitor with his crossbow. Several others joined the assault and soon Ti-ton bristled with arrows, dancing a macabre jig at the multiple impacts.

The prisoners screamed, scrabbling and huddling behind each other to escape quarrels gone astray.

Gralyre used the only cover they had, the dead woman. He flipped the corpse to its side and crouched down behind it as arrows pierced deep into his makeshift shield. "Get down!" he roared protectively. His long arms folded as many women as he could reach into his broad chest and behind the slight cover offered by the body. He thanked the Gods of Fortune for the bars of the cage that deflected some of the wilder shots.

When at last the barrage stopped, Ti-ton's eyes had rolled to the whites and red froth bubbled from between his lips. He still did not go down, though it was obvious to all that he was dead. His sword still slashed through the air in mindless aggression.

At a quiet scrabbling by the cage door, Gralyre spun to see the Rebel woman slowly working the lock open. He viewed her with renewed respect. Where were the rest of the men that Little Wolf had spoken of?

The Rebel woman suddenly dropped to the ground, leaving the key dangling. Gralyre whirled to see what had frightened her.

The livid Count had dismounted and was approaching. Gralyre braced himself for the eminent attack and faced Lord Mallach, leaving the prisoners he had guarded still huddled behind the safety of the corpse against the bars.

"Do you think I do not know you are behind this? Do you think I did not feel your power turn Ti-ton's mind? You think this will provoke me to kill you, it will not! I will have you in the Towers! You will not die this day!" Spittle flew from his lips as he shrieked.

Ti-ton launched himself at his former troops, blocking Lord Mallach's advance. The Demon Riders scattered, yelling and hissing, and for long moments, mass confusion reigned as more died beneath Ti-ton's unquenchable blade. Then someone made a lucky slash, and Ti-ton dropped to the ground, hamstrung from behind.

The Demon Riders fell upon their former Captain, slashing and stabbing, howling at each other. All were eager to give the killing blow that would elevate them from the ranks. Another Demon Rider died, this time by the knife of a comrade.

Lord Mallach moved quickly to quell the fights erupting amongst the remaining Demon Riders. With small gestures of his hands, his soldiers flew off the mangled corpse.

Ti-ton lay forgotten upon the ground. His sword continued to slash, like a reflex, before it suddenly fell still. Seven Demon Riders, including their late captain, lay slain in the clearing. Only eight remained standing with the Demon Lord.

Lord Mallach was breathing heavily although he had not taken active part in the fight. As he glared at Gralyre, his face cleared and resumed its usual expression of evil triumph. "You failed the women again, Hero! You should have chosen a stronger instrument!"

His gaze shifted to one of the caged women. "Here now, is your reward for your sedition!"

Gralyre set his teeth against the skull vibrations from the magic and watched in horror as the head of the woman beside him twisted to face backwards. "No!" he screamed.

Her neck gave a brittle crack and the woman dropped like a rag doll. He recognized her as the same woman who had set his nose and tended his wounds. He had never bothered to learn her name. Curses tore at his throat as he rattled the bars of the cage.

Mallach strode to the middle of the clearing, master of his own world again. "You, and you." He gestured to a couple of dazed and wounded Demon Riders. "Clean up this mess. When the Deathren are reborn with the night, I will have answers for this treachery!" He stalked to his horse and grabbed its bridle angrily as it shied away

Suddenly, from out of the woods, a horn sounded. Clear and true were its tones; another answered, then another. From all directions, peal after peal rang from the forest. The Demon Riders milled in confusion, unsure of where the attack was to come from. Lord Mallach shouted orders that his troops were unable to hear over the din.

Rebel warriors sprang from the forest from all sides, easily crushing the defenders between them. Due to Ti-ton's attack, the small band of rescuers now outnumbered the Demon Riders.

Gralyre strained for a better view between the bars, eager to see Lord Mallach meet his doom. He frowned in concern and confusion, when it was the Rebel woman who walked out to challenge Lord Mallach.

The Demon Lord and the woman circled each other as her men put the last of the Demon Riders to the blade.

Lord Mallach made a gesture. The woman answered with one of her own. The magic buzzed in Gralyre's skull.

Mallach flinched and stumbled. His face flickered with something akin to surprise, before resuming its habitual superiority. "So, it was you who turned Ti-ton against me!" His fingers gestured again. So did the woman's.

Though nothing overt happened, Gralyre could feel the intensity of the magic that flew between them; Mallach's to attack the Rebel warriors, the woman's to protect them.

Mallach flinched again, briefly shaking his fingers as though they had touched a hot stove. He regained his composure quickly. Belaying his dangerous circumstances he now waited quite calmly, a snide little smile upon his face.

Though the Demon Riders were vanquished, the Rebel woman remained focused. Lord Mallach was the only one left to fight, but the warriors encircled him cautiously, as though he were more dangerous then all the Demon Riders combined.

Gralyre recalled the creature's power as he had ripped apart his mind. The warriors were right to fear the Demon Lord. So was the woman.

"Ye are defeated! Surrender now and your death will be quick." The woman's voice rang with power.

The Demon Lord looked at her with the same snide half-smile twisting his narrow lips. "You would challenge me?" His smirk widened as he negligently tossed his unused sword to the ground. "Do you know what I am, girl?" His hands began to glow with a malignant green light as he raised them. "I have no need of a sword to squash you like the vermin you are!" The green light coalesced into a ball of venomous energy.

"Take cover!" a warrior shouted, as Lord Mallach threw the ball of green fire.

Gralyre cried out his own warning as his eyes traced the trajectory of Lord Mallach's magic. It was aimed at the woman, not at her men. Lord Mallach had finally recognized the real threat. The Rebel warriors would be dealt with at his leisure after the Sorceress was dead.

A glowing blue shield materialized in front of her. With a deafening roar, the fireball impacted against it. Green flames flew upwards into the sky before dissipating.

Another ball of energy gathered in the Demon Lord's hand as he drew back his arm. With a shout of exertion he flung the fireball.

The woman's blue shield flickered, but managed to absorb the energy of the second blast. Her body bent with the effort of holding back the impact.

As the flames dissipated, she grabbed the edges of her magic shield and threw it like a discus at Lord Mallach. Only a thin strip of edge was visible as it shot towards the Demon Lord. It made the sound of thousands of angry hornets as it parted the air.

Lord Mallach threw out his hands and the blue swirling disc stopped mere inches from his palms. It continued to spin, whirling and sparking angrily, but it advanced no further. Lord Mallach's face showed his strain, though he laughed derisively.

"Is that the extent of your power, witch?" he hissed insultingly. He slammed his fist down on the swirling disc and it disintegrated into a blue mist.

Far from disabling the weapon, the mist moved to engulf the Demon Lord, burning and searing as he breathed it in. It surrounded him like a thundercloud. Small forks of lightning lashed out at his flesh, making him twitch and dance. His hands slapped at burns as though he had walked into a wasp's nest. His clothing and skin blackened as he hacked and gagged.

For a moment, it seemed he would fall. But then he rallied. He left off trying to stop the mist, and attacked the source of his misery instead. Green lightning streaked from his hands towards the Sorceress.

She screamed defiantly as a new blue shield snapped up in front of her, narrowly arriving in time to protect her. The green fire engulfed her on three sides, yet still could not penetrate her defenses. Little fires sprang up around the glade, ignited by the magical forces being unleashed.

Lord Mallach's barrage increased. Continuous sheets of lightning streaked towards the woman to impact with a deafening concussion upon her defensive shield.

Gralyre gripped the bars of the cage, his eyes fearfully riveted upon the scene. Was her shield failing? Helplessness was rapidly surmounting Gralyre's amazement at the woman's abilities. What if she was defeated? What if Lord Mallach proved too powerful for her?

It was almost impossible to sit idle, but in this magical battle only another sorcerer could help. Anyone else joining the fray would prove a distraction that could cost the woman her life. The warriors she travelled with obviously realized this, for they had taken cover, staying well clear of the combatants. There was nothing for Gralyre to do but watch and wait.

Sweat beaded the woman's face and neck. Her mouth was compressed in a grim line, as she continued to endure the attacks. They were coming so fast and furious the Sorceress seemed unable to continue with her own assault.

The blue mist surrounding Lord Mallach dissipated, revealing the ruin of his boyish good looks. What hair remained upon his head was wispy and blackened. Horrible blisters seared his exposed skin. His fine clothing hung in burnt tatters. But despite this, his strength was slowly overpowering his opponent.

The Sorceress was loosing ground. Her shield had become translucent. Despite his injuries, Lord Mallach chuckled. Sensing victory, he took his time, hissing his terrible laugh as he threw more and more energy at her, savoring her coming death like fine wine.

The ground beneath Lord Mallach's feet rippled like a live creature, throwing him off balance and giving the Sorceress the opening she needed to launch her own attack again. She spun her blue shield at Lord Mallach, but she was not quick enough. He had regained his balance.

As before, he halted it a mere hand's space away and laughed at her efforts to send it further. But he did not dare to touch it this time, mindful of its power. "Stupid witch! Did you think I would fall for the same trick twice? Time for you to die, woman!" Slowly, he began to force the glowing, swirling disc back towards her.

She thrust her hands out, and though this slowed the progression of the deadly weapon, it continued inexorably in the wrong direction.

Hisses of triumph emerged from Lord Mallach as he toyed with her, allowing her to struggle against his superior strength.

Gralyre licked his dry lips, frowning in concern. He did not want to witness her death. His heart was a leaden weight in his chest. He was unsure why her death mattered so to him. It just did.

Then he spied something strange occur behind Lord Mallach's back. A tree limb the length of a man's arm rose from the track, suspended in mid-air. Gralyre's lips twitched into a savage grin as the branch swung and cracked against the side of Lord Mallach's head.

The Demon Lord staggered from this unexpected attack. He lost his concentration and that one moment of inattention was enough for the woman to gain control of her shield again.

In an instant all signs of exhaustion disappeared from the Sorceress' face. Gralyre realized it had all been a ruse to lull Lord Mallach into her trap!

The glowing, swirling disc shot back towards the Demon Lord, sliced into his body and emerged from the other side of his torso. The sudden silence in the clearing was deafening as the shield dissipated into the air.

The Demon Lord shrieked in dismay, clutching at his abdomen, looking for a wound that was not there. "What have you done?" Lord Mallach screamed, frantically clawing and ripping at his stomach.

He snapped stiff and straight as blue light erupted violently from his body. It glowed from his eyes and ears, and as he opened his mouth, a great beam of blue fire shot forth from his lips and muffled his scream. His entire figure glowed with blue radiance that was painful to look upon directly.

Clouds rolled in to cover the sun, creating an artificial twilight. A terrible wind erupted within the glade. It blew through the clearing, scooping debris from the ground, rushing towards Lord Mallach in howling fury. His body vibrated within the maelstrom as sparks ignited the leaves and sticks striking his flesh. The intense blue light threw flickering shades through the moving debris. With a thunderous detonation, Lord Mallach imploded, scattering his flaming ashes to the ground.

As the wind abruptly died, the buzzing in Gralyre's skull ceased with it. The battle was over.

Gralyre laughed, bouncing his fists off the cage as he cheered the victory. *'I told you I would see you dead!'* he crowed silently at the smoldering embers.

The Sorceress turned to her men as they emerged from hiding. As if nothing had occurred, she was all business. "Behead the bodies and be quick about it. We have wasted too much time on this venture and made far too much noise. We canno' risk a patrol happening upon us afore we make good our escape!" The men immediately scattered to do her bidding.

The door to the cage clanged open. It was Wil and his two sons, Rewn and Dajin. "Come on out o' there, lad. We must be well away from here afore we are discovered."

Gralyre winced as he shuffled to the doorway. The women prisoners remained huddled in the wagon. Rescued from their fate for a second time, they were unsure of what to do. In their indecision, they stayed where they were.

Wil helped Gralyre down off the wagon, but even with his help, Gralyre winced with pain as his feet hit the ground. His spine protested loudly as he stood upright for the first time in over a month.

"I surely hope ye can ride, lad." Wil supported Gralyre's weight as he sagged.

"I will stay in the saddle, even if you have to tie me to it," Gralyre promised with grim humour.

"If it comes t' that, lad. If it comes t' that."

"We will get the horses, Da," stated Rewn. He cuffed Dajin on the arm and together they jogged into the forest where their mounts had been left during the battle.

The Sorceress appeared at Wil's side. "I hope he is worth the trouble, Wil," she warned. "I have seen him fight, and felt some o' his magic, but even so, he hardly seems worth the effort." She looked Gralyre's slumped, pain wreaked figure up and down.

"Magic?" Wil questioned, eyeing Gralyre with a hint of wariness, before he shrugged dismissively. "I owed him a life debt, Lady Catrian. T' no' repay him would make me no more than one o' them," Wil chided as he jerked his chin at the headless remains strewn about the road.

Slightly offended by her dismissal, Gralyre looked over her bawdy, ripped and torn outfit and decided she was not such a prize either. Although, he mused, she had a way of carrying herself that went beyond such an insipid label as pretty. The way she moved her tall lithe body, and the level stare that came from her grey-green eyes, intrigued him.

Catrian cleared her throat at Gralyre's overlong perusal and self-consciously jerked up the low neckline of her dress. "No matter. I could no' pass by the opportunity t' kill one o' Doaphin's Demon Lords. Thank-ye for aiding me," she smiled at Gralyre, "Your magic drew his attention from me at just the right moment."

"You are most welcome, Lady Catrian," Gralyre replied.

"This will all be worth the effort if ye can put us in contact with the Southern Kingdoms."

Gralyre started uncomfortably at her words, but remained silent. Wil's life debt notwithstanding, this was the real reason they had rescued him. What would they do when they discovered that he had no clue as to his origins? What would they do to him if they knew that the Demon Lord had recognized him?

Regardless, she had risked her life and those of her men for him. He held out his hand to her and with a reserved smile, she took it. "I shall do what I can to repay you." He made a little motion with his free hand. "I now owe a life debt to you, my lady. I will not forget," said Gralyre firmly as his battered mouth lifted in a semblance of a smile. If she wished contact with these Southern Kingdoms then he would see it done, whatever his true background was discovered to be. He owed her no less for his life.

He bowed low over her hand, a courtly gesture that caused

him some pain. Yet it was worth it somehow. It felt right to him, natural. The delicate feel of her fingers clasped gently in his huge warrior hand stirred something deep within. As he straightened, his eyes travelled back up her long elegant throat to her grey-green eyes. He forgot to breath.

A light blush now covered her cheeks. "I shall wait until ye are less dented afore I collect, if ye do no' mind," Catrian teased him lightly to break the awkward silence.

Wil laughed.

Gralyre reluctantly released her hand as a warrior approached leading a horse. "That is the lot o' them, Catrian. Are ye suffering any ill effects from your battle?" he asked solicitously as he passed her the reins. "For a moment I thought he would take ye!"

"I am fine. The Demon Riders and their Lords are over-confident. 'Tis their weakness. I showed him what he wanted t' see, then attacked from two directions at once. The more vulnerable I acted, the more overconfident and distracted he became," she reassured him.

"If you are strong enough to kill the Demon Lord, how is it ye came to be among the women that I rescued from the wagon?" Gralyre asked.

Catrian's face became shuttered and dark. "That is o' no concern t' ye!" She stepped back, dragging her horse along with her.

Her voice turned brisk with authority as she addressed her man. "Set the wagon horses loose and tell the women that they are free t' scatter where they will. Give them food from the saddles o' the 'Riders. The extra trails they make will cause more confusion for Doaphin's trackers."

With a nod, the warrior hastened to his tasks.

In one agile movement, Catrian swung herself to the back of her horse. The bunched skirt revealed a long length of leg and the dagger strapped to her shin.

From atop her horse, Catrian smiled down at Wil, her harshness of a moment ago banished. "Wil, I have word that your daughter has found our contact in Verdalan. She will be safely t' the mountains by the first snows."

"Thank ye, Catrian," Wil said simply. "I owe ye more than I will ever be able t' repay."

"Please," she interrupted with a wave of her hand, "no more talk o' debts. I was pleased t' aid ye."

"Can ye ride?" she asked, shifting her focus to Gralyre. She waited for his nod of assent before she continued. "Then do so," she ordered. "I will have one o' my men scuff out your trail t' hide your path. We will leave plain enough signs t' draw any trackers away, but in the event ye are followed, do no' return t' Raindell. Ye would do no' but condemn yourselves and the whole village t' death. If ye are followed, try t' lose them and make for Verdalan. There is a tavern there called the Fighting Stag. Go t' the Innkeeper and say these words; 'Running stags canno' fight'. Ye will receive more direction then. 'Tis all the help I dare give, in case ye are seized," she stated tersely.

Gralyre realized from her tight face that such a tragedy had happened before. He wondered at the life she had chosen, a life that meant the constant loss of friends and the constant threat of betrayal by enemies. But then maybe she had been given no choice. Perhaps her powers had chosen her path for her.

"Farewell, Wil." She gave Gralyre a nod, turned her horse and thundered over to where her men were gathering.

Wil's two sons arrived with four horses in tow. "Help him," said Wil to his elder son.

Wincing all the way and frailer than he would like to admit, Gralyre allowed the man to help him onto the horse. When he was mounted, Gralyre leaned down and clapped him on the shoulder. "Thank you... Rewn, is it not?" he asked.

"That is right," Rewn said, smiling as he handed up the reins. "That one," he indicated his brother, "is Dajin." He turned away to his own mount.

The wind blew Rewn's hair backwards and into his eyes, and he paused to brush at the light brown mass before, with a fluid movement, gaining the back of his horse. His father and brother were already seated in their saddles.

Dajin bore a strong resemblance to his absent sister. He was of more delicate build than his older brother, but with the same light brown hair. Dajin grinned at Gralyre now, seeming overly excited for the circumstances as though he viewed the battle and their flight as a play put on for his amusement.

'He is young,' Gralyre decided.

"If ye feel ye are going t' slip from the horse, let us know and we will arrange something. We can no' afford t' go slowly, and I apologize for the pain ye are being asked t' endure," said Wil formally, reclaiming Gralyre's attention.

"I will live... now," said Gralyre with a serious smile. If not for Wil and his sons he would be on his way to torture and death at the cruel hands of Lord Mallach.

They spurred their horses back up the road and away from the distant city. Clinging to his saddle, Gralyre winced and cursed. The beast's rough gait would be the death of him, but if he would keep pace with his benefactors and ahead of any pursuit, he had to endure.

"Where is your wolf, stranger?" asked Dajin.

"He is pacing us in the forest," Rewn answered his brother. "I keep catching glimpses o' him." He nodded his chin to the left. A sudden clearing in the bushes revealed the wolfdog jumping a fallen tree before the leaves hid him once more.

Gralyre opened his mind to Little Wolf. Immediately, he was flooded with the animal's jubilation that he was safe. He felt renewed determination to endure the pain. "There is a farm, about a fortnight's travel from here. 'Tis off the road and will be a good place to rest. The wolf will guide you," Gralyre called out to Wil.

Wil nodded his understanding. "It sounds like a good place t' check for pursuit." There was no more time for conversation as they rode hard into the day.

CHAPTER SIX

During the first few hours of hard riding, Gralyre developed a raging fever. The pounding of the horse's hooves echoed the beat of blood surging in his fevered brow. Slowly, he slipped away into dark mists.

Wil was the first to notice that Gralyre no longer kept the pace. He reined around and rode back to him. "Gralyre, lad, can ye hear me?"

Gralyre was unable to answer for within his fever dream he rode still, pursued by a dark demon horde. Mumbling incoherently, his body twitching and convulsing, he began to slide from his saddle.

"Rewn!"

Wil's son heeded his father's urgent call, spurring his mount around.

Dajin roughly hauled on his horse's reins, bringing it to a blowing, stamping halt. He waited impatiently, eyeing the road behind for signs of pursuit. "Quickly!" he yelled back to the others.

Wil steadied Gralyre as Rewn lashed the man to his mount. To rest here, before they had placed more distance between themselves and the scene of the escape, would be suicide. For the sake of their lives, they had to push onwards.

"I'll lead his horse, Da," Rewn volunteered as he mounted. Wil passed his son the reins, and Rewn hauled Gralyre's horse into motion behind him.

The three men set a hard pace, alternating the gaits of the horses, from walk to trot to canter, to keep them from foundering. The Demon Riders could be easily outrun. It was the Deathren and Stalkers that they feared most. They had to put as many miles behind them as possible before nightfall.

ഇൽ

Miles passed, but Gralyre was aware of none of it. His fearsome nightmares devoured his mind even as fever consumed his body. The pain from the horse's canter breached his dreams and wrought terrible imaginings.

...Arms and legs chained to stone, Lord Mallach shimmers like a mirage in a hot forge.

"You will learn, Hero, never to defy me! You will never escape Doaphin's Towers!" Mad laughter. Bullwhips grow from the Demon's fingertips; snakes of horror, caressing, coiling.

Thunderous cracks snap the air, lashing arms, back, chest. Flesh flays from bone. Hot blood spatters his face, the walls, the floor. Endless pain.

Contorts to escape shackles, screams. The Count's words, the Count's laughter, roll like thunder. "I know who you are! I know who you are!"

Screams, "NO!" Must get away! Escape!

In the real world, Gralyre's fever struggles grew so violent, that the horse began to skip and jitter to relieve itself of its troublesome burden. "Da! He is getting worse!" Rewn warned.

"Bind him tighter. If we do no' calm him, the horse is going t' throw him. Here," Wil tossed his son another length of rope.

Rewn quickly dismounted. "Dajin! Come here and hold the horse's head for me. Keep it still."

"Just leave him! He is slowing us down and is just going t' die anyway!"

"Dajin!" Wil growled reprovingly.

Dajin bit his lip and glanced anxiously back. Seeing the road was empty he threw himself sulkily off his horse and stomped over to grab the bridle. The horse shied at the abrupt approach. "Stay still, stupid horse," Dajin growled.

Rewn made quick work of binding Gralyre's arms and legs and cinching them tightly to the saddle. Before he was finished, Gralyre's body could barely twitch.

He lifted a water skin and dribbled some liquid into Gralyre's mouth, before squirting a bit over his face to do what he could to lower the fever. He paused to gently brush back the matted black hair from Gralyre's battered, bloody face. "Ye are going t' be fine. We will take care o' ye," Rewn promised.

"No more... The Towers... You do not know me!" Gralyre shouted.

The horse reared at the noise and Dajin had a rough moment hauling it back down. Rewn danced backwards to escape the flashing hooves.

"Gods!" Dajin yelped. "Shut him up!"

Rewn pulled a handkerchief from his pocket. He hesitated for a moment, but could see no other way. Quickly, he shoved it between Gralyre's lips to muffle his cries. He met his father's worried look over the back of the horse.

"'Tis alright, son, there be no other way."

"Hurry!" Dajin urged.

Rewn frowned at Dajin as he moved to reclaim Gralyre's horse from his brother. "Do no' be afraid, Dajin. We will stay ahead o' them."

"No' if he trumpets our position t' all the 'Riders in Dreisenheld!" He threw the reins at Rewn, and ran back to his own horse. He waited fitfully as Rewn settled back onto his saddle and pulled Gralyre's mount into position. "Finally!" he groused and kicked his horse into motion.

Rewn watched his brother's back disappear around a bend. He glanced at his father and shrugged.

Wil frowned back. "I should have left him in Raindell."

Rewn grinned. "Ye jest! Imagine the trouble he would find if we were no' there!"

Wil gave a shout of laughter and set his heels to his horse. Rewn joined him and they soon caught up with Dajin.

By binding Gralyre's arms and legs to quiet him, Rewn unknowingly added to the elements of Gralyre's nightmares.

...chains bind, links cut hot firebrands across flesh. The bullwhips crack; Flesh flays from bone, blood spatters and sprays. Endless pain.

"You will feast on your own flesh!" The Demon's words echo. Taunting. In his hands, raw meat, bloody, dripping.

No! No!

Rough hands clamp. Raw meat fills his mouth; blood and fleshy sinew still warm. Chokes! Gags!

A hand stops his lips. "When all your flesh is gone, I will allow you to die."

Heave... Retch... Get it out!

"Da! He is choking!" Rewn was off his horse in a flash, and pulled the gag from Gralyre's mouth just as he vomited. He waited until Gralyre had finished heaving, and then used the water skin to clear his mouth.

Gralyre's face was slack, and his head hung limply against the shoulder of his steed.

"He needs t' rest!"

Wil rubbed his face. "Alright," he decided, "but only for a short time!"

Rewn and Wil pulled Gralyre from his horse, laying him flat and doing their best to get water into him. Gralyre never awoke from his stupor.

Dajin watched as his brother and father worked tirelessly to bring down Gralyre's fever. "Leave him!" he urged once more. "He is slowing us down! The 'Riders will catch up!"

"Hold your tongue, lad!" Wil roared. "We did no' risk our lives t' rescue him only t' give him up now! Find your honor!"

Dajin made no more mention of the matter. A hot flush rose over his cheeks and his mouth set mulishly.

Little Wolf crept out of the bush and cautiously approached. He stopped nervously, his paws dancing, his body swinging first to face Gralyre's supine form, then the safety of the surrounding forest. It was obvious that he wanted to be at Gralyre's side, but was shy of these strangers. His eyes locked to Rewn's.

Rewn froze before slowly reaching out a hand, palm up, for the wolfdog to sniff. "'Tis alright. I will no' hurt ye."

The wolfdog stopped his pacing and leaned forward, his eyes intent, his ears revolving forward and back as he listened to Rewn's voice.

Rewn shivered. These eyes did not belong to a dumb beast. He found himself talking to it as though it could understand. "Gralyre is very sick. We can no' stop for long, but I will do what I can for him. I will no' hurt him nor ye."

Little Wolf paced a wide circle to approach Gralyre's far side, where he flopped down and rested his chin on Gralyre's chest. He sighed heavily, his intent gaze fixed on the slack face of his master.

Rewn let out the breath he had held and looked to Wil for some guidance.

"Go ahead and see if he'll take any more water," Wil advised, ignoring the presence of Little Wolf. "We must away, soon."

When they remounted and continued their flight, Dajin rode out ahead of the others, "I'm going t' scout the trail." The simple reality was that his fear drove him to place more distance between danger and his skin.

"Do no' get too far ahead, boy. And be careful!" Wil warned.

Rewn spent as much time looking back at the limp man tied to the horse as on the road ahead. He did not expect Gralyre to survive the night. The man's injuries were too great.

Little Wolf remained beside Gralyre's mount, effortlessly keeping pace with his easy lupine glide. His eyes remained fixed on his master, as though to blink would be to allow him to die.

Darkness fell, and they were forced to slow their pace, and finally, to call a halt for the night. The horses needed the rest, and so did the men.

"No fire," Wil decided.

Little Wolf curled up next to Gralyre, to offer heat and comfort. His chin rested on Gralyre's chest so that he could maintain his vigil. He was growing more used to the men, and did not shift from position when Rewn approached with the water skin and began to dribble liquid into Gralyre's mouth.

"I will take the first shift, Da," Dajin offered.

"Two hour shift only, then ye wake me. Rewn, ye will take the last post. We ride afore sunrise."

Rewn pulled a cloth bound bundle from his pocket and unwrapped a bit of cold pork. He broke off a piece and put it into his mouth.

Little Wolf glanced at him, nose twitching. His tongue wreathed his muzzle and his ears perked forward. His eyes went from the meat to Rewn and back again.

Rewn sighed and broke a chunk of the pork away and placed it next to Little Wolf's muzzle. The wolfdog snapped it up so quickly that Rewn barely got his fingers free.

"'Tis salty, do ye want water with that?" Rewn asked, smiling wryly. What was it about the creature that seemed so… sentient?

Little Wolf raised his muzzle and looked at the water skin.

Rewn fought back a shiver. "Alright, here ye go." He cupped

his hand next to Little Wolf's chin and squeezed some water into
his palm.

Little Wolf eyed him for a disbelieving moment.

"Well, how else are ye t' get at it?"

Little Wolf leaned forward and lapped.

৪৩৫

Gralyre made it through that night, and the next, though he
grew weaker. Whenever they stopped, Rewn and Wil would try
to get gruel and water into him, but it was a loosing battle.
Gralyre was not going to make it to Raindell.

The men had finally been forced to slow their pace to save the
horses. Death would have found them by now if Stalkers or
Deathren were tracking them. If they were being followed at all,
it was by 'Riders, who were forced to rely on horseflesh for
travel, the same as they. For now the hard pace they had been
keeping had put them well ahead of such a danger.

Little Wolf, if not friendly towards the men, was at least
tolerant of them. He seemed to realize that they were helping
Gralyre. Often when the men called a halt, Little Wolf would
appear with a rabbit or bird in his mouth, supplying meat for the
pack.

During the long days the wolfdog would usually take up
position next to Gralyre's horse. But this morning was different.

They had been underway for little more than an hour when
Little Wolf emerged from the forest to block their path, whining
urgently at the men, and keeping the horses from moving

forward.

"What is he doing?" Dajin yelled. He pulled his sword. "Get out o' my way ye mangy cur!"

Little Wolf's head lowered and his ruff rose. His eyes fixed with feral intensity on Dajin's. The threat was blatant.

Rewn grabbed Dajin's wrist. "Lower your sword," he whispered.

Dajin swallowed heavily, "He is but a stupid beast. He canno' know what a sword is." But he allowed Rewn to push his arm down and he sheathed his blade.

The wolfdog's aggressive stance relaxed, but he continued to glare Dajin's way. He warbled urgently, a sound just shy of speech, and danced sideways towards a faint path into the forest.

Rewn grinned and looked at his father. "The trail t' the farm that Gralyre mentioned?"

Wil shrugged and smiled back. "Smart animal. 'Tis well hidden. We would have ridden right by it."

೮೦೧೪

Gralyre regained consciousness and blinked hazily at the charred remains of buildings. Recognition came slowly. He was in the yard of his farm and Little Wolf lay curled beside him.

The pup thumped his tail happily when he saw Gralyre's eyes upon him. They were lying under a roof of pine bows leaned against the stone hedge that surrounded the overgrown fields.

'Did I never leave? Was it all a dream?' His mind reeled from the disorientation. The last he remembered was being

tortured in Doaphin's Towers… but no that was a nightmare… was it not? Yes, of course, Catrian killed the Demon Lord. There was the battle at the wagon, the wild ride, then the lashing…? His mind shied from the renewed memory of his tortuous nightmares.

Gralyre reached out a trembling hand and anchored his fingers deep into Little Wolf's fur. The pup was the only thing he knew to be real.

"So ye have come back t' us, lad," said Wil, noticing movement within the rough shelter.

Gralyre raised his head shakily and saw Wil advancing on him with a vile smelling cup of liquid. A neatly made camp surrounded a small cook fire, on which a kettle bubbled and perked. Gralyre vaguely remembered other doses of the medicine and his lip curled in distaste.

He was given no choice in the matter, as Wil briskly tipped the cup to his mouth. With his broken, swollen nose still not allowing for the passage of air, it was either swallow the concoction, or choke.

"Your wolf led us right t' this place, just as ye said he would," Wil stated in the cheerful tones one always uses around the ill. He paused in his cup tipping, allowing Gralyre to gasp for a breath.

Gralyre sputtered, trying to remove the foul taste of the medicine from his mouth. His face crumpled in disgust. "What is that? 'Tis vile!"

"Just ye keep a civil tongue, boyo!" Wil grinned. "My dear departed wife used t' douse us with this very medicine when we were ailing. Worked every time to! The children never stayed abed for more than a day or two! They got better just t' keep her away from them with the brew!"

"I can see why," Gralyre growled, coughed and spat.

Wil just laughed. "Ye sound like me when my dear Marji used t' force it down my throat. Trust me, lad, ye will recover if only t' revenge yourself upon me for dousing ye with it."

Gralyre chuckled weakly and then groaned as his ribs protested.

Little Wolf warbled as he sensed his master's pain, and thrust his muzzle into Gralyre's contorted face.

Wil regarded him with rough sympathy, waiting for Gralyre to regain control, before briskly pouring more of the medicine into his patient.

"When we arrived we found a saddle and packs on the ground near the burnt farmhouse. The teeth marks on the leather bespoke your wolf's handiwork. Must have chewed it right off the horse. We placed the packs just there in your shelter," Wil gestured with his chin.

Gralyre turned his head to regard the packs on which he was resting, which also put him out of reach of the medicine cup. A wavering smile of pleasure twisted his lips. It was the pack from the horse that had abandoned him in Raindell and that Little Wolf had led back to the farm.

Its fear of becoming a villager's dinner had outweighed its loyalty to its master. Which was a fortuitous end, for it had born away to safety his most precious belongings. A bleakness he had not known he carried released itself.

"How long?" Gralyre's strength was waning and with it, his voice.

Wil leaned forward to hear him, and stayed to tip the cup to Gralyre's lips again. "We have been here for most of a week and we were on the road for a fortnight and then some afore that."

The cup drained to his satisfaction, Wil sat back on his haunches and rubbed a tired hand across his face. "We thought we were going t' lose ye, more than once, but ye have some strength in ye, lad!"

He gave Gralyre a penetrating look while his finger idly tapped the side of his nose. Finally he seemed to come to a decision. "Ye are no' from the Southern Kingdoms, are ye? Ye said some things during your fever." Wil paused again, uncomfortable with admitting his eavesdropping. "I will no' ask ye o' your loss or who caused it." He paused to indicate the burned out farm. "'Tis obvious enough given your hatred o' the 'Riders." For a moment longer he looked at Gralyre's wan, shuttered face. He sighed heavily. "No matter. When ye are well, we will have the whole story."

Gralyre, unable to support the weight of his swollen head a moment longer, allowed it to loll back against the pack he was resting against.

What had he said while the fever had gripped him? Was it something that revealed how the Count had known of him? A shudder passed through him. The memory of that evil creature left a worse taste in his mouth than the bitter medicine. He closed his eyes tightly, fighting the pain in his soul as much as the pain in his body.

Wil stood and tossed the dregs of the cup into the flames. The fire hissed and sparked as the steam dissipated in the light breeze. Wil rolled his shoulders and regained his sickbed cheerfulness. "For now, we are safe. We are well off the track, so we should no' be happened upon. I have set my boys t' guarding the approach, so we can be well away if we are discovered. Ye just rest easy. The medicine will help ye t' sleep and 'tis rest ye need most."

Wil disappeared from view, back out into the yard. Soon, the sound of tuneless whistling keeping time to the chopping of wood drifted back to where Gralyre rested.

Gralyre's head swam, and he allowed his heavy-lidded eyes to close. Before he passed into a deep sleep, he commended Little Wolf for leading them to the farm. And ordered him to not let Wil near him with that foul concoction ever again.

Little Wolf solemnly promised.

ഇരു

Gralyre steadily improved. Bed rest and good food did much to repair his broken body. Within the week he was able to get to his feet with the support of one of the men.

Much of his weakness was due to the starvation he had suffered in the cage. Now that he was awake and able to take solid foods, his body was recovering much faster, and his frame was regaining its more robust condition.

This night, he had finally felt able to rise from his sickbed and join the men at the fire for dinner, instead of lying helpless upon his pallet and being waited upon.

The moon was full and shone brightly down upon the small party, but the wind was restless, causing chills that forced the men closer to the warmth of their shielded blaze. Clouds scudded across the moon's face causing shadows to spring sharply into being and just as quickly vanish, creating false movement in the darkened landscape. It was a night best spent close to the fire, talking in hushed voices lest the ghosts of the past come calling.

The four men reclined after a satisfying meal of wild onions, mushrooms and rabbit. Into the contented silence Dajin blurted the questions that had been burning in his mind for days. "The graves, down by the river? Who were they? Were they your family?"

"Damn your tongue, boyo! Be still!" snapped Wil at his son's tactless lack of compassion.

"No, 'tis alright." Gralyre sighed heavily. He was surprised they had held their questions for so long. He settled himself more comfortably, and the others, sensing a story, grew still and expectant.

Would they think him mad? He looked across the flames at their honest, wholesome faces burnished in red light. A deep yearning for their companionship welled. Would their friendship be withdrawn if he told them all of it?

His eyes passed over Dajin and Rewn to lock with Wil's penetrating stare. They had selflessly rescued him from a horrific death, doctored his injuries, and guarded his back.

Wil nodded in his encouragement.

Gralyre reached his decision. He would not lie to these men. If they should choose to believe him mad, so be it. He would take that chance. They had risked their lives to save his. The least that he owed them was the truth.

"This spring, I awoke in the forest with no memory of who or where I was. I was covered with blood as from a fierce battle. I was sick and weak." As he spoke, his mind went back to that first awakening, reliving it, even as he told them of it.

"I had but one… memory… if you would. It all began with the Nightmare…"

CHAPTER SEVEN

THE KING'S FOREST- SPRING

Men scream rage and fear. Sword smashes against sword in chaotic battle. Raw grief and despair; his men die, one by one. He stands alone in a sea of blood; the tide is against him. The wave of evil cannot be stopped. It crashes over him, crushes him, brings him to his knees. A prisoner.

A Demon's face slowly emerges from a boiling red mist. Its eyes burn with evil and triumph. An executioner's sword hangs suspended for a wild moment.

Terror! Cannot move! Cannot Escape! I will not cry out!

The sword drops. Sunlight sharpens the edge; his terrified visage, a distorted reflection in metal, chases the blade towards his neck. The sword bites and he is wrenched into the swirling blackness of forever... forever, but not the end...

Agony harries him into an infinite night, a void that has never seen starlight. All is pain. The void pulses, the chamber of a giant heart, flaying his soul in a savage rhythm.

I am lost, I am everywhere, I am the universe...the void pulses...I am nothing, I am smaller than the smallest grain of sand.

For brief flickers between he is himself, eroding with every violent cycle to slip away into the grinding maw of the voracious darkness.

This then, is death; this then, is my punishment for failure.

Wildly thrashing limbs produce no movement. They do not exist here. Screams from blinding suffering go unheard. Infinity swirls and boils, terrifying, with no eyes to shut against it. Whatever power tortures him, forces him to gaze into the face of eternity.

Torment and time. It is forever; it is a split second. Sanity slips further from his grasp. Madness degenerates into soundless howls and disembodied thrashings.

Into the black chaos, colors swirl, growing brighter, forcing the darkness to recede. Vivid greens and yellows, blues and reds, swirl faster and faster.

He fights to escape as he is sucked into the vortex of color, birthed back into the land of the living...

He awoke with a shout, lathered in a cold sweat, his body stiff with fear. He sucked in great gulps of air, starved for it, panting with the effort to slow the wild pounding of his heart. Slowly, he calmed and the fear faded, taking with it some of the contents of the gruesome nightmare.

He lay at the base of an enormous, old oak tree. Sunlight from a cloudless sky filtered through its canopy of leaves and tinted his vision in flickering shades of green. Trees of the surrounding forest rustled busily in the quickening breeze. Somewhere, a bird sang love songs to its mate. Moss and grasses grew thick and fragrant around him, cushioning his body where he lay.

The man drew a deep breath, savouring the rich scents of early spring. He had smelled this before, though when and where eluded him for the moment. Everything was so very peaceful and yet … very strange.

He levered himself up and put his back to the tree. *'I should not be here,'* he mused as he gazed around the glade. Where precisely he should be, he was momentarily unable to recall, but there was a persistent feeling that it was not here.

'I should be…' Terror struck him with the force of a blacksmith's hammer. *'…DEAD!'* His body convulsed in shock and horror. *'No! Not dead! A dead man does not breathe and hear, nor have a head that hurts so badly, it wants to sprout legs and flee!'*

He closed his eyes and pressed a clenched fist to his forehead to soothe the pain of thought as he tried to rationalize his panic away. *'I lay down to sleep, had a nightmare and forgot where I was going and what I was doing? How is this possible?'*

A bursting sense of urgency began to consume him, though the why of it escaped him. Nothing! He squeezed his eyes tighter as waves of panic thrashed through his body and left him quaking.

'I remember nothing but the dream…or is it a memory? What if 'tis a memory?' He moaned his despair. *'What is wrong with me? Who am I? What am I doing here?'*

It appeared to be early spring. The birds were singing, and he could hear a stream murmuring in the distance. Everything was as it should be. *'Except that I have no memory of myself or why I am here when I should be…where? Not dead! NOT DEAD!'*

Something crusty flaked from his fingers as he rubbed his aching brow. Blinking his eyes open, he recoiled in disgust. His hands were coated in dried blood! So were his clothes! His clothing was black, effectively disguising the saturating gore until he noticed the stiffness of the fabric. After an alarmed examination, it became apparent that none of the blood was his.

He drew up his knees and leaned over them, fighting back waves of nausea. '*What is happening? How did my clothes become this way? Was I in a battle?*' His body rocked unwittingly in agitation.

The man looked nervously around the glade. The mossy grass was undisturbed, except for where he had lain. But that meant nothing, for the resilient grasses were already springing up to cover even those traces.

Adrenaline surged through his veins, causing his hands to shake and tremble. With a mighty effort, he forced himself to stop his rocking, and to turn his energies to reasoning out his plight.

'*The blood proves I have been in a fight. Since I am not injured, I must have either won or fled. There is no one else here, so I must have fought this battle elsewhere, wandered here and collapsed.*' Though it seemed a likely explanation, it did not explain the loss of his memory.

'*A blow! A blow to the head could have knocked me senseless.*' He combed his fingers through his matted hair and across his scalp. His head ached like demons were making war within, but there was no lump or other physical injury. Had he witnessed something so hideous that he had fled from the memory of it?

… Battle. Capture. A blade descends towards his neck…

With a cry, he thrust out his hands to ward off the horrific images that momentarily seemed more real than the surrounding forest. They gradually receded, but left a stale residue of fear in their place. His trembling increased until his body quaked uncontrollably.

The place, the time of year, 'twas not right although he could not describe how it was false. *'Should not the ground be rocky, and the weather cooler, like it is…?'*

That cursed dream again! How strange that something so fearsome felt so real that it made the peace around him seem an illusion.

'Is the swordsman of my nightmare hunting me?'

The man scrabbled to look over his shoulder, certain that danger was stalking him from behind. The simple movement of rolling over sent jolts of agony throughout his skull, but did not prevent the hairs on his nape from standing on end.

His nausea increased. Sweat stung his eyes and soft grass tickled his chin as the glade lurched sickeningly around him. The man's forehead drooped to rest upon the ground. He clenched his teeth and fists, and struggled for long measured breaths to control his need to retch.

There must be some truths in his musings, since he was reacting so violently, but what were they? The only fact he had tangible proof of was a battle. For where else could the blood have come from? It would be unwise to bide here when, even now, an unknown foe could be tracking him to this glade!

His legs almost collapsed as he scrambled to his feet. He grabbed a branch on the tree for support until the dizziness and weakness eased. As he shifted, he felt something bump his leg from behind. He swung around with a shout to confront his attacker, and mistakenly cracked his fists into the bole of the tree.

As he fumbled to regain his balance at the abrupt move, he was bumped again, and grimaced at his foolishness. Whatever was touching him was strapped to his back. He flexed his bruised fingers, and reached behind his shoulder, feeling a long, stiff piece of leather. Noticing the thick belt crossing his chest, he forced his sore fingers to work the fastenings.

It was an empty sword scabbard, four feet long, made from oiled and tooled black leather, with an ornate baldric to support the weight of a blade. He touched it in wonder. *'What kind of sword is so large?'*

A strange notion overtook him. He blinked as an image formed of a great steel monster, its four-foot blade sheathed in the leather. The guard was fashioned to look like the wings of a dragon. The tail of the beast coiled around the grip and the dragon's head snaked a couple of inches along the blade. The eyes of the dragon were rubies as was the cabochon pommel stone. In the hands of someone who knew how to use it, such a blade would make the wielder near invincible.

So real was the illusion that his hand reached out, shaped from muscle memory as though to curl around the hilt. The vision shattered. Dizziness rocked him on his feet, sending his hands to scrabble roughly for balance against the tree once more. Darkness crept in on the edges of his vision as he teetered.

'Fool! You have conjured a sword that has never existed!'

Until he had a real sword, instead of phantoms, the sheath was of no use except as a crutch.

As the bout of vertigo receded, he braced himself with the scabbard, and tried to decide which way to go. Indecision crippled him until it occurred that he could choose no wrong direction. He did not know where he was, or where he had been going. No matter his choice, he would have to trust in his luck not to encounter an enemy.

His aching head, soiled clothing and raging thirst decided his direction for him. The creek he could hear beckoned him.

Within one shuffling step away from the tree, his knees buckled. He would have fallen if the stiff scabbard had not been there to prop him up. He was fatigued and trembling, as though he had just recovered from a long illness, and could barely keep his feet, let alone walk. Was that it? Had he been ill? But then, where had the blood come from?

He groaned loudly in frustration as his mind leapt from one possible reason for his affliction to another. His jaw hardened in determination. Whatever the explanation, it made no difference. He had to move, and he needed more support than what the scabbard could give.

He scanned the clearing and spotted a long branch that would function well as a crutch. It would also make a fine staff should he be in need of a weapon.

Collapsing to his knees to retrieve it, he managed a slight smile at his stroke of luck. *'The Gods of Fortune have not yet deserted me!'*

His stomach gave a sudden lurch of anxiety. *'Who are the*

Gods of Fortune?'

He distracted his thoughts with snapping off the smaller twigs from the main branch to leave a smooth shaft. It was no matter. He would think on all of this later, when he had found safety.

Stubbing the butt of the stick into the soft loam, he slowly pushed himself back up to his feet. Leaning against the tree trunk for support, he paused to rest before strapping the scabbard on to leave both hands free to clutch his walking stick. Then, with great effort, he shuffled towards the sound of running water.

When he finally broke free of the underbrush, the man was forced to shield his eyes from the sun-dappled brightness of the water. Silvery darts of light, reflecting off the river, sent arrows of pain shooting into his head. Tears blinded him to all but vague shapes as he dropped to his knees and crawled the rest of the way.

Licking his parched lips in anticipation, he reached out to the murmuring waves, but stopped himself abruptly. His mouth curled in disgust as he beheld the dried blood on his trembling fingers and palms. He could not get a drink by cupping his hands until he had bathed. Pondering the problem for a moment, his vacant mind finally produced a solution.

He dunked his face into the running water, drank his fill, and would have continued to drink if water had not poured into his nose. He snorted in an effort to clear it as he considered the current. In his debilitated condition, the flow here was too quick for him to bathe in.

Feeling somewhat revived after the cool draught of water, the man gathered up his makeshift crutch, and staggered downstream until he found a shaded pool. His headache receded to a background throb without the sun's rays to feed it.

Sighing with anticipation and dropping the crutch, he unbuckled the sheath and let it fall next to his staff. In one fluid motion, he pulled both his black leather jerkin, and homespun shirt off over his head, and suddenly found himself sitting on the ground... hard.

If it was a surprise to have fallen, it was even more of one that he wore a chain mail shirt. As he gazed at it, he forgot his bruised rump.

The armour was woven of a multitude of fine, shiny metal links. It did not appear to be steel, but more like... silver.

'Silver will not stop a sword thrust,' He frowned at the incongruity. *'Still, 'tis better than nothing.'* Removing it, and the white, quilted undershirt that cushioned his skin from the armour's links, he shrugged his shoulders in relief from the extra twenty pounds he had been unaware of carrying.

Releasing the wide black belt circling his waist, he discovered it had an interior pocket filled with gold, silver, and copper coins. Within his absent memory, there was no answer to how much it amounted to. He did not recognize any of the denominations, though he recognized the metals they were composed of. The head stamped upon the coins was also unknown, leaving him no clues as to who this King was. He laid the money belt aside on the growing pile of clothing.

Leery of his spinning head, he stood to unbutton his trousers. As he started to remove them, he saw he was still wearing tall, black boots that would have to come off first. He hissed impatiently through his teeth. He could not even remember how to undress himself!

He eased back to the ground to remove the offending footwear. It took some effort to work the first boot down his right leg and off, for it seemed tailor made to cling perfectly to his calf. He had to rest for a moment before tackling the other. As the left boot freed his leg and foot, a finely wrought dagger dropped away with it. The man pursed his lips in a silent whistle of appreciation as he picked it up.

The knife had ornate, gold and silver bands woven around a steel hilt. The solid pommel was just heavy enough to perfectly balance the eight-inch blade. He flipped and caught the knife experimentally, then tossed it from hand to hand to get the feel of it.

Without thinking, he balanced its point upon the tip of one finger, and then flipped it so its pommel was then thus balanced. He wove it, effortlessly, in a deadly dance around his hands and arms. He flipped it again, so that he now grasped it by the blade, and sent it whirling into a small knothole on a tree, ten feet away. He stared agape at the quivering hilt.

With the help of his staff, the man staggered to the tree. He pulled the knife free, and flipped it again; blade, hilt, blade hilt. He stayed his hand and raised the dagger before his eyes. This felt familiar, an exercise that his hands remembered though his mind could not. What else was he capable of? Would he be able to reproduce *this* trick should the need ever arise? He did not know how he had done it. He had acted instinctively.

A small smile lifted his lips as he realized there was hope that his memory would return in time. The smile slowly evaporated as his mind hunted frantically for more clues to his identity. Finding nothing, his past as blank a page as ever, he fled his anxiety back to where he had left his clothes.

He had to be patient. His mind was injured and, like any wound, it needed time to heal. Until he remembered his past, he had to trust his instincts to survive and at the moment, instinct was telling him to bathe. He could not travel about the country-side looking like a charnel house.

He stabbed his dagger into the ground before shucking his trousers and tossing them on the pile of discarded clothes.

Without his staff, the man tottered to the stream and dipped a cautious toe. The water felt cool and inviting. As he considered the best way to ease into the pool, vertigo once more overcame him. Loosing his footing, he plunged headlong into the river's cool, wet embrace.

The cold water closed over his head for several long moments. It was colder and deeper than he had expected. The current pulled and pushed at his body, confusing him. He did not know in which direction the surface lay!

'Can I swim?' His arms and legs flailed wildly, but failed to stop his decent through the frigid, suffocating water to the sandy bottom of the pool. His air was almost spent! *'I am going to die!'*

His feet found the bottom and, wanting only air, he gave a mighty push that rocketed him back to the surface. He crested out of the water, gasping and sputtering. It took long moments to regain his breath. When he did, he realized he was treading water. His panic had rediscovered the ability to swim.

He must be more careful! He could assume knowledge of nothing! He could have drowned! Until his memory returned, if his memory returned, he had to approach each situation as though he had never encountered its like. It was the only way he would survive.

As he paddled weakly to the shore, he noted that the current had dragged him downstream from his belongings. The lapping water now rose only as high as his chest and he gratefully dug his toes into the sandy bottom as he rested against the embankment, coughing the last of the water from his lungs. The current was faster here, but he judged he could stand against it for the time it took to bathe.

Feeling more secure, his heart now beating at a slower pace, he scooped a handful of sand out of the embankment, and began to scrub the crusty gore and sweat from off his skin. He stumbled slightly as the flow buffeted his body, and needed the support of the bank to keep from being swept further downstream.

Washing himself was like touching a statue; his own flesh was made foreign to him. As he scrubbed he found a tall, muscular man of broad and deep chest, with a stomach that rippled with strength. His long arms and legs held more than enough power to wield the four-foot blade he had envisioned.

What had he been in his lost life to gain such muscles? A Warrior? A Blacksmith? Perhaps naught but a lowly serf, working long hours in a field? He allowed sand to trickle through hands that were large and strong with heavily callused palms. His fingernails, although filthy, were neatly trimmed and pared.

He was still a young man. His tendons held the flexibility of youth and his muscles were hardened stone, even when at rest. His arms bulged and flexed as he twisted to scrub his back. They appeared strong, but at the moment they scarcely held the strength to wash.

He dunked to allow the current to carry away the gritty residue as he scrubbed vigorously at his scalp to remove the matted gore. As he surfaced, his hair coated his face so that he was almost blinded. Brushing most of it away, he brought one strand in front of his eyes to get a better look at it. Holding the lock to the sun produced blue-black highlights within the thick and slightly wavy strands, but otherwise his hair was black as midnight. Its colour matched the light dusting upon his chest, arms and legs.

Though the cool water had soothed his headache, and the nausea seemed to have disappeared, the dizziness persisted. Suffering through another attack, he stood very still, gripping the embankment, to allow his balance to reassert itself. When he felt steadier, he buried his face in another handful of sand and scrubbed rigorously, hoping to finish his bath quickly. Were he to faint while in the water, he would surely drown.

He felt the prickle of whiskers, and realized he had stumbled upon a clue to how long he had been without memory. It was not much of a beard yet. There was about a three-day growth of stubble upon his chin, he decided thoughtfully as he rasped his fingers against his whiskers. How strange to consider that only three days ago he had a name and a history.

Anguish shot through him at the loss. Submerging, he rinsed the sand clear. Three days past... He would not think on this. He could not.

He levered himself slowly up onto the bank, fighting the weakness in his limbs and heart. Looking down at himself, he grinned. If the water had not been so very cold, he would appear well put together in other places as well.

His burst of wry humour faded into a yawn. The man crawled up the bank until he was in a sunny spot, and collapsed upon the soft ferns that grew there. He lay on his side, breathing heavily, collecting his strength.

From where he lay, he could plainly see his discarded pile of soiled clothing resting upriver. He sighed deeply, knowing he must launder his clothes now, or he would never get it done before he succumbed to exhaustion. Once they were clean, he could rest while they dried. The thought proved incentive enough to force him into a sitting position.

It was then, with the sunlight full upon his naked body, that he noticed the scars. Tracing each one as he found it, he counted twenty-six of the silvery lines upon his arms, chest, and legs. Those were only the ones that he could see. There were probably more scars on the backside of him.

It was obvious he lived - had lived - a violent life. That he was still alive to count his scars, coupled with his skill with the dagger, lent him a certain confidence he had not felt before. All the marks were old and faded. Not a serf, and not a blacksmith then.

He was a warrior. His blade skill and the gore he had just washed away made this a valid assumption.

'What if when the time comes, I cannot remember how to fight?'

His short born confidence evaporated as quickly as the water on his skin in the hot sun. Goose bumps shivered up his arms. There was no benefit in worry. Like swimming, perhaps his battle skills would come in time of need.

The man crawled to his clothes, hoping the repetitive chore of laundry would provide a distraction from his direful musings. Amongst the black pile of fabrics, his white, quilted undershirt stood out in sharp contrast. It smelled of sweat, but was mostly free of the blood staining the rest of his garments. He dipped and rinsed it several times, until the stains faded to a sickly pink. He wrung the fabric as best he could and spread it upon a bush. It would dry quickly in this mid day heat.

As he disentangled the leather jerkin from the black, cotton shirt, he noticed for the first time that an emblem was sewn over the left breast of the vest. It depicted a dragon in flight, clutching a crown in one claw, and a sword in the other. The dragon's neck was extended, and its mouth was open, screaming a defiant battle cry.

That crest was very familiar. The recognition was there, if only he could reach it! The jerkin crumpled in his hands as he closed his eyes and strained to catch the fleeting impression. He almost had it when his headache returned with a viciousness that exploded his vision with flashes of light.

He slammed his fist into the ground. His own mind conspired

against him! How would he survive with no memory?

An alarming idea occurred to him. It would explain much; the blood, the feeling of being hunted...

With a decisive move, the man jerked the dagger from where it was stuck in the ground, and used the sharp tip to pick away the stitches holding the emblem in place. If he had deserted it would be rash to continue wearing a coat of arms.

When removed it left a dark patch on the soft, black leather. Anyone looking at it would realize something had once been there, but at least they would not know what. He toyed with the idea of discarding the crest, but decided not to tempt the loss of even one clue to his identity. He tucked the scrap into the money belt. Perhaps, given time, he would remember what it meant.

Next, the man selected the chain mail from the pile. There was not much he could do to cleanse it, save to wipe it down with his dampened shirttail. He did not want to emerge it in water, for that might cause it to rust. Examining it closely, he still could not discern the type of metal it was fabricated from. The fine workmanship of the links offered him no clues.

His shirt was showing wear as he used the sleeves to polish his tall boots. They were of fine workmanship, though worn with much use. When they gleamed he set them aside in favour of the sword scabbard. It had been drawing his attention since he had first beheld it. He took his time wiping away the grime. It had provided him with a vision that may have been a memory. Perhaps it would reveal more.

As his fingers trailed down the tooled leather of the baldric, a notion gripped him. *'There is something about this design...'* His fingers probed gently, and a secret pocket, worked into the pattern on the leather, opened beneath his questing touch.

The man held his breath as he reached gently inside and removed a small roll of parchment. His fingers began to tremble. A broken wax seal guarded the edge of the scroll, stamped with the same design as the crest he had removed from his jerkin. His excitement escalated as he unrolled the sheet, and found upon it a message written in a familiar flowing hand.

It took a moment of staring blankly at the letter before he realized he could not decipher it. That he should be able to read it, he had no doubt, but for some reason he could not.

The man allowed the parchment to roll up with a snap. He stared grimly at it, lying innocently upon his palm. The answer to all of his questions could be in his hands and it might as well not exist! He just stopped himself from crumpling the scroll and tossing it into the river.

Rife with disappointment, he felt within the secret pocket to see if it contained any other treasures. It did. His fingers pulled free a ring, and all thought left him, along with the air hissing out from between his teeth.

The ring had a silver band of a woven design, mounted with a cabochon sapphire the size and colour of a small plum. It was of such a deep blue it appeared almost black.

Examining closer, he discovered the jewel swivelled on its mount. He flipped it over with a flick of his thumb, and revealed a seal etched in silver. Its design matched the crest he had removed from his vest, and mirrored the mark that engraved the wax seal upon the scroll.

Baffled, he fingered the silver engraving, before he swivelled the seal so the jewel was again dominant. It was a ring of state. The seal was that of a noble house. By his rough clothes, he did not think the ring could belong to him, but neither did he feel like a thief.

'Perhaps I am a courier? Someone entrusted with a message to deliver?' He picked up the rolled parchment. *'That would explain this scroll and the gold and silver in my purse. But if I was a courier, why has the seal upon the message been broken?'*

Had thieves attacked him? But if he had been robbed of his supplies, why did he still have his gold? Maybe it was not thieves he had battled, but someone after this letter?

'Maybe there are only more questions,' he thought caustically, *'but never an answer!'*

The man carefully placed the ring and the scroll back into the secret pocket. It would be unwise to allow anyone to know he had such treasures, no matter what the truth turned out to be.

The man was entertaining ideas about why he wore nothing but black as he quickly finished his laundering and hung the remaining clothes to dry. Once the crusty, dried blood was removed, the black clothing disguised any lingering stains.

Feeling desolate, he leaned out over the water, and stared down at his rippling reflection. He glared into the pool. A stranger glared back.

His narrowed gaze flitted briefly over his face, noting overly long hair, a growth of whiskers on a squared off jaw, and a hawkish nose that had once been straight, but now had a hitch in it where it had, at some time, been broken. He lifted his hand

and found the bump with his fingers.

He touched his other features as he visually catalogued them in the water's reflection. His eyes were wide set, large and dark. Long lashes brushed against his questing fingers, too pretty to belong to a man, he thought in disgust. The water did not reflect well enough to reveal a colour.

His eyebrows were very mobile. He spent a few moments amusing himself by lifting them up and down, hitting upon a combination of one tilted high and the other normal that gave his face a cold, arrogant look and felt entirely too natural. He would definitely remember that one.

When taken as a whole, it was a dangerous, forceful face. With the black clothes, dark looks, and muscular height, he was an intimidating man.

His eyes widened as he spotted a small cut on the right side of his neck. *'What is that?'* He ran a trembling finger along the shallow wound. It could not be!

The dream surged back in flickering images of horror.

...setting rays of sunlight glint off the sharp edge. His distorted face reflects in the shinning blade. Wind whistles as the sword parts the air, coming closer! Closer! CLOSER!

'I will not cower before you!'

The cold edge of steel touches his neck and, before he can flinch, he is wrenched into relentless eternity...

Pulling himself back to the present was to find himself curled into a tight ball, shivering and mewling. That was no dream! It was memory! It must be! He had proof!

He uncurled and crawled, trembling, back up the bank to the sunny spot, and collapsed in a heap. *'I should be dead! The sword cut my neck!'* His fingers again sought the shallow wound as he recalled the endless black of the vortex. *'Am I dead? Is this the after world?'*

His stomach chose that moment to growl hungrily. The small sound made it possible for him to regain some control, for he doubted that one would feel hunger if one were dead.

The cut on his neck was naught but a horrible coincidence. He had been in a battle and could have easily received it then. A humourless smile twisted his lips. What a damned fool he was, allowing a nightmare to frighten him senseless. 'Twas only a dream, or the memory of a dream.

The thought did little to alleviate his shivers. The man curled despondently and hugged himself tightly in an effort to abate his fear.

Whatever had destroyed his memory had been very selective. Nothing of a personal nature remained, yet he was able to recall common, everyday objects, like a horse, when it occurred to him that he needed them. For a moment, he was consumed by the question of how he knew what a horse was.

His stomach showed plainly how little it cared about the state of his mind, but his clothes were still baking in the hot sun and there would be no hunting until they were dry.

'Time, then, for that rest,' he decided, as he settled into a more comfortable position. Emotionally and physically depleted, soothed by the heat of the bright sun, his eyes drifted closed.

CHAPTER EIGHT

Gralyre returned to the present and the firelight as Wil cleared his throat. Wil's face bore an odd expression that Gralyre could not decipher.

"These things ye had with ye? Do ye carry them still?"

Gralyre dragged his reclaimed packs into the firelight, riffling them for the objects he sought. "I carry all but the dagger. That was taken from me in Raindell." The men watched in curious silence as he pulled two skin-wrapped packages from the bundles. One was long and skinny and the other was square and bulky. "These are the items I had upon me when I awoke in the forest." He released the last of the bindings.

The men gasped as they beheld the beauty of the chain mail Gralyre held up.

"Maolar! I have heard o' it, but by the Gods, I have never thought t' behold it! Ye hold in your hands a king's ransom, lad!" Wil stated in an awed voice.

"Maolar," Gralyre echoed, running his fingers over the shiny links. "I did not know what it was called. Now that I have heard its name, I know you are right."

"May I?" Rewn asked, holding out his hands. Gralyre hesitated for a moment before handing the glittering armour over.

"'Tis so light!" An expression of absolute delight burst over Rewn's face. For a moment, he seemed as young as his brother, though Gralyre estimated his age to be nearer that of his own.

"Let me feel!" Dajin demanded of his brother, and made similar exclamations as he fingered the workmanship of the metal links.

Wil examined it in turn and passed it back to Gralyre. "Maolar is made by the Dream Weavers t' the east. When Doaphin conquered this land, the Dream Weavers severed all trade routes with our kingdom. They have had no contact with us for three hundred years. Any traders adventurous enough t' brave the mountain passes are never heard from again."

'Dream Weavers... Dream Weavers...' The name resonated strangely within Gralyre's mind as he set the precious armour aside and took up the second bundle.

The men's faces fell somewhat as they beheld the worn leather scabbard. No doubt they had been expecting more fabulous treasures. They would not long be disappointed.

They watched as Gralyre's fingers played down the sheath until they found the pattern in the tooled leather that concealed the secret pocket. He reached gently inside and withdrew the ring.

Exclamations burst forth but Gralyre did not pass the treasure over. Instead, his fingers returned to the pocket and drew forth the small roll of parchment. The men quieted, realizing Gralyre would proceed at his own pace no matter their urgent questions. They avariciously awaited the next treasure to materialize in front of their astounded eyes.

Gralyre placed the parchment and ring to the side and removed the wide black belt he still wore. None of the villagers had suspected its worth and it had been left to him, though his dagger and boots had been stolen. Opening the concealed compartment, he upended the contents to the ground. The firelight glinted off the pile of gold and silver pieces. Gralyre ignored the wealth, picking out two scraps of cloth instead.

He smoothed the crumpled fabric of Doaphin's crest upon his thigh. The flickering firelight made the snakes come alive with black malevolence. "I took this from the tunic of one of the Demon Riders who attacked my farm." With a contemptuous flick of his wrist he cast it into the flames.

He held up the dragon crest. "This was sewn to my vest," he passed it to Wil. "At first I believed myself to be a deserter from an army, so I hid it away. When I discovered this treasure," his hands swept out to indicate the ring, the pile of coins, and the parchment, "I felt I might have been a courier, set upon by thieves or by people trying to intercept this message." He touched the small scroll. "Perhaps after fighting them off, I wandered until I collapsed, my memory lost to injury or illness."

"Or magic," Rewn suggested.

Gralyre was lost in thought for a moment, considering. "Or magic. I never thought of that."

"Best t' finish your story, lad," Wil prompted as he thoughtfully fingered the crest. His face was arrested with a peculiar expression as he passed it back.

Gralyre smiled, and inclined his head. "That first night, I awoke to the nightmare again, but there was more to it this time. I had…remembered…more of it."

"What?" Rewn leaned forward, his face intent and engaged.

CHAPTER NINE

THE KING'S FOREST- SPRING

...he fights no more. He is a prisoner, held on his knees between two guards. Fetid, rotting, breath puffs with excitement against his cheek. He gags.

A Demon's face slowly emerges from a boiling red mist. Its eyes burn with evil and triumph. An executioner's sword hangs suspended for a wild moment, a wide swing that will kill all in its path, including the two who hold his arms.

Terror! Cannot move!

'I will not cower!'

The sword drops. Sunlight sharpens the edge. Fetid Breath dies.

Hot blood sprays over his face. The grip of the second guard slackens.

His terrified visage, a distorted reflection in metal, chases the blade towards his neck. The parted air whistles as the blade gains momentum.

The sword bites his neck and he explodes into the agony of an infinite night, a void that has never seen starlight. It pulses, the chamber of a giant heart; shreds his captured soul in time to that dreadful beating.

'This then, is death; this then, is my punishment for failure.'

His wildly thrashing arms and legs produce no movement

within the pulsing void. They do not exist here. His screams from the blinding agony are unheard. Infinity swirls and boils, terrifying him...

With a violent jerk, he awoke with a yell. He stopped to draw a breath, and bellowed again into the night, for the dream clung tenaciously, and he imagined himself in the void still. A night bird warbled questioningly, and with that sound he awakened fully.

His breath rasped in and out. He felt as though he had fought a battle of epic proportions. Rubbing a hand across his face, he wiped at the thick layer of sour sweat, trying to remember where he was, and what he was doing lying naked on a riverbank.

'I have awakened from this dream before.'

The man was abruptly struck by the notion that the drying sweat on his body was not sweat at all, but blood as with his first awakening. He shuddered with dread, got to his feet, and ran into the frigid river.

He yelled when he hit the water, this time not at night phantoms, but at the cold wetness flowing around his warm body. Ducking underwater, and scrubbing frantically at his skin, he did not stay in long. Without the sun, the water was colder than it had been during the day. His flesh was raw and tingling by the time he emerged.

The moon ducked out from behind the clouds as he climbed up onto the riverbank. It was only a half-moon, but provided enough light to see where he had left his clothes to dry. His mind was clear once more, his shivering now due to the cold water, not to fear.

Shaking his head vigorously, he sent a spray of droplets into the air that glinted briefly in the moonlight before disappearing into the bushes. The movement brought back the previous vertigo, and forced him to sit to dress. He slicked his hands down his body, to wipe away as much moisture as possible, before donning his clothes. As he was pulling on his boots, his stomach reminded him, noisily, that his hunger had yet to be attended to.

The burst of energy he had gained from his nap was quickly depleted. As he was catching his breath, his thoughts cycled into the nightmare, bringing the terror surging back. Placing his hand over his eyes, he fought the dark images, trying desperately to think on something, anything else, but his empty mind held no other distractions.

Gods! He did not care who he was, or how he came to lose his memory! He did not care if all the creatures of the under-world were hunting him. All he craved was a moment's peace!

Action! As long as he kept his mind occupied with a task he seemed to gain a respite from his dark thoughts. He would eventually have to face his demons, but sitting all night worrying at it would gain him neither food nor shelter.

The man returned his dagger to his boot, took up his staff and scabbard, and plunged decisively into the forest. It would have been better if he had hunted under the sun, but he had needed the rest more. For all that he had lost the advantage of daylight, he did feel stronger.

He thought he might cross a game trail by walking parallel to the stream. He stopped mid-stride, surprise freezing him in place as his mind stingily doled out the titbit of helpful information. He searched for more.

A wispy impression; *crackling campfires, camaraderie, the scent of roasting meat fills his mouth with water.*

He clung to the images, but they slid away as his stomach gave a painful cramp of hunger. But the feelings the brief images engendered remained to warm him as he quickened his pace.

About half a league down stream from where he had started, the underbrush thickened, the bank rose, and soon he was scrabbling up a rocky hill. When it finally levelled out, the creek was thirty feet below him. The underbrush cut down the light from the moon. His footing became treacherous as he scrabbled along the edge of the embankment.

Though the way was hard going, he did not abandon it, for he was still hopeful of finding a game trail. The hill finally crept back down to meet the stream again. A little further along, just as his strength was ebbing, he crossed the game trail he had been seeking. He sighed in relief that his hike was over, and looked for a spot to hide that would afford him a good vantage point over the trail.

He settled wearily beside a lightning-blasted stump to wait until something came to drink. The man would need the element of surprise to catch his dinner, for he did not have the strength remaining to run something to ground.

Long minutes passed. The man was nodding sleepily when a plump pheasant strutted down to the stream for a drink. He was instantly alert. The bird was large enough to feed him for a couple of meals.

Tensing in readiness, he waited until the bird bent to drink. As it did so, he burst from the undergrowth and pounced. It probably died of fright before he had wrung its neck.

As he stood triumphant over his kill, he heard a low, threatening growl that froze his blood. Something in the nearby brush was not as happy with his success as he was. Slowly, cautiously, he reached down and grabbed his dagger from his boot, preparing to defend himself and his food. He was too hungry and weak to give up his meal and find another.

The growl came again. This time the figure of a wolf accompanied the sound from out of the bushes. The moon chose that moment to shine her rays down upon the drama about to unfold.

The creature facing him resolved itself not into a wolf, but a dog, albeit a large one. For a moment his heart leapt with hope. Where there were dogs, there might also be people. But as the animal continued to advance, showing no fear of man, he realized it was feral. He would have to defend himself.

He had little time to worry if he would remember how to fight, as the dog leapt at his throat. He swung his dagger in and up. The animal impaled itself as he stepped to the side, its weight tearing the knife from his hand as its momentum carried it to the ground.

It kicked weakly for a moment before succumbing to its wound.

He gasped for air, waiting for his heart to stop pounding and his infernal weakness to recede again, before he bent to retrieve his weapon. Standing hunched over with his arms propped upon his legs, he examined the beast. His mind had given him the trivial information that it was a *Dog*. Aside from this, he knew nothing else about what a Dog *was*.

This dog was pitiably thin and likely more in need of the food than he, for it to attack rather than run. He felt heavy of heart when he noticed the dog had been a nursing female. She surely had pups stashed somewhere that would now die without her. Remorse choked him, and he abandoned the notion of using the dog for meat.

With effort, he forced himself erect. There had been no other options or outcomes possible. At least he had proven his ability to defend himself. The fickle moon hid once more.

Vertigo swept him off balance and he staggered sideways into the brush. He grabbed a stump to halt his fall and his hand came to rest in a notch made by an axe. Glancing about, he realized that many of the trees at the side of the trail bore axe marks, but that the scars were old. Nobody had pruned back these bushes in years, but perhaps the marks would lead to shelter.

Since he had to carry his bird in one hand, he again buckled the scabbard to his back. His staff would balance him well enough as he walked. After one last glance at the dead dog, he slung the pheasant over his shoulder and shuffled slowly up the barely discernable trail.

The staff made rhythmic thumping sounds as it struck the earth. He counted the number of hits to distract himself from his exhaustion. It did not work. His weakness forced him to stop and rest several times.

He had almost decided to camp where he was, when he noticed the path was gradually widening. He broke free from the forest, passed through the collapsed wall of a decrepit stone hedge and was suddenly in a fallow field.

The land was over-run with weeds. It had not been tilled for many years. Small scrub bushes grew here and there, proof of the forest slowly reclaiming its own. In the weak moonlight he could see the vague outline of buildings, so he angled across the field towards them.

The man went cautiously and quietly for, though all seemed deserted, he would take no chances. His narrowly avoided drowning had taught him the valuable lesson of caution.

As he drew nearer, he released his concern. What he had taken for buildings had not been so for a very long time.

He staggered to the burned out shell of a cottage whose four stone walls and chimney were all that remained standing. The walls rose to a height that reached his neck. The fire that had destroyed the building had left the stones blackened and cracked, but they seemed sturdy enough to shelter him for the night. His dagger found its way back into his hand. It would make a good spot to regain his strength from, but he needed to make certain it was empty.

The man cautiously, soundlessly, entered the roofless ruin, dagger in hand, staff thrust forward and leading the way. A quick scan proved it was deserted, and he relaxed.

Spying the fireplace and chimney at the far end of the room, he walked to the hearth and discovered a piece of flint resting where the previous occupants had abandoned it. He smiled with rueful relief, for he had not thought of how he would start a fire. Though he was hungry enough he would have eaten his meal raw.

The ruin was deserted, however there was a musky odour, as of large animals, clinging to the air. He would make certain his fire burned brightly, to scare off any beasties that might come prowling.

He let the bird slip to the ground, where it raised a small puff of dust. If he wanted to eat, he would have to gather firewood. With an exhausted sigh, he stumbled from the ruin, staff dragging, back towards the woods.

$\wp\circlearrowright\Omega$

Silence descended upon the ruin after the man left. After long moments had passed, a scrabbling sounded from the shadows. From out of the darkness, something latched violently onto the bird carcass, and dragged it back into the darkened corner of the hearth.

$\wp\circlearrowright\Omega$

Though the fuel was easily found, the man's lack of strength, coupled with the darkness of the night, caused the task to take longer. Beneath the fleeting moonlight, the tangled forest took on a life of its own, tripping him with hidden roots and clutching teasingly at his clothes with grasping branches. The man fought his way free of the dark woods and back into the fallow fields, toiling under the weight of his meagre collection of deadwood. As he staggered towards his shelter, carrying even this small weight proved too much for him. Time and again, his arms weakened and he was forced to dump his load.

He paused to lean heavily upon his staff as he gasped for air. Only the promise of the coming meal kept him on his feet. At the thought of food, the man fancied he could almost smell roasting meat. His mouth filled with water and his stomach clenched painfully. He eagerly scooped up the fallen wood for the final time and lurched into the burned shell of the cottage.

He swayed to a halt as an uneasy feeling ran up his spine. Something was different... wrong. An oddly familiar metallic scent was present where none had been before. It took him but a moment to recognize the odour for what it was.

'Blood!'

The firewood hit the ground with a crash as he sprang from the doorway to conceal his silhouette. Pressing his back tightly, fearfully, against the wall, he snatched the knife from his boot. He remained in a crouch so his head would not be outlined against the night sky. His previous weakness vanished in a burst of adrenaline.

The man strained his ears for sounds of movement over the loud pounding of his heart. All he heard was the hollow moaning of the wind across the ruined chimney. He cursed the blackness for shadowing the corners from his eyes. His breath shivered from him in fearful bursts and his hands grew slick upon the hilt of his knife.

Nothing attacked; all was quiet. The strain of maintaining his battle stance made his fatigued muscles quake. Despite his weakness, he dared not relax. The thought of backing out of the shelter was stubbornly rejected. He was not leaving without his food.

'There!'

His stomach flip-flopped at a slight noise across the room, near the hearth. He stalked the sound, keeping his back to the wall to prevent an attack from behind.

When he arrived where the noise seemed to have come from, his prey had somehow eluded him. The area surrounding the hearth was empty, except for...

'Damn the Gods of Fortune!'

The remains of his bird were scattered about the earthen floor. While he had been gathering firewood, something had consumed most of his meal. This was where the smell of blood was coming from.

Ignoring the remains for the moment, he carefully searched the corners, but the shelter was empty. There was no place to hide. He was forced to conclude that his ears had played him false.

His mouth firmed into a thin line of disappointment as his gaze rested upon his shredded bird. Whatever animal had stolen his meal had fled. His return may have frightened it off. Perhaps the corners of the walls no longer met and there were places to squeeze in and out? Or perhaps the creature had leapt the walls to escape him?

The man collected what was left of the carcass. There was not much. After it was dressed out, there would be sufficient amount for a small meal tonight, with nothing left over to breakfast upon. He would make do. He was too weak to hunt again tonight. Disappointment bowed his shoulders as he set the remnants of the bird on the hearth and moved with lagging steps to collect the fallen pieces of firewood.

SHUFFLE! SCRABBLE!

He whirled, shocked to the core of his being by a sound coming from a place he knew to be empty! In a flash, his alarm transformed to white-hot anger.

'I fought hard for that meal! By the Gods, I killed for that meal, and will do so again!' Brandishing his dagger savagely, he bolted back across the room - and found it empty!

'There is nothing here! Am I to go mad now?'

Then, by the weak moonlight, he saw that the meat he had painstakingly piled upon the hearth had toppled. An eerie feeling of being watched crept over him.

'There is something in here with me, something I cannot see!'

The fine hairs on his nape bristled as he tried to imagine what sort of creature could hide so quickly when he was a mere body's distance away. He spun, certain he felt a presence creeping towards his back. He spun again, but there was nothing there! His fingers flexed nervously upon the hilt of his dagger.

The sound of the wind's lament across the top of the ruined chimney increased his tension. He stilled, his mouth agape to conceal the sound of his agitated breathing, listening for an attack. By playing a waiting game, he sought to force the creature to make another sound, to reveal its position without revealing his own.

As the tense moment drew out, a notion percolated into the dark emptiness of his mind. Perhaps many creatures, not one, had eaten the bird?

'Rats could cause this damage,' his memory grudgingly informed him.

He felt like a fool as the possibility came to seem more plausible. More likely than not it *was* rats he had heard. It explained the decimated carcass and how the *creature* had disappeared without him seeing it. The place must be infested with the vermin for them to consume so much of the bird in the little time he had been absent.

He maintained his battle stance for a moment longer, but when the sounds were not repeated, he became certain he had found the explanation. Relaxing his tired muscles at last, he shook from unspent adrenaline. He gave a self-deprecating snort.

'Frightened by rats!'

Shaking his head at his folly, he carried the wood to the hearth. No further incidents occurred. The vermin were gone.

Exhausted, he sat on the dirt floor by the hearth and painstakingly whittled some shavings. He laid the thin, wood curls in the fireplace, near the front where he could reach them easier, and struck the flint to the steel knife. Sparks showered onto the kindling. After several tries, the shavings began to smoke. Leaning forward, he gently blew upon the ember, coaxing it into flame. With a small *whoosh*, the shavings caught fire.

As the kindling flared, he distinctly heard a very frightened whimper. Startled, he looked through the flames to the back of the hearth. There, eyes glowing in the light, lay a shivering litter of young pups.

For a long, shocked moment, his eyes locked with the glowing orbs across the blaze. They huddled further away from the flames, crying and whimpering. He had to act quickly or they would be burned!

With little thought for the consequences, he swept the burning kindling from the fireplace. Pain lanced his fingers, but he hardly noticed. He stuck his singed hand into his mouth to soothe it as his mind raced for a course of action.

As indecision gripped him, he shovelled dirt from the floor onto the kindling, to extinguish the last of the flames. He stopped in mid-motion and cursed his witless action. He should have saved an ember. Now he would have to repeat the painstaking process to light a fire.

A yowling cry from the depths of the fireplace returned him to his more immediate problem. It was obvious that the pups had eaten his bird. He had not thought to look within the fireplace when he had initially explored the shelter. He fervently hoped it was only his exhaustion causing his poor judgement and not some inherent idiocy.

He tried to recall the pups' appearances. Were they dog, or were they wolf? The one quick glimpse had been insufficient to determine their breed. He should never have disturbed their den. When their dame came back, if it was not the one he had been forced to kill at the creek, it would not be possible to scare her off. She would fight to the death for her pups. His only recourse was to leave quickly, before she returned. Hopefully, she would not seek retribution for the fright he had inadvertently given her litter.

Picking up some of the wood in one hand and the remnants of the pheasant in the other, he backed quickly out of the ruin. He would make his meal and his bed in the open. The loss of the shelter was a good trade for his continued wellbeing.

If, by the next day, the pups were unclaimed, then it was likely their dame who had attacked him by the stream. If they were gone by dawn, then the bitch had returned in the night and moved her litter to a safer den. Provided he kept his campfire burning, she would be unlikely to approach him. He would be safe. And if the pups were orphaned? Well, they would be safe enough where they were until morning.

Finding a spot to camp next to the fallen stone hedge that bounded the overgrown fields, he again went through the laborious task of starting a fire. By this time, his whole body was palsied with exhaustion. Though he made his bed in the open this night, he knew he would have no trouble sleeping. Even if he had not been tired to the point of death, he would have been comfortable, for the stone fence acted as a windbreak and the evening was warm.

As he sat back, letting the flames catch hold of the kindling, he wondered if he had often spent his nights under the cold gaze of the stars. Through a break in the scudding clouds, a constellation drew his attention.

'The eyes of the Gods of Fortune,' he unexpectedly recalled. *'Always watching, always dispensing luck in equal measures of good and evil.'*

He dealt with this tiny bit of knowledge as calmly as he could, though his heart was pounding hard in anxious hope. Experience from the day had already taught him to expect no further revelations.

With a long drawn sigh, the man released the breath he had been holding and added a few larger pieces of wood to the small blaze, careful not to smother it. His gaze was caught by flares of sparks that danced upon the wind as they ascended towards the sky, not unlike the glints of memory flitting in the empty darkness of his thoughts.

'Will I grow used to having no memory? This useless trivia I keep remembering! Is this what my entire past has been reduced to?' A wave of black desolation crashed over him.

'No! This cannot be all that is left! 'Tis a good sign that I keep remembering these things. It must mean my memory will return!' Perhaps it would not return all at once, just in bits and pieces, but little morsels of knowledge would accumulate until he was whole again. *'I have to believe! I must not despair!'*

He let the sparkling moats of the fire's offspring carry his anxiety away with them into the night sky. As he stared at the hypnotic sparks, his eyes began to droop. Lulled by the snapping pop of the fire, the man slipped into a light doze. Slowly, his head nodded back.

The small movement broke the spell woven by the fire and roused him. He had better eat soon, or he would be asleep before the meal was ever started.

He reached for the pheasant with the intention of dressing it out, but stopped in mid-motion to stare at the dancing campfire.

A frown creased his brow as the feeling he had forgotten to do something gripped him.

'What is it? What am I missing?' Then he realized.

'In the dark of night, the light of a campfire can be seen for miles. It could lead my enemies directly to me!'

He grabbed some tumbled stones from the ramshackle fence, and built a tall fire ring about the flames. He felt foolish at his nervous behaviour for he had no proof he was being hunted, but if the day had taught him nothing else, it was better by far to err on the side of caution.

By the fire's now meagre glow, he dressed out what was left of the bird. When he was done, there was not much left, just scraps clinging to bones. He was now so famished it did not matter that he was eating the leavings of dogs.

'I would have eaten it still, were it the leavings of rats!' he acknowledged to his hunger.

Skewering the pieces of flesh on the whittled end of sticks, he angled them over the flames by wedging them between gaps in the fire ring's rocks. The smell of singing meat filled the air, causing his stomach to twist painfully.

Turning the skewers as best he could to keep the meat from burning gave him singed fingers for his troubles, but he was too impatient to be careful. Hovering over the fire, he urged it to cook faster.

When he judged the meat as cooked, he pulled it from the fire and fell upon it ravenously. It was blackened on the outside and raw on the inside, but it tasted like the finest feast. The hot juices singed his tongue and the roof of his mouth, but he was too hungry to allow the meal to cool.

When at last he was done wolfing down his meagre meal, he reclined beside the small blaze. He heaved a sigh of dissatisfaction as he sucked the last of the drippings from his fingers. The hard edge had been taken from his hunger, but he could have easily consumed thrice that measly amount. The man regretfully tossed the last of the stripped bones into the flame's embrace.

Sparks spat at the sky, lulling him with the sounds of the crackle and pop they made as they left the burning wood. His gaze followed the short-lived moats as they flitted back and forth in the night's light breeze. This time he made no effort to elude their hypnotic beckoning.

For the first time that day, he was almost content; reassured he retained enough skills to keep from dying of hunger or exposure. His appetite had been appeased and he was warm.

'I survived the day. What more can a man ask?'

'A memory.' His answer to his rhetorical, self-directed question shattered his complacency.

He shifted uncomfortably on the hard ground as he realized the moment he had been dreading all day had arrived. Now that there were no urgent tasks dragging away his attention, it was time to examine his plight. There would be no avoidance this time.

As he pondered each of the items he had found on his person, he searched for connections, impressions, and notions, anything that resembled memories. But there was nothing. They were the possessions of a stranger. He clenched his fists in agitation, but was determined to continue to reason it through.

He had a time estimate for how long he had been ill. His beard! Within the past few days, he had shaved and something had happened to him that had stolen his memories. But what? The beheading?

No. That was obviously a false memory, just a nightmare, for witness he still breathed! But if not real, then what of the cut on his neck giving weight to the nightmare images? Was it naught but a coincidence?

He probed at his empty mind, like a tongue at a sore tooth, searching for something, anything, that would trigger a memory.

He had a language, but he had no idea what its name was. He knew how to hunt, to fight, how to start a fire and hide one, but he did not know his name or if he had family. He knew what a dog was, how to swim, how to clean game.

The skills had been rediscovered as the *need* for them had arisen. He had not thought of using a crutch, until he had almost fallen on his head. He had not realized he could use a dagger, until he had started to play with one. He had not known how to swim, until he had started to drown.

But none of these things reflected anything of his true self, his identity.

'How old am I? Am I rich or poor? Cruel or kind? Craven or brave?'

Would he not remember a father or mother until he encountered them? Hope crumbled into disappointment as he recognized that it would not be so simple, for need had not provided for him the ability to read the message on the rolled

parchment. Some element of his amnesia kept him from recalling who or what he was. It was as though someone had taken a
knife and carefully cut away everything he knew of himself,
leaving only that which would prevent his immediate death from
ignorance; common knowledge.

*'Just thank the Gods of Fortune that 'tis so! Imagine my
problems if I knew naught how to track game or which plants
were safe to eat! Things could be much worse!'*

*'The Gods of Fortune? Who were these Gods? How did one
pray to them?'* he demanded of his absent memories as he raised
his frustrated gaze to the stars that twinkled boldly at him from
the constellation he had earlier identified. But his thoughts
remained stubbornly blank.

His memory would return or not. There seemed nothing he
could do to hasten the event. In fact, the more he worried at it,
the more inscrutable it became. Melancholy weighted his soul.

With a listless toss, he cast another branch upon the fire.
Watching the joyful way the flames attacked the wood, he could
not help but feel very alone in his empty wasteland of a mind.
There was nothing to think on except the events of the day.
There were no memories of happier times or loved ones. All he
had memories of were dark emotions, fear, hate, of being
hunted. The nightmare.

As though summoned from a pit, it arose in his mind's eye.
Repetition did little to prepare him for the overwhelming fear.
His heart pounded at a mad rate and sweat glistened on his face
as his body bucked in response to the vivid images of his own
beheading. The man desperately sought a logical explanation for

his terror. Logic was very important to him, he realized.

'My mind is damaged. There is no one after me. I am just experiencing a wounded animal's need to hide.'

He distracted his thoughts from the nightmare by listing what he would have to do on the morrow.

'Find food, find water, deal with the pups. Find food, find water, deal with the pups. Find food, find water, deal with the pups...' He repeated the mantra as a spell to ward off the terror.

He was somewhat successful, for though the fears were too strong to disperse entirely, they did grudgingly retreat. His lips lifted in a small smile of victory. If he could not keep the terror from happening, then at least he had a way to stop it from overwhelming him.

His victorious feeling vanished under a crashing wave of fatigue. He was too tired to think on this more. It did no good in any case, for there were too many missing pieces to create a whole picture. Anything he guessed was pure speculation. When he had more clues, he would try to sort out his ailment again. Until then, challenging the emptiness of his mind brought more pain than benefit.

He summoned a jaw-cracking yawn. Sleep seemed more precious at this moment than all the memories in the world. His exhaustion demanded its due. He had all the rest of his life to challenge his memory.

Judging he'd had enough of the misfortunes of this day, he allowed himself to relax into a more comfortable position. Ignoring the small part of his conscience that mocked him for avoiding his problem, he let his eyes close, and drifted into an uneasy slumber.

∞∞

When he awoke, the sun was high in the sky and shining directly into his eyes. Blinking groggily, he got to his feet and stretched to work out the kinks that the hard ground had given him. He was glad to note that the vertigo seemed completely gone.

Though he had slept deeply, his dreams had been filled with violent images of pain and destruction. He was unable to remember the specifics, but the feelings they had engendered remained. The paranoia of being hunted, the bone numbing terror...

Methodically, he fought back his dread, plucking away the strands of fear clutching at his soul like sticky spider's web. Such dark musing did naught but cripple his mind and steal his will. He sidetracked his thoughts into a more benign direction.

'At least my strength has returned!'

In the warmth of the afternoon sun, he stretched again, glorying in the strength of his muscles, living in the moment, not thinking, just being.

It felt so good to stretch upwards, that he then stretched downwards, touching his forehead to his shins. A sense of familiarity washed through him as he stretched his arms and legs.

Taking up a straight branch he had dragged in for firewood the night before, he broke off a length, roughly four feet long and slashed it experimentally through the air. He did not know why he wanted it, until the random slashes turned into specific designs.

Patterns flowed into patterns, each triggered memory of another, each more intricate than the last.

'This is a block! This is a slash!'

There was a lethal beauty in what he did, fascinating for its masculine grace. Despite the practice sword expertly manipulated through the complex battle forms with a deadly accuracy, his exercise resembled nothing more than a dance.

'Is this a memory?'

The exultant thought broke his concentration. He fumbled the stick in the midst of an intricate move and it tumbled to the ground.

He stared numbly at the fallen branch, his breath coming in light pants from his exertions. The exercise had felt so familiar. First the stretches, then the fighting patterns, the sword dance. He felt a strong sense of ritual, as though his muscles had remembered what his mind could not. Whatever it had been, it was a good sign that his past would return before he was forced to confront the demon who hunted him.

Panic and denial burned through him. It was only a nightmare! Nobody was hunting him. Why would this persistent fear not release its hold? He cast his gaze about, seeking desperately for any distraction. With action came forgetfulness.

'I will go in search of water. That should keep me occupied for a while.'

After some exploring, he discovered a well in the corner of

the yard, near the burnt rubble of a collapsed outbuilding. On hands and knees, he leaned in as far as he dared. He could just make out the glint of the surface, about eight feet beneath him. The water level was high, but he was left with the dilemma of how to get to it. Even with most of his upper body into the moist, dark hole, he was unable to reach the water level and had he reached, there was no way to tell if the water was still sweet.

It was too great a problem to deal with this morning, especially as there was plenty of water to be had at the river.

The man unfolded upright and went in search of the path he had used the night before. With a long, limber gait, he began his hike to the river. From what he remembered of the night before, he expected a half-hour journey, but his well-rested strides brought him to the riverbank in just over ten minutes. He marvelled at how exhausted he must have been.

His face sobered as he spotted the remains of the dog on the path. He would check on the pups when he returned. Hopefully, they would be gone.

It was distasteful to bath in front of the dead dog, so the man took a moment to pile a cairn of river rocks over it, to hide it from view. The chore raised a sweat in the hot sun. When he was done, he shucked his clothing and jumped into the water to wash away the effort.

Refreshed, he dressed and returned to the farm, eager to discover the fate of the pups. He hoped they had been claimed during the night as he crept to the open space that had once been the doorway of the cottage. The man stuck his head cautiously around the corner, bracing himself to get out should the bitch have returned. He relaxed and grinned at the display of youthful enthusiasm he beheld.

There were six pups in the litter. They could not be but barely weaned, for they were still wobbly on their legs as they gambled about, attacking one another. Scanning the interior, he made a point of looking into the fire pit. The sunlight shining down the chimney showed it to be empty.

There was no sign of an adult dog, but then, he had not really expected any. A good look at the pups was enough to convince him they were dog, although a couple in the pack looked as though they had wolf's blood.

One of the pups was industriously gnawing on the oak staff he had abandoned the night before.

'I must not let the pup destroy it, for I might have need of it as a weapon. A man who knows how to use a staff, can defeat a swordsman.' The unbidden scrap of knowledge drifted into his mind.

'Do I know how to use a staff?' After his skills of this morning, somehow he thought he did.

He stepped into view. The pups yelped and raced for their fireplace den. All, that is, but the one working over his staff. The man bent to retrieve it and as his hand touched the wood, the pup growled at him.

Mine - Bite - Chew - Mine!

The man stumbled backwards in surprise. It was pictures, intentions, and emotions all wrapped up into one meaning. The thoughts had not originated from within, but from without. He clapped his hands to his ears. There remained a faint buzzing, but nothing else. Bewildered, he bent for another grab at the staff.

Again he was assailed by the strange images. The dominant impressions were of a fiercely growling monster, bearing a distinct resemblance to this pup, attacking and driving off a pair of tall black boots!

Laughing, the man bent, grabbed the pup by the scruff of the neck and raised it to eye level. "If you mean to attack me, little wolf, you had best attack a more vital part than my feet!" It was the first time he had heard his own voice. It had a deep, rich timbre that pleased him.

He thought no more of his ability to understand the pup, assuming he had been too exhausted the night before for the talent to manifest itself. With nothing to hold up for comparison, he naturally assumed this gift was normal.

The pup squirmed to get away. It let out a howl and the visions of an adult dog, and warmth, and comfort, and need were communicated.

Sadly, the man placed the pup back on the ground and allowed it to scamper to safety with its brothers and sisters. The adult the pup called out for was the same dog he had been forced to kill the night before.

'What am I to do now?'

He had the choice of putting them out of their misery, for without a mother they would die a slow death of starvation, or he could care for them himself.

His instincts rejected both ideas. Something was hunting him. His life was in danger. Death would find him should he stay in one place for too long!

As a long, drawn out howl of distress warbled from within the den, his conscience twisted his thinking in the other direction. He heaved a sigh.

'I killed their mother. Now, when forced to accept respon-sibility for my actions, I would butcher the entire litter because they are an inconvenience?' Six pairs of puppy eyes were riveted fearfully on his face as he decided their fate. The thought of euthanizing the pups was offensive to him.

'Why do I imagine I am so important that someone is trying to kill me? The nightmare? The ring? The message?' He shook his head at his folly. *'If there is someone after me, what is to prevent me from walking straight into their arms? With no memory, by the time I realized I was in danger, I would be dead!*

'The logical thing to do is to go to ground until my memory returns. This place is as hidden as one could ask for. I will have the pups for company, and I will be safe from my own ignorance.'

The man made his decision. If - when - his memory returned, he would leave. By then, the pups would likely be old enough to fend for themselves or he could take them with him. While his mind remained damaged, 'twas too dangerous to travel. Phantom enemies aside, what of customs and laws? A lack of such know-ledge could be just as deadly as the most rabid of foes.

He walked to the fireplace to examine his newly adopted family. Bending low, he looked within at the huddled mass of pups. Two were black, with rust coloured markings on their eyebrows and ears. Two were smoke-grey, and seemed to bear the greatest mix of wolf blood. And two were brown, black, and grey as if leftover colour scraps from the other four had gone into their making.

In build, the pups resembled each other. Their erect ears tapered into peaks with little tufts of fur at the tips, and their snouts were long and pointed. The pups' paws were huge and their tails were long. Their colouring might be that of dog, but their bodies held the promise of the streamlined deadliness of wolf. They would be fierce animals when grown.

Right now, the predominant thought coming from the shivering mob was terror. They did not know what sort of creature he was, but they were certain he meant to kill them.

"Shh, little pups, you are safe. Shh." Awkwardly, he projected feelings of safety at them. It did not work to calm them. If anything, their shivering fear worsened.

Stymied, he dropped back on his haunches. Perhaps the way to win them over lay through their stomachs? They had been more than willing to eat his food the previous night.

Leaving the dwelling, he returned an hour later with three rabbits. The game was plentiful and easily trapped, as though it had never encountered Man before. As he had hunted, he had seen a deer in a clearing. Unafraid, it had stared at him for a long moment before returning to its grazing. He would try for it on the morrow. Now that he had made the decision to stay, his growing pack would need the nourishment.

The man dressed out the rabbits efficiently. One, he kept to breakfast upon. The other two, he carefully deboned and shredded. He took the meat into the den and placed it in front of the pups.

They were in the same huddled mass, as though they had not dared to move for the entire time he had been gone. The shivering started again when they saw him, but as he placed the meat in front of their noses, their fear gave way to hunger.

The images his mind received, swung back and forth between hunger and fear. A black pup, he thought it the same one that had fought for possession of the oak staff, stretched a busily twitching nose towards the meat. With a lightning move, it grabbed a chunk and consumed it with almost no chewing. Quickly, it went back for seconds.

Its actions freed the other pups and began a feeding frenzy. The man sat on his haunches and watched. Now and again, he intervened to make sure all received a fair share.

After they finished eating, they lay about the floor in various states of decorousness, little bellies extended to capacity. They had lost their fear of him, the man was happy to note. They were still young enough to bond with another being besides their mother. Had they been older, they would not have allowed him to care for them and would have surely perished.

The two smoke-grey pups curled up together in a fluffy ball, nose to tail. The two multi-coloured pups harassed them while they tried to nap. The man grinned as he watched their antics, feeling almost carefree. Unable to rouse the two grey pups to play, the multi-coloured pups eventually gave up and joined them in sleeping off their feast.

One black pup rolled onto its back, groaning, paws dangling, and fell into a snoring, twitching sleep within the fireplace den.

'One, two, three, four, five... Where is the sixth?' He double counted to be sure it was a black one missing. He anxiously scanned the room. As he pivoted towards the doorway, the man spotted the errant pup cutting its teeth upon his staff once again. Heaving a sigh of exasperation, he strode forward and snatched the wood from the startled pup.

Mine-Chew-ATTACK!

The pup's intent flashed into his head, accompanied by the vision of the Great-Black-Monster-Wolf attacking a huge pair of black boots. The man laughed as the pup, suiting action to thought, attacked his footwear. It tried valiantly to defeat its enemy until, finally tired, it sat back and gave a yodel of frustration.

The man leaned the staff against the wall by the door and hunkered down beside the beleaguered pup. "Do you give up, little wolf?" He reached out his fingers and ruffled the fur on its chest.

Mother-need-lonely-scared. These thoughts and more the little pup shared with him.

The man picked up the pup and cuddled it gently, settling with his back to the wall. The pup went into an ecstasy of wiggles and licks. In order to defend his face from the pup's aggressive tongue, he rolled it to its back and tickled its little belly. With a playful growl, the pup clamped its teeth around one of the attacking digits.

The man winced at the strength with which the sharp little teeth were applied and used his free hand to unclasp the pup's jaws. "Why I ever thought you were helpless..." He tried to shake some feeling back into his injured finger.

The pup perked up its ears, head cocked to one side in an effort to understand. Its concentration was broken by a large yawn and, with no more thought, it curled up in the man's lap and sighed gustily. The man caressed it with gentle hands, marvelling at the softness of its fur. The pup cuddled closer to the comforting touch and relaxed into a dream of sunlight and crickets.

He continued to pet it. The rhythmic motions soothed him almost as much as it had the pup. A feeling of responsibility, of a need being filled, washed over him. He no longer felt alone and was amazed at what a difference that made. It was strange that these little bundles of fur had accomplished what all his raging logic could not. He had found peace.

The man finally stirred. Now that he had decided to stay, it would take a formidable amount of work to make the farm habitable. He stood and walked to where the rest of the pups slept, and gently laid Little Wolf, as he had taken to calling it, upon the pile.

It opened one blurry eye, and its thoughts of comfort now had the man's image mixed with those of its mother. He sent the pup a warm thought and it sighed contentedly, closed its eye and went back to sleep.

Smiling, he left the pups to their nap and went to cook himself breakfast. *'Now I have a family!'* The thought brought him comfort, and gave him an anchor in a sea of unfamiliar things.

CHAPTER TEN

Wil, Rewn and Dajin proclaimed their disbelief at his ability to hear the thoughts of animals, so Gralyre was obliged to demonstrate. Silently, he called Little Wolf back from his night foraging. The men hooted with nervous surprise as the pup bounded into the firelight and flopped at Gralyre's side.

"Can ye hear our thoughts as well?" Dajin asked suspiciously.

"No," said Gralyre, "just animals."

"Why not?" asked Rewn.

"I cannot remember," Gralyre shrugged, his lips curved in wry humour. "It never occurred to me that it was not a common ability. Have you never heard the animals around you?"

Wil responded with a snorting laugh. "Never! So did ye get better? Did ye remember more o' your past? What more can ye tell us, lad?"

Gralyre grew serious. "I remember that life was good, for a while." He leaned forward and poked at the fire with a stick. "You must understand that with no one else to talk to, I became... an animal. The pack leader. The pups were as my children. I protected them, raised them, hunted for them... In all the ways that count, they were my family.

"I had no past, no name, no identity. I belonged nowhere. So I decided to belong here." His lips tightened as he stared at the burnt silhouette of the cottage. Even after all this time, it still reeked of the fire.

CHAPTER ELEVEN

THE KING'S FOREST- SPRING

He found a cache of tools in a pile of rotting wood that may have once been a barn. In the following days, he fashioned a peaked roof for the burned out farmhouse, and thatched it with bundles of long grasses painstakingly scythed from the neglected fields. The stone house was the only survivor of the fire that had destroyed the farm, and the subsequent years of neglect. It offered the best protection from the coming winter.

The rest of the buildings were too derelict to save, but by utilising the few scavenged boards that were still sound, and wooden pegs painstakingly whittled before his fire every night, he managed to slowly construct a smokehouse. He was in dire need of a way to cure meat for the winter. As his pups grew, the man was forced to hunt for them every day, leaving little time to prepare his shelter for the coming cold storms.

To augment his diet of meat, he ate oats growing wild in the fields, volunteer plants that had taken root from remnants of old crops planted long ago. He found a kitchen garden beside the cottage, containing blackberries and onions. Once, there had been more variety, but these hardy plants were the sole survivors of the weed-choked mess.

Of himself, he still knew nothing. The nightmare continued to haunt him almost every night. When he awakened in terror, there would be a huge sense of urgency, as of an important task left incomplete. The feeling was strong enough at times that he was driven to pace in the fresh night air until it subsided. On other nights, his pups would crowd around him, comforting him as they lay in a great tangle upon the skins he had tanned. The presence of their warm bodies would gradually soothe him, so that he and his pack could drift back to sleep.

In the light of day, it was easy to dismiss his fears as night phantoms. It did not matter what his life had been before. Whatever tasks his memory-bereft brain had left unfinished, were no longer his responsibility.

Early on, he provided the pups with names. They had been born as three sets of twins, one female and one male.

The grey female he named Smoke and the male, Soot, for their colour and for their tendency to steal food from the hearth while he was not looking, soiling their bright fur with ash in the process. Despite their sneaky ways, the black smudges always gave them away.

The multi-coloured female, he called Thatch. She had been a damnable nuisance during that chore as he had fixed the roof of the house. Dogs should not know how to climb ladders. Her twin, he named Thong, for the pile of rawhide strips he had consumed. The thongs were to have been used in the making of a braided tether to get water from the well. The prank had caused a delay of several days, as the man had been forced to accumulate rawhide again. All of the lashings for his snares having been consumed by the pup, there was no worse chore than trying to catch rabbits with nothing but a stick and a knife.

It was convenient to name the pups after their worst debacles. At the mention of their name, they were reminded to strive to do better. At least this was his theory. He soon came to realize his error. The pups bore the names like badges of honour.

The black female he called Spook, for she constantly barked and growled at anything that moved. She sought to dominate all objects before they could attack her, whether it was a piece of wood or a frog.

But his favourite of the bunch was Little Wolf. The pup had shared a bond with him from the very beginning, even though the little villain chewed everything in sight! Everything he owned bore rents and holes from sharp little teeth.

As spring flowed into summer, the man grew content to live out his days here with his pack. He slowly became more like an animal than a man; not a warrior, or a thief, or a courier, or whatever he had once imagined he could be.

He communicated to the pups, and they to him, through their mental contact. Immersed in canine perceptions, he thought and acted as the pups expected him to. The pack leader, an animal. Gradually, the man ceased to talk or make any human sounds. Not speaking helped him immerse further into the fantasy role that he was more than willing to play.

An animal lived a simple uncomplicated life. An animal had no need of a past or future, it lived in the moment. His clothing turned to tattered rags and his beard and hair grew unkempt, thick and long.

The fear of discovery, by whatever he imagined to be hunting him, gnawed at him constantly. His inaction of going to ground, instead of confronting his fears, had him teetering on the edge of madness. Fantasy gradually overtook him.

If he was an animal, he was no threat to the demon hunting him. He was safe.

He cared naught that he was loosing himself. The man he was had died when a dream sword had touched his neck, as surely as if a real sword had lopped off his head. No longer was he that man and he refused to attempt to reclaim a past he could not remember, a past that frightened him.

Even so, he continued his sword dance at the dawning of every day. Though he knew the hypocrisy of his actions, he found he could not give up the exercises. Not only did it give him pleasure, it was also important to retain his sword skills. Just in case.

CHAPTER TWELVE

"A warrior's dance. I have heard tell o' such things in folktales," Wil broke into Gralyre's story. "'Tis a thing no' seen in the lands today. Wearing a sword carries with it the penalty o' death."

"I see," Gralyre mused. "There is much I do not know." He gave a self-deprecating laugh as he swept a hand down his body to reference his current contused state. "Trust me. Lack of knowledge is as deadly as any enemy can be." His mind drifted over his misadventures since he had left. All had been caused by this ignorance. "I was right to hide here."

Into the lull of the conversation, Dajin squirmed forward in his seat. "So the graves by the river...?"

Gralyre's eyes snapped to the younger man's face. They fixed there for a long moment, before they lost focus. His expression grew bleak. "It was autumn..."

CHAPTER THIRTEEN

THE KING'S FOREST- AUTUMN

Summer flowed into autumn and with winter eminent he hunted every day. It was a race against the season to fill his smokehouse with enough cured meat to last him and the pups until spring.

The adolescent pups were large enough now that they could have accompanied him on his hunting trips, but their attention span was still too short. They could not be relied upon to stay quiet and hidden while he stalked game, and so he left them behind. Once the need for meat had passed, he would teach them to hunt. By then, it would not matter if they scared off the prey.

He was bereft of any larger weapon than the dagger, which he had learned to affix to the end of his oak staff and use as a spear. With this awkward weapon, he seldom brought down any large game. Because of this, it was taking forever to store up enough meat in the smokehouse to last the winter. If only he could bring down a deer, his meat supply would be adequate, and he could finish the thousands of chores he had been neglecting.

As with other mornings, he arose early. Leaving the pups asleep before the banked coals, he set out into the morning mists to hunt. If he did not leave before the pups awoke, they would follow after him and ruin his chances with their silly-heart antics.

The sun was just cresting the horizon when he came to the grassy meadow he sought. He found a spot to hide with the hope he could get close to one of the deer that could frequently be found grazing here.

As he waited, his thoughts turned to his family. They were going to be huge when they were grown. Little Wolf was the biggest and smartest of the bunch, the ringleader in all their shenanigans. Hopefully, they would settle down as they matured. He shuddered to think of the damage that the pups could cause if their puppy minds controlled adult bodies instead of their own young, uncoordinated ones. He grinned to remember Smoke tripping over her feet as she ran, planting herself face first into the ground.

Raising a family of dogs was a difficult task, one he was not altogether sure he would complete with his sanity intact. Grinning wider, he settled into a more comfortable position.

He dozed off and on in the early morning sunshine until, finally, his patience was rewarded. A large buck stepped into the meadow and began to graze daintily. Coming alert, the man checked the direction of the wind.

'The Gods of Fortune are smiling on me today!'

He could sneak up on the deer without it catching scent of him. Now all he had to worry about was it hearing or seeing him. Manoeuvring onto his belly with spear in hand, he inched his way across the clearing towards the doomed deer.

∞⊙∞

He was returning from the hunt, dragging the buck on a rough travois he had fashioned, when he felt the change. Something was wrong.

'The PUPS!' His mind screamed. *'Something is hurting the pups!'* He did not question his foreknowledge.

With a snarl, he dropped the deer carcass and sprinted through the underbrush, racing to get back to the farm. He crashed through the woods like a wounded bear, snapping saplings from his path like twigs, knowing he was going to be too late, knowing something was killing his pack!

He ran, legs churning and arms pumping for greater speed, his breath coming in ragged gasps.

'Faster, Faster,' he chanted at himself.

Soon after he began his wild dash, he smelled the smoke. Minutes later, the tortured sound of his pups in pain reached him.

Images filled his brain, reaching out to choke him. Tears of fury mingled with sweat and ran together into his wild beard. He reached the edge of the forest and gazed frantically at the devastation. He ripped his knife free of the oak staff and, with the hilt clutched hard in his hand, ran towards the melee.

⁂○⁖

Little Wolf got up after The Man had left and headed out to the water trough for a drink. He had drunk only half his fill, when he was struck from behind. The might of the blow forced his head under the water.

Sneezing and snorting, he turned to see Smoke standing behind him looking pleased. He snapped at her, but she gambled nimbly out of reach. The chase was on. They cavorted about the yard, playing tag and stalking each other. Out over the fallow fields they raced.

Smoke stopped suddenly and put her nose to the ground, before she was off and running, the game forgotten. Little Wolf put his nose to the spot where she had been.

The Man had passed this way in the small hours of the morning. Perhaps they could track him? He chased out after his sister, into the woods and fast on the trail of their pack leader.

Their hunt did not last long. Minutes into the forest, the sights and smells of too many interesting creatures had them running in nine directions at once.

'Chase that squirrel! Dig in that hole! Mark that tree!'

Finally, panting, they fell in a heap to rest themselves

Far off in the distance, they heard Spook sound off. *'Strange creatures come! Danger! Danger!'* She was cut off in mid bay.

Hearts pounding in fear, they were up and running as fast as they could. For once, their adolescent puppy minds stayed focused. Their pack was in danger! They had to return.

soca

The remaining four pups dozed in the warm sun after Little Wolf and Smoke had left. It was too lazy a day to get up yet. Gradually, they threw off their lethargy and came alert.

The fight all started when Thatch grabbed Soot's tail in her sharp teeth. He yelped and grabbed Spook's ear. The riot in the yard ended as Thong jumped to tackle Thatch, missed, and ended up in the water trough.

Thong crawled from the trough with his dignity diminished and shook himself, splattering his siblings with water. As he was about to exact revenge for his bad luck, he lifted his nose to the air. There was the strangest of smells coming from out of the woods. The others noticed his preoccupation, and they too lifted their muzzles and snuffled the wind.

Odd, clomping, heavy footfalls reached their ears, accompanied seconds later by a strange group of beasts. They smelled of Man, and beast, and of something else, something tainted. They had four legs, and two heads. One head was long, attached to the four-legged body. The other head resembled that of The Man, and sat upon a vertical torso that rose straight up from the centre of the strange creature.

All the pups scattered, except Spook. She growled and barked, trying to bluff the beasts away. It had always worked on rabbits and frogs. One of the four-legged monsters reared up, letting out a long whinny of fear. Sensing a victory, she advanced aggressively. The man part of the monster grabbed up a strange object and pointed it at her.

THRUM!

Spook yowled painfully as a wooden stick appeared suddenly in her side. She must warn the others!

'Strange creatures come! Danger! Danger!' she yelped.

Her warning was cut off as a second crossbow quarrel struck her in the throat.

ဆဝ

The man raced across the fallow fields, dagger clenched tight in his fist. The smokehouse he had painstakingly built was completely engulfed in flames. The roof of the house had caught fire, but was not yet an inferno.

From the distance, he watched as his pups were forced out of the cottage by the smoke and the heat. As they emerged, four men on horseback, dressed in blood red uniforms, took target practice at them with crossbows. The pups ran in confusion back into the burning house to escape the deadly aim of the horsemen, only to be forced back out again as the thatched roof shot flames high into the air.

The man heard the red riders' shouts of enjoyment as they struck down first one, then another of his pups. He was too far away to intervene and could do naught but endure the mental agony, as Thong and Thatch perished. The roof of the cottage suddenly caved in. Anguish as another pup - *'Soot!'* - died in the conflagration.

Out of the woods bordering the yard, he saw black and grey streaks as Little Wolf and Smoke entered the fray. They headed straight for the horses' legs, instinct telling them to hamstring the animals. The man reached the yard just as a laughing horseman shot Smoke in the side.

'Smoke! No!' he yelled within the confines of his mind. Even in his grief, he made no sound, so unused was he to speech. Another red uniformed soldier took aim at Little Wolf, but he had no chance to fire his crossbow.

The man had joined the battle. He yanked the aiming soldier from his horse and twisted his head most of the way around. The red rider was dead before he hit the ground, his unfired crossbow slipping from his limp fingers.

The three other horsemen were thrown into confusion by the deadly wild-man who had suddenly appeared in their midst. They yelled and cursed, as their horses wheeled and dodged to escape Little Wolf's sharp teeth. Having spent their own loaded crossbows upon the other pups, they were having trouble bringing other weapons to bear.

The man snatched up the unfired crossbow of the rider he had just killed, and placed a deadly shot into a red chest. As that soldier flew from the saddle from the impact, the man knocked a third from his horse with a mighty blow from the now empty weapon. He moved too quickly for the red soldiers to defend themselves.

The soldier who remained mounted finally managed to free his sword. He raised it in a swinging arc above his head, but his battle cry became a choked whimper as the shaft of a dagger appeared in his chest. He clutched at it stupidly and folded slowly from his saddle.

The soldier who had been knocked from his horse, crawled to his feet, blood running freely from the blow he had taken to his face. He pulled his sword and rushed at the unprotected back of his attacker. He had taken two strides, when Little Wolf jumped him from behind.

The soldier pitched forward from the impact of Little Wolf's weight. He screamed as the dog latched strong white teeth onto his neck, ripping and shaking the soldier like a rag doll. Blood sprayed in a wide arc as the red rider died from the ragged tear.

Little Wolf looked up from his gruesome task to see The Man crouched beside Smoke. She lay on her uninjured side, panting, giving voice to a high-pitched keen of pain. The Man laid his hand upon her soft muzzle. She gave his hand one last lick, shuddered and died.

With her passing, the man's silence was sundered. He lifted his face to the skies with a primal howl of rage and loss. Little Wolf padded to the man's side and added his warbling voice to the choral of sorrow. The horses scattered in fear.

The man grabbed Little Wolf in a rough hug, his tears wetting the fur of the pup's ruff. He had thought to hide from life, but it had found him with a vengeance!

'Now we are but two.' His thoughts were chaotic and full of rage.

Little Wolf had trouble understanding his words, but not his feelings. *'Now we are but two,'* agreed Little Wolf.

Far in the distance, the wolves of the forest added wailing voices to the echoes of their lament.

₨⌓

It took time to coax the horses back to the scene of the battle, for the man had difficulty concentrating through his over-whelming grief. When he touched their minds, they reacted with fear and mistrust. The minds of the horses were very different from those of the wolfdogs, and he had trouble making them understand. Eventually he got through to them and felt them turn back from their flight.

He gently bore his dead pups to the river and laid them to rest in a cairn next to their mother. Soot was still in the burning wreckage of the cottage and could not be recovered. It made Soot's loss even harder to bear, for the pup would have to travel eternity without the company of his siblings.

He realized sadly that there was nothing left to show he had lived here. All had returned to its original state, burnt and abandoned, a cursed place. Was this what had happened to the farm's original owners? In all this time, he had never before wondered at the fate of the previous residents.

The horses had gathered at the farm by the time he returned from laying the pups to rest. Attached to the saddle of one of the horses was his sword scabbard and within the saddlebags of another, was the money belt and chain mail. The red soldiers had ransacked his home before they had fired it.

He felt a twinge of relief, followed immediately by guilt at being thankful that these *things* had survived, when his family had not. He reeled away from the horses, his fists clenched. He fervently wished the secrets to his past had been incinerated. He would have gladly traded them for the lives of his family.

His back stiffened and his teeth flashed in a snarl, as his eyes found the bodies of the murderers. Who were they? Why had they taken such pleasure in their cruelty? His lip curled in disgust as he knelt by the bodies and roughly searched them for clues about the outside world.

He found coins and weapons, but they carried nothing to

identify them as other than faceless soldiers. After stripping the bodies of any value, he heaved them into the vigorously burning smokehouse. They would receive no proper burial for what they did.

The man left the farm at sunset, as the last of the flames were burning low. Little Wolf had not wanted to leave until the murderers' corpses had been incinerated. When he questioned the wolfdog about its insistence, the pup had not been able to communicate the reason.

'They smell wrong!' was the most that Little Wolf would say.

Urged on by grief driven fury, the man backtracked the red soldiers' trail. Where they had come from, there would surely be more. After months of isolating himself for fear of discovery, he sought the most dangerous route as penance for failure to save his family.

In exchange for the possession of four horses and various weapons, the man left behind the life he had built for himself. But the devastation birthed a new purpose. Revenge!

'I will hunt more of these red soldiers, and they will all pay for the murder of my family!' He was maddened by grief. In his mind, it was his children who had been viciously slaughtered.

Swaying gently from the motion of the horse, he opened a clenched fist and, by the last light of day, once more examined the scrap of cloth he had torn from the tunic of one of the dead men. Two black snakes twined together, standing upon their tails, their hissing heads meeting at the top. They supported a crown between their venomous jaws. The emblem was woven upon a field of red. This was the sigil of his enemy.

Revulsion shook him with the intense need to kill the red soldiers again. Only this time, he would like to do so very slowly.

He could not fight his nightmare beheading, for it was something that did not exist in the real world. He clenched his fist around the torn scrap, crushing it. *'But this is real! This I can fight!'*

The horse sensed its rider's dangerous emotions and shifted uncomfortably, tossing its head. The other horses trailed behind, tethered by nothing more than the man's command to follow.

The man had lost his fear of the outside world, of what he would find over the horizon, and of who would find him. Ironically, it had taken the destruction of his life to force him back to the land of the living. There was no escaping the gaze of the Gods of Fortune. If he merely sat and awaited danger, he would never know when it was coming. If he sought it out, at least he would meet it on his own terms.

Little Wolf whined pitiably as they left the boundary of the farm behind, but he understood the need for revenge the man was experiencing. That need mirrored his own.

CHAPTER FOURTEEN

"That night, for the first time since my awakening, the nightmare changed again. I… remembered… more of it than I had ever before. It was my grief, I think, that triggered the new images."

Dajin grunted dismissively. "'Twas only dogs."

Gralyre's mouth tightened and his eyes dropped as he tried to control the instinctual rage that the disparaging comment about his family's death had caused. It was as he feared. They thought him mad. Perhaps they were right.

Rewn punched his brother in the arm. "Did ye no' hear a word o' his story? That they were dogs is true, but they spoke t' him, as would people. They were his family, just as ye are t' me and Da."

Gralyre grimaced. "You must think me crazed."

"No, no' insane," Wil negated. "Just a man forced t' survive in any way he could, with less skills to do so than a babe in arms. Please, finish your tale."

Gralyre resettled himself. He was uncomfortable now. Hearing his own words aloud, he knew this was not the story of a sane man. But there was little enough left to tell.

"By the time dusk overtook us, we had discovered the road. And my grief was overwhelming me."

CHAPTER FIFTEEN

THE KING'S ROAD - AUTUMN

It had once been a well-travelled road, but was now over-grown with many years of neglect. Ancient ruts were worn deep by the wheels of generations of passing wagons, but no recent travel pruned the tall weeds and small bushes. It would not be too much longer before the forest reclaimed the road entirely.

The path to his farm was almost indecipherable within the thick brush bordering the track. How had the red riders found it? The horrible luck that had precipitated their appearance begged belief.

Always, during his hunting forays, the man had kept to the area near the river that he knew well, rather than risk exploring the boundaries of his world. With every step he took towards the unknown, he recognized his isolation of before.

When daylight had utterly failed and the way ahead seemed hidden in shadowed menace, they made camp. He unsaddled the horses and neatly laid out the ragged bedding that had been in the packs, wrinkling his nose at the sour smell of the cloth. He hoped the night breeze would soon air out the rank body odour of the past owners.

The man started a fire and fed Little Wolf, leaving the horses to forage in the tall grasses growing in the track.

Food was a tasteless exercise. He stopped trying to eat,

listlessly feeding bits of wood to the fire instead.

When it was finally time to sleep, he found he could not. Over and over, his mind relived the murders of his family. There was no escape from the bright pain. He put his back to the fire, preferring the darkness of the endless night. He gazed fixedly into the shadows with eyes rimmed red with suffering.

Sometime during the long dark hours, he drifted into a fitful doze. The image of the roof collapsing on Soot burst with fiery brilliance into his mind's eye and he jerked awake to find that a log had split in the campfire, adding sounds to his nightmare.

He rolled onto his back, tears running freely into his matted hair and beard. He reached out with his mind, trying desperately to sense his pups, knowing there would be no answer, but torturing himself anyway. He was like a man who had lost a limb, but could still feel it itch. There was only one to answer his silent cry.

Little Wolf arose and padded over to the man. The pup whined anxiously, and pushed his muzzle into the man's face as his large tongue licked at the tears. The man pushed the pup's muzzle away, too filled with pain to bear Little Wolf's touch.

In need of comfort, Little Wolf ignored the rebuff and snuggled up to the man's side. With a sad, lonely sigh, he rested his head upon his master's chest.

The man grabbed the dog's ruff to shove him away, but instead found himself clinging tighter. He buried his face in Little Wolf's fur and wept like a child.

He calmed gradually, and finally drifted into an uneasy, exhausted slumber. Even as he slept, he held tightly to Little

Wolf as though to let go would be to lose this pup as he had the others.

The nightmare seeped through, a marauder preying upon his vulnerable grief. It began as it always did…

Battle. Men fight and die, scream rage and fear. Blasts of energy fall, cursing a warrior into black stone, his spear and sword forever raised in challenge. One by one, all die. A menagerie of grotesque black effigies, surround him. Despair crushes breath. He remains untouched.

No longer black statues, but black smoke pouring from his home. The roof collapses.

'Soot! No! Bastards! I will kill you all! KILL YOU ALL!'

But he will kill no one, he cannot move. Two henchmen hold him fast, forcing him to watch while his pups are killed. Fetid breath, the whistling of the sword, the touch of cold steel upon his neck.

'NO! Do not send me into the void!'

Little Wolf appears from nowhere. With a vicious snarl, he attacks the sword wielding Demon Man who evaporates like mist as the dog pounces.

The Void. The Pain. Little Wolf has been sucked into the abyss. Fear intensifies a thousand times.

'No! Little Wolf! Get free!'

The pulsing void attacks Little Wolf though the man tries to protect the pup from the ravages of the nothingness…

Summoning his will, the man wrenched awake, bellowing as

he had not done in many a month.

Little Wolf stared deeply into his eyes, trying to bring the man back to the present. *'I am here.'*

The man gasped for air and shuddered as the dead faces of black stone warriors burned into his mind's eye. What new element of the horror was this?

As the nightmare faded and his pounding heartbeat returned to normal, he rubbed a hand over his face, dislodging the sweat soaked strands of hair that were plastered to his skin.

'I saw the place that you fear,' Little Wolf told him.

The man was appalled. *'You were there! How? I thought it was a dream!'* The nightmare had seemed nothing more than a bubbling cauldron of his most fearful imaginings, the horrors of the past and present joining forces against him.

'While you slept, I heard you cry out. I entered your dream to fight by your side, but there was nothing there I could bite. It hurt! What beast attacks without teeth, and tears without claws? What beast is as large as the sky, and as small as a flea?'

Little Wolf sought an explanation he could not give.

'I do not know. You pose a riddle that I have no answer to. Mayhap we shall find someone who can answer it for us.' He rubbed the pup's muzzle reassuringly. *'Little Wolf, never go into my dreams again. They are dangerous, and I am unable to protect you.'*

Little Wolf gave his promise, curled up beside him and closed his eyes. Soon, sleepy thoughts drifted from the pup.

Somewhat annoyed at the wolfdog's easy ability to dismiss the fearsome experience, the man stacked his hands behind his head, and stared unseeingly at the stars winking out with the approach of dawn. Still, Little Wolf had given him a unique perspective on the nature of the void. The questions the wolfdog posed resonated within his mind.

'What beast can attack without teeth? What beast can tear apart without claws? What beast is as large as the sky, and yet as small as a flea?'

CHAPTER SIXTEEN

"As we followed the back-trail of the Demon Riders, we started to pass through many deserted villages." Gralyre was hardly aware of speaking now. He was held deep in thrall of the memory, just as Wil and his sons were held prisoner by his story.

THE KING'S ROAD - AUTUMN

The first day of hard travel was trying, for the horses made his head ache as they bickered, argued, and gossiped. The experience was made that much worse by his grief and lack of sleep. Like spoiled children, the horses did everything in their power to keep his attention focused upon them. Each vied harder than the other, in vain attempts to upset their rigid equine pecking order.

In a fit of exasperation, the man happened upon the trick of shutting out all thoughts but his own. His mind became blissfully silent.

Frightened that he had done himself harm, he relaxed his will, opening his mind once more. Noise boomed in, wringing a wince of pain. He was not picking up just the thoughts of the domesticated animals he travelled with, but also the fleeting wild thoughts of the creatures of the forest. He had been using the talent for months to aid his hunting, and never realized it.

'Can I shut out all thoughts but the ones I wish to listen to, or am I obliged to sift through the noise to find the mind I seek?' Experimenting, he tried to focus on just Little Wolf.

Startled, Little Wolf looked up from where he was scratching his ear, wondering what the man wanted. He picked up his pace so that he was trotting alongside the horse the man was riding, focussing on his master's face with canine curiosity.

The man carefully filtered out the superfluous noises. First to go were the forest creatures, then the horses. He was not blocking the influx of thoughts, so much as not exerting himself to listen, rather like being in an overcrowded room and attending only to a certain conversation. The horses were still there, bickering, but they sounded far away. Little Wolf was clearly heard.

'You can still smell the soldiers, Little Wolf?'

'The scent is still strong, and it grows weaker.'

'That is good. It means we are getting closer to where they came from.'

'We will find their den?'

'Yes,' the man's hands tightened on the reins. *'And when we do, we will kill them all.'*

Little Wolf approved. His head proudly high, he trotted to the front of the line and put nose to the ground. *'This way!'* The wolfdog quickly outpaced the horses as he scouted ahead.

The man was left alone to mull over his talent. How random his abilities had been before! Why had he never thought to explore these skills fully?

As with all his new discoveries it was necessity that drove him, or in this case the bickering of horses. He wiled away the rest of the day of travel by honing his precision.

Evening was fast approaching when the road opened into fallow fields. In the distance, stone buildings reflected the rosy light of sunset. A village! The man's heart thumped in his chest. He was wholly unprepared to meet people. What if the village housed his enemies? Images of the red riders flooded his mind's eye.

He brushed his hand down his matted beard and forced himself to calm. If he had any enemies, beyond the phantasms of his paranoia, he doubted they would recognize him. He was a far different man than the one who had awakened in the forest. Fortified by this thought, he bravely continued forward.

The man's fears soon proved groundless, for the village had been deserted for years. Cobbled streets were buried under thick layers of soil that had blown in from unploughed fields. Grass and weeds buckled and cracked the stones as they forced their way up through any chink towards light. Though the stone foundations and walls of the buildings remained relatively unscathed, thatched roofs had rotted away and collapsed long ago.

The man searched the village thoroughly for anything that could be of use. Furniture, remnants of clothing and tools, pots and utensils, were still neatly stowed in most of the cottages and sheds as though the occupants had decided to leave on a short journey and had left their homes ready to receive their return.

If he brought everything he found he would look like a grave robbing tinker as he travelled. So he settled upon just the essentials; a griddle, a ladle, a small cauldron with a fire hook, and various utensils not covered in rust, with which to eat.

Mystified at what could have become of the villagers, the man bedded down in the largest cottage. Once again, his rest was fitful as the nightmare images plagued his sleep. He awoke, groggy and ill tempered, as dawn's pink glow washed over the treetops.

He packed his horses with his pilfered treasures and broke camp early, eager to leave the eerie place behind. As he rode free of the outskirts of the village, he spotted the remnants of an old campfire. He called Little Wolf and set the dog to the scent.

The low growl and raised hackles of the pup told him all he needed to know. The red soldiers had camped here. The trail was still fresh.

As they journeyed, the day turned hot and muggy. The man alternated between horseback and walking to alleviate the saddle soreness from the unaccustomed riding.

When he walked, Little Wolf padded beside him. Every so often, the pup would press his nose into the man's hand, needing the reassurance of touch. The pup had not strayed far from his side since the murders.

Towards evening, they encountered another long deserted village. Unlike the first, this one had been the victim of violence. Not a building was left standing. The burned and toppled rubble made it impossible to follow the road through the centre, so the man directed his horses to skirt the perimeter. In the overgrown green at the edge of the village, they passed an old scorched ring where nothing grew.

The man dismounted and walked over the curious patch to examine it more closely. Unlike the rest of the village, here the fire had burned hot enough to turn the ground to slag in spots. He picked up a melted rock. What had caused it?

''Tis the remains of a funeral pyre.'

From the darkness of his memory the thought appeared, and he knew it for truth. The man swallowed thickly as he stepped quickly off the burned ground and back into the tall grass. He wished his amnesia had chosen to keep that information to itself.

It looked fifteen or twenty seasons old. The grasses were only just starting to encroach upon the scorched earth. Whatever cataclysm had befallen these people had happened many years before the previous village's mysterious abandonment. He sighed, and tossed the melted stone into the bushes. Little Wolf bounded after it in joyful pursuit.

There were only two conditions that led to villages being abandoned or destroyed. The first was pestilence, in which case everything, including bodies, was burned, and people left the areas of infection. The second condition was war. If only a few remained to bury the slain, a communal funeral pyre would oft times be the only way to honour the dead.

Deep in thought, the man turned away and strode briskly back to the grazing horses. Whatever the explanation for the disappearances, he was more bothered by something else.

'Why has no one ever returned to reclaim these villages? Not even to scavenge, as I have?'

Something unnatural haunted this land. He gathered the reins of his mount, and ordered the rest of the horses to follow. He would rather spend the night in the forest, than among the remains of this ill-fated place.

೫ೲ

Over the next few days, he left behind many such ruined villages, each either razed to the ground, or abandoned to rot. Deserted or burned crofts passed by, eerily reminiscent of the original state in which he had found his farm. The parade of devastation seemed never ending.

On his fourth day of travel, he finally ruled out pestilence as the cause of the desolation of the countryside.

Within the ruins of what had once been a thriving township, he found steel arrowheads that were still embedded in remnants of charred standing posts in the village square. The wood making up the shafts of the weapons had burned away with the rest of the township, but the barbed metal arrowheads gave evidence of violence. People had been executed here.

The man found the rusted residue of a grappling hook in the rubble, no doubt used to pull buildings apart. And then he found definitive proof. A badly corroded sword peeked from beneath the tumbled stones of a collapsed building. When he shifted a block to free it, the bony hand that had grasped the hilt in death, shattered into dusty fragments.

This ruin was the oldest he had yet seen. Trees claimed the middle of streets, while thick bushes grew in humps over tumbled and burned buildings. He measured the girth of one of the trees with a keen eye. It had been growing for at least forty years. Allowing for the time it took for soil to blow in, and the tree to root, would place this cataclysm at least a hundred years in the past.

The older ruins marked those conquered first. But there remained a mystery in the discrepancy of time between the burned townships, most being a half-century or more in age, and the deserted villages of little more than several seasons abandoned.

'An ancient war lost, those who resisted, destroyed? The survivors fleeing the area over the years?'

His face was grim as he fingered the arrowhead he had prised from the charred wooden remnant of a standing post.

'If they fled, they would have taken their valuables with them, not left them behind. Perhaps, the people of the deserted villages were taken as slaves? But why take slaves so many years after the warring?'

Either way, the conquering forces had taken nothing of value. He could find no sign of looting. Destruction had been the coin with which they had been paid. The proof of these devastated innocents caused confusing, intense feelings.

Guilt. Shame. A wistful pining for a place and people he had no knowledge of. Unable to reconcile the emotional stew, he strode back to where he had left the horses.

This had once been a thriving country, but it was now devastated and abandoned. He changed from fearing to encounter anyone, to fearing not to. Could the countryside be as empty as it seemed? There had to be people left alive somewhere.

The man thought he would find squatters, such as he had been for most of the summer, on one of the abandoned farms he passed, but only field mice and wild animals made use of the rotting structures. He was alone.

As the days continued with no encounters with the living, his confusion grew. Whatever force had vanquished this land, had ground it under its boot heels. What was the use of conquering a people if there were no subjects left alive to rule over?

He was witnessing the work of a madman!

CHAPTER SEVENTEEN

"The work o' a madman," Rewn repeated woodenly. His head was nodding slightly, the agreement of a man who had fought this evil all his life.

"No truer words could be spoken, lad," Wil concurred sadly.

When Gralyre raised his eyebrows in inquiry, Wil smiled grimly. "Your story first. Then we will tell ours."

"It was about then that I encountered the Tithe wagon. I saw the red soldiers again, the Demon Riders, abusing the women! I could not let them pass!" Gralyre said fiercely.

"When it was all over, your daughter asked me for my name. Gralyre. It popped into my head and I uttered it before I could think to question it. I do not know if it is my real name, but 'tis all I have."

Into the drawn silence they all sat silently, watching the sparks dance into the sky like jewelled supplications to the gods. Gralyre tensed as he awaited their verdict.

Rewn looked over at his father and gave a helpless shrug of uncertainty so that it was Wil, in the end, who broke the expectant silence.

"Frankly, lad, your story is impossible t' believe." Wil stated this gently, as though he were speaking with a deranged man.

The bottom dropped out of Gralyre's world. He swallowed around the sudden lump in his throat. "'Tis the only story I have," he murmured quietly, ducking his shoulder. His fingers picked at a loose thread on his shirt. What had he said wrong?

Rewn was staring at Gralyre with deep compassion.

Dajin kept his eyes on the fire, unwilling to make eye contact.

Wil sighed heavily and rubbed a tired hand across his face, scratching absently at the beginnings of his beard. "Ye see, boyo, except for the part about waking in the forest, and your ability t' talk t' the beasties, ye have just repeated a rather peculiar version o' the legend o' the Lost Prince."

Rewn was nodding in agreement even as Gralyre had to ask, "A legend?"

"The way I see it, your mind is using the old tale as memory t' fill in the gaps o' what it does no' want t' remember. 'Tis no' real." Wil gazed with urgent sympathy into Gralyre's eyes, trying to convince him of the truth.

"The Lost Prince?" Gralyre frowned, his head shaking slowly, trying, not for the first time, to jar memories loose from the dark abyss of his mind. "But I know of no such story."

Was it true? Had he made it all up? The Nightmare? The Sword? The Void? None of it was real?

Wil scratched at his ear. "Well, ye no' be remembering it in a full and normal manner, that is plain," he said gently. "Your mind is playing tricks with ye."

Each word was a devastating blow to Gralyre's fragile identity. Everything was a lie? He knew less of himself than ever. He glanced up in time to see the two brothers exchange shrugs of incredulity.

'Damn them, I am not mad!' Gralyre's fingers sought out the scroll. Perhaps the truth was written on the page. It could settle

all the questions, be his validation. Gralyre scanned the three men with a hopeful glance. "Can any of you read?"

"I can read a little," stated Wil proudly. "I learned from my Da, and he from his. Our family were landowners once, afore Doaphin usurped the throne," he finished bitterly. The bringing low of his family's fortunes still rankled after many generations.

Demanding, pleading, Gralyre held the message out to Wil. If his fingers trembled in anticipation as he passed it over, his companions were kind enough to make no comment upon it. "I have never been able to read it. I feel that I must know how, but I cannot remember." Gralyre's frustration with his ailment boiled to the surface.

Wil accepted the scroll and carefully unrolled it. He angled it to catch the firelight, lips moving lightly for long moments, as he carefully deciphered the writings. His eyes widened and air passed from his lips in a surprised hiss. "Was it sealed when ye discovered it?" he asked in a choked voice.

"No," said Gralyre shortly. "It was as you see it now." Impatient excitement pulsed through him.

"Read it aloud, Da," urged Rewn.

"Yes!" exclaimed Dajin excitedly. "Tell us what it says!"

Wil's face held a strange, rapt expression as he returned his gaze to the page, cleared his throat and began to read. "'Tis dated, *'Year Thirty-Five o' the Reign o' Lyre'*," Wil began. He cleared his throat again as his sons murmured their amazement to each other.

Gralyre wanted to know what was so unusual about the date, but was unwilling to interrupt until the whole message was revealed. He almost shouted at Wil to continue.

"*My dear-est son,*" Wil read aloud. The words were wooden and awkward as the older man decrypted the message. "*By the time Lord Fen-nick reach-es ye with this mess-age, your father and King will be dead. Long live the King.*"

There was nothing but captivated silence now as Gralyre, Rewn and Dajin strained to hear this unusual message.

Into Gralyre's mind, the text in whole, memorized, sprang into being. He caught his breath at the impact of the startling memory, and tuned Wil's stumbling words out, for it appeared he already knew them by heart.

We are betrayed from within, though by whom, we know naught. We have retreated to the Keep, and will surely be over-run by first light. Our garrison is crushed and we have been forced to collapse all but our personal escape tunnel to keep the sappers at bay. We have taken a grievous wound, and shall make our last stand within our stronghold. We send to you what troops we can spare and our friend Lord Fennick. He brings to you the seal of our house lest it become a trophy for the cursed usurper.

Lord Fennick carries vital knowledge that we dare not state in this missive lest it fall into enemy hands. He will tell you all. We pray to the Gods of Fortune that he can help you turn the tide of this war. It is too late for Dreisenheld, but perhaps you may yet live to avenge us.

Forgive an old fool who would not heed your words of warning until it was too late. Your affianced Lady keeps a vigil by our deathbed and tends the wounded. She would not leave with the other innocents. Though we both know that when Doaphin's horde enters the Keep all within will die, she refuses to use the escape tunnel to save herself.

She sends her deepest respect and love, and hopes you will keep yourself safe in these dangerous times. Be not aggrieved by her choice, my son, for she does us all a great honour. Her beauty and courage has rallied the men's spirits, and perhaps given us the strength to keep Doaphin at bay long enough for Lord Fennick to make good his escape.

What a Queen she would have made you!

Long live the King!

Wil carefully rolled the parchment and held it sandwiched reverently between his trembling palms. The firelight flickering off his face made it difficult to read his expression. "Well," he breathed. "Well."

"Da, it canno' be real, there is no way 'tis real!" Rewn objected incredulously into the silence, while his brother, Dajin, stared at Gralyre as if he had grown a second head.

Gralyre ignored them all as he picked up the ring and flipped the jewel to reveal the great seal that lay hidden behind the stone. He rasped his fingernail over the embossed silver. In the space of time it had taken Wil to haltingly read the message, Gralyre had gained everything, a father, a fiancée, a life, and then lost it all again. All were dead at the hands of Doaphin.

Gralyre felt strange. He was not sad, for he could not recall the people spoken of in the note, but he was regretful that it was so.

Wil passed the scroll back to Gralyre. "The crest," Wil hesitantly confirmed as he looked at the ring in Gralyre's hands, "is o' Lyre's House." His eyes focussed on the pile of coins, glittering in the firelight. He straightened as something occurred to him. "Pick me out a gold piece, boyo," he asked of Gralyre.

Mystified, Gralyre reached down and plucked a gold coin from the glittering hoard and passed it to Wil. It glinted dully in the firelight as it exchanged hands.

As if he were reaching for a viper, Wil reluctantly accepted the coin. Fearing what he would see, he glanced down at it, and then cleared a sigh of relief. "Here is the flaw in your tale!" A triumphant smile curved his lips as his world righted.

"What is it?" More than before, Gralyre felt himself trapped in the mystery that swirled and boiled around his past.

"This coin was minted by Doaphin. If ye were the Lost Prince, as all these objects and your story would suggest, your coins would carry the crest and face o' the old kingdom."

Gralyre dug through the pile of coins again and came up with a second gold piece. It pinged like a small bell as his thumb flicked it through the firelight towards Wil. The ringing ceased abruptly as Wil snagged it from the air.

Wil's face paled as he examined the second coin, minutely comparing it to the first. He looked at Gralyre, his eyes searching for a reasonable explanation.

The sons kept quiet, almost spellbound by the unfolding drama around the fire. A sudden gust of wind bent the trees with a muted roar. Dajin glanced uneasily at the surrounding darkness and moved closer to the flames.

"I took coins off the Demon Riders who destroyed my farm," Gralyre stated quietly. "The other is what I carried when I awoke with no memory."

"Well, ye canno' be the Legend come t' life, boyo!" Wil burst forth. His accent became more pronounced with his emotion.

"I never said I was," Gralyre snarled back, his confusion making him lash out. "'Tis more likely, I am this courier, Fennick, who was entrusted with this message. Now that I know who it is bound for, I can finish delivering it."

"Oh, ye are no' the Lord Fennick either!" Wil shot back.

"What makes you so certain?" Gralyre demanded.

"Because Prince Gralyre, son o' King Lyre lived three hundred years ago!" snapped Wil. "And might I be the first t' say that ye are a mighty fine looking corpse!" Wil roared to a finish, lifting himself slightly from his seat with the strength of his emotions.

Gralyre sagged, poleaxed, his quest for a past splintering into fragments. He did not know what to say. What was there to say? He was mad. There was no other explanation.

Across the fire, Wil relaxed with a regretful sigh as he saw the pallor of understanding replace the flush of anger on Gralyre's face. "Ye see it now, lad? 'Tis as I said afore. Your mind but uses the legend as memory because it can no' stand whatever the truth may be."

Little Wolf rested his muzzle upon Gralyre's knee, silently offering his support as he sensed his master's turmoil.

Gralyre took a deep breath and released it slowly as the

discrepancies in Wil's logic were thrown into stark relief. "Then tell me where I found the chain mail, the coins and the ring," he demanded, his voice raspy with uncertainty. "Tell me where the letter came from? I did not even know what was written upon it until now! What of the crest that was sewn to my vest?"

Wil hesitated, thinking, carefully constructing a reasonable argument to support the facts. "It be my thought that ye must have robbed a burial mound. T' my view it looks like ye had partners, and when the bunch o' ye saw the richness o' the grave, ye fought over the spoils. Ye won the battle and wandered into the forest with the treasure. Perhaps your memory loss is punishment from the Gods for disturbing the tomb o' the Lost Prince."

Gralyre sat very still, fighting down his instinctive denial of Wil's words, taking a moment to consider their worth. His eyes narrowed in anguish. "I do not feel like a grave robber. I could barely take what I needed from the ruins of the villages I passed, but your explanation makes sense!" For a moment, he rested his hand over his eyes, trying to come to terms with yet another new image of himself.

"Hold a moment, Da," said Rewn. All eyes swung towards the quiet young man who was slowly poking the fire with a long stick. "Parchment and clothing would no' have survived all these centuries in a burial mound. Gralyre thought he might be a courier. He told Dara he was from the Kingdoms t' the South. Might no' what he is carrying be a message t' our resistance, a promise o' help? It has long been held in our company that anyone carrying an old coin is one o' us. 'Tis our secret sign.

Here sits a man carrying a hundred such coins."

Wil smiled at his son. "That makes as much sense as my theory."

Gralyre was also nodding his head at Rewn. "I cannot deny that this theory gives me more comfort. I do not know what to think. Perhaps if you tell me of this Lost Prince, my mind will abandon its stolen fantasy and reveal the truth?"

Wil heaved a sigh, sorry to have caused Gralyre such distress. He reached into his breast pocket and pulled out a pipe. Rewn followed suit.

"Son, would ye have any...?" Wil mumbled around the stem while patting his pockets unsuccessfully, but Rewn was already tossing his pouch of tobacco at him. "Ah," Wil said in satisfaction as he snagged it from the air, "thank-ye, son."

Rewn just snorted as he accepted the pouch back from his father. "He is always without," he complained in a loud aside to Gralyre.

Gralyre's lips twitched at the byplay, but found the matter was too serious to maintain levity at Wil and Rewn's light bantering. He waited impatiently as Wil lit his pipe, settled himself more comfortably and took a couple of puffs.

"I love this story," Dajin exclaimed, scooting closer to his father. "Da used t' tell it t' us around the hearth." His face reflected the memories of better days.

Gralyre felt a burning in his chest at the casual sentimentality that Dajin displayed. How he yearned to have just one such memory of his own family.

Finally, when Wil's head was well wreathed by a cloud of

fragrant smoke, he began to speak.

"This is a tale handed down through our family; a truthful account o' the last days o' the Lost Prince as told by the younger brother o' our great-great-great," Wil flapped his hand to indicate several more generations of greats, "grandfather, who held a commission in the Prince's army. Linus, that was his name." Wil inclined his head towards Gralyre as he offered up the providence to his story.

"Linus was one o' the few t' survive the massacre at Centaur Pass. The Prince himself had sent him over the mountains, t' secure reinforcements from the Dream Weavers for the last battle. But that part in this sad tale comes later."

He paused for another puff upon his pipe, ordering his thoughts.

"Doaphin's forces had taken the capital. The good King Lyre lay murdered in his fortress o' Dreisenheld. He was betrayed from within. A spy had opened the gates t' the usurper. With the outer walls o' Dreisenheld overrun, the King, on his deathbed, sent his court Sorcerer, Lord Fennick, t' the aid o' his only son, Prince Gralyre."

As he said the name *Gralyre*, Wil glanced meaningfully at his subject.

"Lord Fennick found the Prince campaigning in the north, holding his own against Doaphin's forces and steadily gaining ground. The Prince was just getting ready t' push south towards Dreisenheld in aid o' his father. He had no idea that the capital had fallen, for Dreisenheld was a mighty fortress, able t' withstand a lengthy siege had it no' been betrayed.

"When Lord Fennick told the Prince o' his father's death, his lady's death, and the fall o' Dreisenheld, the Prince was inconsolable in his grief.

"Prince Gralyre disappeared into the forest for three days and three nights and returned a changed man. His face was hardened and chiselled, like stone. Where before he was quick t' share a quip with his men, now he held himself aloof. He had left their midst as a Prince and returned from the forest as their King.

"Yet he refused the men the right t' call him King, for he had yet t' reclaim his throne from the usurper, Doaphin."

"The usurper was," Wil paused with a snort, "is… a powerful sorcerer of unforgiving evil. No mere man could hope to stand against him. T' save the Kingdom o' Dreisenheld, they had t' become more than mere men.

"So Prince Gralyre drilled and polished his warriors, the fighting elite o' the kingdom, until they become masters o' the sword, and the Prince, already a Master o' Weapons, became a Master o' all Masters.

"His men loved him and would follow their Prince t' the very gates o' the underworld. But the Prince also loved his men, and never sent them into a danger he was no' in the forefront o' himself. Doaphin's forces could no' stand against their might. Inch by inch they reclaimed the kingdom.

"'Tis said the Prince stood a full head above most men and after the death o' his father, he would wear naught but black…" Wil's voice faltered for a moment as he measured Gralyre's long length, garbed in tattered black. He cleared his throat, took a puff from his pipe and pushed on with his story. "His foes died o' fright afore his blade ever touched them.

"In tribute t' their dead king, and t' their Prince, the army adopted the black dress, and became known t' one and all as the Prince's Black Vengeance. They raged across the countryside, liberating the people from the horror o' Doaphin's occupation. But no matter how many o' Doaphin's armies they defeated it still was no' enough t' assuage the Prince's fury. His thirst for vengeance would only be quenched in Doaphin's blood.

"But Doaphin would no' go quietly. He sent a terrible message by way o' a hideous thing that travelled only by night and hid from daylight. It was a Stalker, erect like a man, with jaws like a shark, and a body o' a lizard. Its hands had razor sharp claws in place o' fingers, and its eyes glowed with red fire." Wil dangled his fingers and wiggled them fiendishly.

The brothers grinned, appearing much younger than their years, as though transported back in time by the familiar panto-miming of their father.

"When the Prince's men saw the creature, they wished t' kill the abomination but the demon had approached under a flag o' parlay, a sanctity which Prince Gralyre would no' violate. The Prince wished t' hear o' the foul plan Doaphin was hatching. So the Stalker was granted safe passage, and allowed t' speak."

Wil's voice roughed and became ghoulish as he mimicked the cadence of the monster.

"'I bear greeting from the all powerful Doaphin. He sends terms o' surrender.'

"The men cheered wildly when they heard this, thinking they had won the war. The Prince waved them t' silence, as the foul creature continued t' speak.

"'Ye will throw down your arms and surrender immediately, or Doaphin will execute your betrothed!'"

Wil's voice changed to take on the deep, ringing tones of the royal hero of the story.

"'Ye lie, foul thing! She fell at Dreisenheld with the King!'

"The creature threw a drawstring pouch at the Prince's feet. One o' the Prince's men rushed forward and thrust his sword into the sack, t' ensure no danger lurked within. Then he used the sword t' spill the skewered contents t' the ground.

"Out shimmered the golden, shorn locks o' the Prince's betrothed, Genevieve the Fair, and a jewel crusted locket that had been the Prince's promise t' her. Her golden tresses lay ruined upon the rocky ground and amongst all that shorn glory, lay a note from that fair lady.

"It read," and now Wil's tone became fluttery and feminine,

My dearest,

They have taken me captive. When the Keep fell, I was forced t' watch them brutalize the bodies o' our fallen. I am sorry, I was no' brave enough t' take my own life, and now they would use me against ye. Forgive my weakness.

I have no' been harmed. They keep me whole t' command your submission. Think no' o' me, my love, for ye fight a greater cause than the rescue o' myself.

"The Prince recognized the hand o' fair Genevieve and grew sore afraid for her. And though she begged him t' give her no regard, he grieved the choice he must make.

"The Stalker was no' through with its threats. *'Ye will come with me now, or Doaphin will lay a curse upon Princess Genevieve o' such horror, the world will shudder at its wickedness for a thousand years!'*

"Prince Gralyre remained silent until his men began t' murmur, wondering what their Prince would choose t' do. Finally the Prince spoke, and such was the rage in his voice that the foul creature fell back in purest terror.

" *'Tell Doaphin, that his days are numbered. Soon he will be dead, and I will rescue my lady, if she yet lives!'*

" *'Ye fear the magnificent Doaphin!'* the creature taunted.

"The Prince drew his sword and set it to the neck o' the Stalker. The firelight glittered off the ruby red eyes o' the dragon that wrapped the handle o' the great sword.

"The demon was afraid t' move lest the Prince take its head. But the Prince was an honourable man, bound by the rules o' parlay. The creature had been granted safe passage.

" *'Get ye from my sight, Demon! Tell foul Doaphin t' crawl back into the hell that spawned him!'* "

"A quick as that," Wil snapped his fingers, "the Prince slashed the Stalker across its scaly face, one perfect stripe down each o' its cheeks, making it squeal and tremble."

" *'Now leave, afore I decide that ye would serve me better dead than as a messenger!'*

The creature fled with all haste from the camp, thankful for its life.

" *'Ye are letting it go?'* asked Lord Fennick.

"'I send it as a messenger t' Doaphin. But it will no' escape me, forever. I will find it again one day, and finish the task left unfinished tonight.'"

Wil mimed the wounds the Prince had given to the Stalker by running a finger down his own cheeks, one on each side. He grinned at Dajin, and Dajin grinned back.

"'Follow it and make certain that it leaves!'

"The Prince's men tracked the Stalker until it had left the confines o' their picket lines and beyond. They were confident it had fled, and so returned t' their camp. But they were mistaken.

"The sly creature doubled back and hid in the bushes t' spy. It had t' be in a hole by daybreak t' avoid the killing rays o' the sun, but it had orders t' discover the Prince's plans, so that a trap could be laid."

Wil paused to relight his pipe, which had gone out as he spoke. Craftily, he rolled his eyes at his sons and then at Gralyre, who were all impatiently waiting for him to continue.

"He always does this!" Dajin complained heatedly. "Always! Just when 'tis getting t' the good part!"

Rewn burst out laughing at his brother's impatience and after a sigh of exasperation, Dajin ruefully joined in.

"Gets 'em every time." Wil chuckled in an aside to Gralyre as he puffed and drew on his pipe to aid the firebrand in its work.

Gralyre's returned smile was strained. Even though he was enjoying the family's byplay as much as the tale, the story was raising feelings and images that he could not reconcile. As Wil told his tale, Gralyre could *see* the Princess' golden hair spilling onto the ground. He had clearly recalled the wounds on the

Stalker's face. The sword Wil had described was the sword from his memory. It could not mean what it suggested, and yet, he knew of these things deep in his soul. How could it feel so real? It was madness!

Finally, Wil's pipe was lit to his satisfaction, and he continued. "Now where was I?" he asked rhetorically.

"Ye are at the part where the Stalker is spying on the Prince!" Dajin exclaimed heatedly.

"Ah, yes," Wil smiled cannily to himself.

"The Prince called his commanders t' his tent t' discuss his strategy. The younger son o' whom I spoke earlier, our ancestor Linus, was part o' this meeting," Wil stated proudly.

"Prince Gralyre spoke freely t' his assembled commanders, unaware that the Stalker had returned and was listening from without. The men loved and respected their Prince and would support his decision if he chose t' rescue his betrothed from the hands o' Doaphin. But that was no' his plan.

"'Thanks t' Lord Fennick's aid, we have found Doaphin's Wizard Stone, and the usurper's destruction is at hand! 'Tis located far t' the north, in Centaur Pass o' the Heathren Mountains.

"'If we turn our army south t' root Doaphin from Dreisen-held, all will be lost, for he is too powerful t' stand against in pitched battle! He expects I will do this in a misguided bid t' win the Princess' freedom, when 'tis likely that Genevieve is already dead.

"'We are too close t' victory t' allow ourselves t' be turned from our path. It rips apart my soul t' abandon her, but I can no' *be ruled by my heart! My first duty is t' the kingdom! If we destroy the stone, we destroy Doaphin's power and my betrothed, if she yet lives, will be released from the spell that Doaphin weaves. 'Tis the only choice!'*

"Tears fell from many an eye over the grief o' their Prince's choice, but the men stood with him. After a moment o' silence t' honour the Princess, the Prince outlined his plan.

"'The Stone will be heavily guarded. Fennick expects there will be a legion standing against us, at least six thousand foot and seven hundred cavalry. We will need reinforcements t' swell our numbers t' ten thousand. If we split our forces and attack from both ends o' the pass at once, we will crush Doaphin's army between us.'

"'But sire, where are we t' find more men?' the Prince's Generals asked.

"The Prince already knew the answer *'Someone must journey east t' the land o' the Dream Weavers, my mother's people, and compel them t' join our fight. If we fail t' stop him here and now, Doaphin will be turning his might against their lands next. 'Tis in their interest t' align with us and remember the treaties o' old.'*

"Our ancestor, Linus, volunteered t' go t' the Dream Weavers and gain the reinforcements. The Prince granted him leave to take ten men and hasten away. If all went well, by the time the Black Vengeance entered Centaur Pass from the west, the Dream Weavers reinforcements would be entering the pass from east and they would crush Doaphin's forces between them.

"The demon Stalker heard all and hurried t' tell its evil

master."

Wil's story was interrupted by Gralyre's question.

"What is a Wizard Stone?"

"Well, lad, ye really have lost your memories," Wil mused. "A Sorcerer, on his own, is powerful enough, but if he wishes t' work great magic, he needs more power than what he can safely hold within his own body. So he stores the magic he needs within a Stone. Think o' the Stone as a bucket. Ye can carry more water in a bucket than cupped within your hands."

Gralyre nodded his understanding.

"The Stone is filled with the life force o' the Sorcerer, and it demands an awful price. The more he uses his Stone, the more o' his soul the Stone claims, until finally, the Sorcerer will cease t' be and there will be only the Stone."

"Then he dies?" Gralyre cupped his hands to the flames to warm them.

"No, lad," said Wil gravely, "then he is immortal. The Stone becomes his body, alive with the Sorcerer's soul. Such Wizard Stones are highly sought after, for the possessor, if he can discover the Stone's Word o' Binding, can bend its power t' his own design, or destroy the Stone and the Sorcerer within.

"Without the Word o' Binding, a Wizard Stone can come t' possess the body o' the unwary. In this way, the Sorcerer can live again as flesh and blood and the poor fool who thought t' be the master, becomes a slave, trapped within the stone for eternity.

"A Wizard Stone is *alive* and has a will o' its own, a will that mirrors that o' the Sorcerer whose spirit it contains. If the

Sorcerer was good, so too will be the Stone. If the Sorcerer was evil..." Wil shrugged. "Well, I think ye catch my meaning."

Gralyre frowned for, though the context of the story now made more sense, an uneasy fear had raised its ugly head. He swallowed heavily as he asked, "The Demon Lord that Catrian defeated at the Tithe wagon. Is he immortal now?" Gralyre shuddered to think that the foul thing could be living on somewhere, untouchable and undying.

"That one?" Rewn chuckled with satisfaction. "He is never coming back. Catrian killed him well and good! He is a Demon, no' a Sorcerer. He has no soul with which t' bind t' a Wizard Stone."

Gralyre smiled as a wave of relief crashed over him. The Demon Lord was gone forever! "'Tis very good news. Please continue," he motioned to Wil.

Wil inclined his head, smiling to himself at the man's oddly imperious gesture.

"Doaphin used magic t' send his orders t' the far ends o' the land, that all passages east through the mountains be guarded t' ensure that the Prince's envoy never made it through. The Dream Weavers would never learn o' Prince Gralyre's plight.

"Doaphin then mobilized his entire might, converging near Centaur Pass t' set a secret trap for the Black Prince. Doaphin went with his evil horde t' personally oversee the defeat o' his enemy and ensure the safety o' his Wizard Stone. There would be no escape for Prince Gralyre. Instead o' a legion o' seven thousand, he would be facing ten times that number."

Gralyre's heartbeat tripled and his body began to quiver. He wanted to beg Wil to stop the telling of his tale. Something bad was about to happen. He could feel it. As Wil continued speaking, Gralyre closed his eyes and unclenched his fists to wipe his sweating palms against the soft leather of his worn britches.

"Linus' trip was fraught with danger. Doaphin's creatures were never more than minutes behind. As the envoy raced through the mountains, his ten companions were taken from him, until he alone was left alive t' carry the message.

"He drove himself and his horse day and night t' keep ahead o' pursuit and reach the Dream Weavers afore the allotted time. He was sore afraid for his Prince. If the enemy knew o' his mission, did they know the rest? Did they know o' the planned attack on Centaur Pass?

"Linus reached the end o' the last mountain and beheld the grasslands o' the Dream Weavers spread out before him t' the horizon. He had made it!

"But disaster felled him as he left the mountain. His horse was struck with a poison dart from the blowgun o' Doaphin's pursuing demons. It fell, and Linus was trapped when the horse rolled upon him.

"The creatures saw that Linus lay broken and pinned beneath his horse and left him t' die slowly, for they are cruel, and would no' think t' end suffering only prolong it.

"But the Gods o' Fortune were smiling upon Linus! He had fallen into a hollow, and the dead horse but pinned him, yet did no' crush him. Still, he was unable t' free himself. For three days and three nights, Linus lay there. Knowing he was t' die, he was inconsolable in his failure.

"Just as life was ebbing from his body, Dream Weaver scouts found him and nursed him back t' health. Even in his fevered state, Linus remembered his duty, and begged the Dream Weavers t' send for an army t' help fight Doaphin's legion and destroy the Wizard Stone.

"The Dream Weavers sent for their high commanders and a Great Debate was held that raged for three days and three nights. Some felt the Kingdom o' Lyre deserved t' fall. But others remembered Gralyre's mother, a princess o' their people, who had died many years before, and that it was her son who called for aid.

"Linus despaired at the time wasting away. For surely any help he received, if he received any help at all, would now come too late. On the morning o' the fourth day, the High Commander o' the Dream Weavers came t' him and pledged t' the Prince's cause five thousand cavalry, warriors and archers all.

"They rode forth with all haste. As they travelled more and more horsemen joined their cavalry until the sound o' their hooves rolled like thunder on the Great Plains. By the time they entered the foothills o' the Heathren Mountains the full five thousand had answered the call t' war. They were unaware that they were stepping into the jaws of a trap!

"Doaphin was very careful. He had no' taken the chance that his scouts had stopped the couriers. He rightly feared the Prince's call might be answered by the Dream Weavers, and so he had placed an army in their path.

"Upon defeating the Dream Weavers, it would be the evil one's army that entered the eastern end o' Centaur Pass. In place of allies, the Prince would find naught but more enemies. Prince Gralyre's trap would be reversed upon him. The hunter would become the prey.

"Doaphin's army sprung their ambush, but the Dream Weavers were no' t' be so easily defeated, though the evil one's army outnumbered them five t' one. They were very canny warriors, and knew that within the thick woods, their horses were a hindrance. So they dismounted and faded away in the forest. They knew they could no' survive a pitched battle with Doaphin's dark forces but enough small cuts will kill as surely as a broad stroke.

"Doaphin's army was left fighting nothing but smoke. They searched for the Dream Weavers in the thick forests but there was no trace o' their foes but for the deadly hiss o' arrows, heard briefly afore their miserable lives ended.

"The Dream Weavers would appear from unexpected directions, their bowmen slaughtering hundreds afore melting away like ghosts, back into the greenery. Doaphin's soldiers died screaming, and nary a Dream Weaver lost further life.

"Doaphin's creatures could find no respite from attack. By day, as they hid from the sun, they would suddenly find the burning light exploding into their holes as the Dream Weavers dug them from their nests.

"By night, when they were strongest, deadfalls and traps killed and maimed if they strayed from their ranks. Yet if they stayed in formation, the arrows would hiss from the trees, piercing and burning with the purity o' the Maolar tipped shafts.

"After five days o' merciless slaughter, the Dream Weavers

defeated Doaphin's army to the last creature. Yet Linus was distraught. It was now plain t' him that the usurper knew o' the Prince's plans. Gralyre was walking into a trap. Would they be in time t' save him?

"With all haste, they rode for Centaur Pass, but the ambush had delayed them dearly. The Dream Weavers arrived at the east end o' Centaur Pass late on the very day set by the Prince for the battle. As sounds o' fighting reached their ears, Linus' worst fears were realized. They were too late."

Wil's gaze turned inward. This dark moment of history sat like a spider in a web, the horror of all that was to come radiated out from this one event, even unto the lives of the men now seated around this fire.

"Days earlier, when Prince Gralyre had arrived with the Black Vengeance, the pass had been deserted. It had seemed that their fears were for naught. Doaphin had posted no army t' guard his Wizard Stone.

"Unwilling t' trust in his seeming good fortune, the Prince made camp and sent scouts t' search the canyon, and the surrounding forests, but all was peaceful. After several days, having received no word from the Dream Weavers, he came t' believe that they had either forsaken him in his time o' need or that his messengers had no' made it through. But the Prince thought it mattered naught, for either way, the stone lay waiting, it was unguarded, and daylight would protect their advance.

"The day o' reckoning arrived. Touting his victory afore him, Prince Gralyre moved the Black Vengeance into the pass. They thought they had won, for Doaphin's creatures could only attack by night, never in daylight.

"But the sun had turned enemy. Doaphin's Horde had marched all night t' arrive at daybreak, t' take the Prince unawares. Their timing was flawless. They materialized from the forest and attacked, driving the Black Vengeance deep into the pass, forcing them t' flee for their lives, for their numbers were too few t' stand against such a wave o' evil. Doaphin's forces should have been falling t' smoking ash in the sunlight, yet they did no'! Doaphin had altered the very fabric o' nature t' create the first Demon Riders, evil demons that could suffer the sun!

"But no' everything was t' go as the evil one had planned! Doaphin's rage was great when he realized it was the Dream Weavers victorious who approached from the east, no' his missing army o' demons. It was a devastating upset t' his evil plans. Prince Gralyre would soon slip from the trap Doaphin had set for him. And worse than that, his Wizard Stone was now in terrible danger. Doaphin could no' allow Prince Gralyre t' reach his Dream Weaver reinforcements.

"The usurper raised his hands and a terrible roar shook the world. The earth heaved and rolled, and from within Centaur Pass a great column o' dust billowed high into the air.

"Fearing the worst, the Dream Weavers spurred their mounts onward only t' find the way blocked by a great landslide. Doaphin had brought the mountain down upon Prince Gralyre's forces. Fully a third o' the Black Vengeance lay buried beneath rock and stone.

"A small remnant o' the Prince's army had escaped the pass ahead of the slide, scouts sent ahead t' ensue a clear path o' retreat. They wept in anguish for their Prince and their comrades, for they knew the overwhelming odds that they faced, and they were unable t' return t' their aid."

Rewn leaned over and touched his father's arm for his attention. He jerked his chin in Gralyre's direction, having finally noted the man's state.

Gralyre's forehead was shiny with moisture, his breath panted out in small gasps. His arms twitched as though reacting to a dream battle in his mind's eye.

"Gralyre? Are ye alright, man?" Rewn asked.

Gralyre recoiled as he was brought out of his nightmare and back to the firelight. He shook his head. "Finish it!" he croaked hoarsely. "Just finish it!"

Wil could not take his eyes from Gralyre's face. An ominous feeling climbed his spine. "Is any o' this familiar t' ye?"

"No! Yes! 'Tis just... I do not know... something... Just finish it. I think I have heard this tale before." Gralyre rubbed a trembling hand across his mouth, taking away the sweat beading his upper lip. *'...or lived it.'* The thought remained unspoken.

"All right then, boyo," Wil said softly. "I'll finish the story."

"The Dream Weavers joined with the remnants o' the Black Vengeance. The Prince's men were frantic, for the last o' their army was trapped on the far side o' the landslide, fighting Doaphin's Horde! Their Prince, if he yet lived, was in mortal danger!

"Unable t' take their horses over the rubble, the Dream Weavers abandoned their mounts. With no regard for their lives they scrabbled up the slide. But the loose rocks could no' support the weight o' so many. They set off little avalanches that buried others climbing the slope behind them. But if they ascended only a few at a time, Doaphin's archers would slaughter them as they crested the top! There was no way t' reach the Prince.

"As they realized this, the Black Vengeance fell t' yelling in anguish and rage, battle cries that went unanswered. Their grief was terrible, for they no' only lost their Prince, their King and beloved commander, but all hope o' victory and peace. The war was lost.

"'We must at least discover the fate o' our Prince!' shouted Linus. He bravely scaled the slide, and carefully peered over the top. What he saw made his blood chill in his veins!"

Wil stopped again, this time to knock the ash from his pipe. He drew a flask from his pocket and took a pull to wet his throat. He passed it to Gralyre, who still looked shakier than he would have liked.

Gralyre took a large swig, savouring the harsh liquor burning his mouth. He took a deep breath and passed the flask to Rewn. The bracing effects were felt immediately.

It was folly to be caught up in a tale. Why did it affect him so? The foolishness of suggesting he was this Lost Prince was becoming more apparent by the moment. But he could see it in his mind's eye, smell the sweat and the blood, the shit and the fear. The screams...

When they had all had their fill, Wil corked the flask and slipped it back into his pocket.

"Linus watched the battle from a hidden place atop the slide.

He could clearly see that the last o' the Black Vengeance and the Prince were trapped.

"Aye, but they made their last stand fiercely," Wil said with pride. "What they lacked in numbers they made up for in skill and bravery. With Prince Gralyre standing foremost in the ranks, no Demon Rider came near without dying.

"The clever Prince had chosen his last stand at the point where Centaur Pass is narrowest. The horde could no' bring its full power t' bear in the narrow space, which negated their numbers. Bodies piled high around the remnants o' the Prince's army and the ground drank deep o' blood that day. Doaphin's soldiers could no' reach the Prince's ranks without that they did no' trod upon one o' their own twitching corpses.

"As long as the Black Vengeance's strength held, they would no' be defeated. They were holding their own for now, but the mon were sure t' tire long afore they ran out o' the enemy. For every creature they dispatched a dozen more were queued t' take its place. They could no' fight forever. Eventually, their strength would wane." Wil flourished a triumphant finger aloft. "But victory by arms was no' their goal.

"Their last stand was a ploy t' buy time for the Court Sorcerer, Lord Fennick, t' find and destroy Doaphin's Wizard Stone. If Fennick succeeded, the Usurper would die, the horde would disperse and the war would yet be won.

"The Prince's Black Vengeance was no' tiring quickly enough t' suite the evil Doaphin. He positioned himself upon a ridge, high above the fighting where he was safe from slings and arrows. His black staff belched forth cracking bursts o' lightning. Every man struck by one o' Doaphin's bolts turned into a statue o' black stone, frozen for all time with sword and shield raised in challenge!"

"What madness is this? Do you mock me?" Gralyre growled. His chest rose and fell in heaves as panic threatened to overwhelm him. The nightmare was breaking through. His head swam with vertigo. The flames of the fire receded as if down a tunnel. His hand travelled to his belt and grabbed the hilt of his dagger, though he did not draw it.

Little Wolf leaped up and growled at the three men. The menacing rumble froze Wil and his sons in place.

Wil leaned forward slowly, carefully. "Calm yourself, lad. 'Tis but a story, that is all. I will stop now. 'Tis clear ye have no' fully recovered from your injuries. Ye need t' rest..."

"NO!" Gralyre shouted. He took a deep calming breath. The fire snapped back into focus. He let go of his dagger and buried a hand in Little Wolf's ruff to compel the pup to relax against him. "Please. I am sorry. I need to hear the rest of it. 'Tis not you. 'Tis the...memory...of the nightmare!" Gralyre drew another deep draught of breath. "You must understand! I dream this," he gritted out between clenched teeth. "Every night!"

Rewn shook his head at his father, not to go on. The stranger and his wolf were too dangerous, and far too volatile.

Wil stared at Gralyre for a long moment. "I will go on, only if ye promise t' stop me if it becomes too much for ye. I am telling ye the same tale ye would have from any bard in the land. I am no' seeking t' mock ye, or cause ye pain."

Gralyre nodded, terribly ashamed by his behaviour. "I am

truly sorry." He ran his hands through his hair, around his nape and up his chin to steeple in front of his mouth. "Please, go on." His eyes closed, clenched tightly, bracing himself for what was to come.

Wil cleared his throat noisily. He noticed that Rewn's hand rested on the hilt of his dagger, and his eyes never left Gralyre's now quiescent form. Wil nodded approvingly at his son and continued his story.

"As each o' his men fell t' the evil magic o' the usurper, it became clear t' the Prince that the only way t' save his men was t' move into the ranks o' the enemy where Doaphin would no' be able t' strike without killing his own soldiers. Prince Gralyre rallied the last o' his men and attacked.

"Though the Prince's strategy was sound, he had no' reckoned with Doaphin's black heart. The Usurper did no' care if he killed two-dozen o' his own t' reach but one o' the Black Vengeance. So the rain o' terrible magic continued.

"As his men died, the Prince's fury intensified, and his battle yells burst from his throat! He became a reaper! Hundreds o' the horde fell t' the Dragon blade, but thousands took their place.

"While the battle raged below, Lord Fennick had scaled the mountainside, having finally located the Stone in a small cave, far up the steep side o' the pass. Upon reaching the Stone, he now had t' discover the Word o' Binding that bound Doaphin's black soul t' the rock.

"Doaphin felt Fennick tampering with his Wizard Stone. He left off his magical barrage, leaving his army t' parish under the swords o' the Black Vengeance once more, and rushed t' do battle with Lord Fennick.

"Linus did no' see the battle between the Sorcerers, but all who survived that day told tales o' the great explosions that rent the air, the molten rocks that rained from the sky and the earthquakes that knocked men from their feet a hundred miles away.

"Without Doaphin t' prod them onwards, the horde fell into disarray. The foremost creatures trampled the ranks behind them as they stampeded away from the killing ground surrounding the Black Vengeance's swords.

"The Prince saw that this was their one chance t' escape, while Doaphin was distracted and his horde in confusion. The outcome o' the war now rested solely upon Lord Fennick's ability t' destroy the Stone.

"The Prince urged what was left o' his men up the treacherous slope o' the rockslide. He chose his best archers and joined them at the base o' the slide, launching volley after volley t' protect the difficult retreat. Prince Gralyre would no' quit the field until all of his men had made their escape.

"From atop the slide, my ancestor, Linus, and several Dream Weavers who had also managed t' make the climb, helped the retreating soldiers t' safety as best they could. Even so, the retreat had scarce begun when their one chance to survive was snatched away.

"Lord Fennick lost his battle afore all o' the men could retreat over the shifting rockslide. The Court Sorcerer came tumbling down the mountainside t' land at the Prince's feet.

"Prince Gralyre held Fennick's broken body in his arms and

wept, and such agony was on his face, that many o' his hardened soldiers shed tears with him. Their last hope for victory was lost, dashed t' the stones o' Centaur Pass.

"Doaphin returned t' his perch, and exhorted and threatened his horde t' attack once more. His mad laughter rang throughout the valley as the Prince, with only the handful o' warriors who had no' retreated, fought for their final survival. Doaphin's staff belched forth its deadly lightning once more.

"One by one, Gralyre's warriors were turned t' black stone, until no one stood by the Prince's side and he fought alone against the army o' darkness. So many o' Doaphin's creatures died under his sword that the ground turned red and bloody and ran with rivers o' it. But even his great strength could no' save him forever. Prince Gralyre was finally brought t' the ground by the sheer weight o' the numbers he faced.

"Only when the coward knew it t' be safe, did Doaphin climb down from the ledge where he had watched the battle. The horde parted for him as he walked t' where the Prince was held prisoner upon his knees.

"The usurper claimed Gralyre's great sword, so weak from his evil conjuring and his battle with Fennick, that he was barely able t' heft the weight o' it. He raised it on high, t' the thunderous cheers o' his army.

"When Doaphin approached the Prince, the victorious horde quieted, so that they might hear his words. Doaphin used some bit o' magic trickery t' amplify his speech, so that even the rocks vibrated with sound of his voice. Linus, atop the rockslide, could clearly hear every word he said.

"Prince Gralyre, held by two o' Doaphin's creatures, struggled still. The fight had no' yet left his body.

"'Ye should have surrendered when I gave ye the chance, Gralyre! Would ye like t' see what has become o' your betrothed?'

"Doaphin wove an image in the air and the fair Princess Genevieve appeared. Shorn o' her hair, her beautiful face distorted with terror, she floated with hands clawed as though fighting t' escape, trapped for all time in a crystal pillar in the throne room at Dreisenheld. A butterfly caught in amber."

Wil's voice assumed the evil, gloating tones of the usurper.

"'Worry not, my Prince, for she is no' dead. She but sleeps. She will sleep until the crystal lies shattered by the will o' your love for her. Since ye are about t' die, she will be trapped forever! Ye had the chance t' rescue her and ye allowed me t' torture her instead. What a lovely gift t' give me. But I feel so bad, for I have brought Ye nothing! Except your death!'

"Doaphin's mad laughter roared gustily from his thin chest, echoing like thunder. His horde laughed with him, and the sound rolled on forever.

"The Prince made a mighty effort t' break free o' Doaphin's restraining Demon Riders. Anguish over the fate o' his beloved contorted his face. But unable to escape, he stilled, and knelt proudly, even unto defeat, for he was a King to the end."

Wil's voice turned heroic and tragic.

"'Ye have one gift t' give me afore I die, Doaphin. Tell me your Word o' Binding, the un-maker o' your Stone! Tell me the one thing that could have vanquished ye. Let me go t' my death

with at least that!'

"Doaphin was unable t' resist gloating. He leaned close t' the Prince and whispered the Word, and whatever that word was, it seemed t' cause Gralyre a great shock, for he paled and sagged limply in the arms o' his captors.

"'Time for ye t' die!' yelled the evil sorcerer. He hefted Gralyre's sword but was too weak t' make a clean strike. So he spun around t' cock himself, t' swing the sword mightily in a great circle.

Doaphin aimed the blade t' kill all three o' the men in its path, no' just Prince Gralyre. The two 'Riders holding Gralyre's arms had also heard his secret word. They could no' be allowed t' live.

Such was the keenness o' the blade o' the Great Dragon Sword o' Lyre, that it passed through the neck o' the first man, and continued unchecked towards Prince Gralyre."

"What happened next, happened so fast, that t' this day, none can say with certainty what really occurred." Wil paused and leaned forward, playing on the intensity of the moment like any true storyteller would.

"As the blade touched Prince Gralyre's neck, there was a great flash o' light. Gralyre vanished and in his place, knelt Lord Fennick.

"It was too late for Doaphin t' turn the blade. It clove Fennick's head from his shoulders before killing the last 'Rider in the line.

"Lightning wreathed Gralyre's blade then, and Doaphin screamed as he was forced t' drop it. Doaphin's skin bubbled and blistered, and the hand that had held the sword withered and died. When the blade hit the ground, the Great Dragon Sword o' Lyre vanished, and has never been seen in the lands since.

"With his good hand, Doaphin held Fennick's severed head by its hair, screaming at it t' tell him where Gralyre and the Sword had gone!

"And the head spoke! The words rang like thunder from the air as Fennick's head pronounced this curse upon Doaphin.

Enigma rise from out o' mist,
Spirit waken with a roar,
Dragon perched on vengeful fist,
Fell Usurper rule no more!

"Doaphin's shout o' rage echoed up and down the length o' the valley, but still, it sounded small next t' the powerful voice o' doom pronounced by the head o' Lord Fennick! The horde dropped t' their knees and grovelled afore this great and terrible magic.

"Doaphin, incensed beyond reason, heaved the head into the midst o' them. It exploded in a great flash o' light and all the evil creatures standing near the spot fell into ash!

"Our ancestor, Linus, was jarred loose by the explosion, and tumbled back down the slope t' the waiting survivors o' Centaur Pass. He told them o' the Prince's fate and the prophecy o' hope.

"The Dream Weavers returned t' their lands, vowing t' heed the call o' the Black Prince should it ever come again.

"Broken and defeated, the remnants o' the Prince's Black

Vengeance travelled deep into the Heathren Mountains, where they fight t' this day." Wil pointed a finger at Gralyre. "Ye met some o' their descendants."

His eyes took on a far away gleam. "In Centaur Pass, stand the black statues, immortalizing the brave fallen o' the Prince's Black Vengeance."

Wil cleared his throat harshly. "'Tis also said," he continued sadly, "that if ye were t' travel t' evil Dreisenheld, ye would still see the beautiful Princess Genevieve trapped for all time within her crystal pillar." His story finished, Wil stared deeply into the fire, his eyes sparkling with unshed tears.

"Doaphin has never ventured forth from his stronghold again," Rewn added to his father's tale. "He is terrified o' the curse. Instead, he sends his creatures t' do his evil will."

For several long moments, all that was heard was the snapping of the fire, and the creaking of the trees as they bent in the wind. The four men sat in contemplation of the tale, quietly absorbing its flavour.

"How is it that Doaphin yet lives?" Gralyre broke the silence.

Wil snorted and shifted his legs to a more comfortable position. "A Sorcerer's life is long, boyo. His evil magic, stored in his Wizard Stone, sustains him."

"So if Lord Fennick had destroyed Doaphin's Wizard Stone, Doaphin would have been killed?"

"If no' killed outright, then at least greatly diminished in power. It would have depended upon how much o' his black soul had already been claimed by his Stone.

"The trick is t' discover the Word that binds the Sorcerer's soul and the Stone together." Wil clasped his hands in demonstration. "Without that Word, ye canno' unmake the binding. Since the Stone contains more and more o' the Sorcerer's soul as the years pass, the Stone is as capable o' defending itself as the Sorcerer is.

"That is why Lord Fennick failed," Wil said sadly, hitting his thigh with a closed fist. "He found the Stone, but did no' have the Word o' Binding t' unmake Doaphin's connection. As he did battle with the Stone t' discover that carefully hidden secret, Doaphin felt his tampering and attacked. Fennick was left t' fight on two fronts. If Doaphin had no' been at the battle, Lord Fennick, given time, would have overcome the Stone and discovered the Word. Doaphin would have been destroyed forever!"

Gralyre broke the ensuing silence within the small ring of firelight with another question. The one whose answer he dreaded the most. "What happened to the Prince and the sword?"

"Well, lad, that is why they call him the Lost Prince. No one knows what became o' him. Some believe he was killed by Doaphin on the field and the rest is just legend. Some think Lord Fennick hid him away, like the sword, and one day he will arise to fulfil the prophecy, and reclaim his throne. No one really knows.

"The truth may be that Fennick sent Gralyre t' the next valley, where the Prince lived out his days in hiding and was laid t' rest in a burial mound that ye may have found."

Wil raised a finger, "The sword, however, is another matter.

Legend tells o' a strange island that rose from the sea at the moment o' Lord Fennick's death. They say that the sword is hidden there, where Doaphin, though he tries, is unable t' reach it. It waits forever, for the Prince t' reclaim it."

Rewn leaned forward. "Did the story help ye at all, Gralyre? Have ye remembered anything?"

"No," Gralyre frowned. "It explained nothing. Why do I carry these things? Why do I have this scroll? This ring?"

"Well," Wil scratched at his ear, "I do no' believe ye t' be from the Southern Kingdoms, even though I suppose your accent could place ye from there."

Gralyre looked up in surprise, "I have an accent?"

Rewn and Dajin nodded in concert.

"There are only two thoughts that come t' my mind," Wil stated blandly. "Ye either wrote that note yourself, unawares, or ye are a spy."

"What?" Gralyre exclaimed.

"A Spy!" The expulsions sounded simultaneously from Dajin and Rewn.

Hothead Dajin leaped to his feet and went so far as to draw his sword.

"Sheath your blade!" Wil roared.

"But Da! If he is a spy we must…"

"Sit, Dajin. Ye will no' violate the hospitality o' my fire!"

Muttering angrily, Dajin sat back down, but his hand hovered over his pommel.

"What makes you believe this?" Gralyre demanded as his hand slowly released the hilt of his dagger, clasped in defense.

"The facts, lad," Wil held out his hands and began to list his reasons upon his fingers. "First, ye have a Sorcerer's powers, yet ye have survived t' adulthood. Doaphin kills every adept that he finds, t' prevent competition.

"Second, there is no way that ye could be the Legend come t' life, so where did ye get your wealth? Doaphin controls the only wealth in this land. Any human with that amount o' coin is a collaborator, plain and simple.

"Third, ye announce your presence in such a way that if there are any members o' the resistance in the area they are going t' take notice o' ye.

"Fourth, ye conveniently have no knowledge o' who ye are. Doaphin has tried t' infiltrate spies before, but we always spot them when Catrian looks within their minds. They can no' hide their thoughts or their past. But ye can!

"Fifth, and this be the worst, ye ranted something terrible while the fever had ye. The Demon Lord recognized ye."

"Gods!" Gralyre choked, sitting back with slumped shoulders. The man's logic was irrefutable and his mind reeled with the implications.

"Wait, Catrian lived to adulthood! She has powers. How is it she survived?" Gralyre grasped at any lifeline to keep from sinking into the whirlpool of Wil's compelling logic.

"She came t' us young and was protected in the Heathren Mountains from the Woman Tithe and Doaphin. Even so, she is a constant target for Doaphin's minions. If ye were one o' us, we would know o' ye. If ye were no' one o' us, Doaphin would have had your gizzards for breakfast afore ye were grown."

Gralyre felt sick to his stomach as he looked at Wil, Dajin and Rewn. To think he could be harbouring a soul as black as the Demon Riders who had murdered his family, as black as Lord Mallach's! Bile pushed against the back of his throat.

"'Tis only a possibility, lad," Wil said gently to soothe his obvious distress, "but it suits the facts. Ye could be a spy, and no' even know it."

Gralyre leaned forward decisively. "Then I cannot continue to travel with you. 'Tis placing you in too much danger." If he were to regain his memories, would he turn on the men? Would he be able to stop himself?

"No, lad, ye must come with us," Wil insisted. "If ye are a spy, we must bring ye t' Catrian, t' be interrogated and dealt with. If ye are no' a spy, we must still bring ye before her that we may discover who ye really are, and where ye found the Lost Prince's treasure." He waved at the glittering hoard still spread out upon the ground.

"If ye found Gralyre's tomb, it may yet contain knowledge that could help us defeat Doaphin. Gralyre would never have taken Doaphin's Word o' Binding t' his grave! Imagine what a weapon that would be! Either way, ye could be carrying important knowledge, knowledge we must have, and only Catrian has the power t' retrieve it!"

"I understand your reasoning, but I cannot believe myself to be a spy, or a tomb robber," said Gralyre with quiet dignity. "However, I must find out who I am, and this seems the only way."

He sighed deeply before pinning Wil with his pensive gaze.

He recognized that until the questions surrounding his lost past were answered he was as good as their prisoner. "I give you my word that I will not try to escape, nor seek to do you or yours any harm, nor allow harm to come to you."

"'Tis good that ye give us your parole, lad, because we will no' be able t' contact the resistance again until the spring. There is no way t' reach the mountains afore the passes are snowed in."

"Spring?" Gralyre rasped, then he cleared his throat. It was too long to wait for his answers, so long to live with the knowledge that he could be a treacherous spy! "What shall you do with me in the meantime?"

"We will bring ye home with us," said Wil decisively. "I will tell the neighbours that ye are a cousin, come t' help us with the farm. A refugee. There be plenty enough o' those in these dark days. In the spring, we will start for Verdalan."

Gralyre nodded his consent to the arrangements.

"Good," said Wil firmly and his gaze roved over Gralyre's face. "In the morning we will cut the hair off ye. Then I challenge anyone in Raindell t' recognize ye when we return."

Wil stood, stretched mightily, and moved towards his sleeping pallet. He clapped a hand to Gralyre's shoulder in passing. "For what 'tis worth, lad, I do no' think ye a spy," he said gravely. With another fatherly pat on the shoulder he moved off.

"What a wonderful choice," Gralyre said cynically to Rewn and Dajin as he scooped up his belongings and retied them into their neat bundles. "I am either a mad grave robber or the spy of an evil usurper!"

Rewn stood to follow after his father. Dajin joined him quickly as though afraid to be left alone at the fire with Gralyre.

"If 'tis any consolation," Rewn said with a quirky grin lifting his mouth, "I agree with me Da. I think ye are mad."

Gralyre rolled his eyes appreciatively at the dig, and felt his anxiety relax just the tiniest of fractions.

With a shout of laughter Dajin clasped his brother about the shoulders, his fear of Gralyre dissipated by his brother's quip. Laughing heartily, the two brothers headed for their sleeping pallets. "Good eve'n t' ye, my Prince," Dajin mocked Gralyre in a falsetto voice. Still giggling to himself, he flopped upon his pallet.

Gralyre found his own bed. Soon after, the sounds of sleep drifted into the night wind, but for Gralyre, rest was a long time in coming. Shivers of revulsion sent gooseflesh popping up over his body.

'Am I in league with the Demon Riders? Am I Doaphin's unwitting spy? The Count said he recognized me...'

'Little Wolf?'

The wolfdog was curled up next to him to share the warmth on this cool fall evening. Little Wolf lifted his head and stared at him inquiringly.

'Am I a good man, or an evil man? Do I smell wrong, like the Demon Riders?'

Little Wolf had seen his mind and had experienced the Nightmare. On two occasions, he had recognized the Demon Riders by the scent of their taint.

'You are good!' exclaimed Little Wolf, poking Gralyre in the

face with his cold, wet nose.

'Thank-you, Little Wolf!'

Greatly reassured, Gralyre wrapped the pup in a bear hug, and ruffled his ears while Little Wolf squirmed happily at the attention. Content within himself that he was no spy, no matter what the others thought, Gralyre drifted to sleep.

ଛୀର୍ଷ

Far away to the west, where the mouth of the great Dreisenscal River meets with the ocean, an evil presence flits through the fishing village of Ghent. It searches for the enemy of the Master. One of Its many minions has told It of a battle that has been fought here. The strife has drawn It as carrion draws flies.

But the Man, for whom It searches, is not here, has never been here. The battle has been naught but a raid by pirates. It must seek elsewhere for Its prey. The Master will not be pleased.

Out of revenge It kills the minion for its error, for taking It so far off the spoor of the Hunt. It makes no effort to hide the body. It knows when the sun's rays touch the corpse it will flame into dust. It moves off into the night, not yet sated by the murder.

A stray dog growls from the shadows as It passes through the village. Without pause, It skewers the animal with one of Its mighty talons, and shoves the squirming beast into Its mouth.

The bones crunch deliciously, but the dog does little to alleviate Its rapacious appetite. However, It dares not stop to feed further as the night is almost spent. It must soon find shelter from the sun.

It shuffles along the rocky coast in search of a cave. It glories in the gouges It carves in the living rock with Its claws. It loses itself momentarily in the fantasy that the rock is the soft flesh of a Human. It hisses with a pleasure that is almost sexual. Tomorrow, Sethreat promises Itself. Tomorrow It will return to the village to feed.

ಬಾಡ

Gralyre awoke before the others, as the sun was teasing the horizon. He stood and stretched, feeling twinges of pain from his ribs. He had been lying in a sickbed for long enough. Before he left his pallet, he strapped his sword around his narrow waist, and pulled on his borrowed pair of boots.

He made his way down the long familiar trail, to the edge of the river where he had laid his family to rest. He spent long moments there, remembering them, grieving.

Closing his eyes, Gralyre allowed the peacefulness of the spot to wash over him. Though it assuaged his hurt, it could do nothing to pacify the rage that still burned in his heart. There was only one thing that would quench that.

Shaking free from thoughts of revenge, he returned to the farm and distracted himself with some light stretching, careful of his mending body. He had no wish for a relapse, not if it meant more doses of Wil's foul medicine. When he finished stretching, he turned his face upwards to the sunrise and sought for the pulse of the dance.

Slowly Gralyre began the forms of the lethal exercise. The movements felt sloppy and weak after his long illness, but it still felt good to be using his muscles. It felt good to feel the cool morning sun beating upon his body.

℘℩℺

Rewn awoke, rolled over, and saw that Gralyre was missing. He bolted upward and grabbed his sword, certain the man had fled during the night, for who would not after being labelled a mad spy?

Little Wolf, who had sleepily moved into the warm spot on the pallet when Gralyre had risen, lifted his head and gazed curiously at Rewn, wondering what the sudden panic was about.

Rewn heaved a sigh and relaxed his grip on the sword. If the man's wolf was still here, then so was the man. He raked his fingers through his light brown hair and sheathed his sword. He would go looking for him.

He pulled on his boots, and tramped into the farmyard. He stopped short in wonder as he found his quarry. Quietly, he sat down to watch.

In spite of the chill of the day, Gralyre was stripped to the waist. The sunlight glinted off the light sheen of sweat on his powerful bronzed back as it flexed and rippled with his movements. His torso was mottled with black, blue and yellowed bruises. Rewn marvelled that the man's strength allowed him to move at all. But move he did.

Rewn had never seen the like. Gralyre swung the sword deftly and surely, one move flowed like liquid into the next. Rewn was mesmerized as he watched the shining blade dance through the sword patterns.

"Well I be dammed," came a hushed voice from above his head.

Rewn glanced up to his father as Wil squatted down next to him. His father's eyes remained locked upon Gralyre's form. "Do ye know what that is son?"

Rewn shook his head.

"He spoke o' it last night, as he told his story, but I confess, I did no' believe him. But this, now, I must believe. The Sword Dance," he breathed in awe.

"Long ago there were men that so excelled at the art o' weaponry and war that when one saw them practice their art it resembled a dance. I had the story at the knee o' me Great Grandfather. Himself never saw it, nor his father's father, but he had the story from his Great Grandfather. During festival times, the Sword Masters would put on a display o' arms for the King. 'Tis a lost art. Doaphin killed everyone who practised it, and out-lawed the songs that celebrated the Dance o' the Swords. The closest t' it that I have ever seen was at a festival in a resistance camp in the mountains some thirty seasons ago... until now. And that was naught but a poor copy o' what we are seeing here!" Absently, Wil clasped a hand onto Rewn's shoulder.

"Da?" Rewn whispered hesitantly. "Is it possible? I know 'tis folly... but... could he be...?"

"'Tis an old wives' tale, son," Wil stated definitively.

Rewn nodded in agreement, "Of course." Though his eyes

were troubled as he turned back to watch the stranger.

Gralyre executed a particularly intricate move. He got only half way through before he gasped and clamped his arms to his ribs. The sword tumbled to the ground with a clang. He breathed shallowly though his mouth until the pain eased, back hunched over to reduce the pressure on his side. Gradually, the cramp receded. He reclaimed the blade and used it ingloriously as a cane until he had the strength to stand upright again.

"Where did ye learn t' do that, boyo?" Wil asked from where he and Rewn sat.

Startled, Gralyre whirled about, his body automatically assuming an aggressive crouch, the sword at the ready. He relaxed immediately as he spied the two men. "I do not know," he shrugged as he sheathed his blade. "'Tis but another of my strange skills," he said defensively.

"Well, lad," said Wil, levering himself to his feet and dusting his hands. "If ye are well enough t' exercise, ye are well enough t' ride."

"Rewn, get your strop and razor and help Gralyre trim up that hair. We do no' want t' be seen travelling with an escaped prisoner."

CHAPTER EIGHTEEN

Beaurice was a large woman with a face that was cast to scare grown men, which worked to her advantage. She was in charge of the fortress' stores of food and weaponry, and ruled the measures with an iron fist. Nothing escaped the Quartermistress' notice, and no one received more than their fair share. The woman wore a crisp white apron over a dung coloured dress that exactly matched the colour of the fat braids of muddy, grey hair that dangled down beside her heavy jowls. She had all the warmth of a glacier fed stream.

Dara quickly learned to keep a respectful distance from the woman's energetic gesticulating as she was given the brisk penny tour of the Northern Fortress on the way to her assigned quarters.

The Rebel hunting party that had brought her the rest of the way from Verdalan to the resistance stronghold had abandoned her unceremoniously with the Quartermistress. Muddy, forlorn and road-weary, Dara was too exhausted to pay attention to Beaurice's running dialogue, and had already forgotten the way to the locations that had been pointed out in passing, such as the communal laundry, and the medical area.

The tent city was arranged in neat, military grids and avenues that all looked identical to her eyes. She would have to start over in the morning when she was better rested. All she craved was the bed she had been promised.

"I have t' get back t' the stores, so this must be quick. They will rob me blind if I am away for too long!" Beaurice groused. "So pay attention. The camp is split into four districts o' two thousand people. Each district is located 'round one o' the four gates; North, South, East and West. Ye will be quartered in the Southern District."

"Each district is overseen by three Stewards. Among other things, they assign all work details such as the hunting parties that supplement their district's meat supply, and the warriors for the sentry rotations at their designated gates. They also adjudicate all petty disputes. Any larger disputes or crimes are t' be taken before the Commanders. Each Steward reports directly t' me."

Dara glanced around at the bustle of activity. She had never seen so many people in one place in her life, and never so many women and children. Still, eight thousand people, not all of them warriors, seemed a paltry number for a resistance effort that she had been hearing stories of for her entire life. She put the question to the Quartermistress.

"This is no' the only resistance stronghold in the land, nor the only one in the Heathrens. Only the Commanders know how many strongholds there are, and their locations. Should one fortress be overrun by Deathren, or Stalkers or 'Riders, they will no' get all o' us."

Beaurice returned to her tour patter with single-minded devotion. "As I said, your district is t' be the Southern District. Should we need t' flee, all items in the camp are designed t' be broken down and packed up within minutes. Learn how your tent folds, 'tis your responsibility, as well as any other duties that the Stewards assign t' ye. In the event o' a withdrawal, your district will exit through the Southern Gate. Listen t' your Stewards. They oversee the evacuation." Beaurice paused and swung around, hands and arms flailing mightily as she emphasized her point.

Dara ducked in the nick of time.

"They each be charged with leading the retreat by a route no' taken by the other three districts. In this way, we can scatter and divide any pursuit by Doaphin's forces. The Stewards are the only ones t' know o' the new mustering place, so do no' get lost." She finished wagging her finger, spun on her heel and was off with a long legged stride.

Dara had to trot to keep apace with her down the sloping avenues between the rows of tents laid out with military unanimity.

The rebellion's Northern Fortress rested near the summit of one of the taller mountains in the Heathren range. The south side of the fort overlooked the valley, and as such commanded a great view of the surrounding area. No army, or small group for that matter, could approach without being in constant view of the camp for almost two days.

The north side was nestled protectively against the mountainside. Should an army manage to approach unseen, their only avenue of direct attack was from the downward slope, giving the Rebels the tactical advantage of the high ground. At the mountain summit, neatly stacked lumber awaited a flame, as a signal to the other Rebel troops in the area should there be need.

At the Southern Gate, controlling all access, two sentries stood guard outside of small gatehouses that were attached to the palisade to either side of the open portal. Fifteen feet above, other warriors paced the catwalk attached to the inside of the wooden wall, their eyes trained through the sharpened pickets to the countryside beyond, searching, always searching, for signs of the enemy.

Three men lounged on chairs around a table inside one of the gatehouses, rolling dice. Beaurice gestured them over. "This here is Jarrod, Hofar and Strier," she named them as they arrived. "They have Stewardship o' the Southern District. If ye have a grievance, ye see them. Ye need supplies? Ye see them. Is that understood?"

Dara nodded to the three men, "Hello, sirs. I am Dara, my father is Wil Wilson who aids the resistance from Raindell."

"So polite, pigeon? Where are your menfolk now?" Hofar's teeth flashed white and strong as he took her hand in a firm grip. He was a handsome young man, with well-groomed hair and kind brown eyes. His beard was clipped short and neat and his clothing was spotless.

Dara fought the tears of homesickness that suddenly prickled. When had someone last shown her kindness? "They will be travelling from Raindell in the spring. I had t' come ahead t' avoid the Tithe."

Strier nudged Jarrod, and the two men shared a look and a secret grin. Dara felt a prickle of unease, and decided immediately that these two were not to be trusted.

"The Tithe?" Hofar shook his head sympathetically. "Tsk,

tsk. How horrible it is t' be a woman o' the lowlands! No' t' worry. We will take good care o' ye, pigeon," he promised with another toothy smile. He hauled her close by the hand he still held, and threw an arm over her shoulders, anchoring her to his side.

Dara felt very uncomfortable, but was too weary to struggle free. She did not wish to seem ungrateful or contrary to people who were showing her a kindness. His flashing white teeth were no doubt meant to set her at ease, not increase her disquiet.

Jarrod stepped between Dara and Beaurice's concerned glare at Hofar's familiarity. "Do no' worry Quartermistress, we will see t' the little lowlander's bivouac." His smile was oily in its sincerity, pulling at his cratered and pockmarked face. Where Hofar was handsome, Jarrod was unwashed and unkempt, his long ratted hair dangled straight from a fringe around his bald pate. The black soil entrenched in the pores of his face made it difficult to estimate his age.

Dara tried not to wrinkle her nose as the light breeze wafted an odour of unwashed body into her face. She switched to breathing through her mouth and tried to pay attention to what was being said. She was so very tired.

"Yea, she is going t' like it here," Strier sniggered, setting his slabs of fat jiggling over his massive, barrel chest. He ran a hand over his hairless head and brushed down the ends of a large moustache that drooped over his upper lip. His hard, glittering eyes swung from Dara to Jarrod and back again.

Dara craned her neck to meet Strier's small black eyes that had all but disappeared into folds of ample flesh. The man was a giant, in both height and form. His pug nose was still wrinkled up with his grin. He was missing a tooth. Something deep inside curdled, as did the smile she tried to give him in return.

"Humph. See t' it that she is quartered and given duties," was Beaurice's parting command as she turned briskly and walked away. Dara resisted the urge to call the woman back.

Jarrod's smile fled the moment Beaurice was out of sight. "Cowardly little lowlander," he spat. "Ye thought ye could come t' the camps and be one o' us? A Rebel? Ye have no' earned the right!" His hand lashed out and struck Dara hard across the face.

Dara cried out and her hand cupped her burning cheek. Hofar held her to his side, not letting her go. Dara searched his face. The warm understanding of moments ago had been replaced by amusement. There would be no help from that quarter. She felt the blood drain from her head, leaving her dizzy with fear.

"Nobody eats for free. Ye want food and shelter? Ye have t' work!" Strier moved in, his jowls twisted in a leer. His beefy hand grabbed Dara's breast and squeezed.

Dara yelped and twisted away from the pain, but could not escape Hofar's anchoring arm. She looked to the guards on the walls, but the men there were studious in their averted stares. She was shocked to her core by this assault. Why did they hate her? It was not her fault that Da had raised his children in the lowlands.

Hofar shook Dara to regain her attention. "So, pigeon. What are we t' do with ye?"

"I... I can work. I can do laundry, chop wood, cook, clean," Dara outlined her domestic skills desperately.

Jarrod's pocked face grew mottled and red with rage. He lashed out with a blow that split Dara's lip. "I have a cook!"

As Dara's head snapped back, her numbness gave way to terror. What was going on? Would nobody help her? Hofar's arm tightened to keep her from falling.

Strier's leer became even more tainted as he rubbed a hard thumb cruelly over Dara's cringing lip, spreading the blood. "And a laundress!"

Dara began to cry. Oh, surely not? Surely these were not the valiant heroes that her father had told her of, the brave and noble resistance fighters who protected the weak from Doaphin's tyranny? It was a mistake, it must be a mistake!

Hofar sighed sadly, "And a woodsman t' chop, and a maid t' clean. What else can ye give t' us, pigeon? Hmm? However shall ye earn your keep?"

෪෮෯

After almost a month at the desolated farm awaiting Gralyre's recovery, the men had been convinced that there was no pursuit from Tarangria. As such, for the remainder of their journey to Raindell, Wil had set a slower pace of travel out of deference to Gralyre's still healing wounds.

What Demon Rider patrols had been on the road, had been easily avoided with the forewarnings supplied by Little Wolf. They had ghosted through the deserted lands without causing a ripple of disturbance.

The men now hovered at the edge of the forest overlooking

the village of Raindell, carefully scanning the area for anything untoward before they moved on to Wil's croft.

"Keep your head down if we should meet anyone," Wil cautioned Gralyre with a worried frown. Though Gralyre had been shorn of his ragged beard and overlong hair, his face still retained the fading bruises of his injuries, which would be sure to draw comment. Wil had given Gralyre a floppy brimmed hat to hide under, but even so, the man's powerful frame and proud stance marked him. Gralyre did not possess the body language of a downtrodden peasant.

"My croft is on the far side o' Raindell. 'Tis a small place, and the rents are high, but it feeds us well enough," Wil told Gralyre modestly.

"What we canno' grow, we poach from the forest!" quipped Dajin. At a sharp look from his father, he hastily amended his statement with a wide grin. "I mean borrow."

Gralyre felt a churning in his gut as he looked down at the village. He had little desire to be any closer. "Do we need to enter?" His lip curled in distaste. Mementoes of his last encounter with Raindell were still healing.

"No," Will answered. "We stay clear o' the village, unless a town assembly is called."

Rewn crouched at the forest's edge, his keen gaze searching the rotting walls of the village, looking for any telltale hints of spying eyes or hidden Demon Riders. "The poor wretches would have a better life were they t' move away from that diseased hole, but they are too frightened. Living without the walls o' a town t' protect ye, brings about its own risks," he admitted grimly. He stood and dusted his hands. "All clear, Da." He quickly remounted.

"We are more than a match for those dangers!" Dajin boasted airily.

"Careful, son. T' flaunt yourself in the face o' those dangers does no' but invite the Gods o' Fortune t' prove ye wrong," Wil warned in a tone that suggested he was often obliged to school Dajin with this old adage.

Dajin hung his head rebelliously at the slight rebuke, his light mood of a moment ago forgotten as they moved out.

They kept to the shadows of the forest's edge as they skirted the village. Gralyre's herd of horses followed obediently behind to their master's command.

Gralyre sighed heavily at the oppressive atmosphere caused by Dajin's brooding. He was glad they had reached their journey's end for Dajin's sulks were wearing thin. At any rebuke from Wil, he was prone to slide into a foul mood.

The boy had no common sense. Were he ever to harness his spirit, he would become a formidable man but he was too often ruled by his emotions and not by his mind. This made him unpredictable and more dangerous to himself than to an enemy.

If not for his father and brother watching over him, Gralyre suspected that Dajin would never have attained adulthood in these troubled times, where to go unnoticed was the best survival practice.

Rewn was his brother's opposite and very much his father's son. Where Dajin was mercurial, Rewn was steadfast, thoughtful and in control. Though he paid his father every deference,

Gralyre could sense a budding disquiet in Rewn to be his own man. It could not be easy for him to be caught in the constant push-pull between his father and brother.

Though he had treated Gralyre with kindness, Rewn had maintained a distance from all overtures of friendship; the cool courtesy afforded an uninvited guest. Gralyre recognized that he had no desire to befriend one who was like to be going to his death as a spy in Verdalan in the spring.

Still, Gralyre could not discount the danger that the Wilsons bearded by sparing his life, by giving him the benefit of the doubt that he was not a spy. Indeed, they had nursed him to health and, at great personal risk, would now house him over the winter. Gralyre had but one coin with which to repay them.

He was not blind to the fact that Rewn watched him practice every morning. The man's longing for the knowledge he could gain was palpable. If nothing else, perhaps Gralyre could earn his keep. "If you like, I will teach Rewn and Dajin the sword," he offered to Wil.

Rewn smiled broadly. "Ye will teach us t' do as ye do?"

Gralyre nodded his agreement.

Even Dajin pulled himself from his sulk to smile in anticipation.

Wil grinned at Gralyre. "That will be fine, lad, just fine!" He kicked his tired horse into a canter. "Come on, boyos! We are almost home!" He burst from the forest, making for a small farm in the near distance.

With whoops of pleasure Rewn and Dajin raced to catch their father. For a moment Gralyre held his mount back, watching the three men shrug their hard life from their shoulders to enjoy the simple, unguarded moment of pleasure. Gralyre could not long resist the urge.

'Run, Little Wolf!' With a wild grin he spurred his mount and raced after the men, the pup loping easily beside him. From behind came the rattle of hooves as the rest of the herd followed their lead.

The croft, when they reached it, was a pleasing surprise to Gralyre. Although not prosperous, it was neat and well kept. Stone hedges surrounded fields of sparsely growing grain, ripe for harvesting, despite the meagre harvest it would be. Leaning against the backside of a small cottage was a large enclosure for firewood. A smaller stone barn placed a small distance away sheltered what grain stores and farming equipment that the family had.

Wil surveyed his golden fields with a cynical eye as he reined in his mount. "Nothing has grown well since Doaphin's occupation. 'Tis as if the land itself rebels against him!" he said bitterly, spitting on the barren ground. "At one time, my ancestors were lords in this province. But that was taken from us long ago."

"It could be that our seed stock is bad," Rewn suggested as he swung himself to the ground. "But there is no place t' find fresh seed. There has been naught but famine for a hundred years. No one will trade what they need for survival." He indicated the fields with a sweep of his arm. "We are lucky t' even have this much growing."

"No' that it matters," Dajin broke in bitterly as he slid from his saddle. "The garrison at Brannock takes three parts o' four in rents! 'Tis no wonder the land and all upon it are dying!"

Wil clapped Dajin on the back, and handed him the reins to his horse. "Dajin, get theses horses hidden in the barn before suspicious eyes turn our way."

"We could turn them loose," Gralyre suggested as he dismounted and gave his horse a rough pat of affection. "They can forage for themselves, and they will not wander if I tell them to stay close."

"We have no way o' explaining where the horses have come from. If they are seen, we will be branded Rebels, or worse," Rewn explained as he passed Dajin the reins to his and Gralyre's mounts. Dajin led them towards the small outbuilding set back from the cottage.

"What's worse?" Gralyre took a moment to order his herd to follow Dajin.

"Collaborators."

Wil unlocked the door to the cottage and swung it wide. "Welcome t' my home, Gralyre," he swept an arm back to indicate that Gralyre should proceed him over the stoop.

The small cottage was of stone with a thatch roof, similar in form and function to the one that Gralyre had left behind at the death of his wolf pack. The similarity ended there, for this was a home, with the trappings and warmth that bespoke a well-loved place. It had a common room with four small sleeping alcoves built into the walls. Colourful rugs were hung in front of each alcove for privacy. A small wooden table, nicked and polished from years of use, sat opposite the fireplace with four benches set around it. Cooking utensils hung neatly off the mantle of the hearth. In the corner, near to the fire, sat a large, ornately carved armchair. Its quality far surpassed the rest of the rude furnishings, a family heirloom that bespoke a once proud heritage. Carefully stitched pillows cushioned its back. A pile of mending rested in a heap beside it. There was one window by the door, shuttered to keep out the wind and weather.

Wil drew back one of the rugs of an alcove. "Ye can rest here, Gralyre. We will make an early night o' it, so that we can have an early start."

Gralyre raised a brow in question.

"Tomorrow we begin the harvest."

ಬಂದ

In the following weeks, Gralyre worked with the men to bring in their meagre harvest. His still recovering body was not up to the heavy task of swinging a scythe all day, so he followed behind, binding the shorn stalks into sheaves and arranging these into stooks. After the grain had dried in the late fall sun, the threshing began.

They worked long hours to separate the dried grain from the chaff before the weather turned bleak. Rewn, Dajin and Wil took turns threshing the grain from the stalks, while Gralyre worked the winnowing baskets with whoever was not on the flail.

"Why do you not hide some of the grain away?" Gralyre asked Rewn, as he measured the pitiful yield they had netted from their efforts so far. The air glowed golden from the motes of crushed grasses that had been teased aloft by the breeze. The haze gilded his view of the twenty sacks of barley stacked neatly against the barn's wall.

Rewn's arms rose and fell in a tireless rhythm as he worked. "The spies will have already marked how much grain our fields will have yielded. The garrison will demand payment on that basis and no other. If we canno' meet the tax, we will be burned out and left homeless, perhaps even taken as slaves until we have worked off our debts." Rewn flailed with slightly more heat. "Every year they leave us just enough grain t' seed our fields, every year we lose a little more ground." Through his heavy sheen of sweat, Rewn's face was grim. Harvest was not the joyful time of celebration as in centuries past.

Wil scooped up a pile of loose grain in his winnowing basket and tossed it high in the air so the wind could tease loose the chaff. "Gralyre, we need t' talk about your horses. We do no' have food for them for the winter, and they canno' be here when the tax collectors comes calling."

Gralyre shrugged, tossing and catching his own measure of barley. Chaff danced and twisted away in the breeze, adding to the golden dust that danced in the sunlight that streamed into the barn through the open doors. "As I said, I can turn them loose in the forest. They will remain unseen."

Wil paused in his labour to pull out a kerchief and wipe the sweat and grime from the back of his neck. "Well, t' that, lad. I know how ye feel about them, but do ye think ye could spare one for slaughter?"

Gralyre froze. Eat one of his horses? "Ah," he hedged, "Wil, you need to understand that I hear their thoughts, I know what they think, what they dream, what they hope. I cannot look on them as food."

"Ye hunt deer!" Dajin glared suspiciously.

"Yes," Gralyre said patiently. "Animal minds that I touch for only a moment. I do not talk to them. Would you eat your brother?"

Rewn grinned at Dajin. "Careful how ye answer, brother!"

Dajin glowered. "'Tis no' the same!"

Gralyre's face went flat and hard. "I will see to it that your family has plenty of meat during the winter. But I will not slaughter one of my horses."

Wil shrugged. "I was no' suggesting the animal for our consumption, but as a bribe. We might have used the meat to buy back some of the grain... But no matter. The preening little collaborator would as like t' have taxed us for having a store o' meat on hand and then charged us with poaching. Just watch, he will be arriving the moment we finish the threshing."

⅏⅏⅏

Wil's prediction proved correct. Almost to the day that they finished processing the fields, an official party of twenty Demon Riders with several wagons pulled by draft horses arrived at the farm to collect the rents. Shuffling behind the wagons, a ragged string of men with metal collars about their necks, and shackles on their ankles, were whipped to a halt.

A gilded, closed carriage, pulled by a team of sleek black

horses came to a shuddering stop. The driver jumped down and opened the door, while a page scurried to the back of the carriage and started to unpack equipment.

With much ceremony, the Tax Master debarked from his ornate vehicle. His page quickly set up a desk in the yard and ceremoniously laid a gold bound book upon it. A folding chair was set before the desk, with a pillow of red velvet to cushion the seat. The taxman threw back his robe with all the flourish of a king as he took his place behind the record book.

During all the affectations, Rewn shuffled closer to Gralyre and murmured, "He's a collaborator who serves the Council o' Raindell. The Council are the human lap dogs o' the Demon Lord. I believe ye met Councilman Cramer afore he was put t' death?"

Gralyre nodded at the grim memory. "I thought the local Demon Lord was dead? Catrian killed him. Would Doaphin be aware of his murder already?"

Rewn nodded. "They know when something happens t' one o' their own. I'm sure Doaphin has redistributed his wealth t' another by now. The new Lord will be well entrenched in the fortress up in Brannock. This year, the collaborators will be doubly vigilant in order t' impress their new master."

"And the slaves?" Gralyre asked, his lips barely moving. One by one, their irons were being struck as they were released from the line and ordered forward.

"Men who could no' make the rent," Rewn's reply was whisper soft.

The Tax Master settled himself and opened the heavy tome,

laying aside a strip of purple velvet that marked his place. His page stood with stiff attention at his shoulder holding a silver tray upon which an inkwell and feathered quill rested.

With elaborate ceremony, the taxman ran his finger down a column. Finding the entry he sought, he motioned to a Demon Rider.

"Forty." He pronounced the levy in a nasal whine of a voice. The 'Rider nodded and cracked his whip. The slaves shuffled to the barn and began to emerge with the harvest. As they loaded sack after sack of grain, the Tax Master made a careful notation in the book. He did not talk to Wil or his sons. They did not exist to him.

When the slaves were finished loading the wagons, only ten sacks would be left in the barn. These remaining stores, the family dared not touch if they were going to sow a winter crop. It was Doaphin's philosophy of rule that healthy starvation kept the peasants docile.

"Who is this man?" demanded the Tax Master, speaking for the first time. "The big burley serf, who thinks he can look me in the eye."

It took Gralyre a moment to realize that he meant him, and that he was indeed glaring. He quickly ducked his head, assuming a more passive mien.

"He is our cousin, Master Findlay, come t' live with us," Rewn bowed smoothly.

The Tax Master made a greedy calculation. "After the Tithe o' the girl, I was told that only three live here. Since it be four, the rent is higher. What else do ye have t' offer me?"

"We have nothing left!" Dajin raged as he took a step forward with his hands fisted for battle. "Ye 'ave taken every bloody thing we own!"

The Demon Riders drew their swords. The rasp of metal caused a deadly stillness to fall over the farmyard. Even the slaves froze in their labours.

Rewn's hand lashed out and pulled his brother back, though Dajin struggled and tried to throw off his grip. "Hst! Dajin! Be silent!" But the damage had already been done.

The Tax Master leaned back in his chair with a chilling smile. "Control that pup or we will do so ourselves!"

At a frightened, censorious glare from Wil, Dajin grudgingly relaxed into a sullen silence. Rewn kept a firm hold on him all the same.

"I apologize for me son, m'lord," Wil said quickly into the silence, and bowed submissively. "He is young and unwise in the way o' the world."

"Threatening an official mission," pronounced the Tax Master, "will cost ye extra!" He sneered at Wil's obsequious bow. "Ye are lucky I do no' take his head for his insolence!"

Dajin's face paled, and Rewn's breath suspended in fear. Wil did not move from his low bow as his eyes clenched shut, awaiting the blow of the Tax Master's decision.

Gralyre's attention flicked from one soldier to the next, planning his strategy. He subtly shifted his body into better balance for a fight.

"Four Dicts fine for threatening me, plus another Two Dicts fine for your cousin's presence on the land! Pay me now or I will burn ye out and ye can work off your debt in the slave line!"

A quiet sigh that may have been a prayer of thanks escaped Wil as he straightened from his bow. "Thank ye, sir, for sparing me son!" But beneath the gladness for Dajin's life, Wil was pale with desperation.

Rewn and Dajin were frozen in place, their eyes on their father. They knew as well as he did that this levy would ruin them. They did not have six gold coins to give. 'Twas a fortune.

To Gralyre it was obvious that the Wilsons did not have the scratch to pay the fine. He had the coin but dared not offer the Tax Master money, as it would be too difficult to explain how he had come by such a large sum. He must give up one of his horses.

Gralyre silently called a horse, forbidding the rest of the herd from following the one he had chosen from out of the forest where he had hidden them.

He would have to present the animal in such a way that this petty bureaucrat would feel he had the upper hand. If the payment were to come too quickly, he could become suspicious and demand additional payment out of greed. The beautiful irony was that every one of his horses was the stolen property of the Demon Riders, and he would be paying their tax with their own goods.

"Well? I am waiting."

"One moment, m'lord," Wil said smoothly and motioned his sons and Gralyre to his side.

When they had come close, Wil looked at Gralyre with quiet desperation. "Ye have the money t' save us, lad. I have no right t' ask, but…"

"Da, no," Rewn whispered back, "it will only make things worse. If he sees Gralyre's gold, there will be questions about how he came by it. And the Gods only know what will happen if he sees the old kingdom's coins!"

Wil hung his head, and cursed. "I know, but what other choice do we have?"

Dajin looked away, and a muscle in his jaw jumped as he ground his teeth in frustration.

"Just wait," Gralyre said with a small smile.

"What?" Wil's head lifted.

"He is almost here…"

The horse rounded the side of the cottage, and Gralyre reacted with surprise and chagrin, laying it on thickly, but the Tax Master was convinced.

"Who owns this horse?"

"I do, if it please your honour." Gralyre ducked his head and pulled on his forelock. He sensed the surprised stiffness of Wil and his sons and could only hope Dajin would not endanger the play. The horse trotted up to Gralyre, nickering in greeting and butting its head against his chest.

"Can ye no' see that he luvs me, your honour? He's the only thing what's mine in the world. Please do no' take him, your honour! Please!" Gralyre begged pathetically, and even managed to squeeze out a tear.

The Tax Master puffed out his weak chest. "I *will* take the beast. It will cover the fine nicely!" It was obvious to Gralyre that he enjoyed the power he wielded through his position.

"No!" Gralyre cried out in grand anguish as one of the guards grabbed the bridle of the horse and wrenched it away. It was soon tied to the back of the Tax Master's personal carriage.

The Tax Master banged his gavel, ignoring Gralyre's wailing as he made a notation in the large book. "Wil Wilson, your duty t' the Lord has been discharged. I have marked your rent, tax and fine as paid in full." With that, he replaced the ribbon, snapped the book closed and stood. The page quickly packed up the book and table.

"Let this be a lesson t' ye!" the Tax Master lectured arrogantly to the four oppressed men. With an over-exaggerated wave of his wrist he summoned his slaves and Demon Riders. He mounted his carriage and led his party onwards to their next appointment.

When they were well out of earshot, Wil apologized effusively to Gralyre for the loss of the horse. He knew how Gralyre felt about his animals. "The man is a thief! Worse! He is a collaborator!" He spit on the ground.

"Ye should have let me kill him, Da," Dajin mumbled rebelliously.

"Think before ye act, Dajin!" Rewn growled. "We were unarmed, they had swords, and as it was ye cost us an additional fine. We might have been able to give him an extra bag o' grain for Gralyre's presence. Ye have t' learn t' control your temper! Ye almost got yourself killed!"

Dajin scowled. "Control my temper so that we can sit back and do nothing?" He glared at Wil and Rewn. "The two o' ye talk big when they are no' here, and bow and scrape t' their

faces!" He thumped his chest aggressively. "Well that is no'
going t' be me!"

Wil grabbed Dajin by the scruff and shook him, pushed to
anger by his son's scorn and his near brush with death. "There
are many ways o' fighting, boyo! 'Tis the smart man who can
fight and live t' fight again. Ye do no' challenge armed men
with naught but your fists, and ye do no' run your mouth about
things ye do no' understand!" he roared.

Dajin's face was white and he was holding back tears as Wil
released him with a push towards the house.

Wil sighed grimly, surrendering his anger as he watched his
youngest stalk off. "'Tis a good thing the taxman did no' see the
rest o' your animals, else they would have been taken as well!"
He said to Gralyre to break the awkward silence.

Gralyre replied with a shrug and a quiet smile, "I gave him
the horse that left me to the mob in the village. I planted the idea
in its mind that those men," he indicated the settling dust on the
horizon, "mean to eat him. 'Tis what made him run the first
time, I have no doubt that he will run again. Then our Tax
Master is going to have to explain to his Lord exactly how he
lost such a valuable asset… if he even recorded it in that book as
he said." Gralyre allowed a slightly larger smile to lift his mouth
as Wil and Rewn guffawed at the jest of it.

"Ye have a truly devious turn o' mind, Lad," Wil compli-
mented him.

☙❧

Almost three hours later, the horse came puffing and whinnying into the yard. Wil, Rewn and Gralyre could not keep their mirth in check.

"What's going on?" Dajin asked as he came out from the barn where he'd been sulking. He had heard the laughter, and could not stand being left out of the joke. "Is that Gralyre's horse?"

Through gasps for air, Rewn filled him in, while Wil sniggered quietly and Gralyre's laughter rolled like thunder out over the yard. The merriment after the trying day was infectious, and soon Dajin was bent double, holding his sides and wiping at tears.

"I had best get him hidden. The Tax Master will be back to find his prize!" With dancing eyes, Gralyre sent the horse to join the herd in the forest and charged Little Wolf to guarding them.

Not long after, when Demon Riders came calling, they found an empty barn and Master Findlay inconsolable over the loss of his beast. There was nothing they could do. The ledger already showed that Wil Wilson had paid his tax. They left empty handed

Wil snugged an arm around his youngest son. "Like I said, boyo," Wil smiled meaningfully to Dajin, "There are all manner o' ways t' do battle, and 'tis a smart man who fights and lives t' fight another day!"

§∞CR

The Sorceress Catrian awaited the Oakhallow Tithe in the poor home of the young couple, Douglas and Lily Martinson, resistance sympathizers who surveilled the blighted territories southeast of Dreisenheld, deep in the black heart of Doaphin's empire. It would be her last opportunity to be taken before the Tithing season came to a close.

"More tea, m'lady?" asked Lily. She waited with the pot suspended over Catrian's cup.

"Yes please, Lily, Thank-ye. 'Tis delicious."

Lily was a lovely young woman, of an age with Catrian, who doted on her husband and child. It broke Catrian's heart that she could not warn the woman of the danger that was rapidly approaching her. Without complaint, Lily had opened her home and her hearth to the unexpected stranger, who if discovered, would be the death of all she loved.

It was unspeakably dangerous for Catrian to be this close to Dreisenheld. She had never been allowed this near to Doaphin's stronghold, and if her men had had their way, she would not be here now.

She was being very careful not to use even the smallest magic for it would send up a flare to every creature in Dreisenheld, but supressing such an instinctual attribute was like remembering never to move her right hand... or blink. The consequences of Doaphin sensing her presence however... she shivered.

"Are ye cold, m'lady? Would ye like a robe for your lap? 'Tis a cheerless day today," Lily remarked as the rain pounded the roof.

"I am fine, Lily, thank-ye," she returned with a smile. If she were not careful, she would grow used to this coddling. "How is young Calum's cough today?"

Lily smiled back, as always, eager to speak of her child. "He is much improved. The poultice ye made for him worked wonders. He was strong enough t' go t' the village with Douglas this morning."

The sound of booted feet on the porch was the only warning before the door was thrust open. Catrian jumped, but it was only the aforementioned males of the family returning from Oakhallow.

"Lily! I have the best news!" Douglas ran forward, gathered up his wife and spun her in a dizzying circle as he shouted with laughter. Young Calum, a youth of seven years, danced and cavorted around them.

Lily giggled, embarrassed for their guest, yet delighted by the play all the same. "Douglas! Put me down!" she slapped him impishly, "What has gotten into ye, husband!"

Douglas cupped her face in his hands and gave her a long buss on the lips. "The Tithe," he smiled when he came up for air.

Lily's face paled at the mention of the sword that hung suspended over the heads of every human woman. "What! Douglas?"

Douglas grinned. "The Council just announced that the Tithe is to be suspended. I did no' even know it was t' come this year! No one did. If ye had been taken…!" He kissed her again.

"No Tithe?" Catrian stood abruptly, and the noise of her chair scraping across the floor parted the couple though Douglas kept Lily clasped to his side. Catrian could not prevent her disappointment from showing.

Douglas grinned. "Aye, may it never come again! Gods!" he

exclaimed, "Ye would have been taken as well!" In his excitement, he misinterpreted her disappointment for fear of the narrowly averted disaster.

"What wonderful news!" Catrian smiled weakly, though inside she was seething mad.

After the mysterious warrior, Gralyre, had attacked the caravan and destroyed her first carefully laid plans for capture, everything had gone wrong. The Gods of Fortune had deserted her cause at every turn.

She and her men had been haring hither and yon to get ahead of a Tithe so that she could complete her mission, but something had Doaphin stirred up like a hornet, for he had changed the Tithe schedules, causing her to arrive too late to be captured, or suspending the Tithe completely in some areas as had just happen here in Oakhallow.

Had she known that her last opportunity to be captured had been when Wil Wilson had convinced her to rescue the warrior, Gralyre, outside of Tarangria, she would have left the man to rot in that cage.

Had her mission been betrayed? How? By whom? Only Boris and his carefully selected protectors had known of her intentions, and she trusted them completely. The ability to look within a man's thoughts was a tool that gave her absolute certainty about who was an ally and who was a foe.

"We must celebrate!" Douglas exhorted. "Calum, down in the cellar behind the potatoes is a bottle o' something that I have been saving for a special occasion. Fetch it for us, would ye lad?"

CHAPTER NINETEEN

"How am I supposed t' learn if ye keep knocking me into the snow!" Dajin roared angrily.

"I would imagine that as soon as you tire of getting knocked on your arse, you will learn the lesson to keep it from happening," Gralyre suggested smoothly.

"Raaaagh!" Dajin yelled and attacked wildly, wooden sword swinging lethally.

Slash! Slash! Block! Thrust!

Crack!

The sound of wood against skull was immediately followed by Dajin's body hitting the snow. Hard. He sat very still for a moment, his eyes slightly crossed. Very carefully, he stood, wooden sword dragging through the slush as he shook his head to clear the droning from his hearing.

Gralyre watched Dajin's progress with serene unconcern, wooden sword angled negligently against his shoulder. The fog that misted out of his mouth in the cold air gave testament to the fact that he was not even breathing hard, unlike Dajin's that rasped in and out in quick puffs. "Never allow an opponent to provoke you to anger. The man who is in control of his emotions is in control of any situation in which he finds himself."

Dajin swiped angrily at a trickle of blood seeping sluggishly from his temple. Gralyre's lessons were going to be the death of him. He set his jaw mulishly, but nodded to show he heard and understood the lesson.

"That is all I will teach you today. You need to find your control," Gralyre stated firmly. He set his wooden practice sword against the side of the house, exchanging it for the crossbow lying in wait. Without another word, he set off across the fields towards the forest. Little Wolf leapt up from where he had been monitoring the exercises and loped eagerly after him.

Dajin staggered slightly as he placed his practice sword next to Gralyre's. For a moment he rested against the wall, shaking his head again to clear it. It did not help.

Allowing one hand to trail against the side of the cottage for balance, he moved around to the door, and with a grunt, pushed it open. A wave of heat greeted him. His brother and father looked up with sheepish sympathy.

"He knocked me down again," Dajin whined. If he was expecting commiseration, he was to remain disappointed. Rewn sported several impressive bruises of his own, worn without complaint. And Wil had no sympathy to give. He was glad his sons were gaining such valuable knowledge.

"Where is he now?" Wil inquired as he returned to his mending. His pipe hung precariously from the corner of his mouth. He settled himself more comfortably in the big chair.

"Went hunting with the wolf," Dajin spat out, angry at the lack of concern he was receiving.

"Good!" exclaimed Rewn. "They always manage t' bring back game." With a groan from his own overstressed muscles and bruises, Rewn limped the few paces to the fire pit. "I had best get the stew pot ready for what he will return with." He hefted the big cast iron kettle off its hook over the fire and went outside to pack it with snow. Their well was frozen by mid-winter, forcing them to obtain water by melting ice.

"Have ye noticed that the worse the mistake I make the harder he hits me?" Dajin complained to his father, still trying to gain a measure of sympathy.

"'Tis so ye will remember no' t' do something so stupid again." Wil grinned and gestured at his son with his pipe. "Good for ye! Toughen ye up," he stated with a twinkle in his eyes.

"I feel more tender than tough!" Dajin groaned dramatically, touching his temple carefully.

Wil just chuckled. "Think o' all the 'Oohs and Ahs' ye will get from the wenches at the Midwinter's Moon Festival when they see your battle scars."

Dajin grinned and began to hum a favourite tune as he poked the fire to bank some hot coals for cooking.

Wil sobered as he watched his young son. There would be all too few lassies at the celebration this year. Only aged crones or young girls would be in attendance due to the Women Tithe the village had been forced to pay this year.

As Wil sunk deep into his musings his fingers stilled in their task of mending. He watched moodily as the door banged open and Rewn entered with the snow packed pot to place by the fire. His sons might never know the joys of marriage and children because of the lack of young women.

'Ah, Marji,' Will prayed to his dead wife, *'did we make the right decision, t' raise our children here in Raindell instead o' the safety o' the Heathrens?'*

Wil knew he performed an important duty for the rebellion as a spy and as a safe way-station, but it had cost him, in the dearest coin there was. He had lost his beloved wife, Marji, and firstborn son, his namesake, to the Demon Riders fifteen years ago when the last Women Tithe had been demanded of Raindell and paid.

Young Wil, a lad of only thirteen seasons, had tried to protect his mother from the 'Riders and had been killed. Dara and Dajin, the twins, had been little more than babes of four years. He thanked the Gods every day that nine-year-old Rewn had been travelling with him, and so had remained safe.

Wil had been returning from Verdalan, where he had been meeting with the rebellion's High Command about Demon Rider troop movements in the area, when word had reached him that Marji had been taken. He had ridden two horses into the ground to reach his wife in time, but had arrived too late.

He had reached the wagons on the evening before they were to enter Tarangria, in time only to witness Marji kill herself rather than submit to the Tithe. Wil had been unable to even bring her body home. The 'Riders had feasted on her flesh in celebration of reaching their destination.

He would never forgive himself for not being there to protect his family, nor would he ever tell his children of their mother's fate. Some knowledge was too much of a burden to share.

Wil's thoughts turned to his most recent brush with the Tithe, and the man who had kept history from repeating itself. Wil had been out of his mind with fear when he learned his daughter had been taken. He would never be able to repay the man for his bravery.

But despite his heroic acts, Wil feared who Gralyre might be. If he were merely mad, he would not possess the ring or the note. Added to this toll was his Sorcerer's power, his ability with a sword, when to even carry one bore a penalty of death, and the wealth of a collaborator in his belt. He had to be a spy!

On the other hand, Gralyre had proven himself a patient, if exacting, teacher for his sons. His sense of honour was infallible and he commanded a great deal of respect from both his sons, especially Rewn who was not easily impressed.

And then there were the nightmares he suffered every night. Surely those could not be faked! When Wil asked him of them, Gralyre would brush aside his concerns and change the subject. If they were nothing, why would the man pace outside in the cold, night after night, as though he feared even the thought of sleep?

'Could he be...?' Wil sighed mightily as the fancy flitted through his mind, not for the first time. He shifted in his chair and took up his mending once more, shaking his head for entertaining the same folly he had chastised Rewn for. It had been three hundred years since the Prince's defeat. The prophecy was just a bard's tale told around the hearth to keep a small kernel of hope alive in the breasts of their children.

Despite his respect for Gralyre, Wil would send him to Catrian in the spring. She would look into Gralyre's mind and ferret out the truth. Or would she?

She never failed to spot the taint of Doaphin that clung to a man's soul, but this time was different, Gralyre was different.

Catrian would look into his mind and see nothing. At a later date, when Gralyre had won the confidence of all, Doaphin could bring back his past and have an ideal infiltrator.

Wil knew what Catrian's response to this unique conundrum would likely be. If one innocent must die to protect them all, then so be it.

Why did Wil feel like he was betraying a friend? Why did the thought of Gralyre's death feel so… wrong?

ဆၣသ

"Enter!" Catrian called out from the depths of her comfortable chair.

The door opened and in walked Matik, one of her most trusted warriors who had travelled with her throughout the summer. He was also her uncle's second in command, and her unofficial keeper.

"Another message has come from the fortress, m'lady," Matik rumbled at her through his thick beard. The axe he wore slung across his back gleamed in the lamplight as he held out the missive.

Catrian's hand moved from within her cloak to accept the sealed scroll. It was always cold and damp in the catacombs of Verdalan, especially in the winter, but the secret ways into the tunnels were secure from the Demon Riders who roamed the streets by day, and the Deathren who roamed the streets by night, and safety was more precious than any warm chamber and soft bed could buy.

The ancient tunnels and rooms bespoke a level of architecture beyond the skills of the humans who now used them to hide. All such knowledge was lost to time, and to the desperate day-to-day hard scramble of survival. Perhaps one day, when Doaphin was defeated, such disciplines would be rediscovered.

She cracked the seal with her fingernail and quickly scanned the letter. Her breath huffed in annoyance.

"Another order t' return?" Matik's heavily bearded face was deliberately bland.

"Yes." She carefully folded the note before feeding it to the brazier that did its best to warm the dampness from the stones of her spartan chamber. The brief flare of light and warmth was most gratifying.

"It be no' my place, m'lady, but ye should heed the Commander."

Catrian grumbled a reply. She had made the decision to over-winter in Verdalan, so that she could attempt to be recaptured by the Woman Tithe again in the spring. She was still convinced that the way to defeating Doaphin, lay through the well-guarded secret of the Tithe. If she could smash that link, it might give the Rebels the advantage they so desperately needed, an advantage that would see the resistance survive for one generation more.

Having convinced Boris once to allow her to attempt her dangerous mission, she would be unlikely to be given permission for a second try. This was the third summons to return to the Northern Fortress that she had ignored.

A dark gravity was pressing in upon her. Something was coming, and preparations had to be made. Now was the time when she could make a difference to the resistance effort. She was not going to waste the opportunity hiding safely in the mountains waiting for the end of all things.

∞∞

"You are doing well, Rewn," Gralyre congratulated as he offered a hand to help the man back to his feet.

When he was standing, Rewn brought up his wooden practice sword. "Show that t' me again, but slow it down. Ye move too quickly!"

Gralyre grinned and slapped Rewn's practice sword with his. "I am moving slowly."

Rewn grimaced, and returned his practice sword to its ready position.

Gralyre's face sobered. "Like this." In extreme slow motion, he showed Rewn the strike.

Rewn's face was a study of concentration, as he nodded. "I think I see where I went wrong." His sword mimicked Gralyre's in turn.

"Now faster, and do not forget to maintain your balance."

Whack, Whack, slide, Whack-whack

"Again, Faster!" Gralrye exhorted.

'That was faster,' Rewn thought with wry amusement as he tried to accelerate the movements.

Gralyre stepped back and lowered his practice sword. "Speed is good, but accuracy is better. Practice this and we will start on something new when you have mastered it."

Rewn nodded.

In companionable silence, the two men stabbed their practice swords into the snow by the edge of the house.

"Gralyre, if I have no' said so, thank-ye for teaching me."

Gralyre glanced away with an embarrassed smile. "You are a good student. You learn fast and ask the right questions."

Rewn shook his head with a shy smile. "I do no' think ye comprehend what a gift it is. Ye make light o' it, but 'tis the truth that no one can do as ye do. For ye t' share this knowledge…" Rewn shook his head and shrugged.

Gralyre nodded solemnly and looked at Rewn from the corner of his eye. He assumed a blatantly feigned arrogance. "'Tis not all selfless you know. I need a proper sparring partner. I have high hopes that eventually you will be able to provide *some* sort of challenge."

Rewn snorted and shoved Gralyre in comfortable retaliation.

Gralyre skidded on the ice. His arms windmilled, and his feet danced a jig, before he landed on his back.

"Remember t' always maintain your balance," Rewn reminded primly as he stood over Gralyre's sprawled form. His eyes twinkled with supressed mirth.

"A cowardly attack! Fetch me my sword!" Gralyre growled jestingly around the grin he could not quite hide.

෨෬

It was the night of the Midwinter's Moon Festival. Traditionally, there would be celebrations in the village this night;

dancing, singing, food and drink. This was the time when the young men declared themselves for their ladies and all were merry as they celebrated the shortest day of the year.

Despite the anticipation of the festival, there would be little to celebrate this Midwinter's Moon. The young lasses were no more, all taken by the Tithe, killed or fled. The young men would drink too deeply of Dolper's brews and seek out trouble.

Wil sighed as he reconsidered his consent to attend the festival. It was a given that there would be trouble tonight. The few eligible women left in Raindell could pick and choose whomever they wished. What woman in her right mind would favour one of the snaggletooth town dwellers, when there would be healthy young bucks like his sons and Gralyre attending the festivities? It was enough to cause bloodshed in a calm year, let alone one that had been afflicted by the Tithe.

Wil gave his sons a covert inspection as they bickered with each other over the use of a scrap of looking glass in which to shave, and found that he did not have the heart to tell them that they would not be going. There was little enough to celebrate in their lives, and he would not be the one to take from them any chance for good memories.

'Ah, Marji, if only ye could see them. They have grown up strong and proud. If only they had a life t' enjoy instead o' this feeble existence we survive.'

Rewn should be married with children of his own by now, and Dajin should be looking forward to a merry life with a young lass instead of slowly twisting himself with rage and hate. If something was not done, all they would have was a life of bleak loneliness. Perhaps it was time to move to the Heathrens?

The door to the small cottage thrust open and Gralyre entered in a flurry of snow. He stamped his boots smartly on the threshold to remove the clinging ice as he slammed the door behind to keep out the cold.

Wil sighed. However handsome his sons were, they could not compare to this stranger. Gralyre had done little to primp for the festivities. His hair was freshly washed and still damp, and his clothes held no celebration. Why the man insisted on wearing black, Wil could not fathom.

'Habit,' Gralyre had told him.

'Maybe so,' Wil conceded at the time, but the attire made Gralyre appear taller and more menacing. Dangerous, handsome and mysterious, Wil now added to his list as he watched the man cup his hands to the fire to warm them.

Gralyre caught Wil staring and smiled, making the skin crinkle around his deep blue eyes. "I have hitched up the sledge. You are sure it will be alright to use the horse tonight?"

Wil smiled back. "It will be fine. I know a place we can leave it where no one will see it. It will be safe."

Gralyre's smile faded, and his brows lowered as he turned away and stared into the flames. Wil thought that he knew the reason for his sudden glower. This would be Gralyre's first trip into Raindell since he was a hirsute prisoner. There was always the risk that one of the villagers would recognize him, despite his smooth shave and trimmed hair, but so long as no one said otherwise, the townsfolk would know him simply as Master Findlay, Wil's cousin from Brannock.

Wil took a moment to carefully secrete a dagger in his boot, just in case.

"Come on, lads. Ye be pretty enough," he teased his sons. "Gralyre has had that horse hitched t' the sleigh for the past ten minutes while the two o' ye primped. Time t' go!"

With one last swipe at an errant cowlick, Rewn turned from the scrap of mirror. As an afterthought, he mussed his brother's hair as he left.

"Quit it!" Dajin exclaimed angrily.

Rewn laughed and bounded out the door. The thought of the party had lightened his spirits.

Dajin, a livid scowl on his face, gave chase.

Little Wolf sighed gustily through his flews from his place in front of the hearth. He was not happy with being left behind. He thumped his tail sadly as Gralyre ruffled his ears. *'I will return soon. Protect the den.'*

Wil clapped a hand to Gralyre's shoulder and led him out of the house, closing the door firmly behind them. "Now remember, lads," he cautioned all the men as he pointed to Gralyre, "his name is Findlay. 'Tis the name we gave the Tax Master."

"Yes, Da," Rewn agreed as he settled himself on the driver's seat. The old sledge had been in the family for years and was only brought out on special occasions if they had a horse with which to pull it. This was a rare treat indeed.

Wil looked up at Gralyre, "Remember that Gralyre is a forbidden name. I think ye do no' want t' see the inside o' Dolper's stillroom again."

Gralyre nodded and a muscle flexed in his jaw.

Wil focussed on Dajin. "Everyone must remember!"

"Why are ye looking at me when ye say that?" Dajin grunted as he climbed up and plopped down beside Rewn on the bench seat. "I am no' an idiot, ye know!"

"Alright, then. Let us be on our way!" Wil climbed up into the sledge, followed closely by Gralyre.

Rewn already had his hands on the reins. An uncharacteristic excitement animated his features, making him look more like his younger brother than he ever had before.

"Rewn, get that horse moving," Wil ordered as he and Gralyre settled in their seats. "We have a party t' get to!" With a smart snap of the reins the sledge jerked into motion and glided towards the village.

Dajin glowered in sullen silence, licking his palms and trying to smooth his hair into place.

༄༅

A welcome burst of warmth and light greeted them as they entered The Running Wolf. It was the only building warm enough and large enough to host the Midwinter's Moon Festival.

The Innkeeper had made an effort to decorate the large taproom with evergreen bows, dried apples and strings of onions. Smoky tallow candles burned brightly in every corner. The hearths at opposite ends of the room, roared and crackled with blazing fires. Spit-boys sweated in the heat as they cranked bits of meat over the flames and carved slices off into waiting trenchers for those who could afford to pay.

But instead of making the event cheery, it had the opposing effect. The harsh light illuminated the shabby filth of the tavern and the gaunt faces of the townsfolk crowded shoulder to hip within the ramshackle room. It showed to the greatest advantage the rags they wore, which were doubtless their finest things.

Smiles were wide but eyes held the haunted glaze of the dying. The tension in the room was palpable, punctuated by brittle laughter and aggravated by toneless music. Set in the corner by one of the hearths, fiddle and fife abused one traditional ballad after another.

Dolper the Innkeeper appeared at their sides, his hands full of empty tankards. Gralyre instinctually stiffened, but Dolper's face held no hint of recognition.

"Brace yourselves, lads," the Innkeeper whispered softly, "The new Lord has come t' call, and he is human." He jerked his chin towards the corner near one of the fires, and walked away.

Wil laid a cautionary hand on each of his son's arms but it was too late to leave without giving insult. Gralyre followed Wil's line of sight past the Demon Rider guards. There, dressed in obscene splendour, sat the new Lord.

His dress aped that of the previous Demon Lord, but there was no disguising the fact that he was a human. His long black hair was clubbed at the back of his head, and his heavy satin coat threw a blue sheen back from the fire. The deep lines on his face bespoke a dissolute life that made it difficult to judge his age. How corrupt must he be to have risen so high in the ranks of the enemy?

"In the name o' ill fortune!" cursed Rewn. "Is that the new

Lord? What is he doing here?"

Wil's lip curled in disgust as he answered. "'Tis obvious, son. What with the Tithe, people are surlier than in past years. Get enough spirits in them and they might decide they can throw down the tyrant. So the tyrant has come t' join our party t' ensure that no one discovers a backbone and comes looking for him. With him staring over our shoulders all night, and with a troop o' 'Riders at his back, there will be little celebrating, and no talk o' rebellion." With an angry snap of his teeth, Wil clamped his pipe tightly and stalked to the slat wood bar for a stoup of mulled wine.

"Watch yourself, Dajin," warned Rewn as he tracked the Demon Riders circulating through the room. "Keep your temper no matter what the provocation, and by the Gods, watch your tongue!"

"Watch your own!" snarled Dajin. He stomped across the crowded room to join his father at the bar.

Gralyre leaned over to Rewn and said in an undertone, "I fear he will be difficult tonight." He nodded in Dajin's direction.

Rewn snorted in agreement, "I would no' take that bet." He steered them towards an empty table. Wil and Dajin soon arrived with a round of drinks.

"We will no' stay long," said Wil quietly. "There is danger here we do no' want t' get caught up in."

"Damn them all," complained Dajin loudly, rocking the table with a pound of his fist. "This is our only time t' celebrate and they have ruined even this!"

Gralyre's hand shot out to cover Dajin's closed fist and

squeezed it in caution. Dajin tried to shake off his hold and gasped when the larger hand tightened painfully. Gralyre subtly shifted his eyes to a spot beyond the younger man's shoulder and then back to Dajin.

Dajin was a rash hothead but he was not stupid. There was a Demon Rider standing behind him. Gralyre released him when he saw the dawning light of understanding enter Dajin's face.

Smiling recklessly, Dajin lifted his mulled wine. "T' the new Lord! Long may he protect us!" he toasted loudly. The others had no choice but to lift their own tankards in salute. With a warning hiss, the Demon Rider moved off to monitor another table.

"This is no game, brother!" Rewn growled. "Get control o' yourself or ye will get us killed!"

Dajin glared sullenly at his brother until, unable to maintain the eye contact, he dropped his gaze to the bitter contents of his tankard. A brooding silence descended onto the table as they sipped mechanically. The sooner they finished, the sooner they could escape.

The door to the tavern burst open and a laughing crowd of people stomped in. They stopped short when they spotted the red uniforms of the 'Riders spaced throughout the crowd and the resplendent Lord sitting in the corner. The men quickly tried to shield one of their number, and to rush whoever it was safely back outside before they were seen.

"Hold!" yelled the Lord. "Who are you trying to hide?" At a gesture, Demon Riders strode forward and pulled the mob of people aside to drag a small rag-cloaked person forward. The outer garments were ripped away to reveal a young woman.

"Damn the Gods o' Fortune!" Rewn gritted out between his clenched teeth. "'Tis Saliana Greythorn!"

"Why in the name o' all the Lords o' the Underworld did her father bring her here! The fool!" Wil hissed.

The new Lord licked his lips and beckoned the Demon Riders to bring the lass forward. A sickening smile lifted his features as the flickering tallow lamp on the table gave his face an evil animation. "So! A little butterfly has escaped the net! I had begun to despair of there being any wenches here! What is your name?" he demanded.

Two large tears escaped to roll down the pale, freshly scrubbed face. Her thin body was trembling in fear as she managed to stutter her name. "S-s-Saliana Grey-th-thorn," she bobbed a curtsy. Her fine white-blond hair added to her fragile presence.

"Bring her father!" ordered the Lord. A Demon Rider leaned into the mob at the door and pulled forth a small man with a large nose.

"Why was she not part of the Tithe? Would you bring Doaphin's wrath down upon us all? Would you allow your sick affection for this *female* to destroy the homes of your friends and neighbours?" The Lord made a slight finger gesture and the Demon Rider clubbed the man to the floor.

"On your knees when the Lord speaks to ye!" hissed the 'Rider. A smile of pleasure curdled its face at the pain it caused.

The father sobbed once then lifted his bloodied face, his hands cupped in supplication. "I beg ye no' t' harm me, m'lord.

She could no' be part o' the Tithe for she has no' yet become a woman. Her curse is no' yet upon her. 'Tis the law. I would no' anger Great Doaphin in such a way!"

The Lord leaned back in his chair and considered the situation. The silence of the room became almost painful. "Is this true, lass?" he asked Saliana gently, a corrupt smile on his face.

She nodded once, her eyes riveted to the floor as a flush of mortification brought false colour to her cheeks. Her terror was palpable. Her shivers had become so bad it was a wonder she was still on her feet.

The Lord licked his lips once more, his eyes roving her thin body. "Come to me, little innocent," he whispered hoarsely.

Saliana did not move. It was not rebelliousness, but simple terror that kept her rooted to her spot.

"Bring her to me," the Lord ordered. His excitement was extreme, and sickening to see.

A Demon Rider grabbed the arms of the lass and dragged her to the Lord. Overcome by terror, Saliana's eyes rolled back in her head and she sagged. Unceremoniously, the Demon Rider lifted her off her feet and deposited her in the Lord's lap.

"Pay the father," The Lord ordered.

The Demon Rider pulled a dull copper coin from his belt and flung it at the cowering man.

Saliana's father snagged it from the air and squirreled it away, thanking the new Lord for his generosity as he backed away, still on hands and knees.

The Lord ignored him completely as he grasped the limp body tightly. He nuzzled Saliana's neck with his mouth and teeth, as his hands ran greedily over her flesh, searching out and finding rich morsels that had been hidden by the rags. He stopped suddenly and lifted his head to regard the room. "This is Midwinter's Moon! I want music and dancing!" He ordered. "Now!"

At his words, the Demon Riders threw tables to the side to open a space for use as a dance floor. That several people were crushed and battered just added to their pleasure.

In a horrible caricature of true merriment, the fiddle and fife began to scratch out a tune, while people about the room were prodded into the cleared area by the Demon Riders' swords and forced to dance.

As the noise level rose, Dajin's eyes remained riveted on the Lord and the limp lass he was groping. "Only one woman comes tonight and he steals her! 'Tis no' fair!"

"Silence, Dajin! Think o' the poor lass!" Rewn looked at his father pleadingly. "Is there naught we can do?"

Wil tapped the contents of his pipe against the edge of the table, sending the ash to the dirt floor as he gazed stonily at Saliana's repugnant father, who was triumphantly showing off the coin to his cronies while his daughter was being publicly violated. "No' if we wish t' see another sunrise." His voice sounded strained to everyone's ears.

At an odd metallic sound, the men turned in time to see Gralyre's empty tankard crumple in his fist. Wil swallowed fearfully as Gralyre calmly examined the crushed vessel in his hands as though surprised to see it. Wil had never seen so murderous a rage before. Most frightening was the will that kept the emotion under tight control. The man's eyes were terrible to see. The blue had fled and only black remained around the pupils. Gralyre's face was like rock, not one trace of emotion did it betray.

Rewn grabbed his father's arm warningly, as Gralyre suddenly stood, his chair sliding backwards ever so gently.

"I seem to have destroyed my tankard," Gralyre said mildly. "I must get another." He walked calmly across the room to where Dolper the Innkeeper served his brews.

"Gods!" moaned Rewn.

"Do no' worry," Wil murmured tensely as he watched Gralyre's progress. "He knows the consequences and will no' endanger us."

"Did ye see his face?" Dajin whispered gleefully. "I wager he could kill all the 'Riders in the room!"

"And then what would become o' us and the village!" Rewn chastised in a harsh whisper. "He would never act with such thoughtlessness!"

"I did no' say that he would," Dajin snarled back, "only that he could if he so chose!"

Wil laid a cautionary hand on each of his son's arms to forestall the argument that was brewing. Both men subsided. Wil did not condemn them their outburst for, truth be told, he felt like snarling and snapping himself.

At the bar, Gralyre quietly handed his crushed tankard to Dolper. A quick glance between the crumpled metal and Gralyre's impassive face warned Dolper to hold his tongue as he dipped a fresh tankard into the mulled wine and passed it back.

Gralyre picked up the new drink, smiling slightly as he realized Dolper had given him a clay bowl this time. He placed a penny on the bar to cover both the drink and the destruction of the vessel.

Dolper's face remained bland as he quickly swept both the money and the crushed mug from sight.

Gralyre lifted the clay tankard in a brief salute to the Inn-keeper, and turned to walk back to the table where the Wilsons waited, but the butt end of a spear landed hard against his chest, stopping him in his tracks. Taking his time, tamping down his temper as he went, Gralyre played his gaze up the length of the shaft to meet the reptilian eyes of the Demon Rider who held it.

The Demon Rider's expression devolved from evil enjoyment to nervous unease. People feared him. They never, ever, looked him straight in the eye as this one was doing. His palms grew damp upon his spear.

"Dance!" he commanded. "The Lord commands ye t' dance!" He shifted the responsibility for the command from himself to the Lord. Perhaps he sought to save himself from the flash of murderous rage that streaked across Gralyre's face.

Gralyre glanced around the Demon Rider to the table where his hosts sat.

Wil's face had gone ashen and his trembling hand was travelling furtively towards the dagger he had hidden in his boot, while Rewn's palms were braced flat upon the table as if he were about to rise and come to Gralyre's rescue.

Dajin's expression was filled with gleeful anticipation, awaiting Gralyre's eminent explosion.

Gralyre gave a subtle shift of his head, telling them all to subside.

The music changed to a slow beating military air that gave him a shiver of familiarity. He shut his eyes briefly, trying to bring forth the memory, and suddenly the knowledge was there!

'The Dance of the Sword! Always performed at festival times.' The Masters would take up their swords and dance in mock battle. As it was against the laws of this land to carry a sword, Gralyre was amazed that this song was still played at gatherings. Perhaps so much time had passed that no one remembered the haunting tune's true significance.

"I told ye t' dance!" snarled the impatient 'Rider, striking him again in the chest with the butt end of his spear.

Gralyre's eyes snapped open and he reached back and placed his drink calmly on the bar. With speed rivalling a striking snake, he snatched the spear from the 'Rider's grip and snapped it like kindling on his knee.

The Demon Rider hissed in surprise as he cowered back, but Gralyre made no further move towards him. Holding a shaft of the broken spear in each hand, he stalked to the dance floor.

The confused Demon Rider looked to the new Lord for guidance, but he was paying no attention, for the lass had finally come forth from her faint and was enlivening their encounter with her struggles.

The Demon Rider knew that he should not let such an insult stand, but he felt a sensation he had never before been given by a human. Fear.

As casually as possible, he glanced around the tavern to see if any of his comrades had noted the incident. No one was looking his way, so he rested his elbows against Dolper's slat-wood bar and stole Gralyre's drink in a fit of petty revenge.

Gralyre glided in amongst the dancers like a panther amongst kittens, and took up his stance in the middle of the floor. He assumed the first pose. Handling the sticks as though they were two swords, Gralyre began to move. The other dancers stepped back in confusion, shifting from his path as he swung the broken pieces of spear.

At the first movements of the dance, the rigidly controlled slashes performed ever so slowly to the beat of the stately song, the crowd standing at the edge of the floor guffawed, thinking he mocked the 'Riders with his movements.

"'Tis the Sword Dance! He is dancing the Sword Dance!" Wil whispered to his sons. A smile of wonder lifted his face from the frown of anxiety that he had worn since they had walked into the tavern.

Rewn craned forward to get a better look at Gralyre's controlled and regimented movements. A quiet tuneless whistle escaped.

Dajin's chair scraped as he stood. "So what! I am getting another drink!" he challenged.

"Dajin!" Rewn hissed after him. "Dajin... Stop... We are leaving...!" A Demon Rider passed by their table and Rewn subsided. He exchanged a speaking glance with his father, before his attention was captured once more by Gralyre's dance.

More people took up the laughter, crowding about the dance floor to see what was occurring. After a few moments, the laughter trickled away as they realized that this was no random gibberish but eloquently controlled movement. Someone in the back began to clap in time to the slow beat and others took it up until the room thundered with a pulse all its own.

Slowly, the tempo of the music increased until Gralyre's arms were a blur of movement as he passed through the complicated steps. Sweat sheened his face from his exertions as he leapt high in the air, his pretend swords whirling with deadly motion. The crowd hooted and hollered their approval as the acrobatic feats became ever more challenging, the pace of the music faster.

The change in the crowd finally percolated through the new Lord's lust. His head lifted and he glared at the man who was singlehandedly rallying the villagers from their subjugation. The crowd had lost their fear. He motioned to the nearest Demon Riders to put an end to Gralyre's dance, but the 'Riders could not make it through the great crush of people to reach the dance floor.

At his Demon Riders' ineffectual efforts, the Lord dumped the girl to the floor. He leapt to his feet, kicking her out of his way.

Sobbing and clutching her torn clothes, she crawled under a table to escape his blows.

"Enough!" he shouted over the din of the clapping. If anyone heard him, they ignored the command. At that moment, the dance ended in a thunderous crescendo. Into the sudden silence the Lord's voice boomed. "Chastise him!"

The crowd of people were instantly cowed by the sound of the Lord's voice. They meekly parted for the two Demon Riders who marched onto the impromptu dance floor and grabbed Gralyre's arms. A third 'Rider rushed forward and slammed a fist into Gralyre's stomach.

"That will learn ye fer stealing me spear!" the 'Rider snarled, brave now in the face of his two comrades.

Gralyre dropped the spear pieces obligingly and bowed to the pain, but his head snapped up as he spotted something. The colour drained from his face. The fist struck again and he doubled forward with a grunt.

"Music! Dance! I commanded you to Dance!" The Lord ordered contrarily. He glared at the fiddler until he took up another scratching tune.

The villagers dumbly took to the dance floor, studiously avoiding the sight of the man who moments before had been their hero, now enduring a beating.

Gralyre made urgent eye contact with Wil and Rewn, then turned his head to indicate the Lord before the next hard fist connected with his gut.

Rewn and Wil followed Gralyre's directions and spotted what his keen eyes had seen. "Gods!" Rewn's disbelieving cry washed away in the din. Both he and his father surged to their feet, but they were too far across the room to do anything.

Several villagers shouted and pointed. The fiddle and fife skirled to a halt. Throughout the room, men were falling back in fear.

Reacting to the cues he was being given, the Lord spun with a flinch, catching Dajin in the act of raising a broken table leg for a blow that was to have crushed his skull.

Dajin froze as he looked into the Lord's eyes. Shock and dismay flitted briefly across his features as dread forced his shaking arms to lower the makeshift club.

Gralyre snarled a curse at Dajin's stupidity, firstly in threatening the Lord, and secondly in hesitating to follow through. Time slowed as the pulse of the dance rippled through him.

The Demon Riders threw Gralyre to the ground as they turned and started to run to their Lord's aid. The crowd parted for them.

Gralyre swept up the business end of the broken spear he had dropped, and jumped back to his feet, hefting the shaft once to get the balance.

The Lord's face blazed in righteous retribution as he drew his sword and placed it against Dajin's neck. He paused to enjoy Dajin's helpless terror before striking. The sword raised.

Across the room, the spear's metal tip caught the light as Gralyre drew back his arm and launched the shortened missile. Somehow the spear found a straight path through the crowd of villagers to reach his mark. It struck the Lord in the back, hitting with such force that the pointed tip exited through his chest as he dropped the sword and stumble forward against Dajin.

Dajin pushed him away with a shriek and clubbed him to the ground with the table leg. Again and again Dajin struck. His rage had taken hold and he was out of control.

The room had gone quiet with the shock of the murder. The wet, rhythmic thuds of Dajin's club as it rose and fell seemed to cast a brief hypnotic spell. Even the 'Riders had frozen in place at the unexpected violence.

Then as though released, the villagers panicked. As one they surged towards the exit, and anything caught going against the tide of their escape was swept under their trampling feet. Including the Demon Riders.

Gralyre threw himself towards the wall to escape being trampled, and watched the three 'Riders who had only just left his side get churned under, unable to rise against the impact of so many feet.

The other Demon Riders were forcing their way back to the Lord's side, but even with threats and weapons they could not part the tide of people. They cut down any villager who impeded their progress but instead of opening a clear channel, it added to the panic and confusion, making it even more difficult to proceed. People and Demon Rider alike were crushed underfoot as the crowd forced its way out to the street.

In the mad rush of bodies and confusion, Wil and Rewn appeared on either side of Gralyre. "We must get Dajin!" Wil shouted over the screaming din.

"Keep to the edges!" Gralyre grabbed the men by the necks of their shirts and heaved them sideways out of the flow. Hugging the wall, they were able to make their way to where they had last seen Dajin by going around the stampede instead of through it. Wil, Rewn and Gralyre were able to press through to Dajin's side before the 'Riders could.

Dajin's club was still hard at work. Fearful tears flowed unchecked, and he grunted with the exertion of each swing.

Rewn halted Dajin's upraised arm, shouting his brother's name, as he was about to pound another blow into the corpse. The collaborator's head lay in a pool of blood and tissue, not even recognizable. Dajin had likely crushed his skull with his first strike.

Dajin turned with a mindless howl to attack whoever had interrupted his work. His face and clothes were bloody from his deed.

Rewn stumbled back in surprise.

Gralyre stepped up and struck Dajin's jaw as hard as he could. As the younger man folded, Gralyre briefly acknowledged how good it had felt after wanting to do it for so long.

Wil shouldered his son's weight, his face strained as he hefted Dajin off the floor. "Get the girl!" he gasped at Rewn.

Rewn reached under the table where the girl had taken refuge and dragged her forth. She came out clawing and screaming. With a rueful look, Rewn knocked her out, as Gralyre had done Dajin, and slung her deadweight over his shoulder.

Gralyre grabbed the Lord's discarded sword, rightly deciding that he was best equipped to cut a path of escape.

They turned to start for the door, but the Demon Riders had won free of the press of people and now blocked their escape. More than one of their numbers lay trampled to death beneath the feet of the villagers.

"Deathren!" A villager screeched as he went down with the hand of a Demon Rider corpse wrapped firmly around his ankle. The corpse hauled him close and set upon him with tooth and nail as the villager struggled and clawed to break free. The screams ended sharply.

Other dead 'Riders began to stir, twitching and struggling stiffly to gain their feet as the power of darkness reanimated them. They mindlessly attacked the last of the fleeing people, their empty hands clawing and their mouths biting.

"*That* is why you have to behead them?" Gralyre yelled in horror.

Rewn paled. "Deathren!" he shouted. "We will no' make it!"

"Dolper was just here! He must have a private escape hatch somewhere!" Wil shouted over the din.

Gralyre remembered his explorations of Raindell as seen through the minds of the rats that had kept him company during his incarceration. As he stepped to the fore with his stolen sword held at the ready, he shouted back over his shoulder, "Yes! 'Tis there, behind the bar! Find a way to open it! I will guard our backs!"

Wil and Rewn shuffled as quickly as their burdens would allow to the far side of the counter, just in time to see a section of panelling settle back into place as Dolper made good his escape.

"He was right, Da. There it is!" Rewn panted.

The first 'Rider to come into reach of Gralyre's blade died quickly the first time, and even faster the second. As the corpse began to twitch and move, Gralyre took the Deathren's head with a clean strike.

Stepping lightly backwards through the overturned wreckage of tables and chairs he crossed swords with the next 'Rider. In the interest of economy of motion, he decapitated this soldier with a mighty swing, thereby saving himself an extra blow for a reanimated Deathren. A third 'Rider came, a fourth, but they had not the skill with a sword that Gralyre owned. Their heads soon joined those of their comrades.

Rewn and Wil lifted the boards hiding the secret passage. "Gralyre!" Rewn yelled, in his excitement forgetting the false name they were to have used.

Gralyre grabbed a lamp and smashed it to the floor, forcing the remaining Demon Riders back with the flames. He sprinted for the bar, diving over it to reach its safety before the 'Riders fought through the fire and saw where they had gone.

He crawled into the cramped passage, and dragged Dajin and Saliana deeper into the darkness after him, making room for Rewn and Wil. The secret panel dropped back into place leaving them in darkness.

"This way," Gralyre whispered. "There is a tunnel."

"How can you tell?" Wil demanded. "'Tis darker than Doaphin's armpit in here!"

"I have enlisted the aid of some guides."

Wil and Rewn shuddered at the scrabbling sounds of rats, but trustingly followed the sound of Gralyre's retreating rustle.

It was hard going, for the earthen tunnel was just large enough for one man to crawl through. With the added burden of the two unconscious bodies to drag, their progress was too slow. Any moment now, the Demon Riders would discover the secret panel. The harsh sound of their laboured breathing filled the passage as they scratched and tugged to reach safety.

There was a crashing sound far behind them. "They have found the entrance!" Rewn, who was bringing up the rear hissed sharply. "Keep moving," he snarled wildly, as his father stopped dead. Urgently, he pushed against Wil, trying to prod him into motion.

"Hst! Rewn! Stop that! Gralyre is doing something!" Wil whispered over his shoulder.

"Hold still," Gralyre's voice sifted softly from out of the darkness. "I have arranged a diversion for our enemies, but they have to get past us to get to them. Just hold still and do not distract them or they may attack us instead of the 'Riders."

"What do ye mean...?" Rewn stopped talking as his question was answered by the sound of hundreds of thousands of tiny, clawed feet echoing from up the tunnel. He made a moaning sound of disgust and buried his face in his arms to protect it.

Rewn trembled as thousands of large rats streamed over him. The tide seemed to last forever, but finally the small army passed him by. Minutes later, horrific screams drifted down the tunnel from the Demon Riders trapped in the dark with the thousands of voracious rodents.

"We are almost to the end! I can see moonlight!" Gralyre whispered triumphantly.

They crawled out of the tunnel and into cold wet snow. They were in the tumbled remains of an abandoned building across the market square from the Running Wolf. At the feel of cold wetness on his face Dajin began to revive.

"Wha...?" he murmured groggily.

"Lie still, son," Wil said. "We are almost free." He pressed gently on Dajin's chest until he was lying flat again.

"I can get up!" Dajin blustered, thrusting aside his father's restraining hand and forcing himself to a sitting position.

"Ye hit me!" he sniped accusingly at Gralyre as he gingerly

rubbed his jaw.

"You were out of control," Gralyre replied dismissively. "Wil, we need to go. The 'Riders will be coming through the tunnel soon. Or more likely, Deathren."

Wil cautiously peered around the sagging frame of the missing back door of the ruin. The snow was undisturbed except for Dolper's tracks running away down the narrow, twisting alley. "All clear. We need t' get t' the sledge."

In the distance could be heard the screams of the people who were still fleeing through the market square. Yells of "Fire!" and "Deathren!" echoed with equal hysteria in the night.

Gralyre's awareness shifted towards an empty hovel at the edge of town where they had left the horse. "'Tis on its way."

Within minutes the animal came jogging towards them down the narrow alleyway, pulling the empty sledge behind. Blowing and snorting in the cold, it pulled up outside of the ruin.

Quickly, they loaded themselves and the still unconscious girl. Rewn took up the reins and steered the horse out of town towards their farm.

Gralyre removed his cloak and wrapped it gently around the unconscious lass. He exchanged a long, speaking look with Wil. "Do we bring her, or leave her?"

Wil knew as well as Gralyre did that because of this night's work, their time here was done. If they wished to survive until morning, they would have to flee. "There is no time t' find her somewhere safe. We bring her."

CHAPTER TWENTY

"Is that the last o' the supplies, Dajin?" Rewn puffed as he slung the heavy sack over the back of one of the packhorses.

"One more," Dajin snarled, working his bruised jaw with his fingers. In his inattention, the horse began to skitter sideways.

Rewn glared at Dajin as he stepped to the head of the horse to hold it still. "Tell me what is biting your arse, brother?"

"'Tis all his fault!" Dajin exploded as he heaved the last pack onto the horse. "If he had no' done that stupid dance we would no' be having t' run away like a pack o' cowards in the night!"

Rewn stiffened, resting a hand lightly against the horse's warm neck. "By 'him', ye speak o' Gralyre," he said quietly.

"Aye!"

The horse Dajin was working on grunted as he cinched the packs in place. It stamped its feet a couple of times, subtly bloating out to keep the bindings slack.

Rewn pushed his brother's hands from the straps and completed the job correctly. "Put credit where 'tis due, Daj." Rewn hauled hard on the leather and buckled it securely. "Gralyre's dance annoyed the Lord, but it would no' have resulted in our deaths."

He turned away from the horse and Dajin stumbled back at the unfamiliar disgust and rage glittering hotly in his brother's eyes. "However, the murder o' the Lord guarantees this village will be peopled by naught but rats and ghosts by morning."

Dajin's lips jutted in a childish pout, and his eyes dropped in the face of his brother's fury. "The Lord deserved it," he carped. "They stole our lands and the tax men sent us into poverty. And he had no right t' claim the best girl at the Festival!"

Rewn growled his frustration at Dajin's obtuse words. "The best girl at the festival! Are ye mad?" He grabbed his brother's ears and forced him to meet his eyes. "What were ye thinking, if ye were thinking at all? The Lord was obviously a tyrant son o' an ass but at least he was human! It would have been better for the people here. Doaphin will replace him with another Demon Lord now! Think how much worse things will be, if there be any left alive after tonight!"

Rewn was interrupted by Dajin's negligent shrug. "Listen t' me, boyo!" he snarled, unconsciously sounding like their father. "If Gralyre had no' thrown that spear true, ye would be dead! Ye are no hero! Ye did no' kill the Lord! He did! He did it t' protect ye! Ye…" he breathed harshly, sputtering in his rage, "What do ye think the 'Riders and Deathren are doing t' Raindell, right now? Do ye have any care for that at all?" With an angry jerk, he released his brother's ears.

"Sorry," Dajin muttered, resentful in the face of his brother's scorn.

Rewn turned away from Dajin, leading the packhorse to join those that were already saddled in readiness for their flight. "It be too late for sorry, Daj," he sighed quietly as he beheld the flickering glow coming from the direction of Raindell.

ༀ

Inside the cottage, Gralyre helped Wil to pry up some of the hearthstones. Straining mightily, the two men worked at the chink in the grout between the rocks using the fireplace poker. With a hollow scraping sound, the stones finally shifted aside.

"I did no' think it would be so hard t' move," Wil panted lightly, wiping a thin film of sweat from his brow with a rag.

"How long has it been?" Gralyre asked.

"Since I was a lad, and my father showed them t' me," Wil stated quietly. He reverently removed several objects from the hole inside the hearth. "'Tis all that remains o' my family's legacy. 'Twas hidden here when they fled their lands after the war was lost. They had t' sell most o' their goods, those that were no' confiscated, just t' survive those first few years. They were nobles," Wil snorted. "What did they know o' farming?"

With a grunt, he stiffly gained his feet while awkwardly cradling the objects. "But they survived." He smiled with pride. "So many could no' adjust t' their new lots, and were broken upon Doaphin's torture machines. But we hid and waited, planned and organized." His words trailed away as he gazed at the family treasures he held before wrapping them in a cloth, hiding them from view.

He lifted his eyes slowly to meet Gralyre's understanding gaze. "Sometimes," he said confidingly, "I think it would have been better had we all died in the wars rather than lived t' see the horrors o' Doaphin's occupation." Shaking his head sadly, Wil carried the precious bundle with him as he stepped outside.

Gralyre scanned the interior of the cottage a final time to ensure that they had not left anything essential behind. All the blankets and clothing they could carry, as well as their meagre stores of food, had been loaded on the packhorses. The vandalized hearth stood cold and empty, its cast iron pot missing from its customary hook. Despite the table and benches and the old chair in the corner, the cottage had already developed an air of desertion.

His gaze settled at the table, where sat the lass they had rescued, huddled under an old borrowed cloak of Dara's. Saliana had not spoken a word since she had awakened. He walked to her side and placed a gentle hand upon her shoulder. He frowned slightly as she flinched away from him. "We must away, lass. We are going to a safe place."

Saliana responded at last, lifting her white, pinched features. "There is no such thing," she croaked dully, sounding older than time.

"Ah, but there is," Gralyre responded quietly. "We go to the mountains, to the Rebels."

For a brief moment, a spark lit her eyes, but it died a stillbirth. "They will catch us."

"Perhaps," Gralyre agreed briskly, "but perhaps not." The change in his voice penetrated her shock and focussed her attention upon him. "But they will certainly capture us if we stay here. Any chance is better than none."

"What o' my father?" she asked, whisper soft.

Gralyre sighed, considered lying to her, but knew that would be worse. "He is dead. Trampled in the tavern."

Her head ducked to hide her emotion, before lifting up once more. A tear ran from her eye, but her chin was as firm as her shoulders. "There is nothing holding me here now," she stated. "I will come with ye." She stood and strode out the door.

Gralyre watched her go, saddened for her loss but marvelling at her strength. He followed her out of the cottage and slammed the door smartly behind for the last time. The brothers were already mounted and Wil was helping Saliana up onto her horse.

Little Wolf trotted up to Gralyre's side from where he had been circling the horses. *'There is an evil smell in the air. Something comes! It runs before the wind!'*

Gralyre stared grimly in the direction the wind was blowing from. Raindell. Firelight glittered on the horizon. Large papers of ash, born by the wind, were beginning to drift down from the sky, declarations of destruction writ by the ravagers of Raindell. The ash peppered the white snow with sooty blemishes.

Only a short span had wasted away while they had packed. Gralyre had expected more time before the Demon Riders finished purging the village and turned their attention to the nearby farms. Of course, anyone at the tavern would have pointed to Wil's croft to find the murderer of the Lord. It would have hastened the 'Riders their way.

The harsh glow from the full moon illuminated the world with a cold blue light of only slightly less brilliance than the midday sun. If they did not leave immediately, they would be trapped in the open. Their only hope was to make it to the cover of the forest. Even then, they would need all the help the Gods of Fortune cared to give in order to slip away.

"Quickly!" Gralyre warned, his voice harsh with tension. "Little Wolf smells the approach of Demon Riders, from the direction of Raindell!"

Dajin spit into the snow and stared fearfully at the empty lane that wound through the fallow fields towards the village. "How did they arrive so quickly?"

"Never mind that now! Make for the trees!" Wil urged.

They rode as quickly as the deep snow would allow, out across the fallow fields, heading for the safety of the forest. Little Wolf whined urgently, easily keeping pace with the horses with bounding leaps that took him up and forward out of the chest high snowpack. Gralyre used his powers to ensure the packhorses stayed close.

They reached the relative safety of the forest, but left behind them a clear trail of churned snow to point the way for any pursuit. The thick woods forced them to slow their horses to a quick walk, but within the sheltering trees the snow was not quite so deep.

All that was heard was the creaking of the frost bound forest and the muffled thud of the horses' hooves. Both the humans and the animals were puffing gusts of fog from their urgent dash. They were all instinctually loath to disturb the quiet.

"This way," Wil whispered, leading them to a hard packed game trail. "If we cut through on this trail for a bit, we will circle Raindell and come out at the road t' Verdalan. Then, 'tis several weeks o' hard travel t' reach the city. We pass close t' the village, but 'tis the only way t' reach the road."

The wind that had been blowing away from them gusted suddenly, changing direction. Little Wolf stopped in his tracks and snarled quietly, his gaze fixated upon the trail ahead.

"Halt!" hissed Gralyre.

The others, upon hearing his urgent command, reined in their horses immediately. The horses snorted the air and stomped their hooves, unwilling to stand still, as they too could smell the taint of evil coming towards them.

"What is it?" breathed Rewn.

"Demon Riders," Gralyre's hushed voice barely carried as he pointed to the woods directly in their path. "But Little Wolf says that they smell different. Their taint is stronger."

"Gods!" Wil's breath huffed urgently with the intensity of his emotions. "Rewn, marked ye how many 'Riders died tonight in the tunnels and in the tavern?"

"More than I wish t' think on," Rewn muttered fearfully.

"Deathren!" Gralyre's mind flashed back to the dead 'Riders in the tavern who had inexplicably regained their feet and continued to kill.

Demon Riders on the main road, and Deathren on the secret paths; Doaphin's creatures were making sure that the fugitives could not flee. "Can we outrun them?" Gralyre mouthed the words at Wil.

"No, lad," Wil whispered back, equally quiet, his face a mask of dismay. "The Deathren can run forever. Our horses will tire a thousand times over afore they ever will. They are no longer alive. Evil moves their limbs like a puppet master. They feel no fear, no pity, only an insatiable urge t' kill and feed. The only thing that can stop them is sunlight, or decapitation. But, I very much fear that none o' us will see the dawn! If there be more than one, they will swarm us before we can take their heads!"

Wil's whisper caught in his tightened chest as panic threatened. "When they catch our scent, they will run us to ground!"

"Look!" Rewn's urgent command was hushed as he pointed through the sheltering brush at their now distant cottage. A column of 'Riders had appeared in the lane from Raindell, trotting their horses steadily towards the farm.

"I told ye we would no' escape," Saliana whispered forlornly.

"We canno' go forward or back!" Dajin whispered urgently. "Why are we stopping?" Dajin's softened voice was pitched high from terror. "Ride! Do something!" His horse jittered restlessly as his hands tightened on his reins.

Gralyre ignored him as his mind raced for a strategy. "If we turn back, the noise of battle with the 'Riders will draw the Deathren, and we would still have to face them. The Deathren are the more dangerous, but we need only elude them until dawn, and the less enemies we need face at once, the better."

Gralyre's lips tightened into a determined line. "I say we go around the Deathren, slowly and quietly, and hope the wind will not carry our scent to them. If they do not sense us, we may be able to win free. When they cross our trail, we will hopefully have a far enough advance to stay ahead of them for the night!"

Despite his prisoner status, Wil instinctively responded to Gralyre's intrinsic authority. "I can think o' no better plan. So be it! We go forward. But quietly! Even if we make it past them, we may have only moments afore they cross our trail here and the hunt begins, so be ready t' fight!" Wil drew his sword quietly from its sheath.

The three younger men also drew steel before moving the

horses slowly forward. They left the game trail and pushed into the dense bushes. Within moments of leaving the path they were forced to dismount and lead their animals. When the horses would have balked, Gralyre chastised them, keeping them quiet and cooperative.

Every jingle of harness and thump of hoof made them wince, but the thick woods and soft snow muffled the sound beyond a few feet. Moving as fast as they dared, they made a large loop.

At one point, as their detour drew them closer, the sound of screams and crackling fires reached their ears, but the thick forest hid from sight the atrocities that were befalling Raindell.

Judging that they had travelled far enough, they finally cut back up onto the trail. Before coming out into the open, they examined the path carefully for signs that they were now behind the Deathren.

Gralyre bent and touched a hollow left in the snow from a naked human foot. The ridges crumbled away, bespeaking a fresh made track. Many prints, both shod and bare, led away down the game trail. They had managed to circumvent the Deathren.

"Does the Wolf sense anything," Wil asked in a hushed voice as they examined the empty path ahead and behind.

"No," Gralyre replied just as softly. "They are no longer in front of us, but they could be just around the bend behind us. Even Little Wolf cannot scent them against the wind."

Rewn tensed. "But the Deathren may be able to scent us."

"Alright," Wil breathed, a plume of fog wreathing his craggy face as he spoke. "We take the trail, but we keep the horses t' a walk. Only when we know for certain we are beyond earshot can we afford t' run. Keep your swords ready."

A long drawn out howl arose from the woods behind them. It echoed sinisterly amongst the trees, defying them to judge the distance of the monstrous baying. For the figures huddled at the edge of the trail, it was a sound they knew came straight from the throat of darkness.

Saliana gave a moaning, choked off little keen as Gralyre's hand smothered her lips before the sound could gain volume.

"Easy," Gralyre murmured to one and all. "'Tis just noise. They do not have our trail yet."

At another baying howl, a packhorse reared in fright. Gralyre reached out with his mind and soothed it before it could make more noise.

But the beast's panic seemed to ignite the same in Dajin. "Quick! Mount up!" Dajin cried out wildly, grabbing his horse's reins and suiting action to words. Before they could stop him, he was pounding away down the road and it was too late for stealth.

Wil's face drained of colour. "Dajin!" Will mouthed soundlessly in horrified disappointment as he watched his son abandon all in his mad panic to flee.

Rewn cursed softly and vilely, his panicked gaze scanning the darkened woods behind them as the Deathren let loose with full voice. The echoes of the frenzied howls in the woods behind bespoke clearer than words that The Hunt had begun.

"Ride!" Gralyre yelled.

The rest of the party mounted up and was away after Dajin's panicked flight.

"Dajin, son, stop!" Wil roared over the pounding hooves.

Dajin either ignored Wil or was unable to hear his father's harsh plea over the rushing of wind past his ears. He soon outdistanced them all, lost in the bends and twists of the snow packed trail.

∞⚭

The face of the Demon Rider Captain was painted in flickering amber on one side, from the flames that roared into the sky from Wil Wilson's cottage, and in icy cold blue on the other from the harsh moonlight. The uncanny effect was all the more chilling as it highlighted the duality of his nature, that of both Warrior and Monster.

His troops were searching and despoiling the crofter's outbuildings when the Deathren's ululating cries of the hunt shattered the night. All around the yard, 'Riders paused to listen to the triumphant bayling of their brethren.

The Captain turned to his men and raised his fists in victory. "The Deathren will take care o' those murderers who 'ave fled. Mount up! We head back t' the village for the rest o' the Midwinter's Slaughter!"

The 'Riders cheered as they put spurs to their horses and charged down the lane towards village. By the time the night was over, there would be nothing left standing and nobody left alive.

∞⚭

The horses dodged and slid through the moonlit shadows on the icy trail, obeying the galloping instinct to flee the horror that was hunting them.

Rewn dropped back to where Saliana struggled to stay in her saddle. He had already noted that the lass was an inexperienced rider. If she could not keep pace, she would fall behind and be the first of them to fall victim to the evil that stalked them.

When Rewn's horse fell into step beside hers, Saliana glanced over at him gratefully.

Over the rush of the wind and the pounding of hooves, he yelled instructions, showing her a better way to hold her reins and sit her saddle.

Necessity made a quick learner and she soon gained confidence to be able to pick up the pace, but when the horse jumped a deadfall that crossed their path, she almost lost her seat. Panicked, she slowed once more.

Patiently, Rewn began his encouragement again. The urgency of his lessons was punctuated by fearful glances over his shoulder.

Gralyre bent low over his horse, its mane whipping into his eyes, as he tried to catch Dajin. The fool would founder his horse if he kept the pace of his panicked flight, not to mention that one slip on the ice, and the horse could break a leg and all would be lost! And if he got too far ahead and ran into another party of Demon Riders... Enough!

Gralyre reined his horse to a blowing halt and reached out with his power, forcing Dajin's horse to stop.

Far beyond the bend in the road, he heard a screech of rage as the animal obeyed. For good measure, Gralyre took control of all the horses, bringing everyone to a safe standstill.

"Gralyre! What...? Dajin...?" Wil's breath was coming in hard, harsh pants.

"Catch your breath. I have stopped him. He is going nowhere until we reach him."

On the trail behind, a packhorse was whinnying its panic, for its load had shifted during the mad dash and threatened to slide under its belly. Gralyre dismounted, as did Rewn, and they worked together quickly to redistribute the packhorse's load while Wil checked the girths on the other animals to ensure they were holding.

They remounted and Gralyre set the horses to a brisk, ground-eating trot. Saliana, in particular, looked very grateful to be riding at a more manageable speed.

"Is everyone alright?" Gralyre asked.

Wil nodded, but Gralyre suspected that the flush in his cheeks owed as much to embarrassment over his son's cowardice as to the biting wind.

They trotted around the bend to see Dajin cruelly slapping his beast with the flat of his sword while spurring bloody gouges into its soft flanks. The trembling animal cried from the pain yet stood still as Gralyre had demanded.

Dajin was out of control. Again.

Gralyre cursed when he saw what was happening and urged his horse into a canter, outdistancing the others. He reached over as he rode up, and grabbed Dajin's shoulder in a punishing grip while wrenching away the sword he was using to beat the horse.

When Dajin lost his weapon, he turned on Gralyre with a snarl, hands clawed to fight.

Without flinching, Gralyre shook him hard enough to rattle his teeth, plucked him from the saddle and dumped him to the snowy ground. "Come back to us, Dajin! We must stick together and remain calm, or we are all dead!" he urged with a hard edge to his voice. There was no time to gently jog the younger man from his panic madness.

"Let me go!" Dajin keened, a high note of terror breaking in his voice and making him sound even younger than he was as he jumped to his feet and hauled on his horse's bridle, trying without success to move the beast forward, his feet slipping and sliding in the snow as he threw his bodyweight against the horse's strength. "They will catch us! We must go faster!"

Gralyre snarled, lifted Dajin from his feet, and gave him another bone rattling shake that sent him sprawling back into the snow. "Use your head! How far do you think you would get with running your horse that hard? In short time, it would have foundered and then you would be dead, and us along with you when we stopped to defend you.

"The Deathren move only as fast as a man at the run. The horses will stay ahead of them only so long as we save their wind! I should make you walk for your stupidity, save that it would slow us even further." Gralyre threw Dajin's sword contemptuously into the snow next to where he lay and rode onward.

Dajin rested on his back, panting harshly with confusion as his family came abreast him. Why were they not stopping? "Da?

Rewn? Are ye going t' let him speak t' me that way?"

"Ye are a disgrace, son. Get on your horse!" Wil's voice was heavily tinted with condemnation as he rode by with Rewn and Saliana close behind.

Rewn kept his face averted as though he did not even want to look at him as he passed.

His father's contempt brought Dajin to his feet, much subdued but still defiant. The horse shied away from him, spinning in a circle as he mounted, untrusting of a rider who would cause it pain.

Dajin paid it no mind, more afraid of the Deathren howls behind and the enigmatic prisoner ahead, who had somehow taken control of everything. That Gralyre was right made no impression. Dajin swiped at tears as he stared daggers at Gralyre's back. The warrior rode at the head of the line, setting the pace for the group

Why was his father allowing Gralyre to take the lead without a word of protest? The man was their prisoner!

He probably only wanted to go slow so his stupid wolf could keep up, Dajin sneered. He ignored the fact that the long limbed wolfdog was loping along over the snow with less difficulty than the horses.

At a particularly gruesome bay from the Deathren, Dajin could not contain his shivering fear. He rudely squeezed his horse past Rewn and Saliana on the narrow track so that he rode in the middle of the line behind his father, unapologetically placing more bodies betwixt himself and danger.

He glanced back in time to see the girl, Saliana, drop her

eyes, but she did not look away quickly enough to prevent him from seeing the cold contempt. Dajin's jaw clenched.

First Gralyre killed the Lord, robbing Dajin of the honour, and now the girl he had rescued was sneering at him! They were all against him!

Dajin looked back again, and noted how Rewn was riding protectively at the back of the column. His perfect brother defending their rear flank.

A Deathren roared, and Dajin's attention snapped forward. He shook with the urge to race his horse again, but he did not quite have the courage to defy Gralyre's edict.

But his Da was not afraid of Gralyre, for see, he was riding ahead now to take the lead. A smile of pure, overindulged satisfaction contorted Dajin's face.

It was about time Da regained control of their prisoner and reminded him of his place! Dajin watched avidly so as not to miss a single moment of Gralyre's comeuppance.

Wil took advantage of a widening in the track to move his horse abreast of Gralyre's. "I apologize for my son's behaviour," he began hesitantly. "I am t' blame. I have been far too lenient on him, shielded him too much from the horrors o' the world. Perhaps if I had given him more duties..." his shoulders shrugged in helpless uncertainty.

"He is young," Gralyre interrupted him and then changed the subject to alleviate the older man's embarrassment. "How much further until this trail intersects the road to Verdalan?"

"Another two leagues or so."

"We must keep the horses to the slowest pace we can and still maintain a reasonable distance from the Deathren. The longer we can go without having to run them, the better chance we have of winning through until dawn." Gralyre fell silent as another chorus of inhuman howls rent the air. Though still far behind, were they beginning to sound closer?

His eyes met Wil's. Silently they acknowledged that despite their precautions, this was probably their last night to live.

Wil fell back and let Gralyre take the lead.

"Da!" Dajin hissed as he spurred his horse even with his father's. "What are ye doing? He is our prisoner! He should be following our orders!"

Wil shot his youngest son a look so full of rage and worry that Dajin cowed and shut his mouth with a snap.

"If we live through this night, 'twill be o' no thanks t' ye, boy! 'Twill be because o' that man," Wil pointed at Gralyre. "I will no' hear one more word from your mouth, Dajin!" Wil's voice broke. "Ye have... may have... killed us all... How can I protect ye from yourself?" Wil hung his head and bitter tears flowed from his eyes, freezing in the cold before they could fall, leaving icy trails across his cheeks.

Dajin swallowed heavily and allowed his horse to drop back, his body wracked by shivers of shame. Nothing that had happened this ill-met night had touched him so hard as this; not the murder, not the destruction of Raindell, and not even his terror of the horrors that dogged their trail.

Just this.

His Da's crushing disappointment, not in Dajin, but in his own failings as a father. It was the first time Dajin could remember seeing his father cry.

�❧☙

Little Wolf, scouting the road ahead, signalled Gralyre that all was well. The group had reached the intersection of the trail with the king's road to Verdalan and had paused for a quick rest while Little Wolf reconnoitred their route.

Gralyre had kept the horses moving in a slow walking circle so that they would not grow stiff, while the people supped some water and did what they could to steel themselves for the night ahead.

Behind them, the howls continuously shattered the crystalline stillness of the moonlit night, drawing everyone's nerves taut unto the breaking point. During their brief stop, the Deathren had definitely drawn nearer.

Gralyre examined the road pessimistically as he made note of the deep snow that was pristine save for the tracks made by Little Wolf. The horses would be breaking trail all the way, and their pace would be slowed.

"Time to go," Gralyre announced.

The small group mounted up and rode onto the wider track of the road to Verdalan. The road was flat and straight, with none of the encroaching wilderness that had slapped and torn at them on the game trail, but as Gralyre had feared, the deeper, uncompressed snow was no friend to their pace. He could only hope that the drifts would also slow the Deathren.

As the moon waned and the stars spiralled indifferently across the heavens, they alternated the gaits of their tiring mounts, coaxing as much speed and as many miles from them as they dared.

Despite all of their efforts, the unceasing shrieks grew louder and closer.

The forest gave way to a plain, and were it not for large rocks placed at intervals along the edge of the track, there would be no way to delineate where the road ended and the flat open land commenced.

Without trees to break its power, the wind gusted and swirled. In places, the road was swept clean as from a broom and their pace could increase. But the bounty of the wind swung both ways. Into every dip and hollow, deep drifts of snow left their horses floundering and kicking as though swimming in mud, bogging them down until they would finally break a path through. Every delay shortened the gap between hunters and hunted.

Without any trees to shelter them, there would be no hiding when the Deathren caught up. The only thing standing between them and the pursuing death was the endurance of their gallant horses and the slowly approaching sunrise.

Large boulders littered the plain. Their size and shape, along with their thick, snowy caps, gave the impression of abandoned dwellings. The bright moonlight created shadow and illusion, and more than one rider turned to stare at a boulder in passing, seeking a phantom movement spied from the corner of the eye.

Dawn was eminent. The stars had begun to fade, though the sky had yet to lighten, when Wil spurred his horse to the front of the line and fell in beside Gralyre once more. The baying Deathren were now very close. He shivered mightily at the bitter wind blowing into their faces, and the bitter fear blowing through his heart.

"Our mounts are all but done," Wil warned.

Gralyre left off watching Little Wolf struggle to keep up. The pup was exhausted, as were they all. He released his reins and put his freezing hands to his mouth, blowing hot breath into his cupped palms in an effort to warm them. He met Wil's eyes. "You have an idea?"

"Hangman's Tor is only a league or so further. 'Tis the only hill in the area. 'Tis highly defensible..."

"Plus the sun will shine on the top of the hill first, a couple of minutes before it will strike the flats," Gralyre comprehended.

Wil nodded grimly. "A couple of minutes could make the difference t' us. Rewn thinks he saw one of them, but 'tis hard t' tell the moonlight from movement at this distance. If they are so close, we will be lucky t' reach Hangman's Tor afore they drag us from our mounts, let alone keep ahead o' them t' the top, but 'tis our best chance."

Neither man addressed the odd shift of power that had happened between them as they fled in the night. Now was not the time for divided leadership. Though Wil was advising courses of action, it was Gralyre who was now making the decisions. His natural air of command and instincts of a seasoned campaigner had impressed itself upon the group's consciousness. Prisoner or not, they were all looking to him to save their lives.

As though to emphasize the nearness of the danger, a howling ululation echoed from the road behind. It was far closer than any of them had anticipated. As one the group turned startled eyes to search back along the flat road.

The exhausted band looked to their leader. "Time to run!" Gralyre shouted. "We make for the top of Hangman's Tor!"

For the first time that night, he allowed the horses to gallop. This is what they had been saved for. Even so, they would have faltered in their exhaustion had Gralyre not explained why their speed was necessary. The horses leapt ahead without further encouragement, bearing their weary riders to safety with their last strength.

False dawn began to lighten the sky and Gralyre risked a glance behind. Horror almost stole the heart of him. To the end of his days, he knew he would have nightmares about his first sight of the Deathren who were running them to ground.

The snow was reflecting back the slowly lightening sky, brightening the night to a dark grey. Eight figures ran effort-lessly along the track behind them, easily gaining on the foundering horses. Their legs cycled tirelessly, never faltering, never slowing.

Their arms dangled limply at their sides. They ran not as men ran, for men would be using their arms vigorously, pumping them up and down in an effort to gain more speed. These creatures ran using only their legs. Their slack jaws bounced with their rough gait, but no fog of breath exited. Some bore gaping wounds from their deaths earlier in the evening, but the injuries hindered them naught. Without a pause in their mechanical strides they lifted their heads and screamed at their fleeing prey. The panicked horses leapt ahead even faster.

"Look!" Rewn yelled over the rushing wind and the strident howls. "Hangman's Tor! We made it!"

Ahead of them, silhouetted black against the bruised sky was the Tor. The tall, cone shaped mound was manmade for the purpose of exhibiting Doaphin's executions to all who passed. It was at least fifty feet to the crest upon which Gralyre could make out metal cages swinging from poles.

Gralyre glanced back over his shoulder. Gods! 'Twas going to be close; a race between the horses, the Deathren and the Dawn!

They left the road using the cart path that led to the Tor, their horses in a flat gallop. As they began their assent, they abandoned the deep snow of the long serpentine cart trail that wound to the top, for a quicker straight-line assent, where the wind had swept away most of the snow.

The horses slowed drastically as they fought against the pull of gravity and scrabbled for footing on the loose shale that made up the slope as they lunged upwards.

The Deathren slowed not at all. Their relentless howls shattered the night, screeching of pain and hunger.

Dajin sobbed his fear, frantically spurring his horse faster. This time Gralyre did nothing to stop him, for he was frantically whipping his own mount for more speed.

The horses tried valiantly to obey the frenzied commands, but the hill was made of loose shale and rocks, slicked over with ice and snow. Even in the best of weather, the way would have been treacherous.

The inevitable happened. Saliana's horse jumped sideways to avoid a large rock, and then stumbled on the slick surface and fell. Saliana's short scream ended abruptly as her head hit the rock her horse had leapt to avoid. With a sigh of relief, she slipped into darkness. She would not be awake to meet her death. The horse lunged to its feet and plunged up the hill without its rider.

Rewn heard Saliana's cry as her riderless horse careened past him. With a curse, he spun his mount and spurred back downhill towards the fallen girl. He screamed her name as he rode towards her, but she did not move.

He thought he would have enough time to grab her up and ride again, but he had not counted on the speed at which the Deathren were making their assent.

Wil turned in his saddle when he heard Rewn shout Saliana's name. Taking in the situation at a glance, he did not hesitate before urging his horse back down slope towards his son.

Dujin twisted his head incredulously to watch as his father fly past. When he saw Rewn's danger, he almost turned back, but he found that he could not overcome his panic. Instead, he put spurs to his horse's heaving sides, demanding more speed from the beast to reach the summit of the Tor.

Dajin's shame was great, and he turned his face away as Gralyre thundered past, chasing Wil back downhill. Even the wolfdog had responded to the danger, following closely on his master's heels.

Rewn arrived at Saliana's side in a spray of gravel. Already turning his horse to flee uphill he leaned too far over in his saddle, intending to scoop her from the ground and continue on. But the Gods of Fortune denied him as his horse overbalanced, stumbled, and slid upon the loose shale.

Rewn fell hard, just missing the unconscious lass. He grunted as he painfully jumped to his feet and drew his sword, though he felt curiously calm as he spun to meet the evil that accelerated towards him from less than twenty feet away.

There were too many of them. He could not outfight the swarm, but perhaps he could outrun them.

He slung Saliana up over his shoulder and sprinted upwards, using his sword for balance against the slippery rocks as he aimed for the summit. At any moment he expected to feel the Deathren's teeth in his neck. His chest laboured in gasps of exertion as his long legs carried him higher and higher. Everything around him slowed and time was measured by the beats of his heart.

Like a dream, the false dawn blushed a warm, pink hue. Then it happened. Sunlight suddenly gilded the top of the Tor. Rewn had never seen anything so beautiful. It illuminated the rime of frost around the thick bars that made up the ghastly cages, turning the cold iron as glowing white as the skeletons within.

But Rewn was still in deep shadow. Off his left shoulder a Deathren howled in his ear… he felt the swipe of a clawed hand skid off his cloak… he was not going to make it…

Wil roared past, ramming his horse through the pursuing Deathren and knocking most of them over with the force of his passage. Shouting the ancient battle cry of his forefathers, Wil's sword hacked away, buying his son the time to escape.

Rewn grinned at his father's heroics and redoubled his efforts to meet Gralyre, whose horse was fast approaching.

The Deathren ignored the blows that would have been the death of any mortal creature. They did not cry out in pain or fear as they were struck by Wil's blade again and again. Only the howls, the insane shrieks. Their dead flesh had frozen hard during the night. Wil could not get his sword to bite deep enough to take their heads. His horse danced and spun with fear as he tried to disengage himself from the losing fight.

Gralyre reached Rewn's side just as a Deathren slipped past Wil's blade and eviscerated his mount. With a shrill death scream the horse toppled, trapping Wil's leg, pinning him beneath its dead weight. Unable to escape or fight, he screamed as the Deathren fell upon him, their hands tearing, their teeth ripping.

"Wil!" Gralyre yelled. His horse reared in fright, delaying him the precious moment when he may have been able to still come to Wil's aid

Rewn turned back to look. "Da!" he screamed. His blade came up and he threw Saliana from his shoulders like a damp cloak. But even as he took two shuddering strides to come to his father's aid, it was already too late.

With his last breath, Wil screamed out but one word. "Run!" The word was severed with finality.

Rewn stuttered to a halt and his chest heaved with anguish as he watched the Deathren swarm over his father's bloodied body.

"Rewn, get on the horse," Gralyre shouted, leaning down and

offering a hand but Rewn was frozen in shock and did not seem to hear him.

"Gods!" Gralyre cursed and dismounted. Wil had sacrificed himself, so that his son and the girl could live. His selfless act would not be in vain.

Gralyre rocked Rewn with a sharp slap across the face, refocusing the grieving man to the eminent danger. "Get on the horse!" Gralyre shouted again and shoved Rewn towards the quivering animal.

Rewn resisted, his face wild with grief as he gazed back at the pack of Deathren. Momentarily silenced and distracted by the warm flesh they consumed so greedily, they feasted upon his father and the horse. With tears streaming down his face, and sobs of rage tearing from his throat, Rewn complied with Gralyre's order at last and leapt into the saddle.

Gralyre scooped up Saliana with the ease of a child lifting a ragdoll, and draped her across Rewn's thighs. He swung himself up behind and spurred the horse towards the summit, heading towards the light. The horse struggled under the triple weight, moving too slowly.

Gralyre's eyes narrowed contemptuously as Dajin, far ahead now, galloped over the summit into the safety of the sun's haven. The packhorses followed after him.

The Deathren left off their feeding as the frantic movements of escaping prey caught their attention. With their howls echoing greedily off the icy slope, their Hunt continued. They shot after the fleeing horse, their bloodlust even greater than before, now that they'd had a taste of it.

As the sunrise advanced, the shadow of the hillside lightened and the Deathren smouldered and sparked as the brightness of dawn began to consume their flesh. Heavy smoke and ash began to stream from their bodies, and their skin began to crackle and blacken as the bright demarcation of sunlight from shadow rapidly approached. Yet they were still safe in the shade of the Tor. Only full sunlight would destroy them.

Even with the slight head start that Wil's sacrifice had bought them, Gralyre knew they would not make it with his exhausted horse carrying a triple burden. Far above, he could see Dajin silhouetted by dawn's first light, holding the reins of his mount in one hand, his sword in the other, watching them race the Deathren to the top. Gralyre's rage built as he did nothing to help.

Dajin still quaked with terror. His heart was twisted with grief for his father and fear for his brother but he was petrified to leave the safe shelter of sunlight. He rocked back and forth on his heels as he watched the horse lose the race.

Mere strides from reaching the edge of sunlight, the Deathren caught up. They leapt from behind, grabbing Gralyre by his shoulders and pulling him from the lunging horse.

Rewn spun the exhausted mount in a tight circle, knocking down three of the Deathren who had flanked him, before he flung himself from the saddle with no thought but to protect one of his own, and avenge his father.

His sword clenched tightly, an uncharacteristic battle snarl distorting his features, Rewn slapped the horse on the rump with the flat of his blade and sent it careening for the safety of the light, carrying the limp Saliana with it.

Two of the Deathren gave chase, but the horse, with its lighter burden, easily outran them now, bursting at full gallop into the rosy glow gilding the flat top of the Tor.

The Deathren followed mindlessly, howling their inhuman challenge. But as they touched the light, their shrieks ceased and they burst into flames. The sunlight consumed their flesh within moments. All that remained was black ash darkening the melted snow upon which they had stood.

Rewn reached down into the mob that was pinning Gralyre and grabbed him by his hair, the only part that could be seen, and pulled him upright and free of the Deathren's clutches.

Gralyre was bleeding from several wounds, but the evil creatures had not had time to inflict much damage. He nodded his thanks as he quickly pulled his sword. "Look out!"

Rewn ducked an attacking Deathren as Gralyre neatly side-stepped and severed the head with a mighty blow. It dropped like a marionette that had lost its strings. That left five to be dealt with.

Back to back, Gralyre and Rewn retreated step by hard fought step up the slope.

The creatures cared naught that Gralyre and Rewn carried swords, for what had they to fear of death, they who were already dead? Their attack was tireless and unflinching, as one creature of many parts, desperate for a portion of the warm living blood that pulsed through the veins of the men.

Gralyre swung his sword into the neck of a Deathren whose mutilated face attested to its encounter with the tunnel rats the night before. The blade bit deep, but failed to severe the head completely.

Even while its head lay upon one shoulder, attached by only a sliver of meat, the Deathren's clutching, clawed fingers still searched for flesh, and its jaws still snapped closed with harsh clicks of teeth. Black, congealed blood rife with ice crystals seeped sluggishly from the stump of its neck.

Its glazed, frozen eyes were obscured in a shifting billow of smoke from its own burning flesh as, with a sickened snarl, Gralyre hacked again, this time completing the job.

The four remaining Deathren used the opening to crowd in, clawing and ripping at the two men.

Circling the Deathren nimbly, Little Wolf darted in and out of their legs. He attempted to hamstring the creatures, but on his first attack he burned his mouth on their smoking flesh. From that moment, all he could do was growl and snap, not causing any harm, but creating a useful distraction.

When the Deathren turned to include the wolfdog in their attack, it gave the men the opening they needed to advance a step closer to light.

Fingernails raked Gralyre's face, burning him, but he could no longer swing his sword due to the Deathren's tight proximity. He threw an elbow and was gratified to feel a nose break, but the creature took no notice. The Deathren's strength knew naught the limits of the flesh. Their death had freed them of any human frailties. At his back, he could feel the desperate movements of Rewn as he hacked and stabbed for their survival.

Gralyre thrust at the belly of the creature to force it away, but wearing its rictus grin, the Deathren impaled itself, walking its smoking body up the sword to get at the warm living flesh it craved. It had its teeth in Gralyre's hand before he could fathom it. With a cry of pain, Gralyre loosed his sword and kicked the creature away.

As it stumbled over a rock and tripped, Gralyre drew his dagger just in time to stab another attacker in the eye. He used his massive strength the throw it back, but there was no respite to be had as another took its place.

Dead hands still bloodied and slick with Wil's blood clawed across Gralyre's chest. He slashed at the fingers with his dagger but the Deathren did not flinch. The burning arm seared Gralyre's skin as the nails clawed deeper. He could not force enough distance from the burning Deathren without a sword.

His eyes dipped to check out the weaponry still strapped to the Deathren, and he almost laughed his relief as he saw the sword belted to its waist. Gralyre grabbed for the hilt just as teeth ripped into his other shoulder from a second attacker.

He slashed his short dagger at the throat of the biting Deathren, but it had already circled behind him to try its luck at Rewn. Movement flowing with the dance, Gralyre thrust the point of his pilfered sword against a metal chest plate to push the first Deathren off balance and away.

Rewn chanced a glance upslope and saw that they were only ten feet away from the safe edge of sunlight. They could make it if they had help!

"Dajin, help us!" Rewn yelled as a corpse sporting a blade through its torso attacked him. He recognized Gralyre's sword in a small corner of his mind as he fought it back.

Dajin took a step forward as though he were going to come to his brother's aid before he buried his face in his hands with a terrified moan, and sank to his knees. Refusing to help, refusing to watch his brother's death, he rocked with his eyes squeezed shut, his hands pressed tightly to his ears to block Rewn's cries.

"Dajin!" Rewn begged again. His brother's name turned into a scream of agony as the teeth of a Deathren sank into his arm. He thrust it away with a shout of rage. It left with a bit of fabric and flesh, only to dart in again for another taste.

The wind eddied with ashes and smoke, choking Gralyre and Rewn, making it difficult to fend off the lightning fast attacks of the frenzied creatures who ripped chunks of flesh from the men and dodged away, only to advance again in another spot. They never stayed still long enough for Rewn and Gralyre to defend themselves

"Dajin!" Rewn continued to scream, unable to believe his brother would abandon him. The sun was rising slowly but they would not live long enough for the light to reach them upon the shaded side of the slope.

Atop the hill, Dajin was petrified by horror and shocked to insensibility at his father's death. He keened and rocked, kneeling on the cold shale in a shaft of sparkling safe sunshine.

But someone finally did heed Rewn's call

Saliana gradually regained awareness of her surroundings. Still draped over Gralyre's horse she struggled to right herself, and wobbled as the horse's heaving, panting sides briefly overbalanced her. She placed a trembling hand to the lump on the side of her head. The pain from touching her injury brought her senses sharply into focus.

'*I am still alive,*' she thought in jubilation, and discovered herself glad for it.

The cries of terror and battle finally seeped into her pain soaked mind. With a wince, she turned her head to see Rewn and Gralyre, beset by four Deathren, slowly being ripped to pieces.

Their clothing was tattered, and their bodies bled fiercely from numerous wounds. The smoke from the burning Deathren briefly obscured them from her sight, but did not prevent her from hearing Rewn scream for his brother's aid.

What had happened?

She saw the remains of Wil Wilson's body on the slope of the hill, in the spot where she had fallen, and realization blazed through her heart. They had come back for her! They had sacrificed themselves so that she would live. In that moment, Rewn's battle enraged features imprinted forever on her soul.

In her family, no man had ever placed such worth on a female. It was inconceivable to her, she who had grown up knowing that some day, the 'Riders would be coming for her and that the men in her family would gladly sacrifice her for their own safety.

She had escaped the Tithe when a strange warrior had attacked the caged wagon. She had not returned to the village for fear of the repercussions and had been too scared to accompany some of the women into the mountains where they said there would be safety.

Saliana had lived alone in the forest for weeks until she could no longer survive, and shame, hunger and loneliness had driven her back to her father.

She had been sorely grieved to discover that the rescuing warrior had been taken by the 'Riders, but she was safe, she had stayed away long enough to avoid the second Tithe.

Her father had beaten her bloody for defying Doaphin and Saliana was left supping on the bitter dregs of her wasted chance to have escaped forever to the mountains.

When her father had willingly given her into the clutches of the new Lord, she had promised herself that if given another chance at life, at freedom, she would never again squander it so cheaply.

Her adulating gaze was riveted to Rewn's face. How handsome he was, how gallant! Throughout the night, he had ridden beside her, encouraging her when he could as easily have left her to fall behind.

She glared at Dajin, willing the man to save his brother, but she quickly recognized his petrified state. She saw in Dajin all that was wrong with the men she had grown up amongst. Cowardice, selfishness, hate. The two of them alone, safe inside the golden barrier of sunlight would survive. Her heart turned to ice at the thought. He would treat her no better than the men in her family had, likely worse, for he was no blood relative.

No, she decided fiercely, Rewn is the one I want to survive!

She had been given a taste of self-worth. She would cling to it, but what good was it without the man who had nurtured the small spark alive during the cold, horror soaked night?

Rewn and Gralyre were only eight paces from the sunlight,

but without a way to break free from the swarming Deathren, it might as well be a mile. It was obvious that Dajin was not going to bestir himself. Help would have to come from her.

With a determined twitch of the reins, Saliana awkwardly jerked the horse around. Spurring it harshly she forced it into a reluctant canter. Each pound of the hooves sent arrows of agony through her skull, but she would not be deterred.

Even if she died, it was preferable to living, having done nothing. If she did not take responsibility for the good and bad around her, she was no better than the weak men of her family who had sacrificed her to the Tithe and to the Lord, and no better than Dajin, sitting in his safe sunbeam and quaking with fear!

She flew past the kneeling man and out of the protection of the sun. Saliana entered the shaded hillside and the temperature seemed to drop with the loss of the light as she rode full tilt at the Deathren.

Rewn felt the shudder of hooves and turned thankfully to praise his brother for finally overcoming his fear to come to their rescue. To his amazement, it was not Dajin who rode so bravely, but Saliana.

Blood matted the hair at the side of her head from her fall. She swayed precariously in the saddle, clinging tightly to the speeding horse, as she advanced upon the dreaded Deathren armed with nothing more than the resolve on her face.

With a clatter of hooves on the loose shale, the horse mowed through the creatures, sending them sprawling. They were up again in a flash, but the distraction was enough to give Rewn and Gralyre the space they needed to make a break for safety.

One of the Deathren broke off to chase Saliana, but she was already pounding back up into the light at the summit of the Tor. The Deathren disappeared in a burst of flame and ash as it mindlessly chased the horse into the sunshine.

Gralyre and Rewn raced for the edge of sunlight with Little Wolf hard on their heels. Stumbling the last few paces, they supported each other with arms wrapped tight about the other's shoulder.

Inches away from the grasping fingers of cold death, they dove into the warmth of Dawn.

The lifeless shrieks of the remaining three Deathren ended abruptly with three distinct *whumps* of ignition. All was silent and there was naught remaining of their foes but black ash drifting down around them in clouds from the heat of the sunlight wrought cremations.

CHAPTER TWENTY-ONE

They gathered as much of Wil's remains as they could find. It took some time, for the Deathren had torn him to pieces. Though Gralyre offered to attend to the heart-breaking task for him, Rewn refused. He would honour his father, who had sacrificed his life for his son's.

When they shifted the dead horse that had fallen upon Wil, Gralyre retrieved Rewn's legacy from the saddlebag. It was the package he had helped Wil spend precious moments prying from the family hearth. With deep sorrow flooding through him, he now passed the bundle to Rewn. "Wil would want you to have this. 'Tis what is left of your family's heritage."

As Rewn accepted the small bundle from Gralyre's hands, a convulsion of sorrow shook his strong frame. He cradled it close to his chest as his legs gave way and he collapsed to sit on a large rock. For the first time since his father's death, Rewn lost his composure, buried his head in his bloodied hands, and wept.

Gralyre rested a heavy hand on Rewn's shoulder. There were no words that could express his sorrow at Rewn's loss. He had known Wil for only a short span, yet the generosity and integrity of the man would live with him forever.

With fingers that seemed almost angry, Rewn tore at the twine that held the package closed. He did not notice when he ripped a nail, the small pain was occluded by the greater pain in his heart.

At last the contents of the bundle lay spread before him; a small pouch of coins, a fine dagger missing the jewels that once had graced its pommel and guard, and a golden chain of office dangling the seal of his family's ancestral crest. Sobs rattled his frame as he rocked back and forth over his meagre legacy.

As the weight of responsibility that was owned by the head of the family settled firmly about Rewn's shoulders, Gralyre turned away and left his friend to his grieving. Rewn needed time to come to terms with the evil the Deathren had wrought this night.

Gralyre drew his sword and began the laborious task of hacking a grave into the frozen ground. They would lay Wil to rest on the Tor, near where he had fallen. Neither man could stand the thought of Wil resting beneath the crow cages at the summit.

As Gralyre began to dig, Rewn raised his head from his hands. "We fought the Deathren for longer than Da, why did they no' kill us?" His tears had worn riverbeds through the blood and ash from the battle, lines of grief and exhaustion. Neither he nor Gralyre had yet seen to their own wounds.

Gralyre shrugged. "It was brighter when we fought them. Perhaps their strength had begun to wane." His grief clouded his vision as he swung a hard chop into the frozen ground that would become Wil's grave.

"Can I help?" Dajin's hesitant voice intruded upon them. He had been uncommonly subdued in the aftermath of the battle, hovering at the periphery of things while Rewn and Gralyre prepared Wil for burial.

Rewn stiffened and turned his face away, his mouth working

in rage.

Gralyre hesitated as he glanced between the two men, before passing Dajin a sword. "Here, you can help me dig."

"Thank-ye," Dajin accepted the sword but tarried to begin. "What is that ye have, Rewn?" His tentative question seemed more designed to engage his brother in a conversation than to satisfy any curiosity.

Rewn swept the package back together and out of sight into his shirt. "Nothing." That one snapped word contained all the disappointment, grief and anger that he was feeling towards his brother.

"Oh." For once, Dajin accepted his brother's rejection stoically, turned away and began to stab at the ground.

In the end, the earth was too frozen to dig anything but a shallow grave. When they laid Wil to rest they used the loose stones of the Tor to build a sturdy cairn over him.

There was no ceremony, for they were all too grief struck and exhausted for eloquence. Instead, they grouped around the cairn on the hillside while the buffeting north wind played a lament through the rocks, and bowed their heads in silence.

It was a quiet and morose group that made its breakfast at the top of Hangman's Tor. They cooked some leftover rabbit in an iron pan over the flames and soaked chunks of hard stale bread in the drippings.

Huddling over the small blaze, they sought to warm the cold of their hearts as much as the chill in their flesh. They ate with little interest in what they consumed, chewing more out of habit than of any will to do so.

Rewn had yet to say a word to his brother. Dajin had begun a weeping apology for failing him, but Rewn had turned away, cutting him off. Now Dajin sat in sullen silence, nursing his self-pity as was his wont.

"Is it likely that the column of Demon Riders followed after us from the farm?" Gralyre asked into the strained silence.

"No," Rewn croaked through his cold chapped lips, his voice hoarse from his tears. "They knew the Deathren would catch us. There was no need for them t' come after. They will have returned t' Raindell. The village will be gone by now." His lips compressed into a hard line and tears spilled from his eyes unchecked as he looked to the spot where his father should have sat. Now that he had eaten, he had nothing but his heartache with which to occupy himself.

"That being the case, we will rest here for today and tonight. The horses are done in and so are we. We will set forth again tomorrow morning," Gralyre announced.

Dajin's head snapped up and he glared at Gralyre. "Who made ye the leader?" he challenged thoughtlessly with a complaint that he had harboured all night.

There was no anger in Gralyre's quiet, confident stare as he waited for Dajin to figure it out for himself.

Dajin was squirming in moments. He dropped his eyes and threw a stick in the fire, his mouth set in a moue of childish defiance from the intimidation of those self-assured blue eyes.

That level stare was worse by far than the harshest word or a hurtful cuff. Dajin was left with no doubt that not only was Gralyre in complete control of everyone, and everything, but that insolence and selfishness would no longer be tolerated. Punishment would be swift, and meted out with cold calculation, not heated anger. That one look had Dajin quaking in his boots.

Saliana approached Rewn hesitantly with a skin of water, a jar of salve and some bandages that she had gotten from one of the packs. She addressed his feet in her shyness. "I can dress your wounds..." Her eyes flicked to his face to gauge his approval, and then to Gralyre's, "... and yours," She drew a breath for courage. "... if ye would like."

Rewn nodded his assent, though his gaze was far away, held captive in a vault of suffering. He took little notice as Saliana crouched beside him, and began to clean and bandage the bite and claw marks that riddled him after his battle with the Deathren.

Across the small cook fire, Dajin, feeling the victim of persecution, watched Saliana shuffle closer to his brother. His lip curled spitefully as all the sorrow and shame that was consuming him bubbled over.

She had been playing Rewn for the fool all night! Now look at her, tending his wounds, cooing and clucking over him until he wanted to puke. *What about me? I lost my father too, but she has no sympathy t' spare for me!'*

The vision of her noble ride to rescue Rewn and Gralyre seared a path across his mind's eye and his shame whiplashed into rage. Dajin's fists clenched tightly, popping a couple of his knuckles. "Ye should be dead, no' Da!" Dajin snarled at Saliana, unable to contain his venom one moment longer.

"Dajin!" Gralyre exclaimed, horrified to his core.

Saliana's hands stilled in her task. The bloody rag she was using crumpled in her hand and her body tensed as Rewn slowly focussed on his brother.

"What did ye say?" Rewn's expression was stark.

"Ye will listen t' me for once, brother!" Dajin spewed. "If she had no' fallen and if ye had no' played the fool and gone back for her, we would all be safe! Da would be *alive*!"

"And Saliana would be dead!" Gralyre reminded him through clenched teeth. One glance at Rewn made him subside. This was a family matter for the brothers, but if Rewn did not handle it, Gralyre would. Dajin would not be allowed to harm Saliana.

"So what!" Dajin shouted. "Better her than Da!" He gave Rewn a disgusted headshake. "Brother, she has been playing ye like the whore she is! Shoving her titties in your face, making like she did no' know how t' ride so that ye would stay beside her all night! Slowing us down so that the Deathren could catch us!"

He held up his hand righteously, speaking loudly and quickly to finish his accusations before his brother could silence them. "And then! Then! Just when we were nearly free o' them," he sputtered emotionally, "she *slips and falls*!" He sneered in a falsetto voice. "We should kill her! She wanted us t' get caught! She is a collaborator, one o' *Them*, Rewn! Can ye no' see that, or is your pecker doing your thinking for ye?"

Saliana drew back with a gasp of fear, poised to flee although she knew she had no chance of outrunning the men. Rewn was silent for so long, she began to despair that Dajin's viperous words had reached him. The golden image she held of him began to tarnish with her dread. *'Please do no' let him be like the others!'*

She could not know it was rage that held him silent. Finally Rewn spoke, his voice a hoarse croak. "Dajin, in the past ye have said and done things that I have found distasteful, but I always put your actions down t' the inexperience o' youth." Rewn shook his head despairingly, confused and disgusted by his younger brother. "This is the first time I have seen clearly that your actions have everything t' do with cowardice and spite!"

Dajin's face paled as his brother spoke and he began to shake his head in denial of the betrayal that rolled though him. Rewn looked like he wanted to kill him, his own brother! Why could he not understand? Had the girl gotten her claws into him so thoroughly? "But... Rewn!" he sputtered.

Rewn made a slashing motion with his arm, cutting Dajin's words. "'Tis past time for ye t' grow up, boy! 'Tis past time t' accept responsibility for your actions! If I was looking for a collaborator, I would be hard pressed t' find one better suited than ye, who have caused the murder o' a Lord, the ruination o' a village, the destruction o' our croft, plus the horror o' being hunted down like stags at a hunt, all in one foul night! Ye have outdone yourself!"

Tears rolled down Dajin's cheeks and he began to rock with agitation, as these lances of truth hit him, barb by shining, hurtful barb.

"This girl has done nothing t' earn your ire, save t' act when ye would no'! She saved my life! She saved Gralyre's life! So let me be very clear with ye. If ye ever speak such vileness in my presence again, I will thrash ye senseless! If I see ye attempting t' hurt this girl, I will beat ye t' within a thread o' your miserable life. Now apologize t' Saliana, and let me never hear such offensive nonsense cross your lips again!"

After a long moment, Dajin muttered an apology, making it obvious it was done under Rewn's coercion. "Sorry." He flung himself to his feet and stomped away.

Gralyre's anger boiled his grief away, but its target was not entirely Dajin. His bitter rage was aimed squarely at where it belonged, at Doaphin, the ultimate author of every misery in this crushed and desolate land. Even after surviving the horrors of the night, once more Doaphin's taint had reached out to smite them, this time setting brother against brother.

Gralyre could kill every Demon Rider and Deathren in the land and never bring back Wil, or the women of the Tithe wagons, or his pups, or the people of Raindell. To end the nightmare, he had to remove the head of the snake! *Doaphin!*

If joining the resistance would allow him that opportunity, so be it. His desire to meet the Rebels no longer just revolved around reclaiming his lost memories and proving his innocence.

"I must find forage for the horses," Gralyre stated abruptly into the unnatural silence that Dajin's accusations had left. *'And make doubly certain no Demon Riders followed behind from Raindell,'* he left unsaid so as not to alarm the others. Little Wolf leapt to his feet to accompany him.

Rewn began an offer of help but his words stilled upon his lips as he saw the expression on his friend's face. He nodded his head instead.

Saliana also witnessed the emotions that briefly twisted through Gralyre. She shuddered and shifted closer to Rewn for comfort.

It was not Gralyre's rage and grief that scared her, for they were natural and right to be feeling at this moment. It was the iron control keeping the overwhelming emotions on a tight leash that frightened her.

That strength of purpose made him capable of any act, any feat and any atrocity. Gralyre would succeed at any cost because *he willed it so!* She shuddered at the insight. *'May he never be my enemy,'* she prayed.

After Gralyre had left, Saliana stared into the fire, exquisitely aware of the man beside her, yet uncertain how to approach him. "I thank ye for standing up for me," Saliana offered awkwardly.

The fight with Dajin had only compounded Rewn's sorrow. He nodded and stood with creaking effort. "Ye had best rest. 'Tis a long way t' Verdalan. I can no' bear t' stay upon this accursed hill a moment longer!" He strode away in the opposite direction from that his brother had taken.

Saliana watched Rewn's back disappear over the slope of the hill, down towards his father's cairn. She never wanted to see that look on Rewn's face again.

She vowed to make peace with Dajin. No matter that she feared and distrusted him, she would not be the cause of bad blood between the brothers again.

CHAPTER TWENTY-TWO

Catrian looked up from the papers that she was studying as the door to her room opened unexpectedly. "Matik? What is it?" The Rebel moved aside, and her face chilled over as her uncle stomped into the room, tracking muck and snow and the smell of pine and winter with him.

"What part o' *'Return at once'* were ye unable t' comprehend?" Commander Boris boomed sarcastically in lieu of a greeting.

Catrian glared around Boris' cloak-bulked body at Matik, her traitorous protector. Matik's gaze would not meet hers as he closed the door with a politic little thump.

Boris threw open his cloak and held his hands over the hot coals in her brazier. He flexed and clenched his fingers to encourage them to thaw. "Ye be an expert on ignoring letters," he turned to glare at her, "so why do ye no' try it t' my face!"

"I am no' a truant child t' be collected!" Catrian shot to her feet angrily. Damn the Gods if she was not feeling exactly like that!

"Are ye no'?" Boris sneered. "Because from where I stand, it seems the price o' your powers has been paid with your common sense!"

Catrian's hands balled into fists.

"Glare at me all ye like, but ye are returning with me. Ye stayed away out o' childish, wilful defiance, because ye knew I would no' let ye return in the spring." He glared at Catrian's belligerent stance. "Admit it!"

Catrian threw up her hands. "Aye! I admit it! I did no' want t' have this argument, so I stayed away! But ye wish t' talk o' childish acts? How would ye describe a grown man who would beard winter and storms just t' confront me for my defiance?"

"I never said I was here just t' collect ye!" Boris yelled. He sighed gustily and sat heavily in a chair, seeming to shrink as his rage drained away.

"No' a single foraging party returned t' the fortress afore the snows. No' a one!" His voice was suddenly whisper soft, as he hunched over and rested his forearms on his knees to prop up his sagging, exhausted body.

Catrian squinted at him as her anger came to terms with his abrupt change in demeanour. "What?" She gasped as the implication struck home. "Why did ye no' say so in your letters! I would have returned at once with the stores from Verdalan. Precious little that there are!"

Boris' head snapped up. "I did say so in my letters!"

"Ye did no'! I would have... remembered..." In the pregnant silence that followed her assertion, Catrian sank slowly into the opposite chair and placed a guilty palm over her mouth. Her wide eyes met her uncle's.

"Aye, and ye read them all, did ye," Boris prompted softly.

Catrian blushed guiltily. She had burned the last letters, unopened. She looked up at the ceiling as her intentions fell to ruins. "No," she admitted and tears sparkled her eyes. "Uncle, I am sorry. I should no' have acted in such a way. 'Twas no'... I do no'… ye know I would never behave like this!" He was right. Her obsession with the Tithe had driven away all reason.

The mountainous isolation that was the resistance's greatest ally in hiding from Doaphin was also their greatest enemy during the long cold winters. The lack of arable land in the rocky hills precluded the growing of many crops, making the fortress extremely dependent upon the outside world for supplies.

In the spring, more than one foraging party was sent to the lowlands, greatly increasing the odds that someone would find and return in the fall with the needed provisions. Every year, the famine that the land endured made finding those stores less likely.

'No one returned!'

The missing men had either fallen or, having been unable to find supplies of grain, had chosen to remain in the lowlands to place less stress on the fortress' resources.

Catrian had not thought to investigate whether the stockpiles of food in Verdalan had been collected and delivered to the fortress. It was unlike her to overlook such details. She must release her grip on her obsession with the Tithe.

It was late in the season to be returning to the mountains, but Catrian knew that the journey could not wait. By now, the need for supplies would be urgent. With insufficient food stores available, the Rebels of the Northern Fortress had to be in the grip of starvation. The stockpile in Verdalan would mean the difference between life and death for many Rebel warriors.

"I will began preparations at once," Catrian announced quietly.

ഇൗൠ

It was a cold and travel-weary group that finally arrived at the gates of Verdalan. Their journey had been fraught with blizzards and ice, and the frigid animosity hardening between the brothers. Eager for the end, they had pushed themselves hard in the past two days in order to reach the city. The promise of warm food, a soft bed and company other than their own, had spurred them forward to the end of their endurance.

Just out of sight of the city gates, Gralyre halted the horses and dismounted. "Give me your swords," he demanded as he sliced a blaze in a tree and began to dig down through the snow to create a hollow.

"We canno' go unarmed into the city!" Dajin sputtered.

"Let that be comfort t' ye when the 'Riders have taken your head for breaking the law in carrying a sword," Rewn reminded his brother scornfully as he unbelted his weapon.

Dajin glared sullenly, but in the end, complied with Gralyre's edict.

Gralyre lined the hole he had dug with an oilskin and a heavy wool blanket to protect the weapons from the damp. Into this, the men dropped all the swords that they had in their possession. To the impressive pile, Gralyre added the oilskin wrapped bundles that were his most precious possessions; the sheath with its secrets, and the chain mail.

Before Gralyre filled in the hole, Rewn added one more package, the family treasure that he had inherited from his father.

Thus disarmed, and denuded of their most precious things, the ragged party rode boldly past the suspicious stares of the Demon Rider sentries, through the gates with their tall watchtowers to either side, and into the city of Verdalan.

The sun was just beginning to burry itself behind the mountains, yet the streets, though still crowded, were already emptying of citizens.

Verdalan was little more prosperous and healthy than Raindell had been. Open sewers, that would have flowed freely down the choked gutters had they not been frozen over, accumulated filthy mounds and buried the cobblestones in muck.

The buildings, though decrepit, lacked the general desolation that had so plagued the smaller village of Raindell. The ancient, soaring architecture bespoke a once glorious past. The beauty of the stonework could still be seen, even beneath the abasement caused by the occupying 'Riders.

"Which way?" Gralyre asked Rewn as they led their weary horses down the wide avenue between crowded buildings and shabby shops. Humans and 'Riders, more beings than Gralyre could remember seeing in one place, streamed by on all sides in a kaleidoscope of movement and voices.

"It was a couple o' years ago that I was last here with Da, but I think that I can find our way." Rewn's head swivelled as he walked, looking for landmarks. "The Fighting Stag is this way."

Gralyre quickly realized that their horses were beginning to draw far too much attention from the Demon Riders. The few humans they saw wore rags and carried themselves furtively and fearfully. Their eyes darted with anxious vigilance as they fled the streets. Most were as thin as the bundle of sticks that many carried across their narrow backs.

But it was not just the horses drawing stares. There were no women to be seen. Despite the cold, Rewn pulled off his cloak and swirled it around Saliana, drawing the hood up to cover her head. "Keep yourself covered," he warned. Though she wore a cloak of her own, its threadbare state was unable to hide her form thoroughly.

The company spotted a human dressed in fine clothing and knowing him for the collaborator he was, ducked into a side street to hide. Here they encountered a Demon Rider column marching smartly along.

"Out o' the way, scum!" cried the Captain.

Forced onto their knees in the filthy gutters, they bowed their heads in deference as did the rest of the humans on the putrid street, until the 'Riders marched past. They sprang to their feet and dragged their mounts onwards, hastening their steps in their fear of discovery.

A town crier passed them by. "Curfew time! Curfew time! Return t' your dwellings or face the Deathren! Curfew time! Curfew time! Return t' your..." His voice dissipated into the distance and was swallowed by the city's noises.

"Which way, Rewn!" Gralyre watched the streets emptying before his eyes; doors were slamming, bolts were sliding home. Without the cover of other humans they would soon be standing out even more than they already were. Until the Deathren were released.

"This way, I think..." Rewn turned them down another side

street and onto a larger thoroughfare.

"Ye think?" Dajin yelped, fairly dancing with the need to get to shelter.

They picked up their pace until they were almost running, moving quickly through the deserting streets. Now that curfew was being called, they despaired of finding their safe haven before the Demon Riders released the Deathren who would patrol the city until dawn.

After a couple of false starts and wrong turns, Rewn finally led them safely to the Fighting Stag, the Inn that was their first step towards contacting the resistance. They all breathed sighs of relief as it came into sight.

By now, Rewn was shivering with the chill, but he did not seek to reclaim his cloak from Saliana. He ushered them to the side yard of the two-storey Inn, where a seemingly deserted stable overlooked empty water troughs.

Rewn pressed Saliana down to sit upon the edge of one of the troughs. "Rest here," he ordered kindly and took her horse's reins from her. From the depths of his shrouding cloak, she gave him a weary smile that he did not see.

The men led their horses to the entrance of the large closed barn that stood ready to house wayfarer's chattel. A slight smile lightened Rewn's face and he nudged Gralyre. "What shall ye do with Little Wolf? I doubt the innkeeper will be overjoyed t' have such as he under his roof."

"Little Wolf will stay hidden in the barn with the horses," Gralyre replied quietly, not joining his friend's attempt to leaven their circumstances. Verdalan might mean safety to Rewn, but for Gralyre it likely meant his death as a suspected spy and collaborator. Tension was already knotting his muscles to prepare to fight for his life. "I have a feeling we will have use of him as a guard. Our horses and packs attracted much attention."

Gralyre turned away to greet the stableboy who had finally roused himself from his warm loft once it became apparent they were not going away.

The stableboy was a thin youth, his clothes held to his scrawny body as much by filth as by threads. The boy twitched and fidgeted so, that Gralyre was unsure if it was due to fear of the eminent danger of nightfall or the lice infesting his clothing.

The boy's eyes quickly measured their wealth and adjusted the rates. Only collaborators rode horses. "The 'orses can stay, but yer mutt 'as t' sleep outside. Half a copper fer each 'orse, fer each day."

With only a slight turning of his body and a small shift of his expression, Gralyre was suddenly a menacing presence. What had seemed a harmless traveller to be fleeced had suddenly transformed into a looming threat. "The wolf stays with the horses," Gralyre stated with quiet authority. "And I will pay two coppers for the lot, for the duration of our visit. Plus decent feed," he tacked on.

"A Wolf!" The boy squeaked, looking closer. Even in the waning light, Little Wolf's obvious lupine attributes sprang out at him. He marked the grim features of the man and thought better of being anything further but accommodating.

He knuckled his brow in deference and defeat. "As ye say, sir," he mumbled ingratiatingly, even as he turned a cunning eye to the horses and the bundles they carried. The wolf could be dealt with later, when the man's attention was no longer upon him.

Gralyre motioned Dajin forward and pressed three coppers into his hand. "Settle up for the horses," he ordered. "Make sure they get fresh feed with no mold and some hot mash. They deserve it after their hard journey. With what is left, see if you can haggle for some blankets to warm them."

"Do it yourself," Dajin snarled. "I am no' your slave!"

He had not quite finished speaking when Gralyre calmly grabbed him by the front of his filthy, ragged jerkin and with an effortless flex of muscle, lifted him several inches from the ground. "You eat our food, you travel with us for protection, you will carry your own weight and do your own share of the chores." Gralyre's words were made more menacing for the mildness in which they were spoken. "Do you understand me?" He gave Dajin a slight shake, giving the impression that he could hold him there all night if the notion took him.

Dajin arced his eyes towards his brother and saw that he would receive no help from that quarter. Beyond Rewn's disillusioned features, Dajin took in the smirking of the filthy stableboy and was sufficiently humiliated into compliance. "Yea, I understand," he snapped with all his pent up hostility firmly intact. He hated giving way but at least Gralyre was allowing his feet to touch earth again.

As calm as he had been throughout the entire confrontation, Gralyre released Dajin's cloak and gently smoothed out the creases he had made. "Good lad," he stated approvingly, as though the altercation had never occurred. His intention was not to punish the boy but to encourage him to become a working, supportive member of their group, with all the perks and responsibilities that went along with that privilege. Enduring Dajin's sullen selfishness had come to an end at Hangman's Tor, but Dajin was slow to abandon the habits of a lifetime.

While Dajin took his humiliation out on the stableboy, Gralyre pulled the packs from the animals and left them in a heap in one of the corner stalls, only separating out those saddlebags that held their personal toiletries and clean changes of clothes.

"Little Wolf," he called.

The wolfdog came to attention and left off marking his territory to trot to Gralyre's side.

'Guard the horses and the packs. Let none come near.'

The wolfdog was not happy to be separated from his master and the other humans of their pack, but understood the importance of protecting the horses.

Gralyre watched Little Wolf enter a stall and make a nest for himself in some discarded straw. He threw him the last of their meat and watched the pup tear into his meal with enthusiasm.

Gralyre shouldered half the saddlebags and gave the rest to Rewn. They left Dajin haggling over the quality of feed, and dragged themselves back out into the yard to wait.

"The way ye treated him," Rewn shook his head ruefully, "he is going t' hate ye."

"I do not care if he hates me now. He will not when he finally begins to earn our respect. The path he is on is spiralling towards a dark place, Rewn. Dajin blames himself for so much that has happened, but worse, he imagines we blame him. If we do not give him a way to regain his confidence in himself and us in him, we could lose him forever."

Rewn looked at the faint outline of Saliana sitting alone on the horse trough as they walked towards her. "I think we have already lost him."

Gralyre snorted and arched an eyebrow. "Do not make me pick you up and shake you." His comment teased a huff of laughter from Rewn. "Give him a chance. He will come around," Gralyre encouraged. "We must hold him accountable for treating us with the same level of esteem with which he would have us treat him. When he gives respect, he will receive respect. He is not a half-wit. He will learn."

"I hope so."

Dajin caught up to them at Saliana's side. "Do ye remember the passwords?" he asked snidely.

Rewn gave his younger brother a cold glare and did not bother to answer. Such was the nature of their exchanges now.

Dajin subsided into his habitual sulk, where he had lived since Hangman's Tor.

Their behaviour left Gralyre wanting to knock both their heads together.

Rewn rapped smartly at the kitchen entrance. "I only hope they will remember and accept me as they would have Da. If they do no' know me, we are in as much danger now as ever we were with the Deathren. If they decide we are no' who we say, they will no' leave us alive t' tell others o' how t' find them."

Gralyre placed a hand on his friend's shoulder, but was unable to offer advice to alleviate the strain, for Rewn's assessment was correct. "Let us procure a hot meal and a bed. Then we can decide what we should do next."

A kitchen wench opened the door. "Good eve'n, masters," she simpered. Far off in the distance a claxon sounded and her face congealed to a consistency to match the stains on her apron. "Come in, quickly! The Deathren 'ave been released!" she shooed them past her into the warmth of the kitchen.

While his fellow travellers were revelling in the heat that was tingling life back into their frozen hands and faces, Gralyre's keen eyes watched a potboy run out of the kitchen towards the front of the house. He quietly allowed his hand to rest upon the dagger he had hidden in his shirt.

The owner sailed from the taproom, her apron starched white, her hands held out in welcome. She was the tidiest thing in the room, greatly improving their hopes of a decent meal and clean bed. Gralyre allowed his hand to slip away from his weapon.

"Ah, ye poor dears, travelling in such weather. You will be needin' a room t' be sure, and perhaps a hot meal. A half-copper a night per room, with either breakfast or supper included. There be a bathhouse in the back with clean, warm water and new linens on the beds every other day for one copper more," she cheerfully rattled off her prices.

Rewn began the passwords that would see them safely to the resistance, speaking as softly as possible. "Running Stags canno'..."

A look of alarm crossed the landlady's face. The welcoming

hands went to her ample chest as though to keep her heart from leaping away from her.

Gralyre quickly drowned Rewn out by stating in a loud jovial voice, "We shall need two rooms then, my good lady, and a hot meal and a bath are just the thing to warm our bones on this fearsomely cold evening!"

Rewn frowned at Gralyre, a question poised on his lips. Gralyre shifted his eyes towards the taproom and Rewn, following the silent signal, finally noticed the cluster of red uniforms that could be seen through the sliver of the kitchen door.

He sucked in his cheeks, his face flushing at the nearness of danger. "Yes, a room is just the thing."

The kitchen wench, though having retreated to peeling spuds over a bucket of water, was also taking avid interest in the conversation. This was neither the time, nor the place for the password.

The landlady gave Gralyre an especially warm smile at his quick wittedness. "Why, I shall just bring ye straight away up t' your rooms, then. Your poor wife looks t' be dead on her feet. How are ye doin', dearie?" she asked Saliana kindly.

Saliana gasped her fear and tried to hide herself further into Rewn's large cloak. The landlady did not give her an opportunity to answer before rattling on. "I bet ye could use a laydown before ye eat, hmm? Why, all o' ye look all but done in, poor dears," she continued to mother them. "I will be more than happy t' carry up a dinner t' your rooms," she craftily provided them an excuse to escape the presence of the 'Riders in the taproom.

"May the Gods of Fortune bless you and your establishment, dear lady," Gralyre said smoothly, giving her a short bow. "That sounds wonderful."

The matron blushed prettily at Gralyre's courtesy. "Cook made some delightful tarts today. Usually I charge extra, but seeing as how 'tis so late in the day, I shall include them on your tray free o' charge," she offered with a warm graciousness.

Gralyre took her hand and raised it, his slowly spreading smile a symphony of flirtatious nuance as he brushed a light kiss across her knuckles. "You are a good and kind woman."

Her blush darkened and she giggled like a young girl as she reclaimed her hand and cuffed Gralyre playfully for his boldness.

Rewn was agape at the sight of this hard man charming the stuffing out of their matronly landlady. He had never thought of Gralyre in any light but that of warrior. This new facet of his friend was a definite surprise.

"Off t' the rooms then, friends, and I shall bring your meals t' ye shortly! This way," she prodded them to follow her up a narrow flight of stairs, situated off the kitchen, and likely those used by servants who were to remain unseen.

With lagging feet, they followed her up to the second floor where seven small sleeping chambers were located. Their party took up two of them, while her continued rambling discourse on the amenities led them to rightly believe that some of the other rooms were occupied.

When Rewn once again tried to speak to her the code, she held up a shushing hand and covered up his voice with what seemed on the surface, nothing but nonsense babble.

"The one unfortunate thing," she rambled, "is the thinness o' the walls. Why, just last week I had one man complaining about the snoring o' another, who was situated all the way at the end of the hall and t' the left. Can ye believe that the next night, the one was gone and the other was lodging the same complaint against the new guest in this room?" She raised her brows to Rewn, who nodded quietly in understanding.

The rooms proved surprisingly comfortable and clean. They gladly paid the price that she demanded.

"Mind ye keep the windows latched during the night. I have never known the Deathren t' climb t' the rooftops, but better safe than sorry." She took her leave, promising to return with a meal for them all.

Saliana sank down on the bed in the small room, and stared with blinking eyes at the flickering candles as Rewn, Gralyre and Dajin put their heads together to talk in hushed voices.

"She did no' give me a chance t' speak the code," Rewn complained, his voice whisper quiet.

A door slammed in the hall and there came the sound of footsteps retreating to the stairs and clumping heavily downward. They held their breath until the noises had faded.

"This is foolish," Dajin whispered. "How does she know we are who we say, if we did no' give her the proper code?"

"I think she understood our meaning well enough," Gralyre stated with a quiet smile. "I imagine there will be someone here by morning to lead us on the next leg of our journey."

They quieted again at the returning sound of footsteps in the hallway followed by a knock. Gralyre cracked the door and peered around the jam. The sudden relaxing of the tension in his shoulders had all the others releasing their pent breaths. He opened the door further, and stepped back, beckoning, and their landlady bustled in with a tray of food.

"Have ye no' the brains o' a sheep?" she whispered harshly to Rewn. All aspects of her affable landlady act had vanished.

Gralyre assumed that the guest they had heard leaving was their only other neighbour at this time and that the rest of the floor was now vacant.

"The walls o' this place are thin enough t' hear flies in the other room buzzing, no' t' mention the kitchens, where that wench would sell her mother for a copper! There's a reason she was missed from the Tithe this spring!" She set the tray down on the table sharply. She drew in a fortifying breath and whispered, "Ye may say the warding-words now."

Rewn, Dajin and Saliana all seemed surprised at her change in demeanour. Gralyre only smiled as he looked into her eyes. This was the true face of someone who could survive in a city of 'Riders and still help those fleeing the tyranny of Doaphin's reign. "Running stags cannot fight," he enunciated softly.

She smiled back at Gralyre. "Alright then," she nodded decisively. "Eat up, and rest. Someone will be contacting ye soon. Mind what I said about the walls." She moved quickly to the door, pausing just inside the hallway.

Looking back at them, she was again the affable proprietress bustling about the Inn's important business. "Sleep tight. Mind ye that breakfast will be served in the common room. If ye want me t' continue t' bring your meals, 'twill cost ye extra!" she stated loudly for show. With that she was gone.

"I never would have guessed," Saliana whispered, surprise still written upon her tired face.

"Did you expect the first contact to be a vacant minded Innkeeper?" Gralyre asked. Admiration tinged his voice. "She plays her role well."

They all quieted at the sound of heavily booted feet ascending the stairs. Loud voices called affable insults back and forth, while one man sang the refrain of a drunken ditty with a toneless monotony. The voices wished each other '*Good eve'n!*' as doors slammed.

A body moved in the room next to theirs as the occupant readied for sleep. Unfortunately for them, their neighbour was the one who had the song trapped in his head, and no talent for words beyond the chorus, which he sang with loud enthusiasm over and over, spaced with vacant humming as he tried to remember the actual tune.

"Let us eat," Gralyre prodded, a finger to his lips as reminder to still their words.

The tray contained four trenchers of hearty stew with sweet, nutty tarts for desert. A jug of mulled cider washed it all down. The hot drink was a treat for the warmth-starved travellers. As they supped, the drunken singer gradually fell silent. They could only hope he had settled for the night.

Soon after, they were yawning sleepily and wishing each other, "Good eve'n," as they retired, Saliana to her own room, Dajin, Rewn and Gralyre sharing the larger chamber.

Though tired, Gralyre remained sitting at the table long after Rewn and Dajin had rolled themselves onto their creaking mattresses. He could not stop worrying about their next contact with the resistance. Would his lack of a past jeopardize not only his own safety, but also that of his companions? If the Rebels turned Wil's sons and Saliana away, what would become of them? How would they survive with no land and no prospects?

It would be a death sentence and he had too many deaths on his conscience already, a list that was almost too long to bear.

'Who am I to have caused the deaths of so many?' he wondered sadly. *'A curse, is what I am. An empty shell of a man filled with the nightmares of a legend that cannot be!'*

With a mighty sigh of uncharacteristic self-pity, Gralyre propped his chin on his fist, leaning over the table to trace the fingers of his free hand through some spilled drops of cider.

It had been a long time since the burden of his empty memory had plagued him so, not since he had gone to live with Wil and his sons. Even his nightmares had lessened in frequency. But with Wil's death, Gralyre's fragile identity had been battered anew, leaving him yearning for a past he could claim as his own.

What would the Sorceress find when she looked into his soul? Spy? Collaborator? Grave Robber? Madman? Prince?

His elbow slipped off the edge of the table and he just caught himself before his chin hit the wood. His flailing hand knocked over an empty mug in the process. He was more exhausted than he had thought. It was past the time to turn in.

Gralyre tried to stand and walk to his bed, but his legs seemed to lack the strength and the coordination necessary to complete the deed. He shook his head to clear the fuzziness clouding his thinking, and realization dawned.

Tired be damned by the Gods of Fortune! His eyes swerved past the empty jug of mulled cider. We have been poisoned!

"Little Wolf!" Gralyre cried out for help, and frowned at the slurred sound of his voice. When there was no response he looked around the room for his pup. The walls and beds whirled by in a confusing blur of shapes.

For a moment, his bewilderment lifted and he remembered that Little Wolf was in the barn. He tried, but was unable to focus enough to contact the animal. Black spots converged on the walls, covering more and more territory in his line of sight.

"Rewn! D'jin! Dgrugged, geddup!" he tried, but his mouth was cotton and the words slurred beyond understanding. There was no stirring from either Rewn or Dajin.

With a great effort, he pushed himself to his feet, toppling his chair in the process and stumbling backwards until he hit a wall with a loud thud. He flattened his hands against it for balance as the room tilted and the black spots danced mockingly closer.

Door, where was the door? He had to get the others to safety!

It was his last coherent thought. His legs buckled and he fell into a boneless heap on the floor.

CHAPTER TWENTY-THREE

It has long been on the Hunt but It has found nothing. 'Tis full on winter and It craves the hot, dark hallways of Dreisenheld. Fornicating! Killing! Eating!

Instead It endures the freezing cold, and is forced to hide every morn when the cursed sun appears! But Its resentment is not strong enough to force It home. Fear of The Master keeps It searching until all leads are exhausted, just as It has been compelled to do, on times too numerous to count. Sethreat obeys despite the likelihood of failure. Again.

It gazes at Its servants, looking for one upon which to appease Its hunger for murder and flesh. Its gaze settles on one, recently arrived from the west, who brings news of unrest. It is yet another lead that must be followed, an extension of Its search that will prolong Its exile from Its warm den for the rest of this bitter season of cold.

With a rapid swipe It grabs the messenger. The prey makes a horrified squeal that makes It smile. Carefully, Sethreat plucks the limbs from the sockets, preferring the hot meatiness of the torso to all else.

These Demon Rider larvae disgust Sethreat. All they are good for is food. Tainted as they are with *humanness* so that they can survive the hated light, they are weak and puny. Not fit to be in Its company but more than fit to slake Its hunger!

The prey's screams grow shrill as It splits the ribcage with a swipe of Its claws to expose the warm, living, bloody, succulent flesh It craves.

It strips the shredded, bloodied red uniform from the twitching, limbless torso and throws the offending clothing to the ground. Cloth causes It slight indigestion.

The screaming ends abruptly as the prey is stuffed head first into Its mouth. It clenches Its jaws around the skull, which makes a satisfying *Pop!* in Its mouth as it ruptures. It takes a moment to savour the sweet tender flesh to be found within, grinding and pulverising the bones in Its jaws.

But now the prey has gone quiet. The fun of savouring food ends when it ceases to struggle. The rest of the torso follows as Sethreat's jaw unhinges to accommodate the breadth of the meal.

As It throws back Its head to chew and swallow the bulky portion, It ponders the information the Demon Rider has given It before becoming food.

So much unrest in the pacified interior is odd. Could the Hunt be real this time? A frisson of excitement passes through Its cold scaly chest at the thought. A Hunt is better than the warm halls of Dreisenheld!

It belches mightily then beckons Its creatures forward through the night. The name of the new hunting ground echoes back to Its minions in a grating hiss, "Raindell!"

As It abandons the remains of the food, there is a mad scramble among the minions for possession of the four warm, twitching limbs steaming their heat into the freezing night.

The strongest of the creatures makes off with a leg and an

arm, darting ahead to be near the Stalker, its Master, for protection while it eats. The weakest is killed over the remaining portions and becomes part of the meal to satisfy the group's hunger.

It growls Its pleasure into the cold air. The strong should always feed off the weak.

ഔൠ

"Wake up!"

The yelled command made Gralyre flinch awake just as a bucketful of cold water landed in his face. Sputtering groggily, Gralyre opened his eyes to darkness and realized his arms and legs were secured by twine. He could not see his friends but he could hear their weak movements beside him.

Straining to see into the dark, he sensed movement just before a lantern was unshuttered. He quickly averted his eyes from the light before it could blind him and turned back after they had adjusted.

The lantern was set on a table in the middle of the room, turned low so that it threw only a small pool of radiance. The rest of the chamber remained in darkness. There were two people sitting at the table but their faces were hidden by deep hooded cloaks and by the shadows created by the light.

Rolling to his side, Gralyre could just make out the scared features of Rewn, Dajin and Saliana in the weak light. His anger ignited as he saw their bonds. "Are you injured?" he asked.

"No," Rewn said, while Dajin shook his head. For once the

brothers were not at each other's throats. Rewn squinted at the light, trying in vain to make out the features of the people who sat around the table, while Dajin met Gralyre's concern with a glare, as usual, focussing his anger in the wrong direction.

Saliana sat ramrod straight, staring at her hands clenched tight in her lap as she wept softly. Though she looked wan and scared she appeared to be testing the strength of her bonds.

Coldly furious Gralyre twisted back to confront their captors. "Where are we?" he demanded, blinking to clear the last of the drug from his fogged brain. There was no need to ask who they were.

"Silence!" The man who spoke had a rough voice with a deep overtone of menace. "We will ask the questions! Woe be upon ye if your answers please us no'! What are your names?"

"I am Findlay, this is Rewn and Dajin Wilson, and Saliana Greythorn," Gralyre answered for them all.

"Lie," stated a quiet feminine voice.

Gralyre's eyes snapped towards the voice, the second cloaked figure at the table. He did not question her knowledge, just quickly reassessed the situation. They would not be able to use the cover story they had used in the village. "She is correct," he stated just as quietly. "My name is Gralyre. Because it is a forbidden name, I have changed it to protect the lives of those I travel with."

There was a pregnant silence around the dark table, before the woman pronounced the verdict. "Truth."

Rough Voice spoke again. "Rewn Wilson, ye are known t' me and if ye say this is your brother Dajin, then I accept it. What o' your father? What has become o' Wil Wilson?"

"He was killed by the Deathren on the night o' our escape from Raindell." Rewn's voice was tired and full of sadness.

"And how is it ye were no' also killed?" the voice demanded suspiciously from the depths of the hood. "'Tis no' many alive who can claim a victory over Deathren! How did ye escape? Are ye in league with them?"

Rewn's voice was hoarse with fury. "We raced the Deathren all night after escaping the purge o' Raindell. Dawn was near, and we could go no further, so we made for a hill called Hangman's Tor. We thought that with the high ground we might fight them off until sunrise. Da never reached the summit. He fell, and sacrificed himself so that we could live. It worked, the sun took the Deathren and we survived."

"Truth."

"Who are ye, girl?" Rough Voice changed his focus to Saliana.

"Saliana Greythorn. They rescued me from Raindell," she said, indicating her travelling companions.

"Truth."

"And ye, who name yourself after the Lost Prince, how do ye come t' be a part o' this ragged party?"

"I rescued Wil's daughter from the Tithe wagon and, in turn, the Wilson's rescued me from certain death when I was taken for my crime. They healed my wounds, gave me shelter - and friendship. When Wil died we continued onwards together."

"Truth."

"It was truly ye? Ye are the warrior who saved us?" Saliana

interrupted incredulously.

"Aye, 'twas me," Gralyre said.

"I am sorry. I did no' know ye! I am twice in your debt," Saliana whispered, "For I am a survivor of that Women Tithe." She smiled tremulously at Gralyre through the murk of the chamber.

He smiled back. The woman at the table shattered the moment, bringing them back to the issue at hand.

"Truth."

Question followed upon question. The mysterious woman evaluated each answer as truth or lie.

Knowing that they could not escape her perception, the companions spoke only the truth to each question that flew at them from out of the darkness.

Only Dajin was caught in a lie. He tried to twist the truth to make it seem that he had been the one to kill the evil Lord and rescue Saliana at the Midwinter's Moon Festival. Perhaps he had even convinced himself that was the way it had happened.

When the woman told him he lied, Gralyre could have cheered. For the first time, Dajin was forced to accept his culpability and tell the event as it had actually occurred.

The lantern had burned most of its oil by the time the interrogation ended, and the prisoners were stiff and cramped from their bonds and the seeping cold of the stone floor. As abruptly as it had begun, the questioning was over.

At a signal from one of the cloaked figures at the table, lanterns sprang to life. The sudden light revealed five heavily armed guards placed in strategic locations about the room. They had been so silent the prisoners had been unaware of their presence.

"Is that it then?" Rewn asked wearily. "Are we free?"

"No' quite yet, lad," Rough Voice stated. "We are only partly certain ye are no' Doaphin's spies."

He stood from the table and slung away his heavy cloak, revealing himself to be of average height, with a huge barrel chest and heavily muscled arms. His beard seemed to grow into the soft brown tunic he wore. His eyes were hard pebble brown, as he casually placed a battle-axe on the tabletop in front of him.

After one evaluating glance, Gralyre turned his eyes to the woman. She interested him much more. She was obviously a woman of power, a Sorceress, and as such was more dangerous than the man. He could not see her face for she was still shrouded inside the heavy cloak, the hood pulled up to shield her from view. She had to be someone of great importance if they were not to see her face until they had been fully accepted, but Gralyre had his suspicions.

Rough Voice gestured and two guards stepped forward. They lifted Saliana off the floor and carried her to the table.

"What are ye doing? Where are ye taking her? Stop!" Rewn and Gralyre struggled and yelled, trying to rise.

Dajin whimpered as he worked his hands frantically to pull them free of the rough twine.

Saliana wrenched and bucked but could not prevent the guards from bringing her to stand before the cloaked woman. One of the men bent her in place while the other pinned her head against the wood of the tabletop. Rough Voice hefted his axe and raised it above his head, suspended and ready to swing.

Saliana whimpered and cried, panting harshly with fear, but unable to move with the weight of two men holding her down, readying her to be executed.

The hooded woman lifted a pale hand and placed it against Saliana's temple. Saliana stiffened and cried out in surprise.

Gralyre felt the familiar buzz of pressure against the base of his skull as the woman wielded her magic. "What are you doing to her?" he roared, his muscles bunching ineffectually against his restraints.

After a long suspenseful moment, Saliana went limp. The guards caught her as she sagged.

"She is clean," stated the woman.

The buzz in Gralyre's head subsided. He panted harshly, flexing his muscles and making the twine of his restraints creak under the pressure, but the bindings had no give to them. They had bound him too tightly.

Rough Voice relaxed his stance, and motioned to the guards. They gently carried Saliana from the room as one of the men held the door wide. Gralyre saw a rough passage of stained cobblestone before the guard snapped the door shut and stepped in front of it defensively

"Where are ye taking her?" Rewn demanded as he continued to struggle. They did not answer him "Where are ye taking her!" he yelled, louder.

Rough Voice motioned two more guards forward. This time they pulled Dajin from the floor to be brought before the woman.

Rewn pulled hard against his bonds, cursing and shouting at them to leave his brother alone. "Dajin!" he yelled in a voice of mindless panic.

"No!" Dajin cried out as he jerked his head back to avoid being pinned, but another man joined them and they soon had him bent against the table. Rough Voice raised his axe, and the woman's hand moved forward.

Unable to affect what was happening, Gralyre lay physically passive, but his mind had not been fettered. He sent his awareness outwards, searching until he found the mind of a sewer rat, nibbling a fallen crumb of food in a chamber down the hall. He willed the rodent to catch up with the men carrying Saliana.

Through the rat's eyes, the men seemed like giants towering over him. Gralyre saw them lay Saliana on a soft bed and untie her bonds. Through the rat's ears he heard, "Tell Heta t' warm up some o' 'at stew we had for supper. The poor thing will be needing a bite after tonight's goings on!"

Gralyre would have stayed longer with the rodent, but a blazing pain slashed through his mind. He gasped as his focus snapped back into the room.

"Ye will no' use magic in my presence again," the woman's calm, voice stated. "Or I will kill ye."

Gralyre gritted his teeth against the throbbing pain in his head, and nodded. At least he knew that Saliana was safe for now.

The woman finally managed to touch her fingers to Dajin's temples. He stiffened with a look of absolute horror.

"Rewn! Hst! Rewn," Gralyre gained his attention as the

magic began to vibrate his skull. "Stop struggling. Everything is alright," he hastened to reassure his friend. "Saliana is being well taken care of."

"How do ye know?" Rewn demanded.

Gralyre lifted an eyebrow.

"Oh," Rewn mumbled. Slowly, he stopped his struggles though the muscles in his arms continued to twitch and jump sporadically.

Dajin fell limp and slipped backwards into the waiting arms of the guards. The two who had left with Saliana returned to the room.

"Well?" demanded Rough Voice.

"He is clean," the woman stated.

Rough Voice motioned and they carried Dajin from the room while Rewn was dragged forward for his turn.

Sandwiched between two guards, Rewn acquiesced quietly, not struggling but frightened none the less of what was to come. Slowly, he bent and placed his cheek to the table. His terrified eyes met Gralyre's as a heavy hand on the back of his head held him in place and Rough Voice assumed his stance with the axe raised on high.

"I am going t' look within your mind now," the woman explained emotionlessly, "t' see if it carries the taint o' Doaphin. The more your mind resists me, the more uncomfortable this will be."

Rewn nodded his understanding, his jaw clenched tight in anticipation of her touch. Her fingers brushed his temples and he stiffened, his breath suspended, but he did not cry out. After a long pause, she pulled her hand back. Rewn's eyes rolled up and he collapsed into the waiting arms of the guards.

"He is clean," the woman stated to the waiting men. They carried Rewn from the chamber as she motioned for Gralyre to be brought forward.

Gralyre did not fight the men who lifted him off the floor and hauled him to the table to stand trial. 'Twas the moment of reckoning, upon him at last. Excitement and hope warred with dread.

Rough Voice took his position with the axe. Gralyre glanced once at the razor-honed edge and then looked away. He hoped the man was good with it, and would not take more than a strike to sever his head should it come to that.

Gralyre drew a deep breath and allowed his tumultuous emotions to still within the pulse of the dance. As he calmed, he distracted himself further by trying to make out the features of the woman beneath the encroaching hood of her cloak.

There was a flash of cheekbone, a wisp of hair, the movement of lips as she spoke to him the same instructions she had given Rewn.

Intrigued now by the whole process, Gralyre awaited the first touch of her hand with hopeful curiosity. Would she unlock his past? Would she deem him clean, or would the axe fall? The beat of the dance pulsed strongly.

Her cool, dry fingers touched his temple, and he felt an instant connection as her mind merged smoothly into his.

Gralyre stiffened, remembering the Demon Lord and the horrifying rape of his thoughts and his soul, but this was different. There was no pain here.

His awareness of the room faded as his concentration winnowed inward to the feminine presence infiltrating his thoughts. She sifted lightly and surely through Gralyre's memories, drawing his consciousness along, so that when she paused over a particular event or day, he relived it with her. Where the Demon Lord had conquered, she cajoled and where she beckoned, Gralyre went willingly.

It was the most intimate thing he had ever experienced. She knew him as well as he knew himself. She saw all that he was.

For a man who felt so terribly isolated by his lack of familiar connections to the world, sharing his mind, his memories, and his dreams with this woman was a balm to his battered soul. He began to lead her towards memories that held meaning to him, funny things that had made him laugh, tragedies that had broken his heart, wanting to share all with her.

Who was she? What memories did she have? Could he move through her thoughts as easily as she moved through his? Wanting a reciprocation of his feelings, he reached out and gently stroked her mind, inviting her to share with him as he was sharing with her.

He knew her. *'Catrian.'*

Her name caressed his thoughts. Memories of grey-green eyes, her face, her shape, her presence, all of his impressions surged to the fore.

He felt her reaction, her surprised awareness of him. A woman for a man. Molten electricity arced between them before her mind pushed his touch away, and she became only an observer once more, giving him nothing. Patiently forcing him back to her agenda, she redirected him to where she willed.

She was travelling back in time in his experiences, here she paused over the night Wil died and felt with him the anguish of his passing, the fight for survival against the Deathren.

Back to the sword dance at the Midwinter's Moon Festival in the village of Raindell, the strength of his body as he danced and leaped, slashed and blocked. The murder of the Lord to save Dajin's life.

Here she paused at his experience with the Demon Lord... *"It cannot be, and yet here you are," Lord Mallach whispers. "You sought to hide yourself, but you have been unmasked! You will be my little secret for now, but soon the Master will grant all I desire!"*

Gralyre did not try to impede her from this memory. He knew that his very survival depended on baring his soul to her, even this potentially incriminating episode of his past.

Then further in time, back to the beating he had received in Raindell, back to his rescue of the Women Tithe wagon and their first meeting. When Gralyre would have lingered over the shared experience, she pulled him onwards, back, always back.

Back to the farm.

Gralyre began to fight against her then, unwilling to relive the pain of the pups' deaths. But her will was inexorable, pushing him towards the event. There was Smoke dying under his hand all over again, the flaming roof of the cottage collapsing on Soot, his pups being murdered one by one.

Gralyre struggled harder to escape her, but she would not let go. Pain lanced through his head as he resisted her, reminding him strongly now of his past experience with the Demon Lord.

She released the memories of the death of his family, and Gralyre calmed, but she still was not satisfied with what she had learned. Catrian pushed further into the past, sifting through the mundane events of his everyday life at the farm for the taint of Doaphin. Until, finally, she arrived at the crux of it all. The beginning.

He lies beneath an oak on a spring's day, opening his eyes to blood and gore on his body, unable to remember his past, except for the nightmare. A brief flash of battle, the sword descends...

And suddenly, there was no more. There was nothing left for her to see, just blank emptiness. She pushed and prodded at it, seeking a way through the dark wall in his mind to the wealth of memories that must surely be on the other side.

Excited by the prospect of recovering himself, Gralyre did what he could to aid her. He led her back to his nightmare execution at the hands of the madman. Wil had almost convinced him it was a fantasy that he had created for himself, but it was still the only thing he had held in his mind when he had awakened that long ago day.

Understanding what he was doing, she tore at the fabric of the images, seeking to unravel them, to form a pathway into the locked away regions of his mind.

The sword glints in the setting rays of light... the rotten breath of the henchman... A demon appears from a boiling red mist.

Gralyre felt her sudden fear lash out at the demonic man

wielding the sword. He had no time to ponder the why of it as the sword touched his neck, wrenching them both into the void, into the nothingness that eroded the mind and shredded the soul.

He felt her pain, her terror, as the void bit deeply into her spirit. Gralyre had once used this very memory as a weapon against the Demon Lord. Even Little Wolf, who had entered his dreams and tried to fight his nightmare with him, had become trapped and would have been lost forever if Gralyre had not awakened. This time, it was impossible for him to escape, to awaken, for he was already conscious.

He felt Catrian's control disintegrate and realized she could not pull free. She was trapped in the depths of his mind with no way back to herself!

Fear for her safety, wrenched at him. He must help her! Gralyre summoned the shield he used to tune out gossipy horses and formed it like a bubble around her mind, isolating it from his own. When he severed their link, the nightmare evaporated and they returned to the saner world of his solid memories.

He slowly began to push at the bubble, forcing her away, further and faster, until she left his mind entirely. Gralyre's eyes snapped open as Catrian cried out.

She threw back her hood, stumbling backwards and over-turning her chair in her haste to get away from him.

For the first time, Gralyre struggled against his jailers to come to her aid but was pushed back down by the guards. "Catrian!" Gralyre bellowed. "Catrian are you injured?" He could not see her from where he was restrained and it was making him wild.

The Rough Voice of the axeman intruded upon the chaos.

"Hold that black bastard still! We will send Doaphin a clear message about the fate o' his spies!" he yelled fiercely, lifting his weapon high above his head.

"No Matik! Wait! Stop!" Catrian shouted over the din of overturning furniture and the struggle of the men trying to keep Gralyre's head and neck flush to the table so that Rough Voice's axe could more easily do its work.

"What are ye going on about, lass?" Rough Voice shouted. "He attacked ye!"

"He did no' attack me. I found no taint of Doaphin! But there is much that I did no' see. This man has a blank void where his past should be. 'Tis guarded by a fierce whirlpool o' nothingness that traps the unwary! I would be dead now if he had no' found a way to bring us both out! He did no' attack me, he saved me!" Her chest heaved with emotion and her eyes were wet with tears of pain. She lifted her hands to massage her aching forehead.

Gralyre knew how she felt, wishing he could massage his own headache away. Instead, his cheek was being ground into the texture of the wooden table as they held him bent in place for execution.

"All that I have seen o' his mind, and o' his actions, have given no indication o' evil intent. I will no' see a man condemned where there is no evidence o' guilt," she decreed quietly. "Otherwise, what is it that separates us from the evil we battle?"

Rough Voice seemed to wage a brief internal war before, with a jerky roll of his shoulders, he was persuaded to her argument and lowered his weapon.

He grabbed Gralyre's hair, pulling his head and shoulders up off the table. "Take a good look at her, lad," he threatened. "If ye betray her, I will cut out your heart and feed it t' pigs!" He drew his dagger and severed the twine binding Gralyre's arms and legs.

Gralyre shook off Rough Voice's hold and straightened to his full height, doing his best to ignore the man who continued to stand uncomfortably close. His attention was all for Catrian as he searched her face intently for any signs that he had brought her harm.

"Lady Catrian," he murmured softly, in contrition, in greeting, though they had met on far more intimate ground moments ago. "You are well?" Gralyre could not lose his concern until he heard it from her own lips.

"Yes, I am well, thanks t' ye." Catrian's hazel eyes were just as intent upon Gralyre's face. "I was curious if ye would remember me. You were very ill when last we met." She brushed away a lock of hair that was tickling her cheek.

The movement captured Gralyre's gaze, and he found himself wondering at the texture of her hair, its perfume. Unconsciously, he drew deeply of the air, a wolf testing for scent.

"How did ye survive t' adulthood with your powers? Doaphin executes anyone showing talent. He is afraid someone will rise t' challenge him."

"You survived," he smiled.

She shrugged dismissively. Her eyes still asked the question.

"I do not know. I have no memory of my past," he reminded her.

"And yet ye have a name," she countered, taking a step towards him, stalking him for the truth.

"Aye. A name I likely chose for myself from a common folktale."

"Are ye sure?" A small frown line crinkled her forehead as she circled him warily.

"Wil seemed to think so."

"Enough!" Rough Voice snarled. "Until ye have proven yourself, *Gralyre*," he emphasized, "I will be on ye like a fly on shit. Make one move that I do no' like..." He made a slicing motion across his neck with his finger.

Rough Voice's theatrics hardly registered upon Gralyre, so captivated was he by the Sorceress' presence. He pivoted with her as she paced her circle. "Wil told me Gralyre was a forbidden name. Until my real name returns to me, you could call me Findlay," he suggested with a slight bow.

She stopped pacing, and seemed riveted for a moment. "I shall call ye Gralyre."

Deep within Gralyre's chest his heart skipped a beat. He looked away in confusion. With no memories as a compass, he could not fathom what he was feeling. He found himself unsure of the currents he was trying to swim.

So he blatantly changed the subject. "What has become of our belongings, my horses, my wolfdog?"

Her eyes widened slightly at his unconscious tone of authority. She answered slowly. "They are still at the Inn. Matik will go with ye t' retrieve them. But understand this, your horses and goods are now just as much a part o' the resistance as ye are.

Just as any o' our people collect resources for us, these will be added t' our herds and stores. Ye and your companions will be allowed a horse each for your own use."

Gralyre frowned as he thought on it. He had no quibble over the fiscal loss, as he had stolen all the horses anyway. Thievery was likely how the Rebels acquired all their goods, he reasoned. His horses were like family, but they would be well taken care of as valued assets to the resistance. "I cannot answer for the goods as they are the property of Rewn Wilson, but the horses are mine. Aye, you can have them."

Catrian nodded as if it had been a foregone conclusion and dismissively turned to Rough Voice. "Matik, keep a close watch. There have been far too many Demon Riders loitering in the Fighting Stag's taproom for peace o' mind. Make sure ye are no' seen."

"That is because an idiot paraded a herd o' horses laden with packs throughout the city." He glared at Gralyre.

"He did no' know any better, Matik." Catrian reminded with iron lacing her words. "Take the North Gate and make for the camp. We will rendezvous within the next three days."

"Yes, m'lady."

"And be careful."

"As always, m'lady," he rumbled like a battered old tomcat, sketching a quick bow.

He cuffed Gralyre on the back of the head. "Let's go," he snarled.

Gralyre's hands flexed as he fought back the urge to return the blow. "My lady," Gralyre bowed his leave-taking before following Matik from the room into the maze of dank sewers under Verdalan.

"If there are so many Demon Riders about, should we not bring more men?"

"What? And look like an armed raiding party? Ye would like that would ye, spy?"

"I am no spy," Gralyre replied icily, fixing Matik with a black look.

"How do ye know? Ye do no' remember your past!" Matik grinned nastily as he drew first blood in the verbal sparing. He led the way up a long flight of stairs, to an oak door.

"Quiet now," Matik hissed before he put his ear to the wood, listening intently. Apparently satisfied, he quietly rapped a code onto the surface. At an answering series of knocks, he opened the door to the back of an apothecary's shop. As the shopkeeper hurried them into the street, coins subtly passed hands along the way. It was a smooth and practiced transaction.

Gralyre followed Matik cautiously into the far too quiet avenue. Though Matik had made a valid point about his past, Gralyre still felt like knocking the shorter man down into the filthy gutter and grinding his face into the squalid cobblestones. It was hard to think pleasant thoughts about one who had held an executioner's axe over his head not ten minutes ago.

Clenching his jaw tightly lest he give way to the impulse, he followed Matik down the street. He put his disquieted emotions down to the unique experience with the Sorceress that still reverberated through the deepest pathways of his soul.

CHAPTER TWENTY-FOUR

Boris entered the chamber after Gralyre and Matik had left and came to stand beside the Sorceress Catrian. The guards exited to give them their privacy.

She sat at the rough table, massaging her temples to relieve her headache. Her uncle placed a gentle hand on her shoulder, silently lending his support.

It was a hard warrior's hand that did not belong to a young man. Scars crisscrossed the fingers and tendons strained outward like rope. Yet the hand touched her with gentle compassion.

"Do ye think he suspects?" Boris asked quietly.

She looked up at him, a smile lightening her eyes. One hand left off rubbing her forehead to cover his where it still gripped her shoulder. She shook her head. "He suspects nothing. I wish this subterfuge had no' been necessary, Boris."

"I know lass, I know." Boris moved to the chair opposite to hers. His hair was iron grey, matching his eyes. Wrinkles radiated from around his eyes, caused by squinting in the sun for too many years. His face was like old leather beaten by rough use. Still, there was an ageless quality to him, an air of the survivalist. He had the dignity and commanding presence of an old stag. "Always the intrigue," he shook his head chidingly. "Ye knew the moment they were brought t' ye, that they could be trusted."

"Yes," she agreed, her gaze holding his steadily. "But Gralyre worries me. I can see him as the man he is now, a good man, an honourable man, but there is no telling what sort o' man he has been in the past... or who he holds allegiance to."

"I take it he is no' from the Kingdoms t' the South?" Boris asked rhetorically. "'Tis likely a trap, Catrian, ye know this. As we grow bolder, Doaphin has become aware o' our presence... and yours." He leaned forward over the table towards her, grey eyes narrowed in concern. "This man, Gralyre, could be hiding an evil nature within his mind."

A crooked smile lifted the corners of her mouth. "I did a deeper viewing on him, uncle, while he was still drugged and asleep. But there was nothing. Just a blackness that stretched like a wall in all directions.

"I even built up the process o' looking into his friends' minds in front o' him t' the point where any minion o' Doaphin, no matter how well shielded from the truth, would be in a frenzied state o' panic. No' our man. He was cool, calm and curious. He was so welcoming it was almost..." She blushed lightly and shrugged, unwilling to complete her unseemly thought aloud.

Boris' eyes narrowed sharply.

She fell silent for a moment, rubbing her index finger along her bottom lip, deeply immersed in the problem. "Even he canno' break through the black wall. I thought for sure if I entered his past with him, something would open up, some hole that I could worm my way through t' the other side o'. But there was nothing. And then there *was* something, a vortex that tore at the mind and spirit."

She locked gazes with Boris. "He fears this vortex and he is a man who fears very little. He has a very powerful defense guarding his past!" She made a sound of frustration and slumped back in her chair, rocking the uneven legs of the table as she did so.

"I was trapped, Boris, it was like nothing I have ever experienced before. No up, no down, infinity and nothing all at the same time. He could have attacked me then, left me there t' parish. But he did neither. Instead he saved me."

"He should be put t' death at once." Boris advised. "Better by far t' be safe than sorry!"

"Perhaps ye are right. However, I found some intriguing images... no' quite a memory, yet no' a dream," she trailed off thoughtfully.

"What did ye see?"

She watched Boris with anticipation of his reaction. "I saw him, Gralyre, fighting a battle and loosing. His men were being turned t' black stone by glowing magic falling from the sky."

Boris straightened to attention.

"Then I saw him held prisoner by two men who were wearing Doaphin's colours. Doaphin himself stood before our man with a sword raised high, *The Sword*, the Dragon Sword. This he swung like a reaper, beheading the first man holding Gralyre," she swung her own arms in mimicry of the descending blade.

"And then it happens!" She shuddered lightly at the recollection of Gralyre's memory of the images. "As the sword touches Gralyre's neck, he is no' killed but is swept into the vortex o' which I spoke. His next coherent memory is awakening in the forest covered with blood, this past spring."

"Ye must be joking! The Tale o' the Lost Prince?" Boris

asked incredulously.

"The Tale o' the Lost Prince," she concurred. "He believes the images are his mind's own creation t' fill in the blank holes in his past."

"Surely ye are no' believing this?"

"No… except," she began hesitantly.

"Except what?"

Catrian picked at a sliver of wood in the table. "The Demon Lord I destroyed this summer past?"

"Yes?"

"Gralyre had horrific recollections o' the Demon Lord torturing him, ripping through his memories while he was held captive in the Tithing wagon. What that creature did t' him!" She shuddered again and refocused on Boris' disbelieving face as she cut to the chase. "The Demon Lord recognized Gralyre. He was going t' use him t' curry favour with Doaphin."

"Do ye want t' hear what I think?" Boris asked.

She nodded.

"Kill him. He is a spy. The most elaborate and insidious spy Doaphin has ever sent t' us. Always ye are able t' ferret them out. Doaphin's taint slithers through their memories, making their perfidy obvious." Boris paused and raised one finger admonishingly. "Doaphin takes a while, but he does learn eventually.

"This man has no past ye can see. He has intriguing hints o' images in his mind that suggest he is the Lost Prince Gralyre. He just happens t' be in the right place at the right time t' join with one o' our most trusted operatives, who later dies at the hands o'

Deathren." His hand curled into a fist. "There are no coinci-
dences. The Prince's return is a fable for children, no' something
t' hinge our survival upon. Kill him and be done with it."

"I wish I could be as sure as ye, Boris." She held up her hand
to stop him when he would have argued. "No, hear me out." She
waited for his nod of assent.

She steepled her fingers in front of her face, focussing her
thoughts. "I agree with everything ye have said, yet I have
doubts. I ran this man through every test I could think o' and I
found no' one fragment or hint o' Doaphin's presence. Gralyre
bears us no ill will, and he had no knowledge o' us when he first
came to his senses without a memory.

"If he is a spy, he is from someone other than Doaphin.
Doaphin is like a falling boulder, smashing everything in his
path. His subterfuges are childish and easily unveiled. Doaphin
has no need for intrigue, for he is the master o' the known world.
Anything he wants, he commands one o' his minions and his
will is done. Ye know better than any, how his Demon Lords
think. This does no' feel like Doaphin. If it is a ruse, 'tis too
subtle for it t' be him. This is more like water seeking out cracks
in the walls t' pull them down."

"Yes, Cat. And are we the wall he was sent t' topple?"

She shook her head, holding up a hand to halt his interruption.
"Forget for a moment the hints o' the Lost Prince that I have
found within him, and forget the possibility that he may be a
spy. Though we have no proof o' his guilt, ye know that for the
possible threat he poses I would wield the sword myself. But he
has magic, Boris! We must keep him alive for his power! We

lack any but the most rudimentary sorcery t' aid our cause against Doaphin and his Demon Lords."

"Ye are the strongest Sorcerer t' be born in four generations, Cat!"

"He could be stronger!"

"Kill him!"

"Ye would have me throw away a much needed weapon?" she asked in a hard voice. "I can take one Demon Lord at a time, maybe two, but if they come at us in force, what then?"

Boris was silent. He had no answer for her very real fear. "Kill him," he reiterated, but with less heat, less surety.

"We canno' afford t' lose one person o' magic! T' throw this man's life away without proof positive o' his guilt would be like throwing away water in the middle o' a desert!"

"So what do ye suggest, Cat?"

She released her breath in a rush, glad Boris had deferred to her judgement. "Matik has agreed t' watch him. He is no' t' be allowed anywhere near our high councils. We will keep him busy with useless tasks, nothing important, or life threatening. He will be watched day and night for signs that Doaphin is awakening him. I myself will scan his thoughts whenever our paths cross. It is the safest I can make the situation."

"For how long?"

"For as long as it takes for us t' be sure."

"Ye have overlooked one important factor, Cat."

She pursed her lips in silent question as Boris hesitated awkwardly.

"Ye said yourself that he found ye attractive." He lowered his gaze to avoid her certain indignation. "If ye are peering into his mind every day, ye will be watching that admiration grow stronger. Admit it or no', it will affect ye. He is a strong, powerful and attractive man, Catrian. The admiration o' such a man would be hard for a woman t' resist," Boris finished in a rush and then winced in anticipation of an explosion.

Catrian placed her hands flat on the table, carefully tracing the grain of the wood with her fingers while she formulated her answer. "I am no' any woman," she stated coldly. She raised her chin angrily, her eyes diamond hard with impatience. "What makes ye think me so corruptible as t' put everything we have worked so hard for at risk over any man? Do ye think me incapable o' controlling my emotions?"

She slapped the table and a long jagged crack appeared in the wood. Snaking across the grain, the crack stopped at a gesture of her fingers just shy of Boris' hands. She waited until Boris swallowed hard with worry before she continued. "If I allowed my emotions t' rule me, I, who can destroy at a gesture, my power would corrupt me! I would become no better than Doaphin!"

Boris snorted derisively but leaned back in his chair to cautiously put more distance between them. For Catrian to use magic to make her point shouted that this was an emotional topic for her. He was even more determined to have his argument heard. "And so ye use the fears that others have o' your powers t' keep them from getting too close and making ye feel too much. As ye just did." His own eyes hardened to match hers.

"Look Lass, I know ye do no' see yourself so, but ye are beautiful! Intelligent! Your powers go way beyond the forces o'

nature ye wield. Few men in the camps are no' smitten with ye."
He overrode her protests. "The reasons ye never see them, lass,
is one, ye never look," he listed off on his fingers, "and two, the
men all fear your magic too much t' risk pressing an unwanted
suit." He covered her restless fingers with his own, stilling their
agitated movement on the table.

"I know ye. I have watched ye. I have seen how ye push
everyone away. I know 'tis as much t' protect yourself as it is t'
protect them. I have seen the men who have tried t' court ye over
the years," he sighed deeply for the pain he saw wash briefly
through her face. "They have either run screaming in terror from
ye, or they have tried t' enslave your emotions t' use ye as their
own pet weapon."

He squeezed her hands reassuringly. "I know ye are lonely,
lass, though ye try t' hide it. 'Tis nature ye are fighting as much
as yourself. Ye are a powerful Sorceress, but ye are also a
woman. Now, suddenly, here is this man who is no' afraid o' ye,
who does no' seek t' control your powers, for he has powers o'
his own. He is your match. He admires ye as a woman." He
drew in a deep breath certain now that his meaning was finally
driving home. "Ye will be looking within his mind, at his
deepest thoughts and desires. Searching for Doaphin, aye," he
nodded, "but also seeing his most private feelings, and no doubt
watching his regard for ye grow. Such admiration, seen
intimately by ye every day, is going t' affect ye, whether ye wish
t' admit it or no'." He gave her hand an extra squeeze and then
released it.

"So what are ye saying, Boris? That I am some starry-eyed

twitch who will swoon at the first compliment paid me by a handsome face? By the Gods of Ill Fortune, the man could be a spy!" she snapped.

"No' at all, lass. But if ye develop feelings for him, it might cause ye t' hesitate when ye most need t' act swiftly and decisively. And I do no' need t' tell ye what happens t' those who hesitate in a battle." He frowned across the table at her closed hard face.

"Just," he hesitated, "be careful. We are all susceptible t' loneliness, Cat." Her uncle rose and left her sitting alone at the ruined table.

ᏸᏝᏩ

Gralyre and Matik took a circuitous route through the city. Gralyre realized early on that it was as much to confuse him as to the location of the hidden entrance as to foil any pursuit.

Having all his conversational overtures rebuffed with malice made Gralyre finally give up as his temper frayed from the continuous barbs flung at him by his cantankerous companion. Matik was determined to dislike and mistrust him. So be it.

Walking briskly, in silent animosity, they finally reached the Fighting Stag. As they approached the Inn, something struck both men as strange.

Of one accord, their steps slowed, though they kept walking so as to not appear to be loitering. What few people were passing by, gave the Fighting Stag a wide berth, as if it were running rife with plague.

"Something is wrong," Gralyre murmured, breaking the hostile silence that lingered between them.

"Aye," Matik muttered, his eyes darting left and right.

Gralyre stretched out his awareness and touched the thoughts of a rodent in the taproom of the Inn. What he saw caused his jaw to clench and a growl to escape as he recoiled.

Matik's restless gaze focussed on his charge. "What has got ye by the elderberries, spy?"

"Demon Riders," Gralyre gritted out, his eyes blackening. "In the taproom. One of them is interrogating the Landlady as to our whereabouts. She is being hurt."

Matik's stance stiffened. He grabbed Gralyre's arm, dragging him along in his wake. "We must leave. Your belongings are no' worth our deaths." His voice was emotionless, as though he had frozen inside.

"What of the lady?"

"We can do nothing for her. She can take care o' herself, she has been interrogated before. If we try t' help her, we will do more harm than good and she will no' be able t' explain away our actions or our presence." Matik glanced back in alarm as Gralyre broke his hold and abruptly changed directions, heading for the side yard of the Inn. "Where are ye going? Ye canno' help her! Did ye no' hear me?"

"If I can get my belongings out, it may spare the lady further harm. Stay here," Gralyre ordered. "I will not ask you to risk your life. I will go to the stables alone and retrieve my animals."

"Oh, ye would like that, spy!" Matik glowered at Gralyre's retreating back. The man would not be moved. Short of burying his axe in Gralyre's head, Matik had no choice but to capitulate. "Well, I be coming with ye," Matik snarled belligerently. "Do no' want t' give ye a chance to talk t' all your 'Rider friends!"

Gralyre ignored the barb. He scanned the street to ensure that nobody was paying attention to them before ducking around the corner of the Inn, heading for the stable.

So far, it appeared that all the Demon Riders were in the Inn and out of the cold. The side yard was deserted, but their footsteps slowed as they saw the stableboy peering anxiously into the barn through the crack of the door.

"What are you doing?" Gralyre demanded quietly as he halted behind him.

The stableboy jumped in surprise and spun to face them, guiltily slamming the door. His scrawny throat bobbled as he swallowed nervously. "Where did ye come from? I thought ye 'ad left fer good! Ha, Ha," he giggled nervously.

Gralyre's eyes narrowed. "I have come for my belongings." Under his steady gaze, the stableboy squirmed and jittered.

"Well, ye can no' 'ave 'em," he blurted, "'at is..." he stammered as Gralyre's face hardened, "Ye can no' 'ave 'em 'til ye settle up with me mistress. She figured 'at ye ran out on yer rent. So she is keepin' yer animals fer payment!" He seemed relieved to have found a plausible explanation for his defiance.

Gralyre raised a brow at Matik. Matik gave a slight shake of his head. The landlady had known exactly where Gralyre and his friends were. She had no reason to deny them their property. But apparently, the stableboy did.

Gralyre swung back to the gangly youth and grabbed him by

the throat. The stableboy gave a squawk as he was lifted off his feet and pinned to the side of the building.

"How many thieves did you sell your information to?" Gralyre asked calmly. Behind him, Matik heaved a sigh of resignation as he loosened his battle-axe in its harness.

The stableboy was gasping and squirming. Gralyre shook him like a wolf shaking a rat, before relaxing his grip and allowing the stableboy's feet to touch the dirt.

"I do no' know what yer..." the stableboy gasped.

Gralyre's grip tightened again.

"Four! Only four!" He babbled. "Me friend Chigger tried fer yer 'orses last night, but yer wolf attacked 'im. 'E took 'is money back, so I 'ad t' sell the gig t' someone else. And I figured why not sell t' a few. First come first serve, I say!"

Matik appeared at Gralyre's side. "That would explain the large number o' 'Riders in the taproom. Rumours o' riches spread faster than stink and become distorted for each retelling. By now, the gossips think ye are the Lost Prince himself, with riches t' match!"

Gralyre's glared at his companion for his bad taste in analogies. But the sound of snarls and growls from within the stable instantly grabbed his attention. *'Little Wolf!'*

With the barest of flexing, he bounced the stableboy's head off the wood wall. Not waiting to watch the filthy youth fold to the ground, he threw open the stable doors and strode in.

Behind him, Matik pursed his lips approvingly as he stepped over the comatose stableboy and followed Gralyre into the dark musty stable.

The sound of growling wolfdog and angrily squealing horses was punctuated by the curses of three ragged men who were trying without any luck to reach the packs strewn about the paws and hooves of the furious animals.

It was a horse that spotted Gralyre first. He reared up and let out a cry of welcome. His flailing hooves clipped a thief on the head. With an ugly yelp, the man staggered back to a safer distance, clutching his bleeding scalp.

Little Wolf left off his growls to give a keen of delight, then immediately began to growl threateningly again when one of the thieves tried to move closer. None of the three thieves had yet spotted Gralyre and Matik.

'Finally you have come back to us! You were gone for too long on your hunt. The scavengers thought our den had been abandoned. But I protected us from them all!' Little Wolf stated proudly. *'Was your kill large? We are very hungry!'*

'Yes, I have food. You did a good job protecting the den, Little Wolf, but now it is my turn,' Gralyre told the wolfdog.

"Do ye need any help or can ye handle this pitiful bunch on your own?" Matik asked with boredom punctuated by a yawn and a hearty stretch.

The thieves whirled to face their new threat. Gralyre did not look Matik's way as he gave his answer. Damn the man for destroying the element of surprise! "If I need your help, I will ask for it." His eyes never left the three thieves.

A small smile curled Matik's lips in anticipation of the coming fight. Negligently crossing his arms, he leaned against an empty stall at a safe distance. Lady Catrian would not let him beat on this spy but she had said nothing about letting someone else do it for him!

The three men seemed puzzled and unsure as they faced the unarmed man, while his heavily armed companion settled in to watch. Then, sensing the way the wind blew, they grinned and chuckled, knowing they held the advantage of both numbers and weapons. They spread out to encircle their victim.

Only their opponent was anything but unnerved. Gralyre stood before them, completely relaxed, his eyes not really focussed upon anything.

"Now!" shouted the boldest of the thieves, dodging in to attack. A hard fist met his face and he staggered backwards, cursing and cupping beneath his broken nose to hold back the blood. His companions had not attacked with him. They were still gawking at the speed with which Gralyre had moved.

Matik straightened from the wall attentively. A scowl slowly immerged from his beard as he realized he was not going to get the show that he had hoped for. A grin of enjoyment leavened Gralyre's features even as the smirk on Matik's face fled.

The bold thief wiped his grimy sleeve through the blood dripping from his chin as he pulled a dagger from beneath his tunic. The second thief also drew a knife but the third thief hesitated, eyeing Gralyre's massive size, calculating how easily he had defended himself from the first volley.

"What are ye doin'? Where is yer knife!" the leader hissed at his hesitating companion. He brandished his own dagger ferociously in Gralyre's direction, though Gralyre did not flinch from his relaxed stance.

The third thief reached beneath his filthy shirt for his weapon but his hand stopped short as he met Gralyre's dark, dangerous eyes. He swallowed nervously as he saw his death writ plain in the face of the warrior. His hand released the hilt of his knife and went instead to his still bleeding scalp where the horse had clipped him.

He rolled his eyes at his fellow thieves. "Oy! Me head!" He staggered as if he were going to fall then rushed past Gralyre towards the open stable door. "Yer pardon, Lord," he whispered through fear dried lips as he passed. Gralyre let him go.

"Ye bloody coward!" The leader howled after him. "When I catch up with ye I will slit ye from throat t' balls!"

"I think not," Gralyre countered as his body flowed into the dance, lethal and quick. Almost faster than the eye could follow, he grabbed the wrist of the second thief and twisted the dagger from his grasp. Weapon in hand, Gralyre pivoted lightly on the balls of his feet, and followed through with an elbow smash to the man's face.

Gralyre's pilfered weapon was there to meet the attack from the leader of the thieves. Steel rang against steel as the two men crossed daggers.

Behind the combatants, the second thief, wearing a look of confusion, collapsed face down in horse dung.

Little Wolf stepped cautiously up to the downed man and sniffed at his rank, greasy scalp. He grumbled distastefully as he circled around for a better aim, lifted his leg, and sent a stream of urine pattering down. For good measure, he kicked dirt and straw over the fallen man. Satisfied that the rotten scent was well masked, he sat on his haunches to watch Gralyre dispatch the last thief.

The knives rang from three quick exchanges. The leader grinned nastily with triumph as he attacked and Gralyre parried and gave way. He pressed his imagined advantage. The clashing of blades and whistling of knife-cut wind interrupted the grunts of exertion the thief gave as he attacked. His opponent fought with unnatural silence.

"Hurry it up," Matik snarled. His good mood had been destroyed as he realized how outclassed the thieves were. He kicked at a board, knocking snow loose from his boot. "Ye make so much noise, we will have every 'Rider in the city pounding on our door in a moment."

Gralyre heaved a sigh as he realized that Matik was right. He'd had enough exercise anyway. He countered another thrust, parried one more attack, and then kicked the thief in the groin. The game ender.

The man froze, his hands slowly drawing in to cradle his injury. Behind him, Gralyre heard Matik give a low whistle of commiseration. The thief sank to his knees, his face frozen in a mask of pain. His dagger fell to the dirt with a clunk, loosed by numb fingers.

Gralyre fisted the thief by his hair, raising his arm in preparation of the final blow before he realized that the only thing keeping the man upright was the handful of filthy strands attached to his scalp. He released the man and gave him a push to aid his collapse into the filthy straw.

"Fast enough for you?" Gralyre asked.

Matik gave a noncommittal grunt, shrugging himself away from the stall. Casually, he brushed off his coat. "A little showy for my taste. Rather sloppy work, actually."

"Help me with these packs so we can get out of here afore the next thieves try for my property," Gralyre commanded, knowing that his tone would irritate the other man far worse than any stinging comment could.

Fingering the butt of his battle-axe longingly, Matik joined Gralyre and they soon had the horses loaded. The fallen men still had not moved when Gralyre and Matik led the horses from the stable.

Little Wolf pranced joyfully about Gralyre's feet, eager to stretch his legs after being cooped up with the horses for two days.

Gralyre felt no sorrow at leaving the stinking confined spaces of the city, although he did regret the loss of the warm bed and good night's sleep he had promised himself.

He sighed, watching his breath frost in the cold air as he trod the slick cobblestones of the road that led to the gate. With every step leading him from the confines of Verdalan, he felt himself relaxing. He always got into trouble when he visited a town. He pondered that odd fact for a moment.

ഇരു

Humans with horses and goods were not a common sight, unless they were collaborators, which engendered Gralyre and Matik a hard scrutiny by the sentries at the gate.

"Where did ye get the horses? What was your business in the city?"

Gralyre bowed smoothly and assumed the accent of the land. "I arrived with the horses two day ago. I am but a humble merchant. I travel with me wares. Can I interest either o' ye in a new shirt, or a kettle?"

The Demon Rider showed his teeth in a warning snarl. There would be no sales today. "Who is this?"

"A woodsman who wished t' travel with me for protection. I do no' mind the company, I can tell ye that! Winter be a dangerous time t' be on the road."

The sentry eyed the axe strapped to Matik's back. "A woodsman, eh?" He did not seem convinced.

"I chop wood t' make me living," Matik mumbled humbly, doing his best to look the part of a benign woodsman instead of a steely-eyed Rebel warrior.

The packs were thoroughly searched, and having found nothing more dangerous than clothing, a few household goods, and the Wilsons grain, they were finally allowed to leave.

"Where are we going?" Gralyre asked as they walked away from the northern gate of the city.

"Ye see those two hills, what look like a woman's..."

"I see them," Gralyre interrupted him wryly.

Matik grinned unrepentantly. "Centred between Left Bosom and Right Bosom Hills, ye will find an old cairn. 'Tis no' much, but the 'Riders do no' know o' it. 'Tis where we leave the horses when we are here so as t' no' draw attention t' ourselves. 'Twill offer us some shelter while we await the muster."

Gralyre heaved a sigh, his hand falling to the head of Little Wolf who, for fear of being left behind again, was clinging to his side like a bur. Gralyre's hands curled over the pup's ears reassuringly before he mounted up.

Onto the road leading to the north, they would not leave the track until they were well out of sight of the watchtowers on the walls of Verdalan. The prickling between their shoulder blades told them that the Demon Riders manning the towers were watching with interest as they disappeared over the horizon.

When the towers could no longer be seen, Gralyre left the path and angled south. The packhorses followed obligingly behind him.

"Where do ye think ye are going?" Matik growled a warning, and shifted his axe into a more convenient position across his back. *'What now?'*

"I left a cache of weapons to the south, along with some belongings that I did not want endangered were I taken by enemies." Unruffled by the threatening posture of his keeper, Gralyre continued to walk his horses in the direction he chose.

"Leave them!" Matik glared at the man's retreating back, at a loss in the face of Gralyre's blatant insubordination.

"No." Gralyre's unperturbed voice drifted back as he continued to move away. It was not a tone that invited debate.

Matik closed his agape mouth with a snap. The man seemed to lack any concept of command structure or to care that he should be ingratiating himself to prove his innocence. He behaved as though he was in charge, and the worst of it was it seemed to come as natural to him as breathing.

Matik had the choice of following after, or making an issue of it. Catrian had said Gralyre was to remain unharmed. Gritting his teeth to contain his annoyance, Matik followed.

§ⓒⓡ

Outside her door, Catrian could hear the running feet and hushed whispers of the Rebels as they made preparations. Boris had ordered the evacuation. In a few short hours they would be on their way back to their mountain fortress with the provisions that their agents within the city had carefully, and secretly stockpiled over the summer. Once in the mountains, they would wait out the remainder of the winter in relative safety and plan their battle strategies for the upcoming spring.

Even moving as quickly as they could, it would still take them three days to decamp from Verdalan. To move any faster would be perilous, for there were not enough humans coming and going through the gates to hide their numbers were the Rebels to leave en masse. To dispel the Demon Riders' suspicions, they had to leave gradually, a few men a day from different gates.

Gralyre and the Wilsons had been lucky to still find them in the city. Had this been a normal year, the Rebels would have departed from Verdalan long ago, before the first snows fell, and they would have had to overwinter at the Fighting Stag.

She was glad to welcome the three men into their midst. The resistance was in dire need of new blood. Every year, their numbers were whittled away. Doaphin's horde of evil continued to grow while the resistance died a slow death by attrition. That the Wilson's packs were full of much needed grain was a fortuitous boon that would be added to the stores they were bringing back to the Northern Fortress.

She heaved a tired sigh and massaged the ache in her temples. The persistent headache brought her thoughts back around to the author of her pain. She sucked in her bottom lip and chewed on it as she began to pace.

Her memory flashed with minutia that she had not registered at the time except in passing; lamplight caught in midnight blue eyes, overlong black hair that curled at the ends from the dampness in the room, a small bump on his nose that marred the symmetry of his face, the smooth flex of muscles beneath the ill-fitting shirt...

Gralyre was a problem she had not foreseen. He posed so obvious a danger that were it not for his untrained powers, she would have executed him immediately. But his magic was there, a much-desired carrot to dangle in front of her. But the preposterous idea that he was the Lost Prince...! It was either an obvious trap or, as Gralyre had suggested, a way for his mind to cope with his amnesia.

Her cloak swirled as she spun on her heel to pace back in the opposite direction. If only she could be sure of him! With his magic added to her own they could destroy the evil that gripped their land! Nothing would stand against them! But her yearning for her dream to be so would never change the fact that she could not trust the hidden places in his mind.

Catrian came to a halt, her arms wrapping about her middle

against a sudden chill that came from within. She was so tired of being the lone beacon, the only one standing between Doaphin and the survival of the last free humans. How much easier would life be if she could share this burden?

She stared unseeingly at the seeping wall of the subterranean chamber as she asked herself some hard questions.

Was Boris right? Was she vulnerable where Gralyre was concerned? Had she secretly been longing for someone like him? Someone with whom she could be herself and not have to watch as admiration turned to fear, someone who could handle the worst she could throw at him and not flinch?

With Gralyre, she would no longer stand alone; she could be herself, she could be free. Catrian shivered pleasurably as she remembered the feel of his mind closing around hers, clasping her protectively within him...

She snapped herself back to the present, horrified at the direction her thoughts had just taken. She was acting just like the silly twit she had emphatically told Boris she was not. Once again, her uncle was proving he knew her better than she knew herself.

Gralyre was a man who could prove more dangerous to their cause than a full attack by Doaphin himself. If she faltered in her resolve it would mean the end of generations of sacrifice and resistance - all they had hoped for, fought and died for!

If only she could trust him!

Catrian made a sound of disgust at the circular path her thoughts had taken.

Her best course of action would be to stay as far from him as possible. He was too powerful and too dangerous to toy with. She needed him for the magic he could provide to the resistance, nothing more. She had no room for gentler emotions where Gralyre was concerned. If he were a spy, she would deal with him, as she must.

If he were a spy…

But a spy for whom? For Doaphin?

Her words to Boris had been true. Were this a deception, it was far too subtle a ruse to be the hand of the Usurper. Who then? Who had the power to take every whisper of a certain memory and lock it away?

She froze and sank back into a chair as a devastating thought occurred to her. Could Gralyre have done this to himself? Was he the power behind the ploy?

ഇരു

'I smell a man in that tree,' Little Wolf warned Gralyre as he sat beneath the implicated fir tree and stared upwards with his ears canted forward.

Gralyre immediately reined in his horses. "Matik," he warned quietly. "Someone is watching us from that tree."

Matik grunted and seemed unconcerned as he moved past with his horse at a walk. "He better be if he knows what is good for him." His rough voice rumbled out loudly.

"Ho! Matik! How goes the battle?" A voice boomed back with a jolly tone from the top of the fir.

Matik looked up and waved. "Better than sitting in a tree

freezing me agates! How are ye, Cedric?"

"Can no' complain, but sometimes I still do!" Cedric chortled at his own joke.

Gralyre could see bits of movement from the camouflaged sentry. The bows of the fir tree jumped and shifted as something heavy moved within their shadows.

"I'll signal ye through," Cedric announced.

Gralyre caught sight of a bright glimmer, and realized that the sentry was using a scrap of mirror to flash a code to the camp to announce their arrival. There would be a different set of codes for enemies, he imagined.

The staging camp betwixt Left and Right Bosom Hills was little more than a corral containing a couple of dozen horses, and a small shed that leaned precariously against the split rail fence, sheltering the feed and harnesses of the horses.

A large tent was pitched within the shelter of the trees. Two Rebels sat before the meagre heat of a small, smokeless fire, huddling under thick cloaks to preserve their heat. They did not rise as Matik and Gralyre rode in with their small herd of horses.

"Matik," one of them greeted. "How are ye?"

"Ye know how It Is, Ansell. I canno' complain, yet sometimes I still do," Matik replied.

For a moment Gralyre thought that Matik was retelling the same lame joke he had just heard, but then the rote nature of the comment registered. A warding phrase. Of course.

The Rebels stood from their places by the fire, and their cloaks fell away to reveal cocked and loaded crossbows, lowered to point at the ground now that they knew they were among friends.

"Prepare t' move out. The muster has been called," Matik ordered.

"Aye, sir," Ansell saluted.

The second Rebel propped his weapon against the stump he had been sitting on and motioned to Gralyre. "Come on then, let's get these horses corralled."

∞○∞

Every morning, as was his habit, Gralyre practiced with his weapons. The Sword Dance was a bold exhibition that began to draw an audience from the Rebel warriors who had been trickling into the camp over the last three days. It was inevitable that one of them would ask to spar.

"Sir, my name is Spence," the lad approached Gralyre deferentially, interrupting his morning ritual. "Do ye think ye could show me how t' do what ye do?"

Gralyre's muscled arms came to an abrupt halt with his heavy, wooden practice swords extended in space with nary a wobble. His precision was so extreme that he appeared to have struck an invisible man. Captured in the golden light of sunrise, steam swirled from his body as his sweat evaporated in the cold air, giving him an otherworldly, godlike presence.

Without a word, Gralyre tossed one of his practice swords to the gangly youth, and made a come hither motion.

Spence grinned mightily through his spotty first beard as he attacked, but as hard as he tried, he could not come close to touching Gralyre. Every slash was met, and every swing was blocked. The sweat built as he threw every move in his arsenal at the warrior.

The rhythmic sound of crossing swords drew a crowd of men to circle the combatants. They hooted and called encouragement, even though they could clearly see that the lad was outmatched.

So far Gralyre had done nothing but defend himself, now he went on the attack. In one slick move, Spence's practice sword went flying and landed point down in the snow at the feet of one of the watching men.

"Gods!" Spence grouched. "How did ye do it?" Gralyre had moved too fast for him to figure out the sequence that had left him with numb fingers and egg on his face.

The warrior to whom Gralyre had delivered the sword pulled it from the snow with slow deliberation, capturing Gralyre's attention. He was a man near to Gralyre's own age, with wild ginger hair and a beard to match. Bright green eyes met Gralyre's in friendly challenge.

"Rolf! Ya Rolf!" Someone shouted. "Have a go!"

Spence stepped back into the crowd and watched as Rolf shrugged out of his long heavy cloak.

Gralyre grinned and motioned for the man to step forward. He missed sparring with Rewn, and even Dajin. It felt good to be useful, to share some of his vast weapon lore.

Again he allowed the warrior to throw everything he had at him before disarming him with the same sequence that had disarmed the lad.

Spence looked on with his head cocked in confusion as he

tried to work out how Gralyre was doing it.

Rolf shook his fingers with a hiss, then laughed heartily when he saw that the wooden sword had landed in precisely the same position, in almost exactly the same hole that it had created when it had flown from Spence's fingers - and at the feet of yet another warrior.

Gralyre beckoned and the new man stepped forward, to a similar result. Gralyre looked over to Spence, who was staring with avid concentration into space and working his wrist to mimic what Gralyre had done.

"Did you see how it happened that time, lad?" Gralyre called out as another man picked up the sword and the gauntlet.

Each warrior was followed by yet another. Each stepped forward in challenge and was as easily vanquished, and not just defeated, but trounced in precisely the same fashion.

The men who'd had a turn gathered in a group, discussing the move and how to duplicate it. "I have it!" Spence yelled over the cheers and jeers.

The men quieted as the lad stepped forward. "I have worked it out, I think…"

A warrior drew the wooden sword from the snow and tossed it to Spence as he stepped forward nervously. Taking a deep breath, the lad attacked.

Gralyre allowed Spence to breach his defenses and try the wrapping move on his wooden sword to disarm it. Though the strike lacked speed, cunning and strength, it was performed correctly so Gralyre let his sword pop into the air and he caught it on the downward fall with a wide grin of approval. "Good!

Well done! Now go practice and work on your speed."

The men grinned and clapped Spence on the back as the crowd began to disperse.

"Perhaps I will have a go," came a rough, rumbling voice. "I would like to see ye try that move on an axe."

Gralyre stilled and dropped the shirt he was about to pull over his head. Something akin to satisfaction roared through him as he stared at his tormenter. He smiled, just a little, as he reclaimed his wooden sword, and beckoned the warrior to dance.

Whispers darted like silver fish through the onlookers. "Matik! Matik is going to fight the swordsman!"

Matik found it difficult to trust a man of unknown limits. Add to that the possibility that Gralyre could be a spy, and he had made it his primary mission in life to shatter Gralyre's smooth shell to reveal the nature of the true beast beneath. But the harder he pushed, the more inscrutable the man became. Gralyre accepted each insult and each abuse with an icy regality that was driving Matik mad! Enough! It was past time to see what this man was made of.

Matik dropped his cloak and shirt as he stepped onto the field. Beneath the thick fur covering his skin, his powerful barrel chest, shoulders, and arms flexed as he hefted his weapon. He grinned and swung his axe in a whistling arc at Gralyre's middle.

Gralyre caught the edge on the wooden practice sword and parried the blow, but lost half of his stick, cut away cleanly in the onslaught.

"Gralyre!" yelled Rolf. "Sword!"

Gralyre spun away from Matik's next blow and neatly caught the sword that Rolf had thrown. He turned back in time to block the next swipe.

CLANG!

The attending warriors grew quiet. The game had grown serious.

Matik and Gralyre froze over their crossed blades, their muscles bulging and straining as they pushed at each other. Matik glared fiercely as Gralyre began to smile. With a fierce slide of metal they parted.

Matik walked in a loose, swaggering circle around Gralyre, until the sun was at his back and in Gralyre's eyes.

Gralyre took a couple of practice swings with his borrowed sword to get the feel of it, then took up a smooth stance, eyes squinted against the glare, but relaxed and ready for Matik's attack.

Matik's volley came swift and hard, and Gralyre's sword danced smoothly to meet each swing. It did not take either Matik or the audience of men long to realize that they had seen this pattern before.

Matik's face began to shine with his efforts, and disbelief clouded his eyes as his every move was countered. Even though he knew what was coming, he could do nothing to prevent it.

Gralyre awaited his opportunity and then struck with such speed that Matik was left looking at his numb fingers in disbelief. He glanced over, and sure enough, his axe was blade down in the snow, amongst similar holes from other bouts.

The attending warriors cheered, and slapped Matik on the

back as if he were a conquering hero. "Ye lasted longer than any o' us!" One warrior congratulated.

Matik was left with no option but to put a good loser's face upon the incident. "Alright, the lot o' ye, back t' work," he grouched with a laugh, although inside he was seething with humiliation.

He was counted to be a master with his battle-axe, and Matik was very proud of the distinction, yet he had just been trounced with as little effort as Gralyre had exerted upon the green lad, Spence.

Matik retrieved his shirt and cloak, and plucked his axe from the snow as the men dispersed. He turned his back to Gralyre, unwilling to see any look of triumph. Disgruntled, he began slogging through the snow back to his tent.

In his path, lying in the sun under a tree, Gralyre's wolfdog blinked at him with lupine contentment. Matik could not stop himself. As he walked past he aimed a kick at Gralyre's pet.

Little Wolf yelped as the boot connected and he scrabbled to get away.

Before Matik's foot finished its second swing, he was on his back in the snow, with a bruise on his forehead from Gralyre's fist. He glared up from the cold, wet depression his body had made, preparing to defend himself from more blows, but Gralyre turned away with an indifference that was incredibly insulting.

He crouched beside his wolf, his hands soothing the beast from its fright, as he checked to see if it was injured.

Matik scrambled to his feet with his fists clenched to continue the brawl.

"Not a good idea," Gralyre stated in his controlled way. There was a deadly promise in the deep baritone voice, a warning of eminent danger should Matik proceed.

Matik wisely decided that the insult was not worth the punishment he was bound to receive should he press the issue. Having just lost a good-natured bout, at least on Gralyre's part, he was not eager to experience the man when he fought in earnest. It was time to retreat.

He contented himself that Gralyre had revealed a limit, a vulnerability. The wolf could be used to goad Gralyre to anger. However, after watching Gralyre with the beast over the last three days, Matik sensed that threatening the wolf would be akin to threatening someone else's child.

That was not the rage Matik was after, for anyone would defend their family to their last breath. He wanted to see the man's control snap at normal, everyday stresses, to reveal his weaknesses. So far, Gralyre had shown none.

Gralyre rose to his full height, staring south with an intent expression. His fingers curled into Little Wolf's fur, keeping the pup's large head pressed against him in soothing contact.

"Hst! Matik!" Gralyre summoned.

The urgency in Gralyre's voice made all contentiousness vanish between them. Matik stepped towards him but stopped abruptly when the wolfdog snarled. "What is it? What do ye hear?"

Gralyre's eyes were focussed to a far distance and his head was cocked to a listening angle. "Demon Riders, a platoon. They are riding straight towards our position."

Matik loosened his axe and gave an odd warbling call. The warriors in the camp froze for a heartbeat then dove into action. Breakfast dishes scattered, fires were quickly buried under piles of snow to smother all smoke. All around, the Rebels quietly drew weapons and took up defensive positions. A dart of light flickered against a tree as the Rebel sentry raised the alarm from his position in the forest.

Gralyre measured the Rebels' numbers as being too few to stand against so many 'Riders. An alternative to battle suddenly presented itself to him. Would it work?

"What are ye doing? Where are ye going?" Matik hissed as Gralyre began to run towards Left Bosom Hill. Matik abandoned his men to follow after, the cold edge of his axe readied to find its mark in Gralyre's back, if the man were a spy about to betray their position.

But that was far from the case. Gralyre plunged up the slope, barely slowing to gravity's demand. Matik puffed after as fast as he could, but he was quickly outdistanced. Before reaching the top, Gralyre dropped to his belly in the snow, despite his naked chest, and crawled the rest of the way. Matik followed suit and together they peered over the edge.

Matik went rigid when he saw the column of red riders against the stark white snow. There was no way that the staging camp would remain undetected, for the 'Riders were headed straight for the passage between Left and Right Bosom Hills. What were they doing so far from the main road?

"Whatever ye are going t' do, ye had best make it fast!" Matik breathed urgently.

Matik's words buzzed annoyingly at the edges of Gralyre's attention, for his awareness was already focussed on the Demon Riders' horses. He reached out and gently touched their minds with encouragement to shift their path, stride by stride, to travel to the left of the hills.

Matik watched in disbelief as the horses carried their riders on their subtly altered course. From his position atop the hill, he could clearly see how the animals had gradually adjusted the path they took.

Questions about what was happening rose to Matik's lips, but Gralyre's look of intense concentration forbade any comments. Matik was not about to distract him from his chore.

It seemed to take forever, but the 'Riders passed wide of the camp, without ever becoming aware of Gralyre's tampering presence, or the Rebels who hid just beyond the rise. They continued unchecked into the forest and soon, the column could no longer be seen as they disappeared over the next ridge.

"Well done, lad," Matik commended.

Gralyre's brows canted mockingly at the praise, immediately setting Matik's teeth on edge and plunging him back into his previous combative state.

With a disdainful swipe, Gralyre brushed the melting ice from his chest and descended the hill with long strides.

ॐ

Gralyre roused from where he dozed beside a small, shielded flame as he sensed approaching horses. The Rebels who had been trickling into camp arrived exclusively afoot. Was it the Demon Rider platoon returning?

There had been no signal of danger from the sentry, but Gralyre had not exactly been paying attention. His thoughts had been flickering in flames of rage about Matik.

Matik, who had been a constant thorn in his hide for days; never leaving him alone, never letting up in his relentless harassment. It had been good when the others had begun to arrive to act as buffers, for one more day alone with the offensive, bearded, axe wielding fiend and Gralyre would likely have lost control of his wrath and given Matik the beating he had been goading him for.

With a glance, he sent Little Wolf hiding behind the tumbled stones of the cairn. He drew his sword and buried it in the snow beside the fire, making certain it was within easy reach as he settled his cloak loosely about his shoulders.

Carefully, he reached out and touched the minds of the horses coming towards him. His tense muscles relaxed as he recognized the approaching riders.

A rough hand suddenly gripped his shoulder and with an effort, Gralyre managed to prevent his startled jerk. He glared up at Matik, who grinned nastily in turn for managing to startle him. If Gralyre's mind had not been so focussed upon the arriving horses, Matik would not have had the opportunity.

"Horses are coming. 'Tis friends." Gralyre shrugged off Matik's hand.

Matik loosened his axe in its straps. "Friends, spy? Demon Riders?" He inquired in a threatening rumble.

With effort, Gralyre kept his tongue behind his teeth. Instead he grabbed his sword from where he had concealed it in the snow and straightened to walk away from Matik and his continuous barbs.

"Rrrrraaaahh!" Matik yelled, whipping his battle-axe from its sheath across his back.

Gralyre whirled into a defensive crouch and brought up his sword, scanning the clearing for signs of an attack. Seeing nothing, he glanced inquiringly at Matik. Realization dawned and his gaze hardened contemptuously on the bared axe in Matik's hands.

Gralyre lowered his blade disdainfully, and waited for Matik's flush of mortification to finish its journey up through his thick beard to stain his cheekbones, before he sheathed his sword and stalked away.

Matik slung his battle-axe home across his shoulder, shaking his head with relief and embarrassment. He could now hear the approaching horses that Gralyre had warned him of and moved forward to greet them. He was not ashamed of assuming Gralyre would attack him, for the sudden appearance of the sword had startled him. He could not fault himself for being on guard with the suspected spy.

Matik greeted his commanders as they rode into the clearing, thankful for their arrival.

"Still alive I see, Matik," Boris chuckled as he dismounted and aimed a friendly blow at his arm. "Canno' complain, but sometimes ye still do?"

"Took your time getting here," Matik's disgruntled tone made truth of the friendly jibe.

"We were followed from Verdalan by a platoon o' 'Riders. We had t' confuse our trail some before heading in your direction."

"Yeah, we saw them ride by."

Boris frowned in concern, but had no time to question Matik as Catrian joined them.

The fur lining the hood of her cloak and framing her face rippled in a strengthening breeze. Storm clouds were gathering in the gloom of the late afternoon. "Where is he," she asked without preamble.

Matik hooked a thumb back over his shoulder. Gralyre was watching them, while his wolf hovered shyly around his legs, avoiding the chaos brought by the newest strangers to invade their camp.

Boris gazed after Catrian as she strode purposefully across the snow to where Gralyre was waiting. "Walk with me, Matik. Tell me o' your time here."

Matik nodded his head, and together the two men ambled away, deep in conversation.

Gralyre watched the Sorceress Catrian walk towards him across the clearing and stepped out to meet her. He unconsciously straightened his shoulders, his nostrils flaring to catch her scent on the slight breeze.

She threw back the hood of her cloak as they met and suddenly the day did not seem quite so dull. The breeze teased at loose strands of hair from her tight braid. He cleared his throat and met her eyes as she spoke.

"Our evacuation from the city went as planned. From here we travel t' the mountain fortress t' await the rest o' the winter," she stated without greeting.

"How are my friends," Gralyre asked to keep her talking, as it looked as though she was turning to leave.

"They are well. Ye can ask them yourself," she smiled, pointing to where they were walking their horses towards the paddock.

Gralyre smiled back at her, then returned Rewn's friendly wave. Dajin turned his back and pulled his horse away from the others, almost knocking Saliana from her feet in passing.

Catrian quickly scanned him for Doaphin's taint while he was distracted. She was finished by the time he turned back, his brows raised inquiringly. Of course he had felt her presence. A blush climbed her cheeks after seeing herself through his eyes.

Gralyre saw the blush, guessed the cause, and smiled slowly at her, a warm intimate smile.

Suddenly she felt herself captured into the midnight blue depths of his eyes. Like a person too long in the cold, she felt herself yearning towards the heat she saw flickering there for her.

She broke eye contact with him, drawing in a long controlled breath. Dangerous! Remember the plan! "I had t' know if anything had changed," she coolly dampened her emotions.

Uncertainty streaked across his face. "You mean you wanted to see if I had awoken to evil," Gralyre reinterpreted.

She did not deny the accusation, for of course it was the truth. "Have your horses packed up and ready t' leave by morning," she ordered briskly and walked away.

Gralyre frowned in confusion as he watched her retreat. One moment they had been connected, the next she had turned cold as though the moment had never been.

He tracked her with his gaze as she ordered the men in their duties. She was right to keep her distance. For all he knew, he *was* a spy. For her sake, he must stay as far from her as possible. He would not run the risk of placing her life in danger if he was suddenly transformed into a creature of Doaphin.

He sighed regretfully as he went to help Rewn, Dajin and Saliana set up their camp for the night.

⊗⊗⊗

Matik continued his report to Boris. "His control over himself is staggering. My worst barbs bounce from his thick hide. I was unable to provoke him to anger!" Matik mumbled into his beard.

"He is a coward then?" Boris asked, his gaze darting across the clearing to where Gralyre was talking to an animated Rewn Wilson. Even the sullen brother, Dajin, was smiling for once.

"No. A coward he is no'. If he fears anything, he fears losing control and what he is capable o' should that happen," Matik mused insightfully. "If 'tis anything similar to what he is capable o' when he is in control, we have either gained a much needed ally or a most formidable enemy.

"I had an opportunity o' sparring with him. Ye can tell a lot about a man by how he fights."

"And what did ye learn?"

Matik grunted at the memory of his humiliation this morning. "He is a cold blooded bastard with a vicious sense o' humour. He put me in my place right and proper! He is the most skilled man with a sword I have ever seen," Matik continued with grudging admiration. "Even ye, Boris. Next t' him, your sword-play looks like a novice's."

Boris' brows rose high at this, but he did not seek to discredit Matik, knowing the man spoke only truth.

Matik glared across the camp at the subject of his resentment. "There is no way around that fact that he saved us from disaster with that platoon o' 'Riders."

Boris glanced to where Catrian was organizing their tents for the evening. "Then let us hope that he is no' an enemy, my friend," Boris stated seriously. "Catrian has a plan."

CHAPTER TWENTY-FIVE

The journey into the mountains was a test of their strength and endurance. So late in the season, some passes were buried in avalanches and they were forced to backtrack to find alternate routes that the horses would be able to take. Some valleys were traversed with baited breath and hushed voices, lest the vibrations of their passing cause heavy shelves of ice to roar down upon them.

Every day the Rebels grew more fatigued, as they climbed higher into the thin, frigid air. Man and horse alike struggled to maintain their footing on the icy trails of the steep elevations. This far into winter, their limited hours of trekking were set by the short arc of the winter sun, late to rise, early to set, extending their journey far beyond the time it habitually took to reach the Northern Fortress from Verdalan.

Night had fallen, putting paid to another fruitless day that had seen less than a mile of useful distance towards their destination, despite a hard slog across fifteen miles of rock, ice and snow. The Rebels had made camp in the shallow depression of a plateau to escape the biting wind. Outside of each tent kindled a small flickering campfire; an effort to gain some warmth for the night's sleep.

Gralyre's fire threw little heat and even less light into the faces of the three men and one woman who huddled around it. But unlike the other campfires that were cheering road-weary travellers, this one had a plump grouse turning a golden brown over the coals and sending up a mouth watering aroma that caused more than one envious glare to be thrown their way.

It was a gift from Little Wolf, food he had hunted for the pack. The companions had quickly settled back into the rhythm of the road; the experience and synergy gained during their journey from Raindell to Verdalan.

"Is it done yet?" Dajin asked, his face avid with hungry longing as he stared at the bird.

Rewn smiled at his brother, a real smile after months of estrangement. Their relationship was much improved since their vetting by the resistance. "No' yet." Rewn's fear for his brother's safety when the Rebels had questioned Dajin, his inability to come to his brother's aid, had worked a transformation to allow him to finally begin to forgive.

And Dajin... well Dajin would always be Dajin.

Gralyre grinned as he watched them. It was good to see that everything was getting back to normal.

"Enjoying yourself, spy?" Matik's rough voice was harsher than ever from the cold, grating out of the darkness as he stomped by.

Reclining next to him on the packs, Little Wolf rumbled an ugly response.

Gralyre's grin fled as he gentled Little Wolf with a hand. He watched broodingly as Matik walked on. The abuse had become so pervasive that he was beginning to hear the man's insulting voice in his sleep.

"Why does he say these things?" Saliana condemned angrily,

which was unusual for her. She more often than not worked at remaining unnoticed.

"Catrian was unable to bring back my memories." Gralyre spoke gently, so as not to scare Saliana back into her shell. Though they had been travelling companions for months, and she was definitely a member of their tiny circle, she shied from any direct contact, unless it was from Rewn whom she seemed to trust the most. "He could be right."

Gralyre cleared his throat and readjusted his position against his packs. "In fact, I have been meaning to talk to you all about this very thing."

Rewn, Dajin and Saliana all looked at him expectantly, and Gralyre fought an uncharacteristic lump in his throat. "You all know that I could be harbouring an alliance with Doaphin," he gestured to his head, "in here. There is no way to tell for sure." He drew a draught of air to brace himself for what needed to be done. "This must be our last night together. If I turn, if I am secretly Doaphin's man, you would not see it coming, and I could hurt you all and be unable to stop it. I want you safe. You must keep away from me!"

Although not openly ostracized by the Rebels, Gralyre was not blind to the lack of warmth for his presence around the camp. Warriors would make polite excuses to be elsewhere doing other things. Matik's open hostility to his presence and loud accusations were doing their job well, keeping him isolated within the group but watched at all times.

Even Gralyre's budding rapports, built by sharing his skill with the sword, had petered out. No one was going to make overtures of friendship to a possible spy.

Gralyre would not have minded being an outsider had it not been rubbing off on Rewn, Dajin and Saliana, who staunchly supported him, regardless of the Rebels' opinion. Though Gralyre appreciated his companions' defense, it was costing them a secure place within the resistance. For their own good, he had to sever the bonds and push them away.

Silence had descended over the small group, broken only by the pop of the fire and the hiss of the juices escaping the cooking meat.

Little Wolf responded to Gralyre's emotional upheaval, by laying his head in his master's lap. His golden eyes shifted from one person to the next.

Rewn cleared his throat, and announced clearly and loudly, "What a load o' self-pitying dung."

Dajin looked uncertain, but Saliana covered a smile with her hand, her eyes darting between Gralyre's surprise and Rewn's pugnacious glare.

"'Tis no jest, Rewn! I could be a weapon sent by…"

Rewn's snort overrode Gralyre's assertion.

Gralyre subsided in confusion.

"Brother, maybe ye should listen t' him?" Dajin suggested, an uneasy quiver in his voice as he edged away from the fire and Gralyre.

Rewn pointed at Gralyre from across the flickering flames. "Ye are no' a bad man." His certainty was immutable. "I have fought beside ye. Ye have saved our lives more than once. Gods! Ye even saved *their* lives!" Rewn's arm swept back to indicate the warriors clustered around them. The story of how Gralyre had influenced the platoon of 'Riders to turn away from discovery of the camp, had made the rounds.

Gralyre leaned forward, his face serious, intent. "What if I am not that man? What if it is all an act? What if all my evil is hidden away?"

Again, Rewn's derisive snort cut through Gralyre's words. "Rubbish! Look at that tree." He pointed to a small, wizened pine that clung tenaciously to the rocks. "Look at how stunted it is, how crooked its branches are, how dull its colour."

Gralyre sighed, not seeing the correlation. "So?"

"So?" Rewn smiled as he clarified his argument. "I do no' have t' *see* the unending seasons o' wind, and snow, and poor soil t' know that these things twisted it. The tree tells all. It canno' hide the forces that shaped it." Rewn's eyes glinted at Gralyre, and absolute faith shone from his face and voice. "Ye are a good man, full o' integrity and honour. I do no' need t' see the forces that shaped ye, t' know they were no' the hands o' evil."

Gralyre's breath left him in a soft hiss and he had to clench his teeth to hold in a most undignified emotion. The firelight ran and waivered as tears built in his eyes. "Thank-you, my friend." Gralyre's voice was hoarse with gratitude at this unexpected support.

Rewn watched Gralyre's face closely and his voice gained volume to satisfy the listening ears of the Rebel warriors clustered at campfires all around them. "And I certainly do no' need a bunch o' terrified milksops telling me who I can, and canno' associate with!"

Gralyre could not help the choked laugh that escaped him. He should have known that Rewn would quickly intuit all of his motives in seeking to push them away.

Rewn chuckled back and wagged his eyebrows comically. "Do no' try that again," he warned his friend with a mock growl.

Saliana smiled happily and poked the roasting bird with her dagger. The juices ran clear. "'Tis ready!" she announced.

Dajin's eagerness for the meal was much less than it had been. In the end, he only picked at his portion before rolling himself in his cloak and turning his back on the fire.

ဆာ

So far the weather had been clear and cold, but when they awoke in the predawn, the sky was black, as though the night had killed the day and twilight was the broken survivor of the battle. The temperature dropped ominously.

Gralyre pushed a groggy Little Wolf away from his side where the wolfdog had been curled tightly all night to share heat. He exited the tent and uncurled to his feet as the first snowflakes began to drift downwards. He billowed his cloak with a sharp snap to dislodge the frost that had caked over him while he slept.

"Morning," Rewn was stirring the coals of their fire to heat the kettle.

Saliana was adding a measure of oats to the bubbling water as she looked up with a shy smile. "Morning, Gralyre."

Dajin had already struck his tent and was busy jamming his

belongings into his pack. He did not look up from the task.

"Morning," Gralyre retuned to all as he yawned and stretched. He was surprised at how late he had slept. Usually he was the first to roll out of his blankets.

Gralyre blinked at the turn in the weather and tried to shake off the lingering aftereffects of the disturbing dreams that had plagued him. Though he tried to recall the specifics, the images flitted away like bats exposed to daylight. Roosting in the dark corners of his mind they awaited the night, when they could once again fly and hunt. He shivered and pulled his cloak tighter about his shoulders.

"Rough night, spy?" Matik snarled as he marched past with a pack to be loaded onto the patiently waiting horses.

"Yea, spy!" Dajin said loudly as he jumped to his feet and shouldered his pack.

Matik paused mid-step and looked back, his brows elevated with surprise.

"Did ye have pleasant dreams o' Doaphin?" Dajin's tone of voice, his swaggering walk, perfectly mimicked Matik's as he puffed himself up.

Rewn's face contorted with astonishment and shame. "Dajin!" he snapped admonishingly.

Dajin made eye contact with Gralyre over a nasty grin. "Ye said it yourself, that we should stay away. Seemed like sound advice t' me!" Truth be told, Dajin was salivating at the chance of revenge against all imagined slights Gralyre had given him.

Gralyre kept his tongue behind his gritted his teeth and forced his clenched fists to relax. Briefly he wondered what forces had shaped Dajin into the man that now stood before him.

"Dajin do no' do this," Rewn warned again, his voice filled with sorrow and disbelief.

"I am my own man, brother. I will make my own decisions. Ye may trust your life t' this spy, but I will no'."

Dajin had stayed awake long past the time when the others had slept and assessed from which direction the wind blew. He had no intention of being ostracized by the Rebels for the sake of an unfortunate association with Gralyre.

Little Wolf growled nastily, his lip curled back to expose his gleaming fangs and Dajin suddenly realized he had fallen a step too far behind Matik for comfort's sake.

Matik took in Gralyre's tight face, and a gleam entered his eyes as Dajin approached. "Let's talk," he invited, as he threw an arm over Dajin's shoulders, and drew him away.

Rewn's arm raised and lowered helplessly as he watched Dajin's defection to Matik's camp. He drew a shuddering breath and turned to Gralyre. His face was a study in grief.

"You should go after him," Gralyre urged though tightened lips. White marks of tension bracketed his mouth. "He is your brother."

Rewn's face suddenly contracted with anger. He kicked his pack and sent the contents flying. "He is his own man!" he snarled. "He 'as made his bed. Let 'im lay in it!"

Saliana retreated a safe distance from Rewn's rage and drew her cloak around herself in defense from the violence that threatened. She watched the two men with the wide-eyed fear of a small mouse confronted by hungry cats.

Gralyre glanced down at Little Wolf and saw how the pup's eyes were narrowed and alert, with a hunter's fixation on where Dajin and Matik were depositing their packs. His luxurious winter coat made him appear larger than ever. His amber eyes, a legacy from his wolf father, never left his intended prey. A low rumbling growl, barely audible, chuffed from Little Wolf's throat.

Gralyre rubbed Little Wolf's ears, calming the wolfdog before it turned savage. If only there were someone to gentle him so, before *he* turned feral.

"Ye should no' let Matik speak t' ye as he does."

It took Gralyre a moment to realize that the words had come from Saliana.

"I have lived with bullies. My brothers... my Da..." she shrugged hesitantly. "Bullies gain power by drawing others t' their side," Saliana said obliquely in reference to Dajin's defection. "Even if they hurt ye for your defiance, at least ye keep your self respect."

Gralyre sighed and rubbed a hand against the tensed muscles in his neck. "There is more going on than simple bullying."

"What then?" Rewn asked as his frustration came to a boil. "What would possess ye t' allow them t' treat ye like this? I have seen ye rattle a man for far less!"

"If only I could take action against Matik!" Gralyre snapped and dropped to a crouch to warm his hands on the fire. "But if I beat Matik senseless it will immediately brand me as an enemy in the eyes of Catrian, and confirm their charges of being a spy."

Rewn took a shaky step forward and crouched down opposite

to his friend, having extrapolated the consequence to Gralyre's scenario.

Gralyre picked up a thick chunk of ice and pulverized it with a flex of his fingers. "I would be executed on the spot, and Matik would swing the axe. He is trying to provoke just that response. My only recourse is to not give it to him!"

For a reason that became more tenuous as the days of harassment continued, it was very important for Gralyre to remain with the resistance. That *reason* paid scant attention to him as they journeyed deeper into the snow capped Heathrens.

The oats began to boil over, and Rewn pulled them from the fire with hands that shook. He yelped when he burned his fingers and dropped the pot. Boiling gruel sloshed over the lip.

Now that the men seemed calmer, Saliana felt reassured enough to return to the fire. "Here," she said gently as she took the pot with the edge of her cloak, protecting her hands. "Let me."

While Rewn and Saliana worked on breakfast, Gralyre worked to hold his fury in check. Continuously pushing it down was like building a volcano's pressure in the depths of a mountain. Eventually, unexpectedly, it was going to erupt.

Gralyre lifted his face to the sky, feeling the slight breeze waft feathery snowflakes across his cheeks, butterfly touches that made him shudder with yearning.

'I wish I was the wind, flying free and far across the land, unfettered, unseen!' Nature could not be bound and gagged by politics and prejudice.

Needing the freedom of such a release, he opened his mind to the wind, just as he did with animals, and felt an immediate and strong connection that hummed with a tone of pure power. Magic vibrated through him as the wind stroked familiar fingers across his soul, welcoming him like a long lost son.

The breeze gusted and swirled around Gralyre, and spoke to him, not in the language of humans, or of animals, but in wordless exaltation. It told him of how it had been born by the rushing body of a swift elk in the high steps to the north, of how it had gathered speed and moisture as it rushed down the steep slopes of the Heathrens, gathering momentum until finally, it had reached the top of their mountain, brooding and dark, the merest vanguard of its power caressing Gralyre; the nuzzling of a soft mouth as it prepared to unleash the body of its fury.

Gralyre could feel the coiled power. How the wind yearned to rush and roar! But like him, for the moment, its tension was held in check by the tiniest of balances.

He understood its desire to break loose with all the destructive powers at its command! He envied the wind its violent maelstrom, wishing he could join his anger to the rush of the blizzard, wishing the gale to pluck him from his feet, that he might become a part of it - its eye.

He relaxed and drew back into himself, shutting his mind off from the siren call of absolute power and destruction. Sighing, he opened his eyes and gave Little Wolf one more scratch on the head before attending to packing up his camp.

Gralyre felt more relaxed for having communed with the oncoming storm, as if he had been relieved of his temper, released, unleashed, to the wind. If only wishes came true. He shook his head at his foolish fancy.

'Twas best that this one did not. Such a storm as he envisioned would kill them all.

Across the camp, Catrian stiffened and stared up at the sky.

"What is it?" Boris asked in concern as she slowly stood, her breakfast forgotten as it slipped from her lap.

Catrian drew in a deep breath, letting it go in a long puff of steam as she continued to stare uneasily at the brooding, roiling storm, fast approaching over the far peak. "I felt something odd. 'Tis this storm. It bears watching."

She shook her head after a long searching moment. "'Tis gone now. Mount the men. We should make such progress as we can afore this storm hits."

The horses were loaded with the packs, the group assumed their accustomed positions in the line, and the drudgery of the day began. One foot in front of the other, up, always up, they picked their way cautiously across the sloping face of the mountain. The gently swirling snow confused their eyes and gathered thickly on cloaks and beards.

By their midday rest the gentle snowfall had changed its nature. The wind had picked up, and the feathery snowflakes had turned to hard beads of ice that stung their exposed skin.

Even as they huddled over their meagre traveller's rations, unable to light a fire, the skies darkened from twilight grey to midnight black. The oncoming blizzard gathered in strength and the wind gained a demon's howling voice, whipping hair into eyes and sucking voraciously at the warmth hoarded beneath cloaks.

After a short consultation with Boris, Catrian turned to the fifty warriors who made up their ragged party. She had to yell to be heard over the roaring voice of the wind, and rely on others to relay her message down the line.

"We must find shelter from the storm. Our best chance is t' cross over t' the other side o' the mountain and hope the blizzard's fury will be less felt in the lee. I shall do my best t' lessen the force o' the storm around us as we travel, but I canno' lie t' ye. We shall need all the good fortune the Gods can spare t' survive this."

Catrian nodded to Boris, who strode forward with rope and tied it to her waist, then to his own. He passed the loose end to Matik who sent it down the line, tied man to man, man to horse, so none would become lost when the storm's full fury smote them.

Gralyre pulled a second strap from his pack and slipped a loop around Little Wolf, collaring him to his waist.

The line began to move. They had climbed high above the treeline during the morning. Now, exposed as they were upon the mountain tundra, there was nothing to break the force of the gale as it roared across the glacier, melting all shapes into its white maelstrom.

The warriors bent double to withstand the blizzard's assault. The horses kept trying to turn their tails to the onslaught, as was their natural wont. It took much coaxing from their handlers to drive the reluctant animals forward.

Even lashed together with less than six feet of separation, Gralyre was soon hard pressed to see the bodies in front or behind. Sharp tugs of the tether became his only connection to the rest of the ragged line of travellers.

Gralyre bowed his head to protect the exposed skin of his face, and used a hand to restrain his hood against the wind snatching it away to expose his ears to the frost biting cold. Already, the blowing ice pellets had frosted his beard white.

The stinging wind forced tears from his eyes that flash-froze his eyelashes. He blinked with difficulty, enduring the small, repetitious pain of lashes being pulled apart. He fought the urge to close his eyes completely, and just allow the line to blindly carry him forward, instead of straining and squinting to keep the shuffling figure of Rolf, on the leash ahead of him, within view.

The tugging at his waist reassured him that Rewn was still following behind. This released him to concentrate on placing his feet securely amidst the swirling ice and snow that shifted upon each tread, making him feel as though he would stumble sideways as from a rug being pulled from under his feet.

Little Wolf padded beside him, stoically enduring the leash tied to Gralyre's waist. The miserable wolfdog huddled in Gralyre's lee, using him as a shield against the bitter storm.

The violent wind churned the hard stinging grains of ice into a frenzy that spent in every direction. Phantoms and shapes pulled at the eye, though the whiteout made it impossible to focus. Near or far - 'twas all the same in the blur.

Only the pull of the tether as it disappeared into the turbulent whiteness bespoke the presence of Rolf ahead of him. By the time Gralyre reached his footprints, they had all but vanished. Why had he wished for such an assault as this?

The footing became even more treacherous as the blowing snow created drifted traps over deep holes and left other spots scoured, and polished to slickness. Gralyre stumbled from an unexpectedly strong pull of the rope just as his foot and leg sank into a deep drift, sending him sprawling. With great effort he resisted the urge to rest.

Surely they had reached the other side of the mountain by now? Where was the lessening of the storm that Catrian had promised? Gralyre was suddenly immobilized by the idea that something must have happened to her. What if she had stumbled, as he just had, and injured herself while trying to guide them through the storm?

Little Wolf nuzzled and pawed at Gralyre, encouraging him to stand when he did not immediately regain his feet.

Gralyre's muscles strained to pull free of the drift as he let the tugging of the rope help him back onto his cold, numbed feet. The fading sensations in his toes made it difficult to find his balance. He stumbled once before securing his footing, and chanced to glance up. His worry subsided as he beheld the power of Catrian's spell.

Arching high above the group was a blue, glowing dome, its brilliance shining through the driving snow. Gralyre felt a shiver crawl up his spine at the sight of Catrian's powerful shield deflecting the force of the blizzard, for if the violence of the storm was this bad within the protective shelter, how much worse must it be outside?

An eddy of wind driven hail drove against his exposed throat as he looked up at the shield, the discomfort forcing him to lower his chin or freeze. Even with the help of her spell they were doomed if they did not find shelter soon.

There were many animals in the area. Game had been plentiful while they travelled. The wild creatures had to take shelter somewhere when storms of this magnitude stuck, so where did they go? Where were the shelters they used?

Gralyre scanned to the limits of his awareness for the minds of the wild creatures, searching for any thoughts of a shelter that could hold a party of their size.

He located a den of wolves in the treeline far below them. They were snuggled in a dugout beneath roots of a wind-felled tree. No help there.

Fox and rabbit, hibernating bear and birds, all were curled up in their own cosy little holes and hollows and had no thoughts of anyplace larger.

Just as he was about to give up, he brushed the thoughts of a stag. It was an old magnificent animal, a veteran of many battles of survival. The stag was sheltered by the treeline but was thinking of a safer place in the ice above.

'An ice cave deep within the living glacier!'

From the thoughts of the animal, he gleaned the cave's location and size. Gralyre discerned it would be a tight fit, getting all the people and animals within, but this would only enhance their chances of survival in the freezing temperatures, where body warmth was the only source of heat.

The column had almost travelled beyond the trailhead that would bring them to the mouth of the cave. It he did not get their attention to change direction, they would never reach safety before they all froze to death.

He tried to increase his pace to catch up with Rolf and relay his message up the line, but the weight of the bodies behind him kept the aft tether taut and Gralyre trapped in place. Even so, the time it would take to filter the message through thirty or forty warriors would see them past the point of no return. Even a shout would wash away in the roar of a wind that drowned out all other voices but its own.

If only he could talk to people as he did animals! So far he had been unsuccessful in all attempts to touch the mind of another human.

'Except for Catrian!'

But Catrian had always initialized the first contact, and he had used that contact as a bridge to her thoughts. Could he establish a link on his own?

He had to try!

Gralyre peeled the ice from around his eyes so he could blink again. Staying out in this blizzard was no second choice, it was a death sentence. He allowed his feet to plant themselves by rote, as he focussed his awareness towards the front of the line where he knew Catrian to be.

From his memories he summoned the essence of her, her touch, her scent, her presence. Holding that ideal strong in his mind, he softly spoke her name.

"Catrian."

The wind drove the sound away so that even his own ears missed the words. But Catrian heard him.

Gralyre expelled a sharp gasp as he felt her thoughts suddenly

entwine with his. His body's reaction to her presence was immediate and strong, as usual. His heart doubled its speed and he
swallowed hard in an effort to keep his focus long enough to tell
her of the cave.

Without warning she severed the contact, leaving him bereft,
then angry that her abrupt departure had affected him so. What
was this hold she had on him? More important, had she understood the message?

Gralyre howled a victory and pumped his fist at the storm, for
he could tell by the direction of the wind that Catrian had found
the path, and turned the column. They had started their climb
towards the sanctuary of the ice cave.

Beside him on the leash, Little Wolf tried to sit down and
chew away the balls of ice that had formed in the pads of his
paws.

Gralyre quickly grabbed the pup's feet and performed the
operation for him, pulling the painful ice chunks from the soft
tissues, yanking fur away with the ice but knowing he had little
time to perform the operation before the rope around his waist
tautened and forced him forward. As Little Wolf whined in
distress, Gralyre told him of the sanctuary they would soon
reach.

With renewed energy, the wolfdog picked up his sore paws,
lifting them high to wade through the deep drifts. But the icy
incline soon forced him to pick his footing more carefully.

The grade became steeper. Gralyre feared they would soon be
scrabbling on all fours and abandoning the horses to the storm,
yet somehow the Stag had made it to this sanctuary. Finally, the

trail levelled and they began walking across the slope again. They were very close now.

Gralyre felt an unexpectedly sharp tug from the line behind, then another, and another. His feet dragged out from under him, as he belatedly realized he was feeling bodies falling off the trail behind him. He landed painfully on his back and slid uncontrollably down the glacier.

Little Wolf yelped as his tether bore him along in Gralyre's wake.

Before Gralyre had gone far he ran out of snow and painfully struck a wind-scoured outcropping of rock. With little time to spare, he braced his feet against the stones and grasped the slack aft tether. His back took up the strain as the rope drew taut. If he had been standing, instead of lying braced as he was, he would have been swept from his feet again.

The warrior who had been in front of him, Rolf, slid past with arms and legs windmilling to find a purchase. Gralyre snagged the forward line and readied himself for Rolf's weight to land against the tether. No other men slid past, so someone at the top of the trail had to be anchoring those who had fallen.

Gralyre grunted in pain as Rolf's weight hit, adding to his burden. With one arm holding Rolf, and the other straining against the weight of many, Gralyre slowly felt his arms leaving their sockets. "Hurry!" he bellowed, but he doubted that Rolf could hear him through the howl of wind.

Little Wolf whined and licked at Gralyre's face excitedly, disoriented by the fall.

'Get back Little Wolf! Calm down!'

Rolf quickly relieved the strain of his weight as he crawled and dragged his way to Gralyre's side. He jammed himself into the rocks, and his strong hands joined in helping to support the weight of the dangling bodies. The relief to Gralyre's arms was extreme as, together, they began to haul in the weight of the fallen.

Instead of pointing off into the blizzard across the slope, as it should have, the rope was drawn sharply back down the mountain. Gralyre forced his numb fingers tighter around the icy tether, pulling mightily, hauling the fallen warriors upwards.

The line slackened and Gralyre assumed Rewn had regained his footing. He smiled with relief and felt his chapped bottom lip split open. He sucked it into his mouth to relieve the slight pain, as he sagged back with the relief of relaxing his overtaxed muscles. Beside him he felt, rather than saw, Rolf flop back as well.

'What has happened?'

Gralyre sat upright when Catrian's mind touched his.

'Some have slipped, but I think they are almost back to their feet. We have almost reached the cave?'

'Yes. Pull twice on the rope when they are ready t' continue.' She was gone.

Rolf pounded him on the shoulder for a job well done, and got to his feet to start back up the slope. Gralyre stayed where he was until he was sure there would be no further slips to protect against.

After an eternity of isolation in the driving wind and snow, braced against the rocks, his only contact to others the vibrating umbilical of the rope, he saw Rewn climb towards him through the flurries. Gralyre got to his feet and gave two sharp tugs on his rope. It would take a moment for the signal to be relayed to the leaders at the front.

In the interim Rewn caught up. He put his mouth close to Gralyre's ear to be heard over the scream of the wind. "That was close! If the horses anchoring the other end had slid away with us, we would have been lost! By the Gods of Ill Fortune, we still might be if we do no' find a place t' rest soon!"

"We have almost made it to a cave!" Gralyre yelled into Rewn's ear in turn. The rope gave a sharp tug and he was drawn back up the glacier to the trail. He could only hope Rewn had heard the good news.

After an eon of battling the violence of nature, they finally reached the cave. The line paused before moving forward in fits and starts, as each warrior took their turn entering the haven. As Gralyre moved forward in place, he eventually saw the tether descending into a faint glow emanating from an opening in the glacier's icy face.

The weak lamplight was as welcome a sight as any Gralyre had ever seen, bringing with it thoughts of warm, crackling fires. Stumbling wearily, Gralyre and Little Wolf entered the mouth of the cave and left the driving wind behind. He heaved a sigh of relief to be out of the icy storm, and let the pull of the rope draw his frozen feet down a long curving ice passage.

CHAPTER TWENTY-SIX

The tunnel was large enough for a man to walk comfortably, and curved slightly downwards to the left. The aquamarine glacial ice of the walls gave way to rough grey granite stone before the passage opened up into a large cavern that was roughly circular in shape and about fifty paces across.

It felt uncommonly warm after the deathly cold of the blizzard. Steam wafted from the bodies of the warriors as they groaned from the painful reawakening of their deadened limbs.

The tether suddenly jerked Gralyre forward in a stagger. Matik, sneering at him as usual, drew him away from blocking the opening, while coiling the ice-coated leash over an arm.

Rolf, the warrior ahead of Gralyre, had already been released from his binding and had lurched to the wall and collapsed. Wisps of steam feathered away from his sodden cloak.

"Ah...warmth!" Rewn groaned in relief as he arrived in the main cavern on Gralyre's heels.

Gralyre was fumbling with stiff cold fingers to undo his tether. "Was anyone injured in the fall?" Releasing himself from the leash, he ignored Matik as he turned to help Rewn unknot himself from his own iced tether.

"I do no' think so," Rewn answered through chattering teeth. "But I am no' sure how many o' us went down. Could no' have been but minor scrapes for the line moved forward fairly well after we got our feet under us."

Rewn wearily turned from Gralyre to help Saliana from her bindings as she stumbled into the cavern. A small bruise marred her cheek and he winced in commiseration as he reached out to touch it.

Her hand beat his to the mark. "'Tis fine," she asserted as she cupped her cheek protectively and flinched away before he could probe the injury.

Rewn shrugged and moved forward to help the next frozen soul who had reached the sanctuary.

Gralyre's attention drifted towards the Sorceress as was usual whenever he was in her presence. Catrian and Boris were across the room, wearing identical looks of wonder on their faces as they pressed their hands against the stone of the walls. "The living blood of the mountain is warming the cavern," Gralyre heard Boris marvel.

Gralyre touched the cavern wall near to him and felt the heat emanating from the stone. A small smile of delight lifted the corner of his split lip.

No wonder the old stag had been dreaming of this place. To have warmth in the midst of this freezing assault was a grand luxury!

He dropped his sodden cloak and, with a grunt of pure pleasure, flattened his body against the rough stone, his arms spread wide against the hot rock to increase his contact. Sensation slowly returned to his numb feet and hands, making him hiss in pain as pins and needles invaded his flesh. As he pressed his ice bound beard to the hot wall, blessed heat began to penetrate to his face. Gods, but that felt good!

"How do ye know o' this place?" Catrian's accusatory demand sounded behind him. "We have travelled these mountains for generations and never known o' it!"

Gralyre suppressed a groan of aggravation as her tone pierced the bubble of his pleasure. How many times did he have to save their lives before they would trust him? Not only were they away from the storm, but they also had this wonderful heat! How could that not be enough for her?

Rudely, he did not turn to face her, unwilling to deal with her suspicions, and done trying to curry favour. He just wanted to absorb as much heat from the walls as possible. "A stag down in the treeline was standing in the cold dreaming of being here." Gralyre mumbled around where his cheek was pressed to the wall. "I had no idea it was warm like this," his voice purred like a contented mountain lion, "I just knew it was shelter."

She leaned against the wall beside him, her face near his as she glared into his eyes. Vexation at his lack of courtesy exacerbated her aggression. "Let me give ye a healthy piece o' advice. Next time ye are going t' use your magic, let me know. I almost killed ye out there before I realized it was ye, though I thought ye were only talking with your dog. Next time ye might no' be so lucky."

At her threat, anger lit a flame in Gralyre's midnight-blue eyes. He leaned closer, his head angled aggressively, and halted a mere inch from her lips. He watched her eyes widen with instinctual feminine panic as she focussed on his approaching mouth. The tip of her tongue darted out to moisten her lips… hot breath brushed his face... her lashes fluttered closed…

"You are welcome," he snarled coldly.

Catrian's eyes snapped open in humiliation as she gasped angrily. She made a huffy sound and flounced away in a snit. "Ignorant jackass!" The insult drifted back over her shoulder.

Gralyre smiled in satisfaction and closed his eyes to return to savouring the warmth. He jumped when a hand clasped his shoulder. He had been concentrating so hard on Catrian he had not noticed Boris was also present. He glanced back at the Commander, readying himself for yet another battle.

"Good job, lad," Boris commended blandly, giving his shoulder an approving squeeze as he moved away.

The ambiguity of his statement left Gralyre momentarily confused if the Commander was referring to finding the cavern or giving Catrian back what she had dished.

Gralyre flipped over to warm his back on the rock, watching Boris help the men bring in the horses. Though the Commander was not willing to trust him, at least he'd had the decency to give him his due for saving them. Unlike other people.

Gralyre wiped his chin free of the drips of melting ice trickling from his beard, his brooding gaze following Catrian as she organized the setup of their camp. She glanced up suddenly and caught him staring.

Confused and disgusted with his inability to ignore her, he looked away, and found his attention captured by Little Wolf who was rolling ecstatically on the warm rock floor with grunts and growls happiness.

The pup's antics surprised a smile from him. Gralyre sank down to remove the leather thong from around the dog's neck.

He scratched Little Wolf's belly, combing away balls of ice that had rolled and matted into his fur.

Little Wolf kicked his feet joyfully at the sensation before twisting to his stomach to groom his icy paws.

Gralyre gave up his wall space to a newly arrived, ice shrouded warrior, to help unload the packs from the horses. Space was getting cramped, but he did not hear anyone complaining. All he heard were groans of thankfulness as heat began to penetrate cold stiff limbs.

so)co

After three days, the blizzard was still hurling itself violently across the mountains and the forced inactivity and lack of room was winding tempers tight.

The horses and packs filled half the meagre space in the cavern and the sleeping pallets took up the rest. There was no room for cooking, so they survived on cold rations and melted snow.

They slept in shifts, the wakened men charged with keeping the improvised stables cleansed and the entrance to the cavern clear. Shovelling the accumulation of snow away from the opening was a full time chore, that if left would eventually cut off their air. Their haven would become a death trap.

Matik and Dajin passed their time baiting Gralyre's temper. Gralyre tried to move to the apposing sleep shift so that he would not have to be awake at the same time as they, but that just made him vulnerable to the sabotage of his belongings, like finding his boots packed with snow or his pack laced with horse dung.

Gralyre's mood became uglier. Unable to escape their taunts in the close confines of the cavern, his temper sizzled ever closer to the surface, a volcano that was straining to be released. His only victory was to show his tormentors a face that was as calm as ever.

Knowing Gralyre would not, Rewn finally went to Catrian in an effort to get her to halt the constant bombardment. He made sure that Gralyre was occupied shovelling snow at the mouth of the tunnel so that he would not be shamed by Rewn's interference in his affairs.

"May I speak t' ye?" Rewn asked as he approached.

Catrian looked up from a book she was reading. With a slight smile she set it aside. "We have nothing but time t' pass. How are ye settling in with us, Rewn?"

"That is no' what I want t' talk t' ye about, m'lady," he said awkwardly, but firmly as he sat beside her.

"Oh?"

"Gralyre." Rewn named his topic.

"Gralyre?" Catrian echoed.

"There is only so much abuse he will suffer before he retaliates," Rewn warned her. "And you do no' want that! I have seen Gralyre retaliate. It does no' end well for his opponents."

"Matik…"

Rewn cut her off. "Let us no' pretend that Matik does no' sit or salute but t' your biding."

Catrian's eyebrows arched, and haughty anger stirred. No one had the right to question her motives!

Rewn was frustrated by her obstinate reaction. "Gralyre knows if he fights Matik, it will only brand him a spy for attacking one o' your own!"

"If he proves himself a spy, I have the cure for it!" Catrian stated sharply, her ire at Rewn's censoring words glittering in her eyes. Deep within she felt a stirring of guilt at the necessary cruelty.

"Are ye willing t' bet the life o' your man on that?"

"Matik can take care o' himself!"

"No' against a man like Gralyre." Rewn stared down at his clasped hands and sighed bitterly on behalf of his friend. "I do no' know what game ye play, Sorceress," he said the word insultingly, "but 'tis no' one that ye will like t' win."

"Is that a threat, Rewn Wilson? Are ye threatening me?" Catrian growled. "I have my reasons, and I do no' have t' explain them t' ye!"

Rewn looked at her steadily until her eyes wavered. "I have no need t' threaten ye, 'tis but a warning. If Gralyre seeks retribution for his ill treatment, he will no' stand alone, for if ye ask me, 'tis bloody cowardly t' attack a man who will die if he seeks t' defend himself."

Catrian gasped at the insult. "Your brother does no' seem t' think as ye do!"

Rewn flushed an angry red and stood. "On your head be it!" he gritted out and stomped away.

Catrian stared after Rewn with her mouth agape. Except for her uncle, no one ever had the courage to censor her behaviour!

Her estimation of Rewn Wilson rose by several degrees.

Despite herself, Catrian found herself re-evaluating her plan. At the crux was the possibility that Gralyre's amnesia was a ruse created for the sole purpose of infiltrating the resistance. If Gralyre were a skilled Sorcerer, and he certainly had the magical strength to do it, he could have placed that wall inside his own mind.

She knew from experience that it was impossible to maintain the concentration necessary to work magic while in the grips of a strong emotion. The constant needling of Gralyre's temper was designed to make him lose control. While he was in the grip of rage, she would enter his mind and see if the wall guarding his past was still in place, or had weakened to the point she could destroy it.

The problem was that so far, the plan had not worked. Though provoked beyond what good sense would stand for, Gralyre had yet to lose control. If it were any other man, the blood would be flowing by now.

Rewn's words came back to her, and Catrian finally recognized her plan's flaw. Gralyre thought that to retaliate would be his death. Of course the man was holding his temper!

To make matters worse, the abuse and bullying was beginning to make the good men of the group, like Rewn Wilson, angry. Matik was losing face. The constant maltreatment he heaped on Gralyre's head was beginning to make him appear as evil natured as a Demon Rider.

But she could not abandon her plan, not when Gralyre was so close to the boiling point! Catrian had to follow through else all the weeks spent torturing the man would have been for naught. She had to eliminate the possibility of Gralyre as author of his own malaise. Every theory as to the origin of his strange affliction that was explored, and rejected moved him one step closer to a cure, and another step closer to becoming the powerful asset that the resistance desperately needed.

As though summoned by her thoughts, Gralyre strode into the cavern from his shift at clearing snow. She followed his long limbed grace with a moody frown. Why would he not let go?

Gralyre passed his shovel to the next man and exchanged a brief smile and a pleasantry before he sat next to Rewn, against the wall to warm himself. His wolf thumped its tail wildly in greeting from where it had been curled up next to Rewn. Gralyre absently stroked it while talking animatedly about something that brought a smile to his face.

The girl, Saliana, came to him with some rations and sat herself on the other side of Rewn, talking shyly with both men, while Gralyre ate.

Catrian's interest was caught by Dajin, who had come on point like a salivating bird dog on the hunt. As the days passed and Gralyre had not reacted, Dajin had grown bolder in his harassment. He now pushed himself up from where he had been seated and sauntered Gralyre's way.

"Spy, spy, ye are a spy! When ye get caught, ye are going t' die!" Dajin recited the taunting singsong poem he had created.

Gralyre looked up at him with a bland expression, and passed his empty dishes to Saliana, who scurried away to avoid the confrontation.

"Dajin! Stop it! Stop this at once!" Rewn yelled at his brother. "What is wrong with ye?"

The wolf began to growl, his nose crinkling threateningly as he showed his teeth.

"Spy, spy, ye are a spy! When ye get caught, ye are going t' die!" Dajin chortled the rhyme over and over, and as his brother reached out to grab him, he jumped back and began to circle Gralyre in a capering dance.

If Gralyre did not stop the fool soon, Catrian was of a mind to. How bad was it for Gralyre as the recipient, when it was annoying enough for someone watching to want to strike Dajin?

After three refrains of the lyrics, Dajin misjudged his safe distance, and Gralyre' hand shot out and pulled Dajin's foot from under him as he hopped past.

Dajin screeched and landed on his head. Gralyre smiled a dead, feral smile.

The wind increased its fury outside and Catrian felt a light tendril of breeze caress her cheek. She smothered her smile of satisfaction. She reached out with her senses. He was close, but not quite there.

Dajin was white of face, his fearful eyes gripped by Gralyre's blackened gaze. Like a rabbit caught in the jaws of a wolf, he ceased to struggle. The tableau held for several long moments. Conversations around the room hushed to the lure of a fight. Yet Gralyre took no further action.

"Just get away from us, Dajin," Rewn said with mortified disappointment. "Ye deserve worse than that, and I have a mind t' give it t' ye!"

Dajin scrambled to his feet and bolted across the cavern to the protection of where Matik sat.

Outside, the fury of the wind abated perceptibly.

Catrian sucked in a startled breath as a notion occurred to her. But no! 'Twas impossible! She had never heard of such a thing!

As casually as possible amidst her excitement, she walked to where Boris was taking his turn sleeping. She sat beside him and gently touched his shoulder, knowing Boris' warrior reflexes would need no further encouragement to waken him.

Boris sat up, completely alert and ready for action. By the look on Catrian's face, he knew something had happened. "What is it?" He kept his voice instinctively low.

"A couple o' things," Catrian murmured urgently. "First, the reason Gralyre will no' allow himself t' lose his temper is that he thinks he will be branded a spy for attacking Matik, after which we would execute him."

Boris' brows rose at this. "That actually makes sense…"

"And secondly, I think we *have* been pushing him into a rage, but his anger has been taking a different form." Catrian's excited gaze turned inward. "I should have realized that as a man o' power, his response was going t' be different than that o' normal men."

Boris rubbed a tired hand across his eyes. "Get t' the point, Cat."

"The storm! His anger is the storm!" She clarified, watching Boris' face as her statement sank in. The moment she saw understanding dawn in Boris' eyes, she nodded and continued. "Somehow, he is using the storm t' release the anger we have built up in him. Every time he is enraged, the storm's fury increases. When he relaxes, the storm relaxes with him!"

"Gods! Such power! Is that possible?"

"I have never heard o' such a thing before! I have heard o' powerful sorcerers o' the past who were able t' direct the force o' a storm, but never before have I heard o' someone connecting themselves emotionally and physically t' one!"

"What does this mean, Cat?"

"It means, uncle," she stated slowly to be certain he understood her completely, "He is using the wind, perhaps the storm, as his Wizard Stone!"

"'Tis impossible, Cat!" Boris scoffed. "A Wizard Stone has t' be…well…a stone! You are talking nonsense!"

"No uncle, I am no'," Catrian corrected. "The only reason stones are traditionally used is because they are more durable than other materials, like for instance a piece o' wood or the metal o' a sword. But t' use the wind!" She could hardly sit still in her excitement at the discovery. "How do ye destroy the wind? Or stop the wind? Even if ye were t' discover his word o' binding, it would do ye no good, for ye could never destroy the vessel o' his power! His Wizard Stone is impervious t' harm!"

Boris shuddered and grabbed Catrian's arm in a hard grip. "Kill him, Cat! Kill him right now, before the binding has grown too strong and we are unable t' defeat him!"

Catrian jerked free from her uncle's claw-like grip. "No, Boris. I will no' do it! No! My reasons remain the same. Besides, at his age the binding t' his Wizard Stone must have been forged many years ago and will be too strong t' sever without the Word o' Binding."

Boris did not look happy. Catrian rushed to reassure him. "I am no' even sure my theory about the wind is sound. I must test it." Her inspired gaze wandered to where Matik sat sharpening the blade of his axe.

"And what o' your other strategy? The bloody abuse the man has been taking t' satisfy your need t' get beyond his memory wall?"

Catrian's face went cold and calculating. "Perhaps we can see t' both at the same time. This is what ye must do." Quickly, she outlined her plan.

Boris went white around his mouth as he heard her instructions, but he did not question her decision further. Muscles knotting with apprehension, he rose and went to Matik's side. He bent and whispered his orders into his ear.

Matik looked up into Boris' grim face, and felt sweat break across his brow. On the far side of him an eavesdropping Dajin grinned nastily. Matik threw off his cloak and gripped his axe more firmly. "Ye be sure 'tis what she wants?"

Boris nodded. "Good luck my friend."

Matik got to his feet and stretched out his kinks. "Thanks Boris," he rumbled from within his beard. He hefted his axe and strode purposefully across the cavern to where the unsuspecting Gralyre sat.

"I have got t' see this." Dajin chuckled in anticipation, swinging around Boris to get a better view.

Boris frowned down at Dajin, unable to see value in the youngster's thirst for blood. He shuddered to think that this boy was to help carry the fight to the next generation. He returned to Catrian's side.

Across the cavern, Matik glanced back at Boris and Catrian one last time. They nodded for him to proceed. Matik sighed deeply, stopped in front of Gralyre while flipping his battle-axe sideways, and blindsided him with a blow to his head. The flat of the blade made a dull ringing sound as it impacted.

With a curse of pain, Gralyre slumped sideways. He glanced upwards, and his eyes widened as he twisted from the path of the blade as it descended in a whistling arc. It clanged as it hit the cavern floor where his head had just laid.

Gralyre jumped to his feet, wobbling slightly. His hand clutched the split in his scalp that seeped blood down the side of his face. "By the Gods of Ill Fortune! What are you about, Matik?"

"I have had all I can take o' ye, spy! Ye sit innocent as can be, yet I know ye are plotting some evil! Ye seek t' destroy us all! But I know what ye are!" Matik yelled as he swung the deadly axe again.

Gralyre jumped back and narrowly missed being bisected by the massive blade.

Men scrambled to get out of their way. Pressing themselves against the walls, they began to lay bets, screaming encouragement to the combatants, eager for excitement after days of forced inactivity.

Rewn dug frantically through the packs in search of a weapon. "Gralyre! Sword!" He shouted and slid the blade towards his friend across the rough stone of the cavern floor.

The symmetry of this fight to the previous sparring match with Matik was not lost upon Gralyre as he dove aside, nimbly avoiding another swing of the battle-axe. Rolling across the hard stone, he came up with his sword in his hand, and his stance ready for Matik's next attack.

The pain and dizziness from his wound faded away as he embraced the rhythm of battle. Win or lose, this fight would mean his death, and he found himself fiercely glad for it, glad that Matik had finally sought the culmination of his abuse.

The storm shrieked loudly, its intensity more furious than ever before. Catrian glanced meaningfully at her uncle.

Boris nodded but was distracted by the fight.

Little Wolf snarled and barked, but at Gralyre's command, stayed away from the battle.

Matik's powerful muscles expertly swung his axe in a punishing arc, but Gralyre easily sprang from its path and Matik was pulled momentarily off balance.

Gralyre's sword flicked like quicksilver, opening a wound on Matik's temple similar to the one he had received. He could kill the man now, but after the weeks of abuse, he was savouring his need to humiliate and abase his tormentor. Then he would kill the hirsute demon.

Rewn's face was pale as he watched the fight. His accusing gaze sought out Catrian, and when she looked back, he mouthed his previous words. *On your head be it!*

Catrian's mouth tightened as she looked away.

Matik howled as his blood flowed down his face, truly angry now instead of just performing the duty that Catrian and Boris had set for him. He backhanded his battle-axe towards Gralyre's head.

Gralyre, not expecting the move, felt the whisper of wind from the blade's passing as he twisted from its path. As he dodged he kicked Matik in his knee.

Matik cried out and grasped momentarily at his injury before shrugging off the pain. Battle madness overtook him. He swung his axe with speed and fury, but Gralyre was faster, always able to anticipate the course of the axe blade.

Again and again, Gralyre's sword whispered and a line of red answered, opening up dozens of small painful cuts in Matik's flesh. Gralyre's eyes were hard with satisfaction and enjoyment as he let the point of his sword flay his opponent, exacting a painful revenge for every abuse suffered at Matik's hands.

The shouting, screaming men watching the death match never noticed the cold breeze that circled inside the cave, though many of them pulled their cloaks closer even as they screamed encouragement.

Matik charged Gralyre, slamming him with his shoulder and spinning him off balance. His axe followed with lethal power.

Gralyre used his overbalanced impetus to spin away from the dangerous cutting edge. He shook his head to remove the blood that had dripped into his eyes and the room lurched around him as he regained his footing.

His head wound was sapping his strength, and his reflexes were slowed. He barely turned the axe on its next pass. Time to end this.

Seeing an opening, Gralyre stepped into a blow. Catching the axe against his blade, he braced himself against the impact even as his sword shattered. With all his muscles straining, he threw his weight into the momentum of his strike, and forced the axe to slam to the cavern floor.

Gralyre stomped on the battle-axe, pinning it, forcing it from Matik's hands.

Matik remembered well the last time he had sparred with Gralyre, and the crushing defeat he had suffered. He had thought at the time that he never wanted to cross blades with the man when he was truly angry. He had been right to fear. He shuddered, embracing his approaching death as he straightened from losing his axe, the jagged, shattered bit of Gralyre's blade was at his throat, following him upwards as Matik stood.

The surrounding warriors quieted at the tableau of death. The moment hung, the tension built.

Gralyre's eyes flicked to Catrian, and a grimace contorted his face at her devastated sorrow. He reversed his grip on the broken sword and hammered Matik in the face, laying him out cold. He flung the broken weapon to the side.

Gasping from exertion and staggering dizzily from the blow to his head, Gralyre slumped momentarily against the cavern wall.

The watching warriors, who had fallen silent as their champion lost the bout to the *Spy*, began to boo and jeer at the victor. Angry shouts echoed loudly in the small space, growing louder and more abusive.

Gralyre glared at them bleakly from where he stood victorious over Matik's unconscious form, feeling his rage pushing at his restraint. He was sickened that his fears had proved correct. In defending himself, he had signed his own death warrant.

A blast of arctic wind swirled through the cavern, ruffling the warriors' cloaks in its passing. None of the wrathful men took notice.

Gralyre staggered several steps to the centre of the cavern, holding his palms out from his sides to show them as empty and harmless. He had known this would be the result of a confrontation with Matik, and now he would accept his death. He was done trying to prove himself, and past done being the whipping boy for the resistance's paranoia. Perhaps it was best this way. Everyone would be safe. He raised his head proudly, defiantly.

"Stop it!" shouted Rewn, stepping in front of the agitated men, coming between them and Gralyre. "What are ye doing? The man was defending himself against a cowardly attack!"

The breeze in the cavern stuttered and began to calm.

"Get out o' the way!" A warrior grabbed Rewn by the arm, and slammed him into the cavern wall to the roar of approval from the Rebels. "We all know 'at ye be the spy's friend," he spit rabidly. He pinned Rewn's arms to prevent him from interfering.

The wind roared to life as Gralyre started for the man restraining his friend. "Rewn!" he bellowed.

"Boris!" Catrian yelled. "This is getting out o' hand! Control the men!"

"Die spy!" Dajin screamed from within the protectiveness of the pack as he heaved a rock at Gralyre's head.

"Dajin! No!" Rewn hollered as he struggled against the arms pinning him to the wall.

Dajin screamed in victory as the rock struck true. Gralyre staggered and went down on one knee, felled in his headlong rush to come to Rewn's aid.

The warrior holding Rewn grew tired of his resistance and slammed his fist into his stomach. Rewn gagged as he fell to the floor.

The wind cycled around the perimeter of the cavern gaining speed.

More rocks followed Dajin's, cast at Gralyre's defenseless form. They meant to stone him to death! He held his arms up to shield his head.

Little Wolf leapt protectively in front of Gralyre, barking and snapping, then yelping as the rocks began to target him as well.

Catrian gripped Boris by the arm, as he would have started forward to put an end to the stoning. "I thought ye wanted this stopped?" Boris yelled over the shouts of the men and the rush of wind.

"Wait! Can ye feel it? He is almost there!" She yelled to be heard over the cyclone. Her cloak flapped rapidly, making her look as though she was about to take flight.

Boris held up a hand to deflect a pot that flew at his head. "Feels like he is there now!"

As if the wind had gained enough power through its cyclonic rotations around the room, it turned against the stoners, slamming the men against the walls and pinning them there. They dropped their rocks, scrabbling against the rough stone for an anchor to hold, as the wind dragged them with hurricane force along the granite walls.

The cyclone had gained a voice; the yells of fear from the men trapped in its eddies, the clang of loose equipment, the scream of horses. Little Wolf howled, adding his ululating voice to the cacophony. Visibility decreased as dust and bedding went airborne.

"Catrian!" Boris begged as he clawed to hold his position against the rocks while the wind pulled at him. "Put an end t' this!"

The horses squealed and bucked, trying to pull from their pickets, but were luckily too heavy for the wind to lift yet.

Arm raised to shield her face, Catrian used her magic to anchor herself against the tug of the cyclone, and pushed step-by-step towards the centre of the cavern where Gralyre stood as if in a trance, bleeding from the many wounds made by the stoning.

Here in the centre, there was no wind. Gralyre was the eye of the storm. Catrian reached up and gripped his face between her hands. She needed a close contact for the connection to be as strong as possible. He had still not acknowledged her presence when she invaded his mind.

She reeled from the strength of Gralyre's power. His rage was focussed, uncaring and unstoppable, consuming his attention to such a degree that he did not even notice her invasion. Perfect.

Catrian crept her way through to the wall surrounding his memories. But instead of having grown weaker, the blackness was stronger and deeper than before.

This was no accidental amnesia. It had been deliberately constructed to imprison Gralyre's past. It fed off Gralyre's magic, but like an invading parasite, not as a symbiotic construct that had been self-created.

Relief left her giddy. She felt like laughing as her fears evaporated. Gralyre was a step closer to gaining her trust. Her plan had worked.

Gralyre came back to himself as her uninvited presence finally intruded upon his perfect wrath. Outrage flooded his soul.

'You have no right! If you want my secrets, you are going to have to give up some of your own!'

'Wait! Ye do no' understand...!'

Catrian screamed as Gralyre's magic slammed into her mind.

The cyclone contracted. Bearing dirt and loose equipment, it cycled faster and faster, forming a solid wall of debris that isolated the couple from the rest of the cave in an impenetrable funnel.

Boris yelled in fear as Catrian and Gralyre disappeared behind the wall of wind and equipment. He rushed forward, but was unable to penetrate the debris field without injuring himself.

Rewn grabbed Little Wolf by the scruff, hauling the animal back when he would have dived through the funnel to reach his master. Though the animal snapped and growled, Rewn did not let him loose. "Easy, Easy, Little Wolf. He is fine. This is a battle only he can fight."

Little Wolf whined and looked into Rewn's face for more reassurance, as his body quivered with the need of fight or flight.

All around the cavern, battered and bruised warriors crawled shakily away from the twisting cyclone. Those that were more able bodied sprinted for the outside world.

"HOLD!" Boris shouted.

The men who had fled halted in their tracks and returned, though their limbs shook and trembled from their fear.

"Crossbows!"

Boris' order had the Rebels diving for weapons within what packs were not cycling in the funnel surrounding Gralyre and Catrian.

Within the privacy of the eye of the storm a battle raged. Gralyre ruthlessly bared all of Catrian's guilt, easily finding her part in directing Matik's abuse, her reasons, her suspicions. His anger filled her to overflowing.

Static crackled through their hair, sparking off metal buckles and buttons.

Catrian struck back. She showed Gralyre how she perceived him. A mysterious stranger with power enough to destroy them all, with a hidden past that could prove him innocent or guilty in one quick moment.

'I am not a SPY! I am not Doaphin's creature!'

'PROVE IT!'

The time for subtlety and deceptions had passed. She attacked Gralyre's barrier with all her considerable power, determined it would fall before her.

He howled his anguish as pain exploded in bright flashes throughout his head. The maelstrom echoed his cry with the hum and whine of wind whipped debris.

'STOP! Gods, you are killing me! Catrian!'

Catrian disregarded his agony. She applied even greater pressure to the task, certain the wall would give at any moment.

Though Gralyre's power at least equalled hers, he had not the skill to wield it that she did, and was defenseless against her superior experience. He could not force her from his mind, so he pushed all his pain into her instead. He made her feel the agony she was causing.

Catrian gasped as his suffering washed into her, pounded into her soul. She hardened herself against it.

'I canno' let up now! No' when I am so close t' breaking through! Just a little longer!'

She pushed harder and screamed as Gralyre's torment rebounded into her mind. She finally faltered as the horror of what her pride was doing to him struck home.

''Tis beyond bearing! Gralyre! I am sorry!'

She stopped assaulting the barrier and tried to sever their connection, to draw back, to end this terrible confrontation.

'Gralyre, let go! Please!'

Now that the pain had abated, he wanted retribution for her assault of his mind, so like the rape he had endured at the hands of the Count. He was insensible with rage, and it made him too strong to use her superior skills against.

She tried to gentle him but he rejected each overture.

'I was trying t' help ye!'

'NO!'

'I am so sorry, please let me go!'

'NO!'

Hoping she was not making a terrible mistake, she dropped

her defenses, and opened her mind wide to his presence, no longer trying to force him out, trying instead to placate him with her lack of resistance, calm him with her cessation of aggression.

He wasted no time in taking total advantage of her sacrifice. She shuddered as he exposed all her dreams and desires, longings and fears. He pulled her worst nightmares from the depths of her soul and forced her to look at them.

She used the weapon he had deployed so effectively. She transmitted all the horror, humiliation and pain caused by his invasion back into him.

His probing stopped immediately and she felt his revulsion at his actions. He was still enraged but had started to regain his control.

Gralyre pulled back from her mind, but as he was leaving he unearthed the one secret she had hoped to keep from him. Her desire for him.

He pulled the knowledge out like a triumphant toddler finding a lost toy. Cruelly, he flaunted the knowledge, taunting her with it as his frustration at her elusiveness boiled over.

Her submissiveness disappeared in a white hot flash.

'Ye have no right t' mock my desires when yours are as strong!'

Her reaction was purely that of a scorned woman. Catrian pulled Gralyre's head towards her with all the hurt that his ridicule had caused. She rose on tiptoe and mashed her lips to his, intent only on forcing his acknowledgement of his own turbulent feelings. It was a tactical mistake, for that kiss distilled all their conflict into a torrent of lust.

The sensation of his hard lips detonated through her senses. She felt Gralyre's shock, then his desire. Her blood caught fire at his uninhibited response.

Gralyre's arms pressed her tighter against his chest and graphic images of his passionate intent flowed unfettered into Catrian's mind. Tightly linked emotions rebounded and grew stronger between them. Catrian could not discern between his passion and hers. It felt as if the fabric of their souls was merging. Isolated from the rest of the cavern by Gralyre's wind funnel of debris, their passion deepened and grew richer, filling their senses.

She tasted the blood of his wound on his lips and felt regret at his injury.

He felt her regret and finally began to forgive, concentrating instead upon the texture of her desire as he lifted her closer against his hardness.

Catrian gasped from the intensity of their emotions and tried to pull away. His teeth bit down gently on her bottom lip, a punishment, keeping her where she was as he ravaged her mouth.

She moaned throatily as she finally pushed away from him. He tried to bring her back into the embrace but she had regained her reeling senses and held him at arms length.

He shifted his arms from around her back, trailing his hands up over her shoulders, her neck, to her face, and finally brushing shaking fingers over her trembling lips.

Her desire flashed to life again.

Still enmeshed in her thoughts, he felt her response. His

midnight-blue eyes burned hotly over her upturned face as he dropped a careful, soft kiss to her lips, letting his hands trail away while his mouth stole one last taste.

He pulled from within her mind even as she released her grip upon his, declaring a truce though they knew the war was far from over. They stared at each other, breathing harshly from their battle, from their desire.

Gralyre allowed the cyclone to die at last, returning them to the presence of the others. The wind had been his to command all along.

"So am I good or am I evil?" was his parting shot as they turned to face the waiting group… and the dozens of crossbows pointed their way.

"Fire!" Boris yelled as they reappeared. With a harsh note, the arrows were released.

The End

of

The Exile

Lies of Lesser Gods - Book One

Coming Soon

The Rebel

Lies of Lesser Gods - Book Two

About the Author

Linda G.A. McIntyre resides in beautiful Vancouver Canada, where she works as an Executive Producer for Film and Television. A self-proclaimed writing addict, Linda has devoted her life to a pursuit of the creative arts.

Connect with the Author

Visit our website for insider news and giveaways
www.lgamcintyre.com

Like us on Facebook
www.facebook.com/lgamcintyre

Follow us on Twitter
@LGAMcIntyre
@LOLG_theExile
#theExile

Made in the USA
Columbia, SC
23 July 2018